ASSASSIN BOOK ONE

A JIM ABLE ADVENTURE

ED CHARLTON

Assassin Book One by Ed Charlton

ISBNs Paperback 978-1-935751-73-1

eBook 978-1-935751-74-8

**Subscribe to Ed's monthly newsletter
edcharlton.com
Free eBook for new subscribers.**

Also available

The Jim Able Offworld Trilogy

Beauty Rising, Larc Ascending, Time

The Aleronde Trilogy

The Problem with Uncle Teddy's Memoir, Saint John's Ambulatory, Aleronde the Great

and

Hoyle Station

THE STORY SO FAR

Previously, *Jim Able: Offworld* began (in *Beauty Rising*) with Jim employed as a bureaucrat resolving competing claims for first contact rewards. After a mission to Turcanis Major V-I, his associate, a chameleon-skinned Neraffan named Tella, created a new job for Jim within the External Intelligence Agency.

Jim has befriended a canid from Gul Tanna named Ernot Dirl Marhan. Marhan is traveling in a stealth warship, one of the few remaining from a large fleet that Jim destroyed on his first EIA mission (in *Larc Ascending*).

Jim was thrown into a mystery on Pec Sonloi—a planet near where he grew up—after meeting a being unlike any other at the temple of Tuanomena. He also met his late father and a daughter, yet unborn, and lost the T-switch, a time machine (in *Time*).

Marhan has an aunt who has led a secret life as an assassin. A device she used to conceal her presence while she worked is now in Jim's possession. In discussions with her, Jim has declared two people he thinks should be stopped before they do more harm. She is now training him as an assassin—a career change he had never imagined.

PART ONE

TRAINING

CHAPTER 1

CH'GARRATT

Jim always thought it odd—as he woke in the middle of the night—that the injury to his face wasn't what he felt. The explosions seemed always to hit him in the stomach.

The rockets had destroyed the terminal at Sin Har's Ch'Garratt spaceport. They had almost capsized his career. They had almost killed him.

Through all the thinking and the talking it over, through endless counseling sessions and nights drinking, he still found himself awake in the dark, sweating.

His fingers gripped the blanket as they had the robe wrapped around the elderly Har. Her face, so solemn, so perplexed, silently asking him across the many months, "Why?"

Though he had helped the injured in the smoke-filled aftermath, the faces of the dead filled the dark of the nights that followed.

He could talk about it dispassionately. He could recount the events. He had even learned to express how he felt.

But he could never answer her question.

CHAPTER 2

JACK KATRIGG

"He killed about a hundred people and injured about as many others," Jim said with a sigh.

"Is that where you got the scar on your face?" Betih asked.

"I thought that had almost disappeared."

"To your eyes, perhaps."

"Yes, I was injured. My colleagues—you met Anne and a guy called Rob—spirited me away from the Sin Har hospital when it looked like someone was coming after me."

Betih sat at the galley table, wrapped in her pink bathrobe, her furry ears slightly flattened, her long snout pointing straight at Jim. She changed the subject. "You know, it makes me happy to hear you and Marhan laughing together so much."

Jim nodded. "Yeah, he's teaching me a few important phrases in Dewghu."

"Can your feeble mouth pronounce our language adequately?"

"Trall-gah hogh," he replied with a straight face.

Betih threw back her head in laughter. "How rude!"

Jim watched the canid's eyes. They bulged a little more than Marhan's, perhaps a sign of her advanced age. He wondered what they saw. She wasn't used to dealing with humans. As he talked with her, he was constantly unsure how much he needed to explain.

His favorite way of getting to know aliens—individually or as a group—was to learn how they swear and insult each other. It had a twofold purpose. Firstly, it helped him avoid mistakes. Secondly, it involved everyone letting their guard down and allowing humor to reduce suspicion and unfamiliarity.

Languages can be learned in their pure form, but colloquialisms permanently keep one step ahead of academic recognition. Book learning, Jim thought, resembled being in orbit looking down on a whole planet; he wanted to be on the ground, risking everything on a vulgar one-liner to connect with one individual at a time.

But as much as trash talking can be good grounds for commonality, the gaps in understanding between species, between worlds, are always filled with unspoken dangers. None more so than with Guls from the Tanna system.

Betih looked like a large, upright wolf. But, dressed in a pink robe, she created an illusion of fragility and old age. Jim had seen through that illusion. Guls can become aggressive faster than a human can blush. Their claws—though retractable—like their teeth are never completely hidden.

This Gul, sitting quietly across the table from him, also had a secret. She had been an assassin, using her natural aggression in cold and calculated ways. That doubled Jim's suspicion that her assumptions would be different from his. Her conclusions, arrived at slowly or in an instant, would likely be—quite literally—inhuman. However, she had also lived the life of a professor of ethics at a theological university. He hoped keenly for possible points of mutual connection.

This was the sort of relationship Jim found fascinating—what he lived for.

"Tell me more," she said, "Jack Katrigg. Tell me everything."

"He's a courier. He's a business fixer. He's a favorite of a certain type of operator—the dodgy kind."

"When did you first meet him?"

"Oh, several years ago. A ruined flier was found with no one aboard; I can't remember where now. In it, the investigators found a security permit for Phobos-R base. That raised a few eyebrows. The permit showed I had authorized it with Jack Katrigg as the assignee."

"Go on."

"So, I interviewed him. Someone in the Office of External Affairs found him. The signature wasn't mine. The document codes didn't match anything issued by the Office of External Affairs. At the time, he worked for several well-known shipping companies. All aboveboard. Courier work, some logistical subcontracting. Nothing special. He told me he hadn't rented the burned-out flier and had documentation showing he was working elsewhere. So his story checked out."

Betih waited, pulling her robe tighter as if she were cold.

"He was a real pain in the ass. He wouldn't sign anything. Only digital signatures. So, I couldn't easily match his signature on the paper permit."

"I've heard Earth has odd ways of doing business."

"There are good reasons for using physical documents sometimes. Even combustible, losable paper can be more durable than electronic records."

Betih laughed. "You say that like it's a good thing. There are many matters best not remembered."

Jim chuckled back. "I guess so. He really got under my skin though. He kept glancing at his watch, like, 'See how much of my valuable time is being wasted by this annoying bureaucrat.' Some people's mannerisms just irritate. His was the constant twisting of his hand. His watch was on the inside of his left wrist, you know. He was constantly checking the time."

"What's a watch?"

"What? Oh, it's a timekeeping device. Worn on one wrist or the other. Not common nowadays, although my brother keeps one."

"Something he used to distinguish himself."

"I guess so. My remembering it"—he nodded—"is sort of the point. The OEA was doing the audit in the Sin Har port called Ch'Garratt. I was part of the team, interviewing pilots and ship owners. His name came up on my list." Jim sat, remembering. "He was friendly enough. I said I remembered him. He might have remembered me; I wasn't sure. The audit"—Jim waved a hand vaguely—"I won't bore you with it. But at the end of the interview, I had to ask him to sign a physical document to show he agreed with the statement of what we'd done."

"He wanted to do it electronically?"

Jim sighed. "He read it over quite carefully. Then I offered him my pen, and he signed the form. He even smiled."

"Interesting."

"The inspectors cleared his ship, and I took him back to it. That was the first time he checked his watch. He was wearing it on the outside of the other wrist."

"Is that unusual?"

"Sure, people strongly prefer where and how they wear something like that. It will hardly change over a lifetime."

"And you noticed. That's very good."

"No. I didn't. Not then. Not when it counted. I escorted him to the boarding gate where he'd docked his ship. We said good-bye, and he left." Jim sighed. "He took off at the same time as another craft—a police flier. One missile brought down the flier; he fired five more into the terminal where I was still standing."

Betih watched Jim's face.

He continued, "It wasn't the same guy, and I guess he thought I had noticed. Obviously, he had something important to conceal."

"Since your friends 'spirited' you away, have Katrigg or his people tried to kill you since?"

"Someone tried when I was on Flereat with Marhan. I was following a lead about Katrigg; I don't think it was a coincidence. But then Marhan gave me another lead. I went to Stacco Ila 32. I found out two important things. First, there are more than two Jack Katriggs. It's a whole big institution. If you have a problem with authorities somewhere and need someone to lie for you, he—they—will do it. If you need doubt thrown on an investigation by his proving he was somewhere else at the time, that's no problem."

"How very useful. But after he tried to kill you so publicly, the authorities must be seeking him."

Jim shrugged. "He was somewhere else and can prove it. Can't have been him. Was someone impersonating him? You can make up your own story. The doubt cast by the evidence of another Katrigg is enough."

Betih's eyes were focused elsewhere. "The galaxy is large, and those investigating crimes are stretched thin." She nodded. "I can see it. I can see it working."

"Marhan's contact told me how I can hire one."

Her eyes snapped back onto Jim's face. "Good!"

"What I don't know—yet—is how I find *my* one. They all look the same and can coordinate lies about their movements. I don't know how I will get to that particular individual."

Betih nodded vigorously. "Good! From a large population of possibilities, you have narrowed your search to a much smaller one. A finite population who looks alike and have the same name. They are all criminals or supporters of criminals." Hardly missing a beat, she added, "You could assassinate them all."

Jim thought, *And here comes the cultural gap. Is she serious? Do assassins eradicate groups of people or only individuals?*

He asked, "Are you joking?"

Betih snapped her jaws at him. "Perhaps. A mission like that might become a lifetime's work. I think you are too impatient for such a large-scale undertaking."

"Right. I want to do it the clever way. Avoid unnecessary bloodshed. I don't so much care about the organization or the others or what they do. This individual stepped way outside the normal bounds of fraud and deceit."

"Your morality has interesting boundaries. You pick and choose."

Jim shook his head. "Not really. I don't want my distaste for the rest of them to get in the way of the main point—stopping this one from doing it again."

"Or succeeding where he failed before."

"I was thinking more of the people in the terminal who I couldn't save. Some died in my arms that day. I won't forget them."

Betih was silent. Jim got up and fetched a drink for them both.

"This is a complex mission," she said quietly. "Katrigg is a man who works for others. He is no politician who can be found easily in public spaces. You will need to become part of his life, be where he is, be with the people he is with. It will not be quick."

"But, I think, worth doing."

"Will the common good be increased by your actions or decreased?"

"There's the professor of ethics talking!"

"No, that's the assassin talking. That is the first qualification for any mission. If the galaxy will be worse off after someone is dead, do not kill them. Simple as that."

"Isn't that just picking and choosing? Your morality shouldn't be bound by whether the job is of some great worth or not!"

"Now you make fun of me! Impudent puppy!"

Jim smiled, silently toasted her with his mug, and asked, "So, you'll train me?"

She rolled her eyes. "What do you think I've been doing?"

"When? All we've done is chat."

"No assassin will kill the wrong person—or even the right person —if they should not be killed."

"Okay. So far, I approve of that."

"How is such specificity achieved?"

"What do you mean?"

She shook her head. "The job of the assassin is to be sure. It is not to kill; the killing is the least part. The death is quick, certain, nonnegotiable. Why? Because the work has already been done. Everything has been investigated, checked, verified, checked again. You kill when you know, not before. How do you spend your time? Investigate. Study your target. If you can, get to know them in person. How will you become certain? How is such specificity achieved? Answer me!"

"You mean my feeling sure isn't enough?"

"Who are you to meet out death on such a basis?"

Jim knew the answer, but it still made him feel uncomfortable. *This isn't going to be easy.* He replied, "Okay, you need the facts—like the police would." He nodded, "An objective judgment."

"He begins to see. Marhan said you were quick for a monkey."

Jim narrowed his eyes. "We Earth monkeys may appear slow. That's just because we are trying not to let things, like unnecessary rudeness, get in the way of otherwise profitable relationships." He smiled.

Betih straightened in her chair and looked at Jim with one eye. "Interesting. Aren't you used to nonhumans? You have worked with many races."

"And few are as annoyingly confrontational as guls."

A smile spread along her snout, revealing her teeth. "Good. So you know us well enough."

And you have no intention of changing.

He took a silver golf ball, called The Cloud, from his pocket. He had acquired the alien object from an officious EIA operative named Sharkey, who had threatened Jim on his first morning with the agency. It was remarkable in two ways. When activated, it stopped all electronic devices from functioning—a dangerous property aboard a spaceship. And it had once belonged to Betih.

He sighed and asked, "You mentioned other tools besides The Cloud. What are they?"

The elderly canid shrugged. "It depends on your needs. But the primary one is The Striker. How do you intend to kill your targets? Once The Cloud is working, no electronics-based blaster will work. A projectile weapon might, but there are better devices."

"The Striker? Do all your tools get fancy names?"

"Your tools, not mine. They come from an ancient tradition, which you will respect."

Jim smiled. "Of course! And I do. What is The Striker?"

"A device so long"—she held her hands twelve inches apart—"a cylinder within a cylinder. When you strike the target, the motion of the inner cylinder causes it to fire. It may have electronic components that prepare its charge, but the final action is mechanical."

"How does it kill?"

"I am no weapons engineer! It kills. Effectively."

"Does it need ammunition? You say it charges. Maintenance?"

"No, yes, and no. It can be ready to use again after firing and once out of the influence of The Cloud."

"Okay. So where is yours?"

"Gone. With The Cloud when it was stolen. Perhaps they were kept together. How will you find it?"

"Me?"

"You. Perhaps the same skills you must show in investigating your targets can be employed in recovering your tools?"

"Okay. Training, huh?"

"What are you waiting for? I am old. At this rate, I could die before you learn anything!"

She had a humorous glint in her eye that Jim had not seen before—an inkling of mutual understanding.

Maybe this is going to be okay.

CHAPTER 3

ROB STUART

Robin Stuart sighed and sat back in his chair. The room was quiet but for the hum of the equipment. He reached over to a nearby display and tapped the control to lower the lights.

He was now in a sea of small indicator lights with a few islands of display screens.

If he were of a less practical disposition, he might have appreciated the beauty of what he saw and marveled at where he was. Instead, he recited a well-worn curse upon his former boss.

When Rob was first demoted to his current job, several others had worked with him. Now, he was alone. He had more responsibility, fewer resources, and unending pressure to reduce costs. All the while, his customers—the agents and staff of Earth's Office of External Affairs—still required constant access to their archives.

The archives surrounded him. The electronic stores and their supporting infrastructure lined the walls of their secure and bomb-proof bunker. Rob's office was the center of the whole operation, literally and figuratively.

And it sucked, in Rob's opinion.

A trained and experienced agent. Qualified space pilot. Qualified armorer. Expert outmaneuverer of bureaucrats. And look what it's gotten me!

The latter skill had been his undoing. His former and much-cursed boss, Liz Curacao, had worked long and hard to place him somewhere he would no longer bother her. Prior to her one victory, he had run rings around her, lived high on inflated expenses, visited planets more for recreation than for work, and trained many other agents in his techniques for making the most of life under the nose of an oblivious administrator. *If only she had stayed oblivious.*

He turned the lights back up and sighed. *Still getting paid though.* He smiled.

A call interrupted his reflections.

"Archives. Stuart. How can I help?"

"Hi, Rob! It's Jim."

"Jim who?"

"Jim Able. Forgotten me so soon?"

"Jim Able? Hmm. Once knew someone by that name. Hauled his ass out of all sorts of trouble, I seem to remember. But that can't be you."

"It can't?"

"That Jim Able is now 'rich beyond the dreams of avarice' and is far too high and mighty to be contacting a humble archivist like me."

"That may be true. I did get a first contact reward. But you, an archivist? Since when?"

"Long story."

"Fair enough. Looking for another job?"

"Doubt I'd get a reference. Know what I mean?"

"I'm looking to fill a vacancy. Want to work for me?"

"What? Hmm. I'd have to think about it."

"Sure. I can send you—"

"Okay. When do I start?"

CHAPTER 4

CLART MUNA

The Artist of Sonloi-AC threw her brush into a jar of spirits. The liquid splashed spots of light blue over the table. She turned, unhooked her smock, and let it drop to the floor. She crossed from her studio into her living room and threw herself into a chair.

She reached behind her head and pulled the three braids of long hair, each dyed a different color, from behind her and placed them to one side.

At once, her tablet chirped with an incoming call. She grabbed it, pressed the button, and yelled, "What!?"

"Hi, Mom. You okay?"

"Jim! Hello, dear. Don't mind me. This painting is not going well. How are you?"

"Doing fine, Mom. I have a question. Do you still work with that accountant you had? What was her name?"

"Clart? Yes, but I think she's retiring. She's not getting any younger. Like me. Why do you ask?"

"I—er—need an accountant. I thought of her. You trusted her, right?"

"Of course! A more upright citizen you couldn't hope for. Wouldn't let your father get away with anything!"

"That's what I remember; he used to complain a lot about her."

"Don't hire her for anything illegal! If you need that, I can probably find you someone."

"What do you mean? Why would you think I'd want that?"

She paused before saying, "Yes, dear."

"No, I want to contact Clart. What's her other name?"

"Muna."

"That's right! Got it. Retiring though?"

"That's what I heard."

"Huh! Might work out."

"You are up to something. Would you like to tell me what?"

"No, not really. I came into some money recently. Just need someone to manage it for me."

"Oh, that's good to hear. Well, both bits. The money, and that you realize you're not very good with all that."

"Thanks, Mom."

"Don't drink your way through it."

"No, Mom. No intention of doing that."

"Does this mean you can afford to come and visit me more often?"

"Sure, Mom. Talk to you soon."

"Bye, dear!"

Clart Muna had already retired. The call from Jim found her sitting on her porch, eating a fish breakfast and enjoying the warm morning air, her husband at her side.

"The Younger Son? To what do I owe this honor?"

Jim replied, "I talked with my mother recently. She speaks highly of you. May I ask about your plans to retire?"

"It's all true! I have retired. I'm enjoying the quiet. You must come and visit! Bring Alfie over and spend some time. My home is in Calamo. It's so beautiful!"

"Sounds great! A visit would be good. You see, I'd like your help with managing some money."

"I did say I'd retired."

"True. But I hope you'll make an exception. I received a substantial payout from a First Contact Claim."

"Oh...congratulations!"

"I'll need help placing the funds across several worlds and setting up a small business."

Her Meoenan voice deepened. "Well, that does sound interesting. But I did promise my husband we would have time together at last."

From across the table, her husband said in an undertone, "It's the Family Able. Of course you'll do it!"

She laughed. "Cal says I'll do it. Well, come and visit so we can talk it over in detail. I'll be happy to help if I can."

"Thank you! Both of you! Of course, I think you'll understand I hope to keep this strictly a private matter."

"Of course, Jim. Of course. Say no more."

"I'll work out a visit to Sonloi and bring Mother over."

"Wonderful! We're looking forward to it."

CHAPTER 5

SHARKEY

Robert Sharkey liked routine. He ate the same breakfast every morning, drove in the same vehicle along the same route to the office, and deliberately arrived before anyone else.

When he had to induct new employees at the External Intelligence Agency's office in Unity City, he did so reluctantly. Some were late. Some were nervous. All had endless questions. He appeared to be an interested, kindly, avuncular figure. However, his job was to impart a set amount of information within a limited time. He preferred it when they shut up and listened.

When no inductees were expected, or no secret or dangerous cargo needed to be carried between offices, he could relax. He could arrange his time as he saw fit. His research—both official and unofficial—could continue beyond the constraints of working hours.

Sharkey's keenest interest was alien machinery. His collection—the official and the unofficial—dwarfed those of many museums.

The agency blessed his research and overlooked his excesses. His boss understood the advantages of a steady and loyal employee. They were also of the same mind concerning the risks that so much alien contact posed to the Earth and all true, loyal humans.

He sat in his office in a large worn leather chair. On his desk lay a folder of papers from a recent find. Embedded in the desk's surface sat a display screen, showing the same documents.

As he studied the diagram of an object on the screen, he jotted notes in the margin of the equivalent paper document.

"No emissions" he wrote. "No smell."

The object, a cube about fifteen inches a side, showed no markings, and no one knew yet what it was for.

His tablet lit up, and his boss asked, "Found anything so far?"

"Not yet, no. I'd like to find another one."

"Another?"

"Sometimes devices talk to each other. Proximity might trigger something within."

"We're unlikely to find one. The wreck this came from had been there a while."

"I know. I can wish, can't I?"

"All you want. File it away until we see another ship of the same kind."

"Another couple of days. My people have a few more experiments lined up."

"Very well. There's a package tomorrow. My name. Collect from the OEA warehouse."

"Going where?"

"My desk."

"Of course."

That's all he asked, and that's all he would be told. He liked the inherent simplicity of his job.

For Tella of Neraff, the job was never simple. Its assignments (and it strongly preferred non-gender-specific referents) often involved standing somewhere naked, cold, and bored. Listening to the conversations of humans, of jorrs, or of guls had limited appeal. But to pass unseen, to soak up nearby colors onto its skin, to smell the currents of alien air, to feel the play of emotions in a room, or to merely retrieve information that otherwise would remain hidden—these were the sources of great joy. Too often, though, it was finding the pleasures of work diminishing. A diminishment it put down exclusively to its involvement with Jim Able.

Jim had introduced it to many new ideas and had an approach to meeting people quite different from Tella's. This odd human rarely seemed to expect a return from an encounter with a stranger. He approached all with equal interest. He might cover it over with an air of cynicism, but it was a cover Tella saw through.

So far, on this mission, Tella still wore its white robe, the hood covering the back of its head. The white of the robe washed through its skin, making its face and long arms visible. Its face, flat nose, thin lips, and almost sunken eyes rarely betrayed any emotion. Such was the norm for a Neraffan-jong.

It drove from the OEA warehouse and through the streets of Unity City following a vehicle whose driver was returning to the EIA main building.

Tella sighed, recalling details of the building. It had worked there for longer than had been comfortable. It had been given a code name, R546. It had even created a job for Jim Able. More recently, Tella had left without a word, without permission, without notice. It was probably being sought by the agency's best—a situation that neither worried it nor induced a desire to rectify the situation. It had seen the agency from within and had assessed its agents lacked the capacity to be a threat.

Jim Able, however, had warned Tella specifically about Sharkey, calling him "dangerous."

Tella would soon see.

CHAPTER 6

ROB'S VACATION

Rob spent a quiet couple of days' vacation on the third moon of Tule Fewar. The locals generally shortened its official name of Ardageth—"Glorious Sight"—to Arda—"a sight"—as a small defiance against Fewar planetary authorities. Rob liked the locals.

The view that gathered tourists from many worlds faded in the daylight but dominated the night. Arching overhead shone the cause of its civilization's rapid fall and triumphant rebirth, the remains of a supernova—the "Glory of Fewar"—glowing in eye-popping colors.

"Pretty, isn't it?" he noted.

"Don't say that too loud. You'll be lynched!" Jim replied.

Rob snorted lightly. "I get bored with the hype."

"You have no soul."

"Well, true as that may be, I appreciate you paying for it."

"It's a one-off. The job won't pay much at first."

Rob sat up from his lounger and gestured to the waiter to bring another famously overpriced drink.

"Going to tell me more about it?"

"Sure. I want you to create a company that finds people—a search and rescue agency, that sort of thing."

"Hmm," Rob said slowly, "a lot of travel. Expense accounts. A big network of investigators."

Jim counted on his fingers. "Yes. No. Not necessarily."

Rob sighed. "Go on."

"Travel? Probably. I have no objection—whatever the work requires. Expenses? Sure, but only based on the company's income. I know you too well; you're not spending my money like you did the OEA's."

"Damn!" Rob smiled.

Jim continued, smiling back. "I want to use existing resources for the search operation, as much as we can."

"What resources?"

"How about the OEA's archive?"

Rob laughed. "So, you knew all along!"

Jim replied, "Kind of. A happy coincidence. Can it be done?"

Rob chewed his tongue. "You're not thinking 'officially'?"

"No."

"Then, probably. How much traffic would you be adding to the system?"

"Not much at first. We'd need room to expand later."

Rob nodded. "A spider program runs in the background of the archives checking data integrity. It randomly hits the data stores, moves damaged files for rescue, swaps storage units, asks the operators to replace suspect hardware...that sort of thing. I've wondered about hijacking it but never saw a reason to."

"Monitored?"

"No. Well, hardly ever."

"Sounds ideal."

"I can see changing it to accept remote requests as input, but I don't know about getting the results out. Not without someone noticing."

"There's a couple of kids I want you to work with."

"Kids?" Rob did not sound keen.

"My nephew and his girlfriend. You'll be impressed, I think. Once they're old enough"—Jim paused—"next year, persuade them to work for the company." Jim held up a finger. "Important to note that I am not involved. This is your company, as far as the galaxy knows. Their fathers would have a fit if they thought I had anything to do with employing them."

Rob laughed. "Families are great, aren't they?"

"Always."

Rob nodded. "Okay. I have an idea of what to set up before I resign"—he turned his hand in the air—"given that I don't know what we're doing with the output. Can the kids work unofficially now?"

"Doing my best to make that happen."

"Where else? The OEA archive has its limits."

"Who else uses the same tech?"

"Oh..." Rob frowned and stared up at the magnificent sky. "...government accredited? Could probably find you some other agencies with the same kind of setup."

"EIA?"

Rob gave him a sideways look. "You insane?"

"Totally."

"Whoa...that would have to be a clean job. Sparklingly clean. Antiseptically—"

"I know. It's an ambition."

"Okay. What about offworld data?"

"Clo—the girlfriend—did something with gossip-nets. I was on Sonloi-AC; my mother had been kidnapped. I was under pressure to find something my father had hidden while keeping myself out of sight." Jim glanced at Rob. "I was meticulous about keeping out of sight. Clo found something on a gossip site about my being there." Jim shook his head. "They found me. She's a real asset."

Rob was staring at him. "Kidnapped your mother to get to you? That's as dirty as it comes. She alright?"

Jim nodded, then replied, "Yeah, it all worked out in the end. Meoenan politics more than anything else."

Rob drank silently.

Jim watched the supernova remnants and waited.

Rob said softly, "So, I see an iceberg company. A little bit of public front—'We find your missing loved ones!'—on the surface.

While underneath is this vast hacking infrastructure spanning...How big do you want it to get?"

Jim nodded. "Bigger, the better."

Rob nodded in return. "Ambitious."

The two sat silent once more, bathed in the multicolor glow.

"Go on," said Jim, "ask."

"I'm not sure I want to. Okay. Why?"

"I will occasionally put in my own requests for information. Targets that aren't missing but might be elusive. Targets that mustn't be forewarned of my interest in them."

Rob laughed. "A revenge machine?"

Jim laughed too. "No, better than that! A justice machine."

CHAPTER 7

TELLA AND SHARKEY

It took Tella a few minutes of searching the EIA parking garage to find Sharkey's vehicle. It fixed a tracking device under the rear and returned to the street.

Large crowds of office workers and tourists jammed the sidewalks. It had to wait for a large enough gap in the foot traffic before stepping out. As it walked, it gave half a thought to the possibility that its feet might occasionally become visible to those walking behind as the colors of the walkway flushed over them.

Sharkey returned home, and Tella followed.

No high-rise apartment for this EIA man, Tella thought.

Sharkey lived, at the agency's expense, in one of the houses on the shorelines of Unity City built originally for ambassadors and their staff; two stories and a black-tiled power-gathering roof, a garden of tropical trees, and a fence high enough to make for a difficult climb.

Someone thinks highly of you. Or you have the dirt on someone important.

Tella parked its vehicle at a nearby café and waited for dark.

Leaving behind its white robe, it went to test the barriers that kept Sharkey safe from intruders like itself.

The gate boasted cameras and motion-sensitive lights.

Of course.

The fence smelled dry and dusty.

Electrified, but not high voltage. Interesting.

Tella touched the fence and stepped quickly against a nearby tree, the bark's shadows and colors flooding its skin. Lights came on over by the house. On one corner of the building, the circle of a lens appeared, reflected distant lights, and faded as the camera panned the area.

The Neraffan examined the entire boundary and found no breaches, no opportunities to exploit, no weaknesses in the defense.

Jim was correct. Mr. Sharkey has something to hide.

The next evening went better but less comfortably. The cargo floor in the back of Sharkey's vehicle smelled old and vaguely of the sea, but the dark matting was a good source of disguise. And Sharkey didn't look closely enough to notice the color mounding higher than the floor.

Tella rose to stand in the shadow of Sharkey's back door. It was midnight, and no sounds came from within. Waves crashed against the nearby seawall.

The rear fence stood closer to the house than elsewhere. Tella could see the patterned wire through the trees.

Gathering a handful of stones from the flowerbed, it took shelter under a window, still close to the door. Waiting a minute or more between each one, it threw a stone toward the fence. Each time a stone made contact, the automatic systems reacted. Quiet beeps and chirps came from near the back door.

After an hour of repeated alarms, lights came on within. The back door opened, and a yawning man in black strolled down the path to check the fence.

Tella had gained the inside before the door swung shut.

. . .

Sharkey's house held an immediate surprise. Tella walked quickly down a pastel-colored corridor into a central area. The décor was similar to—if not exactly—that of the EIA's head office. *Functional, boring, unremarkable.*

The Neraffan looked briefly in two rooms off the central hall— plain furniture, a sofa that seemed never to have been sat upon, a table bare of decorative objects.

Footsteps announced the guard's return from the garden. Tella stepped behind a door in one of the empty rooms.

Watching through the crack of the door, it saw the man open a doorway to a staircase and descend.

A basement? In Unity City? That would take excavating the underlying volcanic rock!

Tella resisted the urge to follow him down the stairs imme- diately.

Instead, it examined the other rooms, listened for noises from the floor above, and oriented itself again to the corridor to the back door in case of an urgent exit.

Tella reviewed what it was learning. *What isn't here? No electronics, not even a television. No books. No paper. No decorations. Where is the 'stuff' that indicates a human lives here?*

Someone climbed the stairs and burst out into the hall. A second followed. They argued.

"It's just faulting constantly!"

"Nonsense! It's state-of-the-art. There's something there! Go check again."

Their invisible watcher smiled. They had left the door to the basement ajar.

The air coming up from the lower level was warmer and less fresh. Tella could smell the warm air from computers and display screens and the scent of several humans. It looked down at the end of the flight of steps and saw a patch of wall it could stand against and perhaps avoid detection.

The lights shone less brightly in the basement. The large room contained several rows of workbenches, like a commercial labora- tory or large school science lab.

Seven humans stood or sat at different places.

Sharkey is not here.

As it watched the activity in the lab, both Tella's understanding and alarm grew.

One woman crouched over an object on her workbench. She had a line of three bright lights immediately above it. A magnifier stood between her and the piece; her hands manipulated long tweezers thrust into the heart of the object.

The green scaley exterior immediately told Tella of its origins—the Glat system, one of the nine stars of the Plett Empire. Having traveled there as a youth, Tella knew humanity and the Plett would not like each other. This object looked like a battlefield weapon, though one end showed irredeemable scorching. *Perhaps parts have been blown off?*

Whatever its condition, the Neraffan worried that a human technician could do herself a lot of damage poking around the innards of such a device.

The other workbenches also held other nonhuman technology.

Jim Able had told Tella that this human, Sharkey, likely possessed a device of the same origin as the small silver ball Jim called The Cloud.

'A device.' 'Possessed.' No, Jim, this is a large-scale operation. I may need to access a catalog of objects to find the one you want.

Tella fought two competing urges. The first was to abort the mission since Jim's expectations and all their preparation had been misguided. The second was to stay and learn more, to find the catalog, to retrieve the device, and to be done in one visit rather than risk another entry into the house.

Juggling the two paths, Tella found itself caught against the wall at the foot of the stairs as Sharkey descended.

CHAPTER 8

DR. SLOTA

The Artist of Sonloi-AC sat back from her painting and smiled. *That's better.*

Her latest portrait, of an older Meoenan girl, had been tricky. The subject had a scar across her cheek that Alfie knew caused pain both physically and mentally. The challenge she had given herself, and nearly failed to meet, was to balance the accuracy of her work with the girl's aspirational hope that her scar should not be the only thing people saw.

The eyes, of course, were the key. Marhan had seen that immediately when the large canid had visited her studio. *Remarkable insight for such a coarse and intrusive creature.*

In the case of this Meoenan girl, the eyes told the whole story.

Alfie's tablet chirped.

"Hi, Mom!"

"Jim! Another call so soon. How lovely!"

"Mom, that Meoenan doctor I used to see when Chapman was away. Are you still in contact with him?"

Alfie tilted her head and asked, "The doctor? Are you sick? Is it that wound on your arm?"

"No. Nothing to worry about. Just looking for a Meoenan who knows which way up humans go."

She laughed. "He's still around. I think I saw him get an award for something recently. He'll be glad to see you again, I'm sure."

"Great! Send me his contact information. I'll give him a call."

"And putting this together with the accountant business, you seriously have to tell me what you are up to."

"No, Mom. My business. But at least you'll get another visit from me when I see him."

"Well, you can tell me all about it then, can't you!"

"Bye, Mom."

"Doctor Slota! Great to see you again."

"A visit from the Younger Son is always welcome!" The doctor extended his blue hand and clasped Jim's warmly.

Jim could see the effects of age on the doctor's face and a faint clouding of the large Meoenan eyes.

"How much do you remember of the human anatomy? Do you get to practice our medicine much?"

The doctor nodded slowly, a gesture learned and applied judiciously by Meoena when addressing humans. "Some, yes. I regularly see your mother for her heart condition of course."

Jim swallowed. "Hmm. Didn't know about that."

"Oh, I'm sorry. I assumed she would have told you."

"No. Perhaps she told Matt."

"Indeed. And how is your brother?"

"As cranky and argumentative as always."

Slota laughed lightly. "The Elder Son! Famous both for his words and his emotion."

"A nice way of putting it."

"So, what brings you to me after all these years?"

"Something confidential. Not just in terms of medical privacy. This has...ramifications."

The doctor nodded and listened.

"That's why," Jim continued hesitatingly, "why, in the end, I got my mother to make this appointment with you rather than risk being overheard making it myself."

The doctor listened but didn't nod.

"I had business on Tanna Gul, a world of canids. I don't recommend it generally. I was attacked—not seriously—but I was unconscious for a while. I think"—Jim sighed—"my attacker may have implanted something into my back."

Slota stared and then spoke. "What does your doctor on Earth say?"

"I don't see one. The last examination I had was by Matt's guy on EBMS. He didn't notice anything. That's what worries me. I don't think it will be easy to find."

"And why me?"

"You're not on Earth. You're not associated with me, recently at least. I trust you. And you know your way around a human body."

"Who was this attacker?"

"A monk of the Praestans Rapax."

The doctor's head rose full on his long neck. "They build spaceships. I have never heard of them either attacking people or implanting things in them!"

"Nor have I. However, the question remains. Did they? Or did he, I mean."

"What an odd situation!"

"If they did something to me, I don't want them to know I know."

He smiled at Jim and said, "And I thought your mother's life was complex."

"Yeah, we're quite the family, aren't we?"

"I presume I will see nothing from an external examination?"

"I doubt you will. But you're welcome to look."

He nodded and gestured for Jim to sit on the examination table.

Jim sat and removed his shirt with a sigh. "I always wondered, doctor."

"Yes?"

"Why do you keep these rooms so damned cold?"

"Ha! You want to uncover our secrets! Of course, we do it to remind the patient who is in charge. We keep you cold and afraid, so you don't answer back when we tell you what to do."

Jim chuckled. "Thought so!"

"Well, I see some scarring. "One, two...seven sites. All similar. Same age. Are these the ones you are concerned about?"

"I was told initially those were scratches from a creature."

"Hmm, I doubt it. These are not clustered. Animal attacks generally show the angles of the different claws and the direction of the swipe. These are all too similar, identical even."

"Okay..."

"Do you think there may be just one implant or one under each penetration?"

"No idea, Doc. I'm hoping you'll tell me."

"Well, put your shirt on. You are presenting me with a puzzle; that much I can see."

"Okay."

"How far do you want to take this?"

"What do you mean?"

"How many scans can I do? Do I book you into the main hospital in Tuanomena? How much time do I have?"

"Ah. I'd rather do everything here. I don't want undue attention."

"Yes. Yes."

"As long as you want. I can pay you directly for anything you need to do."

"Let's start simply then. I'll have my nurses put you through the routine scans. I'll build a picture of what happened, where your body has been healing, and anything anomalous we can see. If nothing shows up, I have only limited resources here to do more."

"How about over on Sonloi-AC?"

"Very good! I'm sure we can ask for the necessary privacy there."

"Thanks, Doc. This'll be a weight off my mind."

Slota chuckled. "If I find something, won't that be more worrying than if I don't? Let's hope for the best."

CHAPTER 9

THE BASEMENT

Sharkey came quickly down the stairs toward Tella. He stopped on the last two steps and looked to his right—away from the Neraffan.

"Pack it all away!" Sharkey called to the technicians in the room. "There's an intruder on site. Lock it all down!"

Relieved he had come no closer, Tella counted two pieces of new information. *Sharkey wears old-fashioned pajamas to bed. They are on to me.*

With great reluctance, Tella looked around the lab one more time. The technicians were sealing objects in storage boxes of similar color and size and placing them on carts for transport.

The Neraffan followed Sharkey back up the stairs. *Sorry, Jim, this part of the mission has not been a success.*

It was easy for Tella to follow a guard out through the back door and into the open. Then came the problem of how to leave the compound alive.

As it walked across the lawn, a beam of light from the house swung across the grass toward it. Tella ducked and ran to the right. The light swept passed and then came back. The Neraffan ran left, trying to outrun the beam, but was caught briefly.

Shouts went up, but his pursuers did not understand what they had seen.

"Animal sighted!"

"That's no animal! It looked like a patch of mist."

"Go and check! Get out there!"

Tella also heard Sharkey's voice but couldn't hear what he said.

Sprinting into the trees, it lost itself to the searchlight among the shadows of the trunks.

At the side of the front garden, the trees grew closest to the fence. Tella climbed one whose branches stretched out along the fence line but not quite over it.

Hidden by the dark and the patchwork of shadows and bark that played across its skin, it waited as the search followed into the trees.

After several minutes, Tella heard Sharkey's voice again. "There. Up there! That one!"

Blaster fire raked Tella's tree. Leaves and twigs burst into flame and swirled in the air.

As the branch it clung to snapped and twisted through the air, Tella thought, *This is going to hurt!*

A loud cracking noise accompanied the branch, the shower of debris, and Tella as they all fell onto and over the fence.

Tella hit the ground and rolled, not elegantly, into the road, bouncing over twigs and burning vegetation.

Sharkey shouted insults at his guards. One shot randomly through the fence, but Tella was across the street and into a neighboring garden.

Limping and gasping for breath, it sank into the dark water of an ornamental pond, its face at the surface near the edge, using ferns for cover.

Oh, and hurt it does!

CHAPTER 10

TELLA REPORTS

Jim's ship had had a parade of visitors at the spare berth on the Europa Biological Monitoring Station or EBMS, where it was docked. Matt Able—administrator or tyrant, depending on whom you asked—temporarily allowed his brother the privilege but was surprised, curious, and annoyed.

"Get your own station!" he yelled at Jim.

"What?"

"You have the traffic to warrant it! Ships coming by night and day, bothering my staff, demanding to dock, just to see you. This isn't what we agreed on. You'd be working elsewhere, you said. 'Be no bother,' you said. Well, you're not elsewhere, and you're being a damned nuisance!"

"It's only temporary. Just while I sort out a few things."

"And what's this rumor about you coming into money?"

Jim replied tersely, "Just a rumor."

Matt glared at his brother and bit back the reply that desperately wanted to burst out. "Two weeks! Clear off my station. Whatever it is you need to do, do it somewhere else."

Jim sighed and said, "Sure, Matt. Whatever you say."

Matt was momentarily confused. Realizing what Jim had said, he nodded briefly and left.

Tella returned.

Escorted by an EBMS security guard, the Neraffan leaned against the docking hatch as Jim opened the airlock.

"You don't look so good."

"I have felt better."

"Shall we get the doctor to visit?"

"Does he have any experience with my people?"

"None. Does that matter right now?"

"No. I suppose not."

Jim asked the guard, "Medical visit, as soon as possible, please."

"I'll have to clear it with Doctor Able first, sir."

"Soon as you can."

Jim took Tella up the ramp from the flight room to the sleeping module specially prepared for Neraffans by the ship's makers. The module sprouted from the ship's upper deck like all the others—a spherical protuberance. On seeing Jim's ship for the first time, many thought it looked more toad than spaceship.

"Rest, Tella. I'll bring the doctor up as soon as he gets here."

"Thank you, Jim. I regret to report my mission was largely unsuccessful."

"Later. Let's get you fixed up first."

Tella sighed and laid back on the bed.

Jim sat in the galley, down a ramp from the flight cabin. Marhan paced to and fro. "So, what happened?"

"I don't know yet!" Jim shrugged.

"It is unlike Tella. He has not failed before."

"I'm sure it has. Remember to call it 'it,' won't you?"

"Yes, yes!" Marhan waved an arm at Jim. "Betih was expecting to see her tools again."

"She will. We'll get them. Some way or another."

"Huh!" the gul snorted.

Jim ignored him and asked, "How is she doing? Is she alright staying here on the ship with us?"

"She loves the attention. She speaks to you for hours each day. You listen and argue rarely. She has as much food and drink as she can swallow! Do you have any doubt, monkey? She loves it here!"

Jim laughed. "I see what you mean. What about you? You getting restless yet?"

"No! Yes. I hear your plans but have yet to see my place in them."

"You're in them, alright. I just haven't..."

"What?"

"I haven't decided if I want to put you in so much danger. I'm going to be doing some risky stunts before long. But I know I will need someone to haul me out of it all—when I mess up."

Marhan pulled a chair over and sat down heavily opposite Jim at the table, his long snout hanging low. "Danger? Is that what holds you back? You fear for me?" The canid laughed, snapped his jaws at Jim, and growled softly.

"No offense meant."

"You have heard Betih and I talk of our belief in the spirit. How it inspires and drives the Raeffs of our world. You, too, may have that spirit."

Jim blinked.

Marhan continued, "The spirit touching an off-worlder is something we have never seen before. Ask her. She is a Luminant; she can tell you better than me. For that chance alone, I will stay with you. I will haul you out of whatever messes you create and gladly."

"Thanks, I think. I don't feel divinely inspired. Not at all."

Marhan's eyes held his. "You are too close to see it.

A knocking sound came from above.

"That's the doctor," Jim said.

. . .

"Okay, Tella," Jim asked, "What did the doctor say?"

Tella answered quietly, "Bruises and burns. No skeletal or internal damage."

"Good! Did he give you anything to take for the pain?"

"No. That wouldn't be wise, given his inexperience with Neraffan physiology."

"I guess so."

"There are some items I would like to order. Foods I know will be beneficial."

"Of course, order whatever you want."

"Thank you. Now, may I make my report?"

"Sure. The table in the galley has become the center of every-thing; we can use it as a conference table. I want Marhan and Betih to hear it too."

Tella wore its white robe but moved carefully as it approached the table. Marhan sat tall. Betih, wrapped in her bathrobe, looked frail and distant.

Jim thought, *She's listening. That's what she does. She looks like she's switched off, but she is all there.*

"Okay, Tella. From the top."

"The top of what?"

"The beginning."

"Yes, Jim. Sharkey has a large operation based in his house. Perhaps I should say his 'compound.' There is an extensive base-ment area. I didn't see it all. In it, he has a large collection of nonhuman technology. He has a team of technicians examining the items. I saw one pulling apart a damaged weapon—without any safety precautions. I'm surprised they haven't killed themselves yet."

"You think my—Betih's—tools are in his collection?"

"Certainly. How they are stored, I didn't see. But items are placed in standard containers, marked only with codes on the outside. We would not be able to browse through the collection. We need access to their indexing system."

Jim sat back with a frown and sighed.

"You were caught?" Marhan asked.

Tella nodded. "Not quite. But they found me by using a scanning device that Sharkey held. He pinpointed me in a tree."

"Probably some sort of infrared scope. They're common enough on Earth. I didn't expect him to have one in his house!"

Tella shook its head. "Not a house. He shows no sign of living there. There are no books, trash, entertainment, or decorations visible on the first level. He sleeps upstairs—where I did not go. Perhaps it is more personal up there."

"Perhaps what you saw is indicative of the person," Betih commented quietly.

"Go on," Jim said.

She asked thoughtfully, "Is he someone devoted utterly to his job? He works in an office during the day and runs a laboratory at night. If that is his life, expect him to cling tightly to it. He will not easily give up something he has collected. If that is all he lives for, the loss of any item will be personal and painful." She shook her head.

"You think he's already hurting because I have The Cloud?"

"Of course!" she said,

They sat, each in their own thoughts.

Then Jim said, "I need to hit him hard. Present him with no real choice but to give up the tools. A choice between losing them or everything else."

Betih nodded.

Jim turned to Tella and said, "I'm sorry. My assumptions about Sharkey were wrong. I thought he was a typical middle-aged EIA agent quietly waiting for his retirement. I sent you into something quite different."

"Different, yes. And well-disguised. I doubt you would have found out without my seeing it in person."

"Don't let him off the hook so easily, Tella," Betih interjected, "He has to know better. He has to gather more information before he puts lives in danger. Perhaps he understands that now."

Jim scowled at her. "I understood it well enough before."

"Not well enough! Do better!"

"Enough Betih!" Marhan shouted, "Show respect."

"I will. When he's earned it!" She stood and returned to the ship's main level.

"Suggestions on how to proceed?" asked Jim grimly.

CHAPTER 11

JIM AND SHARKEY

The café, where Tella had parked previously, hummed with a robust clientele.

At a central table, Jim and Sharkey sat smiling opposite one another.

Sharkey began. "I presume you have activated my jamming device already?"

Jim nodded. "Of course. So, contact with your staff is lost for the moment. But you touch upon the point of our meeting. It wasn't *your* jamming device, was it?"

"That is none of your business."

"How do you know?" Jim locked eyes with Sharkey and smiled.

"You said you were willing to share information about the device."

Jim shook his head. "I know who owned *them*—not just the silver ball—and how they came on the market. I have information about why you should return them."

"I will not be returning them to anyone. You will return the jammer to me. Now that I know you have it on you, I'm not letting you leave with it. Did you really think I would?"

Jim frowned and looked away. "Here's what I thought," he

said, looking back at Sharkey's face, "I thought you would be surly and argumentative, arrogant and patronizing. How am I doing so far? I thought you'd be armed. I guessed—and it was just a guess —that you'd have hired muscle nearby to haul your ass out of a fight if one broke out. Still with me? But I also thought you'd be interested in hearing what I've learned about the items in question."

Sharkey glared at Jim and quietly said, "Proceed."

Jim pulled The Cloud out of his pocket and placed it near his elbow on the table, its surface rippling with a rainbow of colors. "Lay out the other items on the table."

"This is a public place. Such a disclosure is not wise, Mr. Able."

Jim shook his head again. "Surely you realize if the other people here aren't working for you, they're working for me. Go ahead. This isn't in any way public."

Sharkey glanced nervously around the café, noting the faces he didn't recognize. "I see you've done a lot of planning."

"I don't want to spend longer in your company than necessary. Get on with it!"

Sharkey slowly picked up his bag and began to lay out the items across the table.

First came a small, threadbare but still functional bag, the color of old ivory.

Then he placed the cylinder that Betih had described. Its surface showed minor dents and scratches and lines of the same script that was etched into The Cloud.

Next came a thin rectangular slab, mirrored on one side, etched with script on the other.

Finally, he laid out a pair of wristbands. Each held a small disk of the same material as The Cloud and the cylinder.

"There!" Sharkey almost hissed. "Now, tell me what you know."

Jim raised his hand over his head. Betih rose from her seat at a table behind Jim. He said, "Someone I'd like you to meet."

Betih sat with them at the table and looked at the tools but said nothing.

"Who is this?" Sharkey asked.

"Ernot Bard Betwen. She is Professor of Ethics at The Luminary on Tanna Gul. Betih, this is Mr. Robert Sharkey of the EIA."

Betih looked down her snout at him and said flatly, "I know."

Sharkey didn't look at her. To Jim, he said, "What business has she on Earth?"

She answered, "My business is there on the table. Those tools were stolen from me."

"Impossible!" muttered Sharkey. "Tanna Gul, you say? Nonsense! Guls don't have the wits to make things like this."

Betih bared her teeth and growled quietly at him.

"Want to ask us what else we know?" Jim said, smiling.

"I won't be inclined to believe it. Unless you give me a verifiable manufacturer's name and planet of origin."

"Ancient. Too ancient for you to contact anyone about them."

"Which planet? And how do you know?"

Betih laughed. "Stupid monkey!"

Sharkey's face colored. "Watch your tongue! You're on my planet. Don't forget it!"

"Did you buy these tools from the thief, or did you steal them too?" she countered.

Jim added, "For our purposes today, it comes down to one fact. You didn't declare them to the appropriate authorities when you brought them into the Earth's environment. They have never been checked and cleared as safe, have they?"

"I work for the EIA, Able, or have you forgotten? *We* protect the Earth."

Jim shook his head. "Not just you. Import rules and restrictions protect us too."

"If you don't have a planet of origin or a name I can follow up on, you have nothing of interest to say to me."

Jim sighed and smiled but didn't respond.

Betih picked up the ivory-colored bag and put The Cloud into it. She, too, said nothing.

"Really?" Sharkey said, with a mocking smile, "You arranged all this, and that is all you've got? I told you, you were a waste of space, Able! What better demonstration could you make?"

"My friends and I are leaving," Jim said quietly, "and these tools are coming with us."

Sharkey laughed. "Who says? Friends? A senile canid and a couple of ex-OEA pen pushers?"

Betih picked up the cylinder and opened it up to its full length. Something clicked inside. "Can I kill him before we go?"

Jim kept his eyes on Sharkey and shook his head. "No. Mr. Sharkey is about to let us leave peacefully."

"That was never the outcome, Able!"

"You see, Bob—can I call you Bob?—there's something you don't know and I do. And that's the one thing that will finally persuade you."

"Oh, really? And what do you imagine that is?"

"A flier. Isn't it strange how things work out? It happens to be currently hovering over your house. If I don't leave here with these tools, the pilot will fill your house and your basement lab—and all it contains—with enough ordnance that the hole will be toxic for a century."

Sharkey shook his head. "How dumb do you think I am? Never play poker, Able; you don't bluff convincingly."

Jim nodded. "Thanks for the advice." He picked up the bag and put his finger in to deactivate The Cloud. "Ask your minions back home."

Sharkey spoke softly into his sleeve. He smiled at the reply. "Nothing, Able. You have nothing."

Betih held up a small comms unit and said, "You may end stealth mode."

Jim said, "Check again."

Two other patrons stood up from their tables as the reply came to Sharkey.

Jim smiled.

The color drained from Sharkey's face. "You wouldn't dare."

"Wouldn't he?" Betih asked as she put her snout close to his face. "How about me?"

"The interplanetary fallout would sweep you amateurs away! A gul destroying a human residence? You really haven't thought this through—"

"I'm sitting here in a café, monkey!" Betih chuckled. "What proof is there that I have anything to do with it?"

"Tell the pilot to fire," Jim said simply.

"What?" shouted Sharkey.

"Fire!" Betih said into the comms unit.

Sharkey jumped to his feet. Into his sleeve, he shouted, "What's happening?"

Neither Jim nor Betih moved as the cafe's large window shook.

Jim said, "Bob, please, sit down. Sorry about the landscaping. But if he fires again, he won't stop until everything you have has melted."

Sharkey pointed to Betih and began to say "Kill—" but his eyes were on Jim's face.

Sharkey's guards had weapons drawn but waited for him to finish his order. Jim's team had each of them covered.

Jim said, "We'll leave now. And don't try to follow us. Don't be stupid; my pilot can always come back."

Sharkey said nothing but glared at Jim.

Betih collected the tools as she stood. She jammed The Striker onto the table, which cracked and smoked briefly.

Jim followed her out, and Jim's hired muscle backed out after them.

CHAPTER 12

ROB'S NEW OFFICE

Unity City may boast bright areas, wide boulevards, glimmering arcades, and fine glass towers, but it must also admit to streets like Bunden Street.

The lighting shone dull yellow at either end. Traffic moved carefully along the road, hovering higher than normal to avoid the piles of trash. Even if it were clean and well lit—like the places people preferred to go—two vehicles wanting to pass each other would have to negotiate who went up or down or who reversed to the corner.

Only two buildings lined the street. On the north side, the Asteroid Center housed five businesses at street level: a martial arts school with faded fliers and a pile of mail rising behind its glass doors; a tattoo parlor boasting that "all species" were welcome; an electronics repair store; a grocery store run by an ancient alien of indeterminate species; and finally, the Asteroid Take-out, a fast-food hole-in-the-wall serving smoking spicey meats, also of indeterminate species.

On both levels above, the windows showed advertisements for legal firms, travel agents, and notaries.

On the south side of Bunden Street rose the larger Elation

Building. Six stories tall, it housed small apartments on the top three floors. Below them were two floors of offices. The street-level businesses had less obvious purposes than their neighbors on the north side. One sign read "Accommodations." Another "Communications." Inside, they looked identical—a couple of plastic chairs, a desk, walls plastered with rules and regulations, and faded certificates. On either side of the Elation Apartments' main entrance stood one small café and a flower shop.

Rob Stuart had rented the office above the café. He had also found the apartment above the office to be empty and rented that as well.

He placed a poster in the office window reading "#501 Floor 2. We Find People." And the business name: "Robins."

His first business-related call was to the electronics repair shop opposite. The proprietor, an elderly Viking called Ulf, seemed to disapprove of the intrusion into his dimly lit world.

"Hi," Rob began, "I'm just setting up an office across the way. Got a couple of questions, if I may?"

Ulf nodded once.

"Is there a main network access tap under this building?"

Ulf shook his head.

"It's under the Elation building, then?"

Ulf nodded.

"Want a connection?"

Ulf frowned. "Who are you?"

"I'll be needing it for my business. I'll include you in if you like."

"That's illegal."

Rob nodded. "According to some, yes. Others would claim such access should be a right."

"Who are you?"

"Robin Stuart. Here's my card. Let me know if you're interested. I want good relations with my neighbors. And I will want to know when people come around asking questions. You'll find I'm a generous fellow."

Ulf nodded again, took the card, and said, "They already did."

"Who?"

"City detectives. They said they were watching the guy at the market. But they wanted to know about you."

"Appreciate it. That's probably routine."

"Want me to sweep your place?" Ulf asked.

"If you can."

"I can."

"Thanks! What's the clientele at the café like?"

Ulf frowned. "Coffee drinkers."

"Excellent."

"Don't go in there when the commuters come down from the apartments."

Rob smiled. "Even better information! Thank you. Visit whenever you can to check the place over."

Ulf nodded. Rob nodded back and then left, smiling.

In the empty café, he introduced himself to the owners.

"Hope you ain't come to complain about the noise!" said Di, one of the two tattooed girls.

Nef, the other, laughed and said, "Nothin' we can do about it!"

"No, you're fine. No complaints. Just want to warn you my electrician may need to drop a line through here to the basement. I'll pay for any cleanup and such. Won't take them long."

Nef frowned. "What's it for?"

"Just a network cable. Ever seen those junction boxes in the basement?"

Neither had.

Rob continued, "My business needs the right kind of connection. So..." He walked behind the counter and studied the corner where the plumbing pipes descended. "Somewhere here, probably. That okay?"

Di popped her gum and said, "Sure."

Nef shrugged.

"Great!" said Rob, "Thanks a lot."

"What business is it? What do you do?" Nef asked.

"I find people."

"What?"

"I find people. Missing people. Humans. Aliens. Don't do animals though."

The women looked at each other.

Nef asked, "You want to find my brother?"

"Maybe. When did he go missing?"

"Two years ago," she said quietly, "Two and a half."

Rob nodded for her to go on.

"He went to the Hawkins Array for work. Know where that is?"

"Heard of it, for sure. What work did he do?"

"Structural repairs. Atmospheric integrity. Plumbing. That sort of thing."

Rob pulled out his tablet. "What's he called?"

He typed as they spoke. "Fred Neuhaus. Member of the Structures and Buildings Maintenance Union."

"The union didn't help?"

"Nope."

Di added, "Wouldn't even talk to us."

"That's odd. Sure, ladies. I'll put someone on it. Give me your details so I can contact you."

Di smiled, "What, you're not coming in here regular-like?"

He smiled back. "Of course I will. But not to talk business."

Nef said, "Nice." She sighed. "But I suppose you charge."

"Maybe. Good publicity is sometimes worth as much as a fee."

She gave him a cautious smile. "Yeah. Okay."

Rob's electrician called the next day. She was a tall, dark-skinned islander with jet-black hair caught up under a baseball hat. Nef and Di were busy and left her to drill, curse, grunt, and curse some more by herself.

She disappeared several times to the basement, Rob's office, and the apartment above.

Eventually, a pipe, like one of the drainpipes already running from the ceiling to the floor in the corner, was finished and painted the same as the others. All the dirt was tidied away.

Nef said, "Sorry. We didn't ask your name."

"Bernie."

"Hi, Bernie. Want something? On the house."

Bernie frowned. "Thanks. Espresso. That's good of you."

"No problem."

As they prepared the drink, Bernie asked, "You met Rob. What did you think of him?"

Nef shrugged.

Di nodded and said, "Okay."

Nef asked, "You worked for him before?"

"A while ago, I did some jobs for him."

"He said he might help us find Nef's brother," Di said.

"That's good. I hope he can. He tells me he's got a vacancy. I'm not sure, but I might apply. What's this area like?"

Di answered, "The dumps! Very little foot traffic. But it's convenient for everywhere else. We're here 'cos we love the city!"

Bernie nodded. "My family's always been here. Since before the city was built."

"What when it was the islands?"

"Certainly. The older folk told a lot of tales of how beautiful it all was."

"Cool!" Di replied with a frown.

Bernie laughed. "Don't worry! I love the city too, and it's too late to do anything about it!"

Back in Rob's office, Bernie sat close to him, talking quietly. "I told them you had a vacancy, and maybe I'd apply."

"Great! So they'll be expecting you to show up again."

She nodded. "You're all fixed up into the network. No one will be able to trace it among all the other traffic. And the installation is good. Looks like the real thing."

Rob smiled. "I knew you could do it."

She shrugged.

"How are you adjusting to being out again?"

"Still looking for somewhere to live." She stopped and smiled.

"You know, I'd forgotten about people being kind. Those two down-stairs offered me a drink—on the house! That sort of thing doesn't happen in prison."

"I'm sure. If you need, I guess you could use the apartment upstairs."

She shook her head. "No, that wouldn't look right. An electrician can't afford one of those."

"Okay. But let me know what I can do. Like I said, this job has plenty of backing."

"You've already done a lot. Thank you. I'll come by next week."

"Great. Look forward to it. I should have most of the gear set up by then."

"Good to see you again, Rob."

"Likewise, Bernie. Can't wait to get this all started up!"

As she left, she said, "Bunden Street! Of all the shitholes..."

"I know! Perfect, isn't it?"

CHAPTER 13

HAWKINS ARRAY

Rob had never been to the Hawkins Array, and Jim had not recommended it.

Started as a scientific outpost, it had added a small number of traders supplying necessities. To the amazement of all, the trading post became popular. Its growth outpaced its administrators. Businesses had opened with the permission of other businesses—rather than from the station authorities. They docked together and drew up contracts permitting passage through existing modules for both customers and stock. The station had soon become a maze of oddly configured compartments, corridors, and walkways under the control of small fiefdoms. The original businesses froze in place, locked by docking clamps, open airlocks, and old contracts. If a business failed, or its proprietor moved on, died, or disappeared, sometimes no one took over. Empty modules became cold and dark, forcing neighbors to band together to prevent disasters. Fear of atmospheric leaks kept the derelict areas accessible and minimally serviceable.

A community formed of traders, criminals, and lawyers. The administration's continued failure to control was a leak pluggable only by an unusually large police unit.

. . .

As Rob stepped out of his flier and into the antiseptically polished docking corridor, he breathed in deeply.

In the last two years, he had not traveled. He had grown accustomed once more to the blue skies, the noise, the sea, the smells of Earth. His body had almost forgotten the difference. Something in the air of space stations made his skin tighter. A dryness rushed down his respiratory tract—not a scent, but a feeling. If it were a smell, for Rob—long practiced in the art of making his work pay—it was the smell of money.

Police Commandant Ngell Amarno's hair had gone gray. Rob wondered if it happened soon after he took the position.

"Thanks for seeing me," Rob said politely.

Ngell replied with a sigh, "Don't have long. How can I help?"

"I asked to see you personally on the recommendation of Jim Able. You met him a while back. From the OEA."

Ngell's face showed no trace of recognition.

"He was here with a Neraffan called Tella."

A smile lit the officer's face. "Tella! Yes, I remember him. Good investigator. Very competent." He sliced the air with his hand. "Straight on. No nonsense."

Rob nodded. "But you don't remember Jim?"

Ngell shook his head. "Sorry."

"Well, that's Jim for you. Unassuming sort of guy. Likes to stay in the background. Anyway, I'm in search of a missing person, Fred Neuhaus. Came to work here just over three years ago. Remember the case?"

Ngell stood and picked up a large tablet from a shelf. "Let's have a look." He typed in a search and studied the results. "Yeah. Remember this now. No trace. Probably lost in a depressurization. Sad."

Rob smiled. "That's it. There is probably not much point in me digging into it. Probably not much to dig into!"

"'Fraid not."

Rob frowned and said, "I have a couple of questions, though, if you don't mind."

Ngell shrugged.

"Any record of a depressurization on that day?"

"You've not been here long, have you. Some parts of this...construction are better than others. He was working in one of the worst."

"Sure, I understand. Those union guys are brave men. I'm not volunteering to do what they do! But did your alarms go off? I presume that happens when there's a serious breach."

"Sure. We have the same lockdown protocols that any station has. But remember, not all leaks are catastrophic."

"No. No, I understand that. In my younger days, I was into all that sort of stuff—the engineering theory behind building stations, the specifications, the codes...but this is what I'm wondering. A leak strong enough to push a man out is one thing, but it would also have to have been strong enough to send him traveling way beyond the station. Or you'd have found his body floating outside, right? Now, you see, I remember that sort of detail: atmospheric volume per second. That size of leak would absolutely be enough to set off your alarms. At least, it should be, unless there's something wrong with your alarms."

Ngell didn't reply immediately. He looked at Rob, reassessing him. Getting up, he went to another desk and sat before a display. "Give me the date again."

Rob read out the date and time.

"You're right. No alarms that day."

Rob waited until Ngell sat behind his desk again.

They sat in silence, facing each other.

Ngell said quietly, "I don't have time. I don't have the staffing. The case is over two years old."

"He's not out there. He's either still here, or he was taken somewhere else."

"If he's here and dead, someone would have reported the smell.

If he's here and alive, someone would have seen him, or his badge would have been in use somewhere on the station."

"Would you have seen him leave?"

Ngell shook his head. "Unfortunately, there are a lot of ways off this place. On a commercial transport? Yes, we'd have images of him. In a crate? There's no guarantee it would have been caught. Every time we close a rat hole, they open another. We just wouldn't know."

"The last thing I want to do is embarrass anyone or cause you any trouble. But I do want to find out what happened to him. Fred's sister deserves an answer."

"If he was in a crate or taken out a back door, troubling me or embarrassing admin are the least of your worries. You start asking the wrong questions or poking around the wrong places, and I might not be able to protect you."

Rob sighed. "You have a difficult job."

"You have no idea."

"I think I do. But I've taken on a difficult job too. Are you okay with me asking questions and doing some poking?"

"As I said, I don't have time. I don't have the staffing. I recommend you go home."

"I'm not asking for armed escorts. Just for no interference."

Ngell nodded slowly. "I strongly recommend you go home, but I can't force you."

"Can I have his badge number?"

Turning his tablet around, he let Rob copy down the ID.

"Thanks. I'll let you know if I find anything."

"If you go missing, who do I contact?"

Smiling, Rob handed him a business card. "My admin, Bernie. I appreciate the thought."

Rob sat in a modest café near the Hawkins Array's main admin center, listening to the conversations surrounding him.

He had thought to eat in the famous Hawkins Restaurant. The food had the highest reputation with prices to match. But he had looked at the menu with Jim's caution sounding in his mind. *Better earn some money first.*

From the down-market café, he watched the staff come and go from the admin offices. Eventually, two youngsters came into the café and sat together. One was thin and bespectacled, with a scrappy beard and ruffled hair. His companion sported multicolored hair and multiple piercings and carried several large sheets of paper in her arms.

Listening as the girl berated her friend with jargon Rob did not follow, he came to understand something in the flow charts and diagrams filling the small table was a point of contention.

Bingo! he thought.

Waiting until they paused their discussion to sip their drinks, Rob moved his chair to join them at their table.

"Sorry to interrupt, but I hope you can help me with a small problem."

"Umm...Okay," the boy said.

"I'm working with Commandant Amarno on a missing person's case. I'm Rob, by the way." He held out his hand.

"Mitch," the boy replied, shaking his hand.

Rob looked to the girl who, frowning, said, "Tess."

"Good to meet you both! Got this problem, you see, and I don't want to waste police time tracking this down. I have the badge ID for the missing person, and I need a printout of his last day's location points."

"Okay..." Mitch said noncommittally.

"Bet you two could print that off in half a minute without bothering anyone else. It's old data. About two years ago."

Tess said, "Not current, then?"

Rob waved his hand, "No, no! Archival stuff. Nothing live. I wouldn't want you doing anything with live systems."

Mitch frowned and said to Tess, "That'd be in the V25 Monthly, wouldn't it?"

She nodded. "And/or the V32 Periodic."

"Both loaded on the hoard-broker. That wouldn't be hard."

"Easy."

Rob went on, "Now, I don't want anything else—just that last day. Would you be able to get that for me?"

Mitch looked at Tess. She shrugged.

"Great!" Rob said with an encouraging smile. "Here's my address. Best place to send it is there."

Mitch looked at Rob's electronic address and said, "That's a private one. Why don't you want it to go to your HA address?"

Rob looked sad. "It's for his sister, you see. She's never been told what happened. So, I thought if I could paint a picture of his movements, it might help. I mean, there's no way to find him now and no one's got the resources to investigate further, so it's the least we can do. You know...share what little we do have. And as I say, I don't want to bring anyone else in on it. Certainly don't want to waste valuable police time on it!"

Mitch frowned.

Rob pressed, "*Can* you do it?"

Mitch nodded. "I guess..."

Rob pulled a piece of paper out of his pocket. "Here's the badge ID and the day we're interested in. See what you can do. His name was Fred Neuhaus. His sister will be so grateful. It's been a couple of years of hell for her."

Mitch shrugged and looked at Tess for confirmation.

She shrugged and nodded.

"Thanks so much!" Rob got up and left the café.

Mitch and Tess sent the information within fifteen minutes.

Rob sent a copy to his office in Unity City and began to follow the path taken by Fred Neuhaus the day he disappeared.

The badge was recorded entering Court Six and immediately going into the Bargain Break eatery.

Rob stood before the boarded door and whitewashed windows of the Bargain Break.

Next, he followed the electronic trail up to Court Eight and the electronics store run by a Huracken called Melha Melha.

The storefront was clean and bright. The displayed items had small price tags, each turned just out of sight from anyone looking through the window.

I see what you did there.

"Good morning!" Rob called from the doorway.

"What do you want?" came the reply.

"Something in your window caught my eye. Is that a Lascon stunner?"

"What? No! Such things are prohibited."

Rob advanced to the counter. Melha Melha sat behind it in a circular wicker chair, a length of chewing string hanging from his mouth. His hair hung unbrushed around him in the typical Huracken style.

"What's that in the window then?"

"A theatrical prop. It doesn't do anything."

"Oh, right. No impulsor."

"You know about such things?"

Rob noted the retailer's guarded interest. "I do." He looked around the otherwise empty store. "Can I get one *with* an impulsor?"

Melha spat his string into a bucket under the counter. "They're illegal. You might be able to buy an impulsor on its own, but it'd cost you."

"I can afford it."

The Huracken scratched himself and stood. "Wait here."

Rob watched Melha—reflected in the mirror behind the chair—retrieving the device from the window. He returned to scrabble under the counter, finally emerging with a small black block with a red warning label hanging from it. He ripped off the label, then pulled open the stunner and inserted the block.

"One theatrical prop. One impulsor. Payment in full."

Rob turned over the small price tags and didn't blink. "Of course," he replied with a smile, handing over his payment fob.

As he pressed the fob into his terminal, Melha asked, "Want 'em wrapped?"

"No need."

"Pleasure doing business," Melha said as he sank back into his wicker seat. "Your discretion is appreciated."

"Of course. I wouldn't want to make trouble for either of us. Just one other thing. How do I get to Eight-Four Forty-Second Alley?"

Melha snorted. "Why?"

"I have some business there."

"You'll need more than that," he said, nodding toward the stunner.

Rob nodded slowly and waited.

Without turning or getting up, Melha said quietly, "Through the green curtain. Don't go up the ladder. Keep going straight. You'll see two green arrows; at each one, go the other way."

"Thank you. Have a nice day."

Melha Melha chuckled.

CHAPTER 14

MORE TRAINING

Betih laid out the tools on the galley table. She sighed.

"You okay?" Jim asked.

"I am sad. These were my friends for many years."

He nodded, not knowing what else to say.

"You suspect already what this is." She held up the cylinder.

"You threatened Sharky with it. I guess it's The Striker, and I saw it do something unpleasant to the table in the cafe."

"It kills. Surely and quickly."

"How does it work?"

She snapped her jaws. "How would I know?"

"No...I mean, how do I work it?"

"Better. You pull out the inside until it clicks. You push the end against your target. It fires something into them. As they die, you step away. You have already planned and memorized your exit. You do not look back."

"Can I try it?"

"No."

"What? I'll have to practice with it. Get a feel of it."

"There is no safe way to do that."

"Why not? What the hell does it fire?"

"Antimatter, I hear."

Jim blinked. "You're joking!"

Betih shrugged. "What do I know? I suppose it must be a small amount. Just enough to do the job."

"So, if I accidentally prime it, I'd have to find an unsuspecting table to blow up?"

"Perhaps. Do you hate tables so much?"

"I can't remember. Does antimatter irradiate when it goes off?"

"Perhaps."

"Am I going to get irradiated every time I kill someone? Did we leave a mess for the café staff?"

"Perhaps."

Jim shook his head. "You've never checked?"

"Fool of a monkey! How would you check such a thing? An assassin does not reveal herself."

Jim looked away. Wagging his finger at her, he said, "You said something like that before...You said no one names an assassin. What would happen if someone did?"

She shifted uncomfortably in her chair. "I don't know. But I heard it once happened long ago. Other assassins came, and the person with loose lips was killed."

"Oh, I see. But you've never been called to do such a communal thing."

"No."

"Interesting."

"Do not experiment with The Striker. It will serve you when necessary."

Jim picked it up from the table and turned it round in his hand. "Wait a minute. I have to press this *on* my target? I'm that close? An arm's length?"

She said nothing, her eyes on his.

Jim frowned and looked away. "Fair enough. Just a bit more...intimate than I imagined."

"Death is a personal experience for both the target and the assassin."

"But that's way close enough to get hit by whatever radiation is generated."

"Perhaps. If the amount of antimatter is small and the target is fat, perhaps not."

"It injects? Or deposits on the surface?"

"Injects at speed. There is an explosion within the target. It kills. Surely and quickly, I already said. You used the word 'unpleasant.' What did you expect? Birds to sing? Crowds to cheer? Grow up, monkey!"

"Fuck you!"

She reached across the table and picked up the wristbands. "Put these on!"

Jim frowned but obeyed.

Betih stood and walked across the galley.

"Touch the surface."

He put his finger on the silver disk on his left wrist and then on the right. Both disks showed the rainbow haze he knew from The Cloud.

"What are they?"

"Shields."

"Oh! I have some protection?"

Betih threw something across the room at him. Jim instantly brought a hand up near his face to catch it.

A small blade hung in the air just beyond his fingers, pointing at his eye. It, too, shimmered with a rainbow of color.

He reached with his other hand, took the handle, and gently placed the knife on the table.

"That is how they work," she said with a smile.

"Have you been carrying this knife all the time?"

"Of course."

"Good to know. These wristbands, I presume, I can practice with?"

"You may. But you should never show them off in public. Nor should you rely on them. Do not imagine they will save you from your own foolishness."

"Can they stop blaster shots?"

"Yes, if your hand is already in its path."

"I see. There isn't a version of these to cover the whole body?"

"I've never seen one."

Jim turned off the wristbands and sighed. "Do you know anything about where this tech comes from?"

"Only that it is old. Through generations, they have been suffi-cient for the assassin's purpose and not more."

"Okay. I get that."

"At last, you begin to learn!"

"I'm learning about you. You could have taken my eye out!"

"I could. And, in doing so, would have proven my nephew wrong. Is there a loss in that outcome?"

"So, what? It's scarier for you if he's right?"

She nodded. "That the spirit could work through the likes of you is unheard of. The Luminary's library is full of books—from end to end—not one even mentions such a possibility."

"I hear you two say things like that. You mean something more than me taking up your assassin's duties, don't you."

"We do. What that is, I may yet discover."

CHAPTER 15

THE TRAIL

The green curtain revealed a door opening to a ladder and a wide gap in both floor and ceiling. To the right, just wide enough for a foot, a ledge led around the ladder and into the corridor behind.

There was little light to guide Rob down the length of several modules. At an intersection with another—thinner and darker—corridor, he saw a piece of card taped to the wall: the first green arrow.

The air in the thinner corridor bit his nose. *Damn, it's cold. Must be close to a gap in the structure.*

As he walked, he felt the walls. *These were in space. Someone's docked them and later sealed it all up.*

At the next intersection, warm air wafted up from below. A ladder ran up into the ceiling and down into the dark. Another green arrow pointed up.

At least it'll be warmer.

He slowly climbed down, looking for clues about what lay below.

On the next level, he stopped and stepped off the ladder. He heard the hum of machinery but also the distant sound of voices.

Rob stared into the dark. To the left and right, he could make out the rectangular outline of another corridor. Behind the ladder, there was a difference in the shadow. He stepped around and felt along the wall.

Got you!

His fingers curled around the thick fabric of a black curtain. He felt behind it and found a door handle.

The light stung his eyes for a moment. He was in a storage container, empty except for a free-standing lamp and a bowl of plastic petunias.

The doors at the other end were open outwards. Poking his head nervously round into the next room, he sighed.

One side of the room consisted of five other storage containers, rammed up against each other, doors all open. Against the opposite wall stood empty tables.

He could see piles of crates through a glass door to his left. The voices were louder.

He quietly opened the glass door and hid between two columns of crates.

The voices were not clear. Several people, he thought, were whispering to each other or perhaps muttering to themselves. That they weren't arguing, shouting, or even laughing helped him relax.

Taking a deep breath, he stepped out of hiding and walked around the room's perimeter until he found an anteroom and another door.

Rob's heart sank, and he almost swore out loud.

In the next room, he saw Fred Neuhaus's final destination. Several men were moving around worktables, unpacking small capsules—seeds or pills, he thought—from large boxes and repacking them in bags.

Their skin, pale in the bright lights, was raked with sores and bruises. They were naked apart from diapers. Around their heads, they wore mechanical headbands. Rob could see old blood caked around the edges of the bands.

Each man repeated phrases to himself, "Repack one-quarter kilo." "Unpack five kilos." "Repack one-quarter kilo."

Another voice sounded behind Rob in the crate room. "Ha! Such a joker. Wait till your wife finds out!"

Several others laughed.

Rob stood off to the side of the anteroom.

Six humans appeared, with two other people Rob didn't immediately recognize.

One man caught sight of him and said, "Who are you?"

"Don't worry!" Rob replied cheerfully, raising his hands, "I'm meant to be here."

As his right hand reached just higher than his head, he activated the Lascon stunner and dropped to his knees. A blue flash filled the upper part of the room. All eight crumpled to the floor with nothing but the sound of the breath being knocked from their bodies.

He ran back through the crate room, the container, up the ladder, and through the corridors. He burst out by Melha's counter and stopped himself long enough to assess who was in the store.

Six customers and Melha—four close to the counter, two by the door.

Rob raised the stunner, angled it down toward the counter, and fired. The two by the door were out of range, but the other four and Melha dropped immediately.

Rob shouted, "You two! Get Commandant Amarno here! Do it now!"

With looks of alarm, they ran from the store.

Rob looked down at Melha slumped in his wicker chair. *Okay. Nice doing business with you too.*

He worked his way around the Huracken to the payment terminal. Reaching down, he took the till controller from Melha's belt.

He refilled his payment fob from the store's account.

Smiling, he unhooked the controller, stopped, reconnected it, and filled two more fobs.

A pleasure.

Through the shop windows, he could see Amarno and several other officers running through the court.

Before Amarno could ask, Rob was shouting instructions.

"Medic team for these people! Another team to follow us in to Eight-Four Forty-Second Alley. You'll need your backup to trace you as you go—can they do that? Follow me!" He led them back the way he came.

Amarno asked several questions. Rob only answered, "You've got a big problem. We have to move fast."

Startled by the prone bodies in the anteroom, Amarno shouted, "Wait one moment! Who did this?"

"The medics can sort these folks out. Your problem is in there." He gestured to the police commandant to look through to the packing room. The repacking activity went on undisturbed.

Amarno looked. He seemed to Rob to have stopped breathing. "I see."

"Yeah, and no. Your problem is more than just these guys. It's getting us out of here alive; now they know we know."

Pointing to the unconscious on the floor, Amarno said, "They won't be talking yet."

Rob shook his head. "This isn't all of them. Someone's monitoring those mechanized slaves. And you can be sure they have eyes on every room here."

Nodding, Ngell replied, "Okay." Looking back into the packing room, he spoke into his comm badge, "Sergeant on Duty, do you read me? Listen carefully. Call in the nearest medical ship. We need emergency evac. Try EIA, OEA, commercial, whoever is closest, I don't care which. Tell them at least a dozen patients in dire medical need beyond the capacity of this station. I need armed response to my position, three teams. One from Court Eight. One from Level Six, moving up. One from Level Nine, moving down. They are to arrest anyone they meet who's moving quickly." He looked back into the packing room, turned to Rob, and said, "Damn you!"

Back in Amarno's office, Rob sat and watched the commandant's face.

"That something like this could be going on—under my nose— it makes me sick."

"Yeah, I know. You'll let me know if one of them is Fred Neuhaus?"

"Of course. Soon as I hear."

"And...if you don't mind...let me know the names of the others too."

"I shouldn't. But okay."

"And...again...to stretch a point. The names of the organizers, the people you arrest."

Ngell shook his head. "No way. You can ask for the judge's records and see what's on the public declarations. I can't name anyone who doesn't get convicted."

"Hmm. Yeah, that's the problem, isn't it? The ones who walk free. The ones who know who you are and who I am. It puts us at a disadvantage, don't you think?"

"That goes with the job."

"Not mine, it doesn't. I'm just a concerned citizen."

"A concerned citizen who brought some kind of illegal stunner onto my station."

Rob smiled. "I can categorically state I did not bring it onto the station. I bought it from Melha on my way through."

"He's already been convicted three times of shit like this. He crawls back out every time."

"You need to take care."

"I know. I have your details; I'll send you news when I can."

"Thanks."

"Now go home. Don't come back."

Rob sat with Nef and Di in the empty café.

"I'll tell you more as soon as I know. Fred was definitely one of them. And...not all of them will survive. It's a difficult surgery to remove controllers like those from a brain."

Nef nodded.

Di muttered, "It's like slavery but with hardware."

"That's exactly what it is. It goes on in less civilized parts throughout the galaxy. Very difficult to stop."

She shivered. "It's horrible."

Nef said, "Well, anyway, you sending me a bill? We don't make a lot here."

"I know. I don't want you breaking the bank. I, umm, got paid from another source while I was there, so I won't be losing out. Maybe give us a testimonial instead? Success stories are great advertising."

PART TWO

MRS. KATRIGG

CHAPTER 16

MAKING CONTACT

A member of EBMS staff escorted Rob Stuart to the airlock of Jim's ship.

"Rob!"

"Hi, Jim!"

"Come on in. This is the ship!"

"Praestans Rapax! You can always tell their work. Too clean. Perfect—horribly perfect."

"Yeah, I know what you mean. How was Hawkins?"

"Dangerous."

"Told you."

"You did. I told Commandant Amarno I knew you. He didn't remember you."

Jim snorted. "Typical."

"You need to make more of an impression on people, Jim. Don't blend in with the scenery so much."

"Up yours! Hungry?"

"Sure."

"The galley is also the conference room."

"Sounds ideal."

. . .

Jim and Rob slouched together at one end of the galley table, laughing.

Tella took a seat, and Jim introduced it to Rob.

Rob nodded and said, "I've heard a lot about you."

Tella replied, "And I, you. Both from Jim and from contacts in the OEA."

Rob thought, *Damn, that doesn't sound good.* He asked Jim, "You been spreading rumors again?"

Smiling, Jim said, "Who'd believe me?"

Rob laughed.

Betih and Marhan came into the galley together. Rob caught his breath at the sight.

"Rob, this is Ernot Dirl Marhan and his aunt, Ernot Bard Betwen, from Tanna Gul."

Rob said, "Pleased to meet you both."

Marhan said, "Jim has spoken of you."

Betih said, "You are smaller than I thought you would be."

Rob frowned.

"You can insult her back if you want," Jim commented.

"I...umm," Rob stuttered, "wouldn't want to cause any friction amongst your team, Jim."

Marhan fixed Rob with a stare. "Wise monkey."

Betih snapped her jaws and smiled.

Jim said, "You first, Rob. How is Bunden Street?"

"Robins is up and running. First case successfully concluded."

"What about the underlying tech?"

"Underway. What about your nephew?"

Jim checked the time. "If he can sneak out, he'll be here in an hour or so."

Rob asked, "And everyone else here knows all about that?"

Jim nodded, as did the others. Then Jim said, "Thanks, Rob. Now, I want to talk through my next step. I'm going to hire Jack Katrigg for a job."

Marhan asked, "Which one?"

"I guess whichever one they send. Once his job is done, I'll start making complaints. I want to see how high up the organization I can reach."

"Aren't you worried about using your name?" Rob asked.

Jim shook his head. "I think I have to. From what I learned on Stacco Ila 32, my name is already out there. Certain folk are worried about me. About who I am. I hope that'll be useful in this case. It won't be as suspicious as if I was still with the OEA or the EIA."

Marhan growled. "I still think it foolish."

Tella added, "Again, Marhan and I agree. There is great risk."

"That's what I need your help with. Once I contact Katrigg's organization, I'm relying on you guys to have my back."

They all nodded.

"Before we go too far though," Jim continued, "I'm going to disappear for a while."

"Anywhere nice?" Rob asked.

"Sonloi-AC."

"Visiting your mom? Okay."

"I'm going to have some minor surgery done."

Marhan barked and said, "At last!"

"Anything we need to know about?" Rob asked quietly.

"No. Not going into details here. Suffice to say, this ship is too clean, like you said, just not clean enough."

Rob's eyebrows shot up, and he put his finger to his lips.

Tella asked, "What will you ask Katrigg to do for you?"

Jim sighed, "I don't know. Something simple. Deliver something to Rob at his office?"

Rob shrugged.

"Deliver what?" Tella asked.

Jim raised his hands. "Wasn't going to decide yet, but..." He stood and walked over to a food locker. "This'll do."

He tossed a small can to Rob, who caught it and spun it onto the tabletop.

"Mackerel? In sauce?"

"I can't see any of us being in so much need that we'd actually have to eat it. So, yeah, why not?"

"I'm already looking forward to its arrival!"

Returning to the table, Jim said, "Tell me everything you can find out about Katrigg when he visits. Scan him, photograph him, weigh him if you can!"

"Got it! Shoe size, inside leg, color of earwax. No problem."

Betih spoke. "DNA?"

Rob cocked his head and looked at her.

Jim smiled sadly and said, "May not be possible."

Rob shrugged. "I'll see what I can do."

A knock sounded at the airlock door. Jim said, "Davey, I hope."

He walked up the ramp to the flight room and down the corridor to the back of the ship. As he approached the door, he heard raised voices.

Outside, Davey and Clo's faces were turned to the floor.

Davey's father wagged his angriest finger at them both.

"Matt?" Jim said, "Is there a problem?"

"Damn right, there is! I've told you before—no contact with EBMS personnel. That includes these two!" To the kids, he shouted, "What the hell are you doing here? I'm still waiting for an answer!"

Davey looked up to Jim but didn't speak, his face red with embarrassment.

"Matt, listen—"

"No! I'm done listening to you. You never change. I do you a favor, letting you dock here, and what do you do? Same as you always do, you ignore the rules. You take advantage. I'm done." To Davey, he said, "Grounded. Your room. One week. Go!"

Davey glanced at Jim again and shrugged.

To Clo, Matt said, "Go see your mother. If she doesn't ground you, I'm putting you in the brig. Go!"

As the kids walked away, hand in hand, Matt said quietly to Jim, "You, your visitors, and the rest of your freak show leave within the hour. Don't come back."

"Matt...really? Listen, let me explain.

"No. Don't come back. If you're not gone in sixty minutes, I'll have my engineers cut your ship away."

Jim bit back what he wanted to say. "Sure, Matt. Whatever."

Back in the galley, Jim announced, "Slight change of plan. Rob, off you go. Everyone else...we're looking for a new home. Matt's on the warpath. He caught Davey and Clo sneaking over to see us."

Rob asked, "So, no help from the kids?"

"Are you joking? Davey has a whole week grounded in his room with nothing else to do! Just make sure Matt doesn't trace your communications."

"Got it!"

Marhan asked, "Where will we go?"

"Sonloi-AC. It's earlier than I wanted, but it's a nice place."

Marhan told Betih, "Jim's mother paints portraits of the Meoena. You might find it interesting."

Betih put her head to one side quizzically but didn't reply.

Jim sent a message to the address he was given for Jack Katrigg.

From: Jim Able Private Citizen Sol Earth
To: J Katrigg Courier Superincumbent Logistics Company

I need a small package picked up from Pec Sonloi Sonloi-AC and delivered to Robins, Bunden Street, Unity City, Sol Earth.
I require speed, discretion, and confirmation of delivery.

CHAPTER 17

THE COMPLAINTS DEPARTMENT

Rob's data on Jack Katrigg's visit was far more extensive than Jim expected, though it wasn't all intelligible. *That's a whole lot of electronics you must have bought. I hope you're not bankrupting my company before it gets going!*

From: Jim Able Private Citizen Sol Earth
To: Courier Superincumbent Logistics Company, Tak Balun Rel 25

I wish to register a complaint about the recent delivery service performed by your courier Jack Katrigg. Please advise me of your procedures in dealing with inadequate service.

The reply came quickly.

From: Courier Superincumbent Logistics Company, Tak Balun Rel 25
To: Jim Able Private Citizen Sol Earth

Complaints may be registered at Service Desk Courier Superincumbent Logistics Company, Tak Balun Rel 25.
Thank you for your business.

———

From: Jim Able Private Citizen Sol Earth
To: Service Desk Courier Superincumbent Logistics Company, Tak Balun Rel 25

I wish to talk to someone regarding the inadequate service performed by your courier, Jack Katrigg.

———

From: Service Desk Courier Superincumbent Logistics Company, Tak Balun Rel 25
To: Jim Able Private Citizen Sol Earth

Please supply the contract number, service date, and copies of all signed documents relating to this contract.

———

From: Jim Able Private Citizen Sol Earth
To: Service Desk Courier Superincumbent Logistics Company, Tak Balun Rel 25

Documents attached. Please contact me in person. I want to talk to someone in charge.

———

From: Service Desk Courier Superincumbent Logistics Company, Tak Balun Rel 25
To: Jim Able Private Citizen Sol Earth

We have reviewed the contract in question and have concluded the service provided was within expectations.

From: Jim Able Private Citizen Sol Earth
To: Service Desk Courier Superincumbent Logistics Company, Tak Balun Rel 25

I want to speak directly with someone in charge.

From: Service Desk Courier Superincumbent Logistics Company, Tak Balun Rel 25
To: Jim Able Private Citizen Sol Earth

No one is available to speak with you.
We have reviewed the contract in question and have concluded the service provided was within expectations.

From: Jim Able Private Citizen Sol Earth
To: Service Desk Courier Superincumbent Logistics Company, Tak Balun Rel 25

I am not satisfied with your previous reply.
I want to speak directly with someone in charge.

From: Service Desk Courier Superincumbent Logistics Company, Tak Balun Rel 25
To: Jim Able Private Citizen Sol Earth

No one is available to speak with you.
We have reviewed the contract in question and have concluded the service provided was within expectations.

———

So, Jim thought, *I'm dealing with an automated system. So far, so good.*

From: Jim Able Private Citizen Sol Earth
To: Service Desk Courier Superincumbent Logistics Company, Tak Balun Rel 25

Please put me in touch with Jack Katrigg.

———

From: Service Desk Courier Superincumbent Logistics Company, Tak Balun Rel 25
To: Jim Able Private Citizen Sol Earth

No one is available to speak with you.

———

Tella came down the ramp from its module to find Jim working at a display to the right of the flight cabin. "How is it going?"

"Okay, so far. Seventy-five messages to the complaints department, and I've yet to find the magic combination of request and insult that gets a live person to respond."

"I admire your tenacity."

"It's just a matter of triggering the right line of code."

"Would threatening legal action work?"

"Tried that. And I've tried threatening exposure on the gossip nets."

"Have you tried asking for Jack's boss?"

"Yep."
"Supervisor?"
"Yep."
"Landlord?"
"Not yet. But I might."
"Rabbi?"
"Good one!" Jim made a note.
"Hairstylist?"
"Let's not get silly. But I'll try his family members if I have to!"
"I admire your tenacity."
"See you later."

From: Client Relations Courier Superincumbent Logistics Company, Tak Balun Rel 25
To: Jim Able Private Citizen Sol Earth

Please provide the reason for your request to see Mr. Katrigg's mother.

There's a Mrs. Katrigg? And she's part of this organization!

From: Jim Able Private Citizen Sol Earth
To: Client Relations Courier Superincumbent Logistics Company, Tak Balun Rel 25

My desire to contact Mrs. Katrigg dates from August 2098 when Jack Katrigg was involved in a mandatory audit at the Sin Har spaceport of Ch'Garratt.
He tried to kill me and, in doing so, killed over a hundred other people and injured as many.

From: Client Relations Courier Superincumbent Logistics Company, Tak Balun Rel 25
To: Jim Able Private Citizen Sol Earth

Please supply the contract number, service date, and copies of all signed documents relating to this contract.

From: Jim Able Private Citizen Sol Earth
To: Client Relations Courier Superincumbent Logistics Company, Tak Balun Rel 25

I cannot supply any contract details since either a) someone else hired Jack Katrigg to kill me, or b) he decided to do so of his own volition. This matter obviously cannot profitably be discussed by an automated system. It requires personal contact between me and Mrs. Katrigg.

Around the table in the galley, the remains of a meal cooled as they talked.

"I haven't had a reply for eight hours."

Tella said, "I wonder if Mrs. Katrigg is another artificial system? Will you be transferred from one automated routine to another?"

Marhan laughed. "I think you are wasting your time with this approach."

Betih shook her head. "I think you have moved into the real world. Systems can reply instantly. Either you will never receive a reply, or it will be from a person. People are slow."

"I hope you're right."

Two days later, Jim received the following.

From: Mrs. T. Katrigg, Superincumbent Logistics Company, Rinfar Molc, Isnard, The Mansion
To: Jim Able Private Citizen Sol Earth

Dear Mr. Able,
I find it hard to believe the story you tell of being the target of an attack by my Jack. However, I have done some research and found an incident did take place at Ch'Garratt and that Jack was employed there at about the same time.
I also read that you behaved creditably in helping the injured.
For this reason, I invite you to tea so we can discuss this matter further. I hope to clear up this misunderstanding as soon as we may.
I will have my staff send you the details of where to land, as I understand we are otherwise a little difficult to find.

Yours,
Talia Katrigg, Mrs.

"Congratulations, Jim! This sounds like a success," said Tella.

"You cannot go alone," Marhan warned.

"She sounds genuine. She doesn't write like a system."

Marhan pressed, "Her 'staff' may yet waylay you."

Jim nodded. "I know. But what do you make of this?" He showed them a display with two planets listed. "Here is Rinfar Molc. This is Acep Five. Her address is Molc, but the coordinates they sent take me to Acep. The planet is otherwise uninhabited, so no formal name yet."

Betih offered, "It has all the marks of a trap."

"Does it, though?" Jim wondered. If you want to conceal your actual location, this is one way to do it. List everything in one place, and only tell people where things really are when you absolutely have to."

"You cannot go alone," Marhan repeated. "Such deviousness itself is a warning."

"True. We'll all go. But I'll go to tea in the flier." Jim indicated the solo craft held in the belly of the ship. "You'll be in orbit, ready to rescue me."

"It would be better if we were closer," Tella said.

"Only I got the invitation, and I don't want to spook her."

CHAPTER 18

TALIA KATRIGG, MRS

Acep Five would traditionally have been called an ice planet. Such a designation would require two things: first, a planetary survey confirming that no part of the world warmed beyond the freezing point of the predominant liquid, and second, someone to care sufficiently to mount such a survey.

I doubt anyone has bothered, Jim thought as he watched the white surface approaching him.

The flight was the first real trip he had taken in the solo flier the Praestans Rapax had provided with his ship. The interior, though comfortable, was snug.

Upon leaving the main ship, he engaged the stealth systems and turned them off once he landed on the clearly marked pad.

A path had been cleared ahead of him, straight through the snow and up to the front door. The wind was wild and bitingly cold.

The house was huge and built in the style of an elegant Earth mansion. Few properties in Unity City could match it in beauty or nostalgia. Two wings stood four stories high, with neat windows and chimneys. A grand staircase led up to the oversized double doors.

A comfortingly archaic plume of smoke drifted from one tall chimney.

Jim checked in with the ship. "You guys seeing all this?"

Tella's voice replied. "We are. We do not see any concentration of people. The building is largely empty."

"Understood."

A butler opened the door before Jim knocked.

"Good afternoon, sir. May I view some form of ID, if you please."

Jim showed him an old OEA ID card. "I'm Jim Able."

"Indeed, sir. Thank you. Please follow me."

"And your name is?"

"I am Jenkins, sir. I have the pleasure of serving this house."

"Okay, Jenkins. It's good of Mrs. Katrigg to see me."

"Yes, sir. She does not request many visitors. It is an honor bestowed on very few."

Once through the vestibule, Jim saw the hall rising to the roof. The dark wood of the rafters was repeated down the staircases to the paneling of the first floor.

"You will meet with Mrs. Katrigg in the drawing room. But first, I must be assured you carry no weapons, sir."

"Well, I came prepared for any eventuality. I have never met you or Mrs. Katrigg and had no idea what kind of reception I would find."

Jim removed his blaster from its holster and offered the handle to the butler.

"Thank you, sir." Jenkins took the blaster and placed it carefully on a tray at a side table. "And now, if I may?" He picked up a scanner from the table and walked around Jim slowly. "That all seems to be in order, sir. Thank you."

He led Jim into a bright carpeted room.

It's like an antique store in here!

The furniture spoke of a long history—a distinctly human history. Several mirrors adorned the walls; each frame sparkled with gold. Stern-faced ancestors frowned down from their portraits on the otherwise happy scene. The fire burning in the oversized fireplace gave off a faint scent of apples.

"Mr. Able, Madam."

"Oh, Mr. Able! How wonderful. You are prompt. I do appreciate that."

She didn't rise from the wing chair but gestured to the sofa nearby.

"Thank you for seeing me. It's a pleasure to meet you."

As Jim sat, he quickly assessed Mrs. Katrigg. *Older than she sounds. That face has seen a lot. The jewelry—if it's real—could buy a planet!*

"How is the weather outside, Mr. Able? Not too bad a walk from the pad?"

"A little chilly, but no problem. Thank you. And please, call me Jim."

She looked up at Jenkins, who still stood by the door. "Tea, Jenkins. Be sure the water is properly hot."

"Of course, Madam."

"Now, Mr. Able. Tell me a little about yourself. Are you from Earth?"

"I am, though I grew up on a station, and I've traveled a fair bit."

"Ah, yes. Sonloi-AC, I hear."

That's effective research. Shouldn't expect anything less. "That's correct. And I've spent many years at the Office of External Affairs."

"Ah, yes. Have you ever been to Rinfar Molc before?"

What? "N-no, I haven't."

"Well, it isn't what it once was. I haven't seen it without snow for nearly twenty years. So sad. But then, climates are not things to be trifled with. Ah, here comes the tea! On the table here, Jenkins. We'll serve ourselves."

Jim had never held such high-grade porcelain before. It felt as though it would shatter under the pressure of his fingers. The pattern depicted horses and a fox.

"Are your parents still living, Mr. Able?"

"My mother is; she's an artist on Sonloi-AC. The locals, the Meoena, have a high regard for her portraits of them."

"Oh, how wonderful! It's so good for one to have a hobby."

She sipped her tea as Jim wondered if his mother had just been insulted.

"Now, Mr. Able, from the beginning, please tell me why you think my son would be involved in those dreadful events on Ch'Garratt."

"Sure. August 2098, I was part of an OEA audit of trade going through Ch'Garratt to Earth. One of my interviewees was Jack Katrigg. Our interview went well. The examination of his ship was fine. I escorted him to the docking bay in the terminal. He went on board, but"—Jim shook his head at the memories—"as soon as he took off, he fired a missile at a police flier and then five more into the terminal building."

She looked horrified. "So distressing!" She sipped her tea.

Jim squared himself to face her. "I'd like to find out why he did it."

"Well, of course! One would."

Jim put down his cup and looked back at her.

She looked at him with a slight furrow on her brow. "You seem an honest man, Mr. Able. I have no reason to doubt you, except I know I raised my son better than that." She put her cup down and continued, "Can you describe the ship for me?"

"The ship? Sure. A golden saucer. Quite distinctive."

"Oh, then easily traced, I imagine."

"It should have been. It was never seen again."

"How curious."

"I didn't mention one more thing. He left mines in orbit of Sin Har. They were nasty pieces of ancient technology. It took some clearing up."

She shook her head slowly and pursed her lips. "So strange! So strange!"

"I presume his actions were to cover up something. Something he thought I had discovered."

"I can see that, yes, that you would think along those lines. But..." She sat back in her chair. "So many elements of your story are hard to believe."

Jim half shrugged and held his palms up.

"Let me see," she began counting on her fingers. "A golden ship—so ostentatious; Jack wouldn't own something like that. There was a booking on Sin Har—I checked—but I saw nothing of meeting you. As for firing on the innocent and dropping mines...no, no. Not my Jack."

"Mrs. Katrigg, you should know that I know how your organization works. I know there is more than just the one Jack Katrigg."

She blinked. Her face creased into a puzzled frown. "Of course there are. Jack has so much business and so many requests for his help; there is no way he can do it all by himself!"

"Is it possible one of the others has gone rogue?"

"Well, that's a more comforting thought than of my son murdering people in cold blood. But, also, so unlikely. I would have heard other reports. Yours is the only complaint that has reached me in years!"

Jim smiled wryly. "There might be a reason for that. You have an effective automated system for stopping complaints from getting through."

She dropped her head and looked at him under her eyebrows. "Mr. Able, I have an effective automated system, full stop. My late husband spent many years developing it. It allows me"—she gestured to the room—"a very pleasant life."

"You mean all the Jacks and all the contracts are all arranged by the system without any personal supervision?"

"Such supervision would require employees, Mr. Able. Employees, generally, are sources of irritation. One automates wherever one can."

"So, it's just the system, your son, and the others who look just like him?"

"Oh yes. Well, let's just check." She rang the small bell on the table. Jenkins appeared in the doorway. "Jenkins, do we still employ anyone?"

Jenkins frowned and replied, "I don't think so, Madam. Once we outsourced the legal department, I think that was it."

She nodded. "Very good. Thank you, Jenkins."

"Madam."

"Now, Mr. Able, to your idea that one of the alternate Jacks could go rogue. My husband would have addressed this possibility early in the construction of the system. Their contracts are monitored. Likewise, feedback from clients. Also, of course, the cost-effectiveness of each contract. The performance of each Jack is constantly compared with the others. Rest assured, activity such as killing clients would be flagged as a deviation from the norm."

Jim smiled. "Perhaps I'm just special."

She smiled back. "I mean no offense, Mr. Able, but I doubt that."

"Right." *That told me!* "But how do you arrange them covering for each other in the event of...problems, investigations, and so forth?"

She smiled. "More tea?"

"Thank you, no."

"So, you bring me a puzzle, Mr. Able. I'm not sure whether to be grateful or annoyed."

"I'm sorry to hear you no longer have employees. It'll be tricky to investigate further, won't it, Mrs. Katrigg? Let me volunteer to investigate for you. Let me know where that particular Jack is now, and I'll go and see him and find out what happened."

She shook her head. "I cannot do that, Mr. Able. To compromise the identity of one unit would be to compromise the whole."

"He already did that! His face is on the Most Wanted List on every world Sin Har is in contact with. None of your Jacks can work anywhere near those systems."

She smiled. "But you said you knew how the system operates! Of course they can work. Let the authorities arrest the next Jack they find. The system can deal with that most effectively."

Jim nodded. "Of course. He'll prove he was somewhere else at the time."

"I'm a little surprised that didn't all happen within the first few days. What were the Sin Har police doing?"

"Mopping up the blood, Mrs. Katrigg."

"Don't be gross, Mr. Able. Are you seriously saying we could subcontract our investigation to you? Would that not be a conflict of interest?"

"I think of my personal involvement as an incentive."

She sat back in her chair and sighed. "Perhaps so." Leaning over to the table, she lifted the bell again.

"Jenkins?"

"Madam."

"Is my son available for a conference?"

"I will find out, Madam. Will you be including your guest?"

She nodded, and Jenkins returned to the hall.

"I hear you have recently become independently wealthy, Mr. Able," his hostess commented.

"I had the good fortune to make a first contact."

"Congratulations. I remember the news of several early ones. Such hope there was for humanity, for business. Such youthful enthusiasm soon fades. So sad."

"Earth has a growing reputation among the other planets."

She smiled. "Well put. Be careful out there, Mr. Able. We are ill-equipped for the dangers that await us."

What does she mean? He smiled. "So far, so good."

A sound filled the air beyond the room—the beating of wings, cries of sorrow.

"Oh, Mr. Able, do go to the window and see! Every afternoon, the flocks of geese fly overhead. Do go and look!"

Jim stepped over to the window and looked up. A huge number of creatures swooped and whirled over the snowbanks. Their long beaks and leathery wings spoke of something far distant from geese. Their cries filled Jim with dread.

"Geese?"

"Aren't they sweet? Every day, they come by."

Jenkins reappeared. "Young Jack is waiting for you, Madam, in the office."

She rose from her chair, saying, "Come along, Mr. Able! Come and meet our one and only Jack."

The office, across the hall, sported the same dark wood paneling. Devoid of all furniture, the carpet dominated the room.

A lone figure stood in one corner, the holographic simulation of Jack Katrigg.

Jim's breath caught as he saw the familiar face—the ghost of so many nightmares.

"Jack, my dear! How are you?" asked his mother.

"Fine, Ma. How are you?"

"The same. I have a visitor."

Jack did not look happy. "So I hear."

"Now, don't panic, dear. Jenkins has done all due diligence before allowing Mr. Able to be here."

"Hello, Mr. Able. Who are you? How do you come to be visiting, Ma?"

"Mr. Katrigg," Jim replied. "Have we met?"

Jack shook his head. "I don't believe so."

"I have met one of your alternates."

The hologram nodded warily. "Okay."

"He tried to kill me."

Frowning and shaking his head, he replied, "Nonsense."

"Ch'Garratt spaceport on Sin Har. Remember?"

Jack thought before replying. "I have heard of it. I have heard of the incident."

"I was there. I saw a Jack Katrigg onto a ship that then fired missiles at me. It's not something I will forget." Jim continued before anyone else could speak, "The ship left mines in orbit and was never seen again. If that Jack is still operating, I need to find him. You need me to find him."

"To do what? What are you suggesting?"

"If he's a rogue actor, your company's reputation is in danger. He could do it again! I don't know why he did it, do you? What's to stop him from slaughtering more people? That he hasn't since is small comfort, I'd say."

"The company's reputation is *our* business, not yours."

Mrs. Katrigg interrupted. "Jack, I'm seriously considering taking Mr. Able up on his offer to investigate."

"Why, Ma?"

"He represents an opportunity to conclude the Ch'Garratt

matter. I hear he has both the requisite skills and the time."

"If you want it dealt with—after all this time—I can get someone to work on it."

"Yes, dear. You miss my point. If Mr. Able and the alternate in question have something to resolve, perhaps it would be best to let them do so."

Jim caught a glint in the holographic eyes that unsettled him.

Jack answered, "Oh, I see. Yes, sure. Go ahead.

"Thank you, dear. So nice to see you. Do visit."

"Will do, Ma. Bye now!"

The image disappeared.

Mrs. Katrigg looked Jim in the eye. "You may proceed. Jenkins will provide you with the information you need. And since you are enjoying the fruits of your recent good fortune, we will not be paying you for your services in this matter."

Jim hesitated but said, "Okay."

She held out her hand. "So nice to meet you, Mr. Able. Jenkins will see you to your craft."

Jim shook her hand and said, "Thank you for the tea."

What did I miss? That was way too easy.

CHAPTER 19

DEBRIEFING

In the café on Sonloi-AC that looked over to Pec Sonloi, Jim sat with Rob, admiring the view.

"Thanks for the trip," Rob said, "Nicer station than EBMS."

"No problem. While I met Mrs. T, you met one of the many Jacks. What can you tell me about him?"

"A lot. I borrowed some really good tech from the shop across the road."

"You didn't tell them why, did you?"

"Of course not! Jim, it's me! When did I ever give someone a straight answer?"

"Okay. Just checking."

Rob gave him a sideways glance and continued. "Not human. Human-like, for sure. Not clear where he's from."

Jim frowned. "That's not all that helpful."

"True. This might be though. Carbon isotope mixture was odd, way out of whack."

"Meaning?"

"Again, not certain, but it could mean he had been in a cryo-tank."

"Really?"

"Folks that were frozen for long-distance travel, you know, before they got D-switches, would often have isotope profiles like this."

"Okay. So, yeah, that's a thing...a planet far out that developed its own way of getting about using cryo-tanks. Then they heard about D-switches and started using those."

"You see, Jim, they're still cropping up—those original ships! They're like time capsules. Who knows how long ago they launched; they're still arriving."

Jim nodded. "Okay."

"And here's the thing; one of the side effects, sometimes, on some species, is epidermal degradation."

Jim, remembering something he had once read, said, "Right! Ice melt, or something, they called it."

"That's right! Plastic surgery all round. Which means..."

Jim's eyes widened. "An excellent opportunity to make yourself look like someone else!"

"Right. They wake up in the future, and it's tough for them. The galaxy isn't what they expected. They don't have jobs. Maybe no one left back home who's interested in what happened to them."

"Unemployed *and* ugly."

"If your friends at Super-Recumbent Logistics are looking for people to hire, these are great candidates!"

"Super-Recumbent? Ha! I see what you did there. But, yeah, they're the people who would be drawn into that kind of occupation. Okay, I'll call that a result!"

"Don't forget, at the time, on Sin Har, we suspected Katrigg wasn't actually human."

Jim nodded. "Right! The brothel. Didn't you go there?"

Rob squirmed. "Bit embarrassing. Probably not my best moment. The Sin Har girls thought it was hilarious, and"—Rob held up his hands—"I can see the funny side better at this distance than I could at the time."

"But Target Katrigg recommended it to me."

"Possibly in a moment of candor, forgetting he wasn't addressing one of his own kind."

"So, he changed his face, maybe his hands, but nothing else. *And* he did it to get the job."

"I think we're getting more of an idea of who he is—who they are."

"Good work!"

"A pleasure, boss, a pleasure. When..."—he crossed his arms —"are you going to tell me about this 'minor surgery'?"

Jim shook his head. "Best not. No offense. Keeping this private."

Rob frowned but didn't ask further.

Later, back aboard Jim's ship, Tella announced, "Jim, I wish to rewatch the recording of everything that transpired at the Katrigg mansion."

Jim sighed. "I don't need to go through it all again, do I?"

"Yes. There is much to be extracted from your trip."

Jim sighed. "I hate listening to myself. I sound so...lame."

Rob added, "And I already had to listen to you being lame once."

"The canids should watch with us," Tella added.

"Really? I love giving Marhan more chances to laugh at the Earth monkey!"

Tella leaned close. "I thought we were getting used to them. It's business, Jim. It isn't personal."

They gathered again in the galley around a screen Marhan had set up to watch the playback.

"What do we know about the butler?" Marhan asked.

Jim shrugged. "Nothing more than we see. He didn't click or drip oil. Seemed to be human."

Betih added, "Likewise, the female seemed human?"

"I think so," Jim said.

"Let us continue with the recording," Tella said.

Jim narrated as the images from his bodycam played across the display. "First look at the drawing room. Real Earth antiques. Real fire; smelled great!"

Rob asked, "How did she smell?"

"Behave! Nice bling. If that's real, business has been good."

"Here," Marhan interrupted, "I don't understand this. You ask her to call you 'Jim,' but she continues to call you 'Mr. Able.' Why? What does that mean?"

Jim frowned. "Yeah. That's...that's a power thing. She's keeping me in my—lower—place. She's not allowing us to be equals or friendly, just formal."

Marhan nodded. "I see."

Betih commented, "She knew your background before she asked. Why did she waste time asking you questions?"

Jim shrugged. "To see if I'd lie? I think she's just being polite."

"But not friendly," Marhan added.

"Right. Now, here," Jim continued, "she asks if I've been to Rinfar Molc. I didn't get this."

Rob commented, "Their official address."

Jim added, "As if she didn't know she was on Acep Five."

"Odd," Betih said, nodding.

"Later, when those creatures fly over, she calls them geese. Weird."

They listened as Jim, on the recording, recounted the events at Ch'Garratt.

Betih asked, "Is her reaction genuine? She seems concerned."

"Almost impossible to tell. A calm but thoughtful appearance...could be real...or not."

Tella sat up straight. "There! When you mention the mines and that they are ancient technology."

"What about it?"

"She does not react. Most people, when you say that, are interested or alarmed. She is neither."

"Perhaps she knows all about them?" Marhan suggested.

"Perhaps," Tella replied.

"That part fills me with dread," said Betih.

"Why?

"I lack the experience to deal with automated systems; they do not have their own ethics. Give me living beings, and I can find my way. If she knows about such devices and is comfortable with them, she is truly dangerous."

"Oh, Jim! I liked this bit," said Rob with a smile.

"Which bit?"

"When she tells you you ain't special. I started liking her then."

"Concentrate, monkey!" growled Marhan. He leaned forward and they watched Jim persuading Mrs. Katrigg to let him investigate.

Betih muttered, "She thinks Earth people are not thriving in the galaxy. She knows of some danger to you."

Jim shrugged. "No idea what. Oh, here come the geese. Did you guys see much other wildlife from orbit?"

Marhan shook his head. "It is a bleak place."

"No one sane would live there," Tella added.

Betih said, "That is the point, I think. Either she is made safe by its isolation or sidelined so she cannot interfere."

"That," Jim said, nodding, "would be useful to know—which is it?"

Rob nodded in agreement.

"How did you feel seeing the real Jack Katrigg, Jim?" Tella asked.

Jim frowned, sighed, and answered, "Unsettled."

Betih shot him a glance and said, "Note that, human! Be aware of your feelings. They can unintentionally delay action."

"I know. Understood."

"Here! We come to the most interesting part," Marhan said loudly. "Due diligence! A fancy term for a boring exercise."

Rob pointed at the display. "And she didn't do the 'due diligence'; Jenkins did!"

"Not just a butler then," Tella added.

"Pause it. Pause it here!" Marhan said.

"Okay. What do you see?" Jim asked.

"Hostility. The Katrigg wants nothing to do with you. He resents your being in his mother's presence, yes?"

"Good summary. Yes."

"Play on!"

Jim started the playback again.

"Stop there! See, his expression changes. What did she say? I don't read humans well enough to understand this."

Tella quoted, "If Mr. Able and the alternate in question have something to resolve, perhaps it would be best to let them do so."

"Why would that convince him?" Marhan asked, "It completely changes his mind."

After a brief silence, Rob answered, "Because she just said that Jim could take out the rogue Katrigg and cheaply resolve a potential problem."

Betih added, "Or the other way round. That Katrigg might kill Jim."

Marhan nodded. "Yes, and that would resolve the Real Katrigg's problem of Jim interfering in the company and his family's business. That is what he understood!"

Rob pointed at Jim. "So that's their strategy! Make you and the rogue confront each other. Either you kill him and resolve one problem. Or he kills you and resolves a different problem. Even better, you kill each other, and they don't have to lift a finger. Nice!"

"'Even better'?" said Jim with a wry smile.

Almost smiling in return, Tella said, "It's business, Jim. It isn't personal."

"So you say!" He put his head in his hands.

Tella looked at the top of Jim's head. "From this, we learn something to your advantage, Jim."

He looked up reluctantly. "What's that?"

"They will warn this Katrigg that you are coming. They will expect him to prepare for your arrival. They may even say you intend to kill him."

Jim pointed his thumb at the screen. "You read all that from what we saw?"

"And years of research into tactics, conflict analysis, and warfare."

"I thought you were into theology and philosophy."

Tella smiled clearly and unambiguously. "They are threads of the same cloth, Jim."

"Great..."

Rob asked, "What next for Robins?"

Jim frowned. "There will be prep for my meeting with Katrigg. I don't want to go in there with holes in my armor. Be on standby at the office. Maybe we'll have you travel with us when we get a destination."

"This isn't a missing person, is it. This is what you meant by having *your* projects for Robins to investigate."

Jim nodded. "Yeah. And I can't always share what I'm up to."

Rob shrugged. "This one is obvious enough. It's about Ch'Garratt. Nail the bastard."

"'Bout right. Don't want him getting away with it."

Rob looked at the distant look in Jim's eyes. "Good luck."

The next day, Jim saw Rob onto a ship back to Earth with a slight pang of regret that they couldn't work together more in person. Soon after returning to his ship, he received a long communication from the Superincumbent Logistics Company.

Jim announced over the galley table, "Here are Katrigg's contracts for the next hundred days. "This gives me some time to prepare and for him to sweat."

Marhan said, "Time for him to prepare. You should kill him before your operation."

Betih shook her head and snapped her jaw at Marhan. "Too soon. You must meet him first. You must hear his story."

Jim asked, "You sure about that?"

"Do you know, for certain, beyond all doubt, that his finger pressed the missile control? Or that his voice gave that command?"

Jim was taken aback. "Sure! Who else would it have been?"

Betih growled. "Have you learned nothing? Find out! Find out who else it could have been. Be sure! Be sure it was Katrigg. You were not in that ship. Find someone who was! What have I tried to teach you? 'No assassin will kill the wrong person—or even the right person—if they should not be killed.' Remember?"

Jim held up his hands. "Calm down! I remember."

She drew the pink robe around her. "I waste my time here. Even the first-year Luminants are better students!"

To Marhan, Jim smiled and said, "I guess that's a real insult." To Betih, he said, "I know. I know I have to talk to him and...convince you he's the right target. The killing comes at the end—when everything else is done."

"It is not me that needs to be convinced," she replied quietly.

"But you are harder to convince than I am. You two are my standard."

Tella said nothing but smiled.

Marhan asked, "What will we do while you are on Sonloi?"

Jim shrugged. "Hang out. Find me more about this Katrigg. Relax before things get ugly."

"Another word for you: waugh-sa."

"What's 'waugh-sa'?"

"The sores you get on your ass from sitting and doing nothing!"

Jim laughed. "So do something! You don't need to wait for me to micromanage your days."

Marhan growled back. "As it should be!"

PART THREE

THE TEMPLE

CHAPTER 20

OPERATION OPERATION

Station Administrator Jayde Duke sat with the Artist of Sonloi-AC at their favorite café table, the splendor of Pec Sonloi shining through the panoramic windows.

Their favorite table was somehow always available; the pair enjoyed the status as a permanent station institution.

The Artist relaxed, her multi-colored hair loose down her back and over the chair. The Administrator, fiercely neat and conservatively dressed, sat bolt upright. The Meoena considered her the best administrator in a long line of illustrious predecessors.

"Why didn't you tell me about your operation before now?" Jayde asked.

"It's really nothing to worry about."

"That's not what I mean. I just thought that...you know, you'd have mentioned something."

Alfie reached out and held Jayde's arm. "It's nothing to worry about. Jim will be with me the whole time."

Jayde sighed. "Sure, Alfie. Don't let me be too nosey." Then she said, "I've been looking at his request for docking privileges."

"And?" Alfie smiled.

"He hasn't put an end date on it. Normally, that would be

flagged as an incomplete application and shot straight back. What's he up to? Did he just forget?"

Alfie sipped her coffee. "Perhaps he isn't certain how long I'll need him?"

Jayde nodded. "Okay."

Alfie watched her friend, the slight frown, the eyes wandering over to the planet. She said sweetly, "Of course, I don't have a dock allocated to me, do I?"

"You don't own a ship!"

Alfie shook her head. "No, no. But if I did, would I get one?"

"Well, of course!" Jayde sat up straighter. "Is he coming back to live here? Why didn't he say so?"

Alfie put both hands down on the table. "Let's not get ahead of ourselves. He hasn't said that to me. But..."

"That would cause quite a stir! The Younger Son has almost a folk hero status among the Meoena."

"Exactly. He does not like a fuss."

Jayde's eyes held Alfie's. "Oh, I see. That complicates it, doesn't it!"

"So, perhaps a request for docking privileges without an end date might be a more discrete way to arrange things?"

Jayde's shoulders sagged as she sighed. "Alfie! You know what a position that puts me in. I'd be taking a berth out of rotation without... We don't have any I could call 'spare,' you know."

Leaning in, Alfie said almost in a whisper, "Jayde, I don't know all that Jim has been up to, but if he thinks he'd rather be here than anywhere else, I hope we can give him a chance to finish...whatever it is. I suspect he and his brother have had another of their fallings-out."

Jayde drained her cup. "Sure, as long as it isn't forever. I can cover it over—list it as a temporary assignment—but, as I say, not forever."

"It'll be nice to have him around for a while."

Jayde covered Alfie's hand with hers. "I know how happy it'll make you."

"Thank you, dear. I'll let him know."

. . .

In her suite, Alfie pulled on her painting smock. "I talked to Jayde about your docking berth."

Jim replied, "Thanks! Did she take much convincing?"

"We left it open-ended."

Jim gave her a sideways glance. "You didn't get a permanent allocation?"

"Not yet, dear."

"Mom! They owe you one!"

"But it isn't for me, is it?"

Jim frowned. "Technically, no. But, as I said, tell her it's for the family."

"Yes, dear. I mentioned that. She'll keep the end date open. I don't want to press it more than that."

Jim held up his hands in defeat. "Okay, she's your friend. Thanks for trying."

"Oh, and she's suspicious that I haven't mentioned 'my' operation before."

"It'll be fine. Just tell them it has to do with your heart. That's close enough to the truth."

"I'll be painting this afternoon. When do we leave?"

"Middle of the late shift, if that's okay. I've booked a private shuttle."

"Will any of your friends be joining us?"

"No. They are all going to a bar to get drunk."

"Lovely." She gave him a sly look. "Jealous?"

"No." He shook his head. "It's a cover, Mom. They are going to make enough noise so that, tomorrow, people will swear I was there with them."

Dr. Slota sat across his desk from Jim.

"We should review the scans one more time."

"Okay. There's something there, right?

The Meoenan's head rose slightly on his thin neck. The large pale blue eyes blinked once. "Something, yes. Something removable, perhaps. Something implanted, I cannot yet tell."

"Understood, doc. Did you find seven of them, one under each wound?"

The doctor nodded slowly. "Indeed. The coincidence of location gives me sufficient cause to explore further."

"Okay. So, you'll take them all out."

"One. First. Then we'll see."

"I was assuming all of them. I don't want to have to keep coming back."

"I understand, Jim. But I would prefer to be cautious. I do not know what they are, what they are doing, or—more importantly for today—what will happen upon removal. So, I suggest removing only one."

Jim sighed and glanced at Alfie, sitting silently in the corner. "You understand I'm highly motivated to get them the hell out of me."

"I do. And that must, ultimately, be your choice. I have stated my recommendation."

"Okay. Be prepared to take them all out. If something goes immediately wrong with the first one, stop. I'll take the risks based on that."

Again, the doctor nodded slowly. "I have our little operating room set up. The nurse will prepare you. I assume a general anesthetic is okay?"

"Can you do it with a local? I could tell you if I feel it doing something as you remove it."

"As you wish. But please remember, no surgeon likes a patient who provides a running commentary."

Jim laughed. "I'll bear that in mind."

Jim lay face down on the operating table. He could see nothing of what the doctor and nurses were doing. He smelled the distinctly medical odors of disinfectant and cleaned gowns. Mixed in were old, familiar scents of Sonloi. He felt he had forgotten so much in his traveling, left so much behind.

As the team murmured to each other, he remembered his childhood friend, Rolo. The Meoenan shared Jim's sense of humor and that deep inner streak of enjoyment at flouting the rules. *I wonder where you are now?*

Jim remembered the day Rolo left for his "walkabout." They had shaken hands, hugged, and said 'Teo Ma!' the Meoenan equivalent of *au revoir*.

Never saw you again, did I, buddy?

Jim heard Dr. Slota swear. It was a simple Meoenan word for "shit," but coming from a doctor with blades in his back, Jim's stomach knotted.

"Doc?"

"Nothing to worry about!"

"Tell me."

Dr. Slota sighed. "I have it. A rectangular strip of tissue. It had been spread out between two muscles. It is now wrapped tightly around one side of my tweezers."

A gloved hand with tweezers appeared in Jim's line of sight. "Okay, so that's good, isn't it?"

"See how tightly it is wound?"

"Not really. I'll take your word for it."

"I've seen reactions like that in tiny organisms, where they bind themselves into smaller shapes to avoid dangers. Whatever this is, it doesn't like being exposed."

"Fair enough."

"Have you felt anything since I detached it?"

"Not a thing."

"Very well. Shall I proceed to the others?"

"Yes, please. Got enough tweezers?"

There was a mumbled comment from one of the nurses.

The doctor said, "Perhaps I can use something else. Now I know how they react; it might ease the extraction of the others."

.   .   .

Jim sat up in bed, against a pile of pillows, in the doctor's recovery room.

"Jim, here it is!" the doctor said.

"I don't see anything."

"There—on the very end of the probe."

"That? It's tiny!"

"I haven't been able to unravel it yet."

"And the others are all the same?"

"The same. What would you like me to do with them?"

"Keep three. Examine them every way you can. I'll take the rest and do the same."

"As you wish."

"When can I get up?"

"Tomorrow."

"Oh, come on, doc! I don't want to waste your time or be a nuisance."

Dr. Slota stood tall at the end of the bed and pointed a steady blue finger at Jim. "You will remain where you are until tomorrow at the earliest. I will take all due measures to ensure your mother is entirely satisfied with what we have done and how you react to it. She is not someone I will argue with. You, however, are."

"Well, that puts me in my place."

The doctor smiled in agreement.

Jim sighed. "Hey, Doc, do you remember Rolo Kerit?"

The doctor began to move his hands to the left in the Meoenan gesture for "no" but stopped and said, "Yes, I believe I do. A name from the past...You were friends! I treated you both for plasma burns after one of your experiments went wrong."

Jim laughed. "Oh, that's right! Yes, that was *you* lecturing us on being stupid kids who could've killed ourselves!"

"Rightly so!"

"Damn, we came close that time!"

"What makes you ask about him?"

"I was wondering where he is. We lost touch."

He gestured right. "I have not seen or heard of him in many years."

CHAPTER 21

IMPLANTS

Jim called Rob to ask, "You know anyone with experience in microelectronics?"

"Not really, no. How micro?"

"Pretty radical."

"Hoo, well. I'd go with someone in academia. Maybe that Professor Whitehorse fellow or someone like him."

"Anyone offworld?"

"Human?"

"No."

"Ah, I see where you're going. Well, the Narptur are good with electronics generally. The Finnig. Misan something...Actually, those, umm, beak-faced people. What are they called?"

"The Limarc?"

"Yeah, yeah. That's the one. They used to be really good with that sort of thing before, you know..."

"I hate those guys."

"Ha!" Rob chuckled, "Who doesn't."

"But, it might do. Find someone for me to talk to on...whatever their planet's called."

"Talair. Lim Talair. Okay, if you want."

"Discretely."

"Of course! Though I'll probably have to go through the authorities on Arun Peer."

"Really?"

"They've got some kind of governorship since Talair got hit. I think the Limarc authorities live there now as well."

"Hmm. More complicated than I thought. See what you can do."

"I'll need something specific to ask about."

"I'll send a diagram. Ask them what it does."

"Probably easier if you send the device."

"Maybe. Not ready to let them out of my sight yet."

"Is this something you bought or something you found?"

"Can't really say. Acquired. Confidential case, this one."

"Yeah. Okay. You're the boss."

Two days later, Rob called back.

"Hey, Jim! I've got a Limarc for you. Professor Zahid Orun is at the University of Wellin on Cob Tac."

"Cob Tac? Don't know it."

"It's a nice place. I spent a few weeks there once. Don't know this city—Wellin—though."

"Who are the locals?"

"Fische."

"Fish?"

"No, Fische with a 'ch.'"

"Okay. Good relations with humans?"

"Well, pretty good. I was only there a few weeks."

"Okay, not long enough to do any real damage."

Rob laughed. "How well you know me! I haven't sent anything yet. Do you want me to send a message or go and see him?"

"Hmm. If he's away from home, it might be worth just going and being friendly. I'll send Tella."

. . .

Tella stood—perfectly still—in the hallway of Professor Orun's house. The walls were hung with multi-colored hangings, and the windows were all intricately cut with circles of color.

Such a nightmare!

The Neraffan moved carefully along the hallway to the room across the back of the house. The professor was alone, quietly reading a printed book. On either side of his beak, his eyes were covered by wide-spaced glasses attached to his ears, buried back under long black hair. At the bottom of the white bony protrusion hung a thin-rolled cigarette. The smell of the smoke tickled Tella's small nostrils.

Such a nightmare!

As it was about to turn and find somewhere else to remain undetected to observe Orun's routine, another waft of smoke caught it unaware.

"Achoo!"

"Who's there?" called the professor.

Tella closed its eyes and swore silently.

The professor was already only a few feet away when it opened its eyes. Orun looked through his glasses, then over them, then through them again.

"What are you? I see you, but I don't see you! Are you a hologram? What are you doing in my house?"

Tella replied quietly, "I am Tella of Neraff. I mean you no harm. I apologize for disturbing you."

The professor searched the air for hints of Tella's body. "Fascinating! Come, sit down! First, tell me where Neraff might be, then tell me why you have come."

"Thank you." Tella sat opposite the professor's chair, a woven blanket casting long streaks of color through its body. "Neraff is one of the original twelve planets and is thus given the honor of having the name of its star, Tyg, omitted from references."

"Ah, like Gron and Kalay! I see, yes, yes. And are all your people chameleons?"

"No, I am Neraffan-jong. We are a persecuted subspecies on our home world."

The professor nodded. "I see. There is much suffering to share across the galaxy, is there not? Now, to what do I owe the honor of such a remarkable visitor as yourself?"

"I have a friend in need of advice. He has a piece of electronic equipment—microelectronic, I should say. Your reputation in the field has spread."

The professor hung his head. "I know something of such things. But so what? He has a device, you say. And?"

"We need to know what it does. We might look, but we would not see what you can see."

Orun laughed. "Seeing you tells me my sight cannot be trusted."

"Will you help us?"

He looked at Tella and said nothing. Then he nodded. "I presume the manner of your coming indicates the matter is secret. There is perhaps something dangerous about the device? If so, no, I would prefer you not bring it here."

"I don't think it's dangerous in itself. Its dangers might lie in the facts of where it was made and where it has been."

"But you don't know what it does?"

"True. That is what we must find out."

He shook his head. "There are many ways for danger to present. You know of our world, Lim Talair?"

"I do. You have damage from something that fell to your world."

"Damage? Yes. And more. If you bring an alien device to me, I will not trust your word that it contains no threat. I cannot. I live here, in exile, because the universities of my home are all shuttered. My family is scattered across several worlds. All our losses began with a device brought to us. I will not have you bring something suspicious to me, my house, my institution, to the world that shelters me. I cannot."

Tella sighed. "I understand. Can we perhaps bring you to it? My friend's ship is in orbit."

Orun sighed. "Is it so important?"

"So much effort was made to conceal its existence that I can only say it is important to someone."

"You make an intriguing case, my transparent friend." He held up his book. "Perhaps the Limarc philosophers must wait for my return."

"Thank you. I will order you a shuttle, professor. What equipment will you need to bring?"

Jim's heart beat faster, watching the Limarc walk down the corridor toward the flight room. The scar on his arm itched in memory of the attack by Limarc thugs on Flereat. This one came alone, but then, so had the Limarc in the Mech-suit forcing his way into the ship when Davey and Clo were on their own.

The professor took control of the galley table without considering how hungry Jim and his friends were getting. He sat back in the chair and grunted.

"Professor?" Jim began, "You have news for us?"

Nodding, Orun said, "I think so. Come and sit with me. Let me tell you what I have learned."

"Would you like something to eat first?"

Cocking his head to one side, he turned to point his beak at Jim. "That would be most welcome. Do you have any ridett, carvu, or hostolla?"

Jim frowned, "I doubt it. I'll ask the others." He moved to the ramp to the flight level but stopped. "Tella isn't the only surprise around here. I have two guls on board. Don't be alarmed."

"Thank you for the warning."

Everyone gathered around the table to eat and hear the professor's thoughts.

"The device is disarmingly simple. It consists of a receiver of input. The input is stored and, I suspect, manipulated in some way. Upon some trigger, the entire store is transmitted. I realize this may not be of much help to you."

Jim sighed. "Something goes in, something goes out. Yeah, professor, color me unimpressed."

Tella asked, "What can you tell us about the input. Is it auditory?"

"No. It is numbers. Not many. A short series of numbers."

"And the output?"

"Again, more numbers. The whole store seems to flush out and reset. Oh, the receiver of the output will be close to the device. The range of the transmitter is short."

Jim immediately asked, "How close? Inches? Feet?"

"Ten feet at most. Depending on any barriers to the signal."

They all looked at each other around the table.

Marhan asked, "Can you tell if it has been in use?"

Orun shrugged. "If it has been receiving input, I would guess it has."

Betih spoke up. "How far can the device be from the sender of the input?"

"Further, but within the confines of a ship, perhaps, or a small house."

"I feel," said Jim, "like I know less than I did when you started."

The professor laughed. "You know much! You know it is not going to kill us. You know it is but part of a larger system; the input is derived from a compatible device; the output goes to another compatible device."

"Why?" Tella asked, "What added value is there in having this device in between those other parts of the system?"

"To tell you that, my friend, I must dismantle it. I will need microscopes of some sophistication. I suspect there is a whole world of function hidden inside."

Marhan frowned and asked Jim, "But you cannot have these things leave the ship, surely?"

The professor interrupted. "There is more than one?"

Jim nodded and watched the professor. "There are seven. They were implanted in my back without my knowledge. What do you think, professor? Dare I trust you with one of these devices before we know what they do? How secure can you keep it?"

Orun sat back and held up his hands. "That is a decision I cannot make for you. I will endeavor to keep it safe. But I am neither a bank guard nor a security agent. I may have to tell a colleague what we know in order to book time on the right machines. The university's resources are not unlimited."

Jim narrowed his eyes. "Is there a fundraiser going on at the moment?"

"Ha! Of course! Always. The chancellor himself has launched a new campaign. He begins to doubt the quality of his legacy; he fears not being remembered as fondly as he hopes to be.

"I'll make a donation. A big one. If he gives you free rein on this project."

"Oh...Well, let's be clear; the chancellor does not like me. Many of the faculty do not think a Limarc should be serving as their equal."

"I'm sorry to hear that." Jim hesitated. "Would it help then if you presented it as a chance to do something no one else has had a chance to do?"

"In what way?"

"The devices were made by the Praestans Rapax. Who, I believe, imagined these implants would never be discovered or examined. It is a chance to see something from their workshops that isn't a spaceship. Something not sold on any market. An insight, perhaps, into technology no one else will ever see."

The beak and its half-hidden eyes turned fully toward Jim's face. "That would be extraordinary! In such a case, I doubt a donation would even be necessary."

Jim smiled.

Jim's ship was in orbit of Cob Tac for eight of its days before the professor returned in a shuttle.

"Welcome back, professor! It's good to see you," Jim said.

"And good to see you. You have given me an intriguing puzzle to solve."

"I hope you've had some success."

Orun nodded, but he didn't look Jim in the eye.

Jim waved him back down the ramp to the galley. He noticed, as the professor moved, the faint scent of food.

All waited with bated breath for the Limarc to begin.

"It is beautifully made. As, perhaps, we all expected. Such craft! Such artistry."

"Please, begin with the input and take us through whatever processes you have discovered," Tella asked.

"Indeed, indeed. Three numbers are received. Judging by the storage allocated, these could be anything from an ID number to an address to a spatial location. There is no way of telling without also seeing the device that sends the signal."

Into the frustrated silence, Jim commented, "But that device is on this ship."

"Oh, yes. And it sends its signal often, I would guess."

"Okay. Why do you think that?"

"The central piece. It contains twenty-one clocks."

Marhan laughed.

Jim said, "What?"

"Beautifully arrayed. Nothing is wasted. Quite remarkable."

Tella asked, "Are they all the same? I mean...do they all tell the same time?"

Orun laughed. "Yes, I would think so. But they don't do it all the same way."

"Please explain."

"What sort of clocks do you use on Earth, Mr. Able?"

"Well...a variety. For accuracy, I think we still use the vibrations of Cesium atoms."

Nodding, the professor said, "Yes, one of the clocks uses the same. Another has hydrogen, another strontium. I also found the use of other more exotic principles than atomic vibration. Such masterful miniaturization of the technologies! But someone was very concerned to measure not only the moment an event occurs, but also how long it lasts."

"I don't understand," Jim admitted.

Orun took off his glasses and sighed. "I see twenty-one precision devices that record the time of the input. They are then interrogated again at the start of the next event. The difference between the two times is recorded—twenty-one times—as well as any differences detected between any two of the clocks."

Jim asked, "W-wait...Why would there be any differences?"

"That, my friend, remains the puzzle. I can speculate that the clocks will occasionally differ because of environmental factors affecting their own peculiar measurement standards. But beyond that, I do not know."

Betih ground her teeth, growled, and said, "They went to extraordinary lengths to achieve this. It is enough—for us—that they did so. It is important to *them*. What else?"

Tella shook its head. "The environmental factors will be the same. The conditions aboard a ship result in one of the most stable environments we know."

"And so," the professor added, "we should expect the times to be the same with no differences. And yet, they record any differences to a scrupulous level of accuracy."

Jim laughed. "Scrupulous? That's the Praestans Rapax all over."

The professor continued, "As has been said, we can tell much from the care and deliberation with which it has been done. We must conclude that they *expect* to find differences undetectable by other—more ordinary—means." The professor put his glasses back on. "What do you do so quickly and so often, Mr. Able? And why should they care so much?"

Jim smiled and shook his head. "It's absurd."

Tella asked, "How many events does the system store?"

"Thousands." The professor waved his hands to indicate more.

Marhan growled loudly.

"Marhan?" Jim said.

"No. I was a weight control clerk. What do I know about things like this?"

Betih snapped her jaws at him.

Jim said, "Go on. Spit it out."

"Three numbers. Three coordinates. Input into your nav-system. Thousands of operations in any one journey. Switch, switch, switch."

"The D-switch?"

Tella spoke. "They are monitoring your journeys."

Betih shook her head quickly. "No, for that they need only to copy the navigation log. With these things, they do something else."

Jim thought and nearly said, *The T-switch*. He looked around the room.

At the expression on his face, the guls and Tella fell silent.

Jim said cautiously, "Thank you, professor. We need some time to think about this."

"Oh...I was hoping we could perform some experiments! I would be interested to see what it might take to somehow induce such a difference as the device is built to record. Do you seriously think something happens when the D-switch is in use?"

Jim smiled and swallowed. "You'll be the first to know when we're ready for that, professor. We won't forget you."

After the professor was entertained and sent on his way, they assembled again in the galley.

"My first thought was it's something to do with the T-switch," Jim began.

Tella asked, "How would they have heard of the T-switch? Your implants came long before your father appeared to you."

"True. However, someone on Sonloi got wind of it before I did. But for the PR to have all this ready for our mission to Tanna... And don't forget, at that time, they thought I was you!"

Marhan asked, "What do you mean?"

"The PR requested the help of EIA agent R546, who, at the time, was Tella. But the EIA couldn't reveal who R546 was, so...we told the PR it was me and that Tella worked for me."

Marhan frowned. "I see."

Tella continued, "So, in thinking that, it was R546's travels they wanted to follow—an unpredictable set of journeys. I have led an interesting life that some would find disconcerting."

"What were they expecting to record?" Betih asked. "What about your travels would give rise to discrepancies in the clocks?"

Tella and Jim both shook their heads.

Jim sighed and said, "I'll have to ask Daum Robertus. Before I kill him."

Betih smiled. "You and he have much to discuss."

Tella stared into the distance. "Inside the body? Inside the ship? What could possibly be different?"

"What?" said Jim.

"Why imbed them in you—in your body—or mine if that was their intent? They pressed this ship upon you. We can assume it is the only one equipped with the devices to send the coordinates to the implants and receive the results. Yet, is it only the D-switch they are monitoring? Do they think there is some discrepancy between your traveling and the ship's?"

"I don't know, and as much as I hate to admit it, the PR are cleverer than we are. We aren't going to find out without questioning one of them—on our terms. The professor has answered our question about what the devices are. He's given us an idea of how they work. But those are always much easier to discover than the why."

Betih nodded. "You monkeys almost have a brain between you; it's impressive to watch."

Jim laughed and said, "Fuck you!"

Marhan barked and said, "Be polite to my aunt!" Then he added, "Betih?"

She answered sweetly, "What?"

"Fuck you! Leave the monkeys alone."

CHAPTER 22

INTO HIDING

Jim received a call during the journey back to Sonloi-AC from Cob Tac.

"Jim Able! How wonderful to see you again. I trust you and your family are well."

"Daum Robertus, this is a surprise. To what do I owe the honor?"

The face on the screen was of an older person, possibly a human. His untrimmed, unruly white eyebrows stood in abrupt contrast to his short gray hair. Jim remembered the monk's gray-blue eyes well; they sparkled with humor and a superiority possibly based on knowing more than Jim did.

"Consider it a courtesy call to one of the Praestans Rapax's best customers. How is your ship? Are you enjoying flying in it?"

"I am. All is well, thank you."

"I saw you had some recent repairs. Of course, I realize you cannot tell me details of your work, but I understand that sometimes your ship may be involved in the kind of events that most of our products never see. Was there any further damage we should know about?"

"Well, I had some repairs to the outer airlock door. The people on Hon Hen Flereat did a fine job on that. And your folks at the docking cradle repaired the control panels."

"Our engineers will happily render a complimentary follow-up visit at your convenience. I don't want anything to have been missed."

Jim smiled. "Well, thank you for the offer. I'll see when I'm next docked somewhere long enough to allow that."

The Praestans Rapax monk smiled in return. "A pleasure to speak with you, Jim. All the best to you in your travels."

Jim sat for a minute after the call and said nothing.

Tella, sitting beside him, was also silent.

"What do you think?" Jim asked.

"Your implants. I don't think he knows for certain you have removed them."

Jim nodded. "Okay."

"But they know the overall system has stopped working. They already are aware that the data transmission has ceased. His first line of inquiry was to ask about damage to the ship. They wonder which end has failed: if the collection of the implant data has ceased or only the data's transmission to their homeworld."

"I told the ship to stop transmitting anything to the PR within the first day I had it!"

Tella shrugged. "I doubt they would allow such a transmission to be stopped. It is probably low-level, independent hardware, not under the ship's control."

Jim gagged and shook his head. "Damn!"

Tella continued, "And they hope to have an engineer come and repair it under the guise of a 'complimentary' visit."

"Yeah, I get that bit."

"You would be unwise to give them access."

"No shit."

Tella smiled at the distinctly human phrase.

Jim sighed deeply. "But a call from the man himself—and so quickly—they've been monitoring me in real time. It's that impor-tant to them!"

Tella laughed. "They do everything with such skill and close attention. It must be worrying for them to have a system suddenly fail without warning."

"Okay. I see what you mean; I won't feel so singled out. It's just something going wrong with a product. An event so rare it would always get high-level attention."

Tella nodded. "Indeed so. And remember, it *is* me they think they are following."

Jim smiled. "Uh-oh! You're not going to let that go, are you?"

"Never." Tella almost smiled.

"Still, something to celebrate. We've scored a point over them."

"One point in a long, long game."

The ship was approaching Sonloi-AC when another call came through.

"This is Jim Able."

"Jim, it's Jayde Duke."

"Hello, Administrator, how can I help? We're just on our way back to you."

"I know. Don't dock."

"There's a problem?" *Has she rescinded my permission for the berth?*

"I don't know yet. But probably. Have you heard of a Meoenan gang called the Parfot?"

"No, what are they, street performers?"

"Criminals. Nasty ones. They came out of Hostac province a few years ago. The authorities are at a loss what to do with them."

"That's unusual for the Meoena. Wouldn't they usually prefer to hire someone else's criminal gang rather than form their own?"

Jayde laughed. "My thoughts exactly. Anyway, three members have come aboard the station. They're asking about you."

"Uh-oh...I hate being popular."

"I wanted to warn you. I'd recommend treating this seriously. You'll need to do better than hiding in the heating ducts this time."

"Ha! If I go somewhere else, you'll keep an eye on my mother?"

Jayde agreed, "Of course, my highest priority. They won't get near her."

"Thanks. I'll let you know what alternative plan we come up with. If you can find out more about why they want me, I'd love to hear it."

"Sure, no problem."

"Thanks, Jayde. Really! I appreciate it. We'll talk soon."

Over dinner in the galley, Jim asked, "Any suggestions as to who it is? Should we face them head on, or should I lay low?"

Tella spoke. "I doubt this comes from the PR."

"Agreed."

Betih bared her long teeth in a smile. "You have a growing collection of people who do not like you."

Marhan laughed. "Go down the list. Who is most credible?"

Jim shook his head. "I don't know...whoever hired the Kevar on Stacco Ila 32? Whoever was behind the Limarc goons on Flereat?" He chuckled briefly. "My former boss at the OEA?"

Marhan offered, "Drinking establishments we stiffed or damaged during our week of celebration?"

Betih gave him a surprised look but said nothing.

"Sharkey," Tella suggested.

Marhan added, "Mrs. Katrigg, her son, or the one you seek."

Jim became serious. "But, whoever it is, Jayde isn't given to sending false alarms. And even if we took these gang members on, there's no guarantee we'd find out who sent them." He stared into the distance. "Where should I go?"

"If we challenge them and they become violent, perhaps your daughter will intervene again," Marhan said with a squint.

"Don't want to hear it, Marhan! She's not part of anyone's plans. Though pencil in her mother at the end of our list."

Tella suggested, "The temple."

The guls stared at him.

Jim replied, "In Tuanomena?"

Tella tilted its head to one side. "There was a Meoenan at tea with your mother. I remember him saying his father worked at the temple."

"Right! Yarl...something or other."

Betih said, "Beware of compromising him or his family."

Jim nodded quickly. "I know. I'll get Doctor Slota to ask Mother to speak to him." After another moment's thought, Jim added, "Oh...That guy on TMV-I. He probably wants to kill me too. Better add him to the list."

When they returned to the flight room, Jim told Marhan, "Take command of the ship. Call Sonloi Orbital Command and ask for a slot for a few days. Long enough for me to get to the temple and to keep you guys off station for a while. You'll attract the gang's attention when you get to AC. Be careful."

Marhan nodded without comment.

Betih said, "Take your tools with you. Not to use, but to keep safe from prying eyes."

Jim replied, "Okay. Will do."

"I will maintain contact with Yarl," said Tella, "And perhaps find out more about these Meoena who are after you."

"Tella, you have to be careful too."

"Of course."

CHAPTER 23

THE TEMPLE

Jim landed his solo flier in a small field between low stone buildings. The farm was deserted, the windows were broken, and plants climbed up the walls and through the roofs.

Yarl stood watching him land.

"Yarl? Thanks for meeting me," Jim called.

Yarl said, "Welcome, Jim. My associates will roll your craft into the barn and conceal it there. Please come with me."

Jim looked at the three identical black vehicles with dark-tinted windows. "Two decoys?"

"Best I could arrange. I hope it will suffice."

"I'm sure it'll be fine." Sitting in the back of Yarl's vehicle he continued, "I really appreciate the trouble you've gone to with all this."

Yarl replied, "The Family Able has only to ask."

Jim sat back and watched the two decoys drive in opposite directions at the farm gate. He and Yarl were soon on the direct road to Tuanomena.

. . .

Jim caught his first sight of the top of the temple many minutes before they came close. The ziggurat dominated the old part of the city.

They drove through narrow lanes to reach the fenced-off receiving area of the greater temple grounds.

Yarl spoke softly. "Please be patient. We must wait behind these deliveries. When I talk to the monks at the gates, please don't say anything."

"No problem."

A tall Meoenan monk waved for Yarl to open his window. "Are you delivering something?"

Yarl leaned slightly out the window and said, "Good morning, Offa! I have something for my father."

"Yarl? Why the tinted windows? Since when did you travel in something like this?"

"Long story. Oh, I forgot my formal robes. Can you get me a set?"

"Hardly! I'm working. Have you seen this line?"

"Sorry! I know it's a nuisance, but I'm stuck. Has anyone got anything hanging in the office?"

Offa shrugged. "Probably, but it'll be dusty."

"I'll take my chance. Thanks!"

Offa was about to wave Yarl on. Instead, he leaned close again and said, "Look, if you're going to the office, park in space twelve. Yinn isn't in today, so it's open."

"Great! Thanks."

Yarl parked where directed, spent several minutes in the office, and then returned to Jim in the vehicle.

"Here's a robe, Jim. Make sure the hood covers your face. Try not to show your feet or hands either."

With much grunting in the confines of his seat, Jim dragged the thick cloth of the robe over his flight suit.

"Ready?" Yarl asked.

"Sure. Let's go."

Yarl led his guest back toward the office but took an unmarked door just before it. Jim was plunged into darkness and ventured a peek outside his hood.

The corridor was narrow. The left-hand wall was made of ancient stone; the right-hand wall consisted of unadorned plaster wallboards.

"What is this?" he asked.

"A souvenir of renovations made a few decades ago. I don't know what they were thinking, but we do better work nowadays."

"I meant more like where does this take us?"

"I think you would call it the 'staff areas' where neither pilgrims nor scholars go. No one but the staff knows anything of them."

"Sounds excellent."

"Follow me. In silence, please, brother monk."

Jim bowed and hid his face again.

Yarl moved at a steady, unhurried pace. He quietly acknowledged anyone they saw but did not stop to talk. He led Jim down stairs; up stairs; along corridors; and, Jim thought, back along the same corridors.

They stopped by a door with a small sign that read the Meoenan equivalent of "F.C.P."

"What is this? Jim whispered.

"Your room. The letters stand for Friend in Continual Peace. It means you are on a silent retreat, and no one is to speak to you."

Jim said, "Umm, that sounds a little duller than I hoped."

"I believe that is the point. No one will bother you in here."

"Got it! Thanks." *So far, so good!*

Yarl left Jim alone in his room with the promise he would return.

The room was small and sparse. It held a bed, a chair, a small table, and a lamp. An archway in one wall led to a tiny bathroom.

Jim studied it all. *Larger than some of the fliers I've been in.*

He sat on the bed, got up, and sat on the chair. There were no ornaments and no pictures on the tan stone walls. He moved his hand over the lamp to switch it on and, again, to switch it off. The only other light came from a small square in one corner of the ceiling: a glow of sunlight, a faint indication of the outside world.

"This isn't going to work," Jim said aloud. "I'll go crazy in here."

He lay on the bed and remembered what he could of the old city. Several restaurants came to mind. *The Cal Merra Bar! That's just around the corner...*

A couple of hours in the library. A good meal. A drink. Okay, not going to go too crazy.

Yarl knocked lightly on the door.

"Come in!"

"Jim! I checked on the library. There are few academics booked into the reading room this week. You will be able to go there without too much chance of being noticed."

"Great! There are several things I want to look up while I'm here. Things my father told me about his studies."

Yarl nodded. "Very good."

"And," Jim continued, "let me know how I can get out again. I'd like to eat at one of the local places I remember from my youth."

Yarl swung his hands to the left. "That is not advisable. I understood you were to remain within the temple walls."

"Sure, I am. But a quick trip just outside should be fine."

"Your description of the situation was that a 'hit squad' is pursuing you. This is one place they may watch—your father's history with the temple is known. It makes no sense to me to disguise your arrival so thoroughly to have you immediately wander onto the streets."

Jim grimaced. "Not wander. I thought I could blend in easily enough with a crowd...a quiet restaurant, a quiet bar."

Yarl's blue head rose on his neck. "I see. May I remind you that you have this room because The Family Able is held in such high regard. That regard itself should make you realize you will be recognized wherever you go. You cannot *ever* blend in with a crowd."

"Yarl, I'm not actually on a silent retreat. I'll go crazy stuck in here!"

Yarl stared at the blank wall, but his thoughts were elsewhere. "Jim," he said evenly, "If you go outside the temple or even stay long in the public areas within, you will be seen and recognized. If I arranged an armed guard, someone would be sure to notice, and rumors would spread. There is no alternative; you must stay hidden!"

"I'm not so sure about that."

Yarl almost swung his hands to the left again but stood tall and said, "Please let me consult with my colleagues. I will see what further arrangements we can make."

"Fine! Thanks."

As Yarl turned to leave, Jim said, "Thanks for what you've done so far. I do appreciate it."

Yarl nodded and left.

Jim laid back on the bed. The sound of distant chanting drifted down from the bright square cut in the ceiling.

The Cal Merra! Dark, mysterious, and the haunt—back then—of a girl called Lesya.

CHAPTER 24

BETIH'S INTERVENTION

A monk knocked on Jim's door and, without a word, handed over a box and left.

Jim nodded his thanks. He unhooked the lid and took out a small comms screen.

With a grin and a sideways glance at the closed door, he chuckled. "Hey, I'm on silent retreat here!"

The device came to life, immediately showing part of a hairy snout and broadcasting the sound of a gul swearing a little too loud. As he scrambled to reduce the volume, the image steadied to a more distant view of Betih's face.

"Jim!"

"Betih. What's up?"

"You're an idiot!"

"Thanks! You had this delivered so you could insult me?"

"Someone has to."

Jim sighed and sat on the bed, his back against the wall. "Okay. What have I done, or not done, this time?"

"Neither. What are you going to do?"

Jim frowned. "I'm going to wait here until you guys get a true threat assessment of the gang members. How is it going?"

"Our efforts are about to fall apart in disarray and ruin!"

"Why?"

"We hear you intend to go to a local bar. Is that true?"

Jim gagged. "No! Wait...Yarl snitched on me?"

"Stupid puppy! We are not playing games. Your life is in danger, and so are ours."

"I know...You make it sound like I intend to go off on a bender!"

"Marhan has told me of your lost week spent drinking with him."

"So?"

Betih said nothing.

"What?" Jim asked. "He was celebrating. I...helped."

"And when you were on that Stacco place, on your own? Did you drink then?"

"No! Well...hardly at all. I wasn't there long."

"You wish to celebrate your retreat from public gaze by going out to a bar."

Jim looked away from the screen. "Kind of. I have happy memories of the place."

"I've never had a student like you."

"Glad to hear it!"

"Fool of a monkey!"

"Listen, Betih, I know what I'm doing. Not sure I appreciate you guys assuming the worst over there. I'll be fine!"

"The monks are preparing to stun you to prevent your leaving."

"Is that a joke?"

"No. But it will be amusing to watch. I, for one, will laugh."

"You guys can't be serious!"

"Jim, you must stop. Take a deep breath," she said calmly. "Listen to me; I'm old and have gathered some measure of wisdom in my years. In following me in my work, you must make decisions and abide by them. Now, sit back, close your eyes, and listen!"

"More inclined to end this conversation, Betih. Don't see it's worth pursuing."

"Then return the tools; you can go no further!"

"No! Don't...take on so. I'll listen. I don't guarantee I'll agree with you."

Betih stared at him from the screen, long and hard. Finally, she began, "Marhan has told me how impressed he was when you described the time machine to him. He says you understood straight away the danger it represented. He says you showed a humility he had never seen in you before."

"You can tell him what he can do with his backhanded compliments."

"What was it—in your past—you were tempted to change? What would you want to prevent yourself doing?"

Jim did not smile. "How...how do you know I'd want to change something in *my* past...and not in someone else's?"

Betih snarled and snapped her long jaw at him. "Think, puppy! Look into your own heart. What does the spirit tell you?"

Jim pointed at the screen. "Not sure I believe in all that spirit stuff you talk about."

She did not reply.

He sighed and continued, "Okay, yes. There are many, many mistakes I've made that could benefit from a different outcome."

"And?"

"And what?"

"How many of them started in a bar?"

"Fuck you!"

She growled. "Return the tools! I will not inflict a drunkard assassin on the galaxy."

"Drunkard? You...you don't know me! You don't know what you're talking about."

"As you have pointed out before, I do not feel the need to be polite to you. You cannot be the person you aspire to be by making old mistakes. You have already seen the shape of the changes you would make when you resisted the temptations of the time machine. Use what it taught you and apply that lesson to the present!"

He thought, *Who the hell are you to tell me what to do!* But he said, "Sure, no problem. And I know somewhere very nice to sit and think about it all."

"Your room. That's what it has been for—for centuries. Think of the souls who have sat on that bed, listening to the quiet. I'm sure that room has never been empty. So many come to the same point that you have. Listen to them saying, 'It's time for a change.' 'How do I do it?' 'How do I proceed?' 'How do I change?' Sit there and listen to the spirit!"

Jim dropped the screen onto the bed and stood up. He had thought the room empty, but it seemed suddenly—and claustropho-bically—full of previous guests, all with troubles, many worse than his own.

He turned to see Betih's snout still pointing into the screen. "So what?" he asked grimly, "What do you want me to do?"

"Where are you? Why can't I see you?"

"'Cause I...I'm over here." He picked up the unit.

"That's better. What do I want you to do? I want you to do everything we have been talking about since I came aboard your ship! I want you to avoid being stunned by the monks"—she snapped her jaws—"too often. I don't want those pursuing you to succeed. But, most of all, I want to finish my work with you, and then, perhaps someone will let me go off alone into the wilderness and die as I should have long ago. That's what I want! Any questions?"

Shit! Don't say that. Don't die, Betih! "No. No questions."

CHAPTER 25

NIGHT AT THE TEMPLE

Jim saw the hole in the ceiling darken as the sunlight faded over Tuanomena. He waved his hand over the small table to turn on the lamp.

Distant sounds continued to flow through the opening and perhaps the walls. Gongs marked transitions; chants rose and fell; soft conversations drifted by—just too quiet to make out; even fainter still, air traffic or perhaps a space-bound craft flew by.

Eventually, Jim lay on the bed and covered himself with a thin sheet. The flow of air through the opening in the ceiling barely challenged the warmth of the room.

In hours of half-sleep and half-wakefulness, Jim remembered his days growing up on Sonloi-AC, visits to Meoenan cities, vacations in the countryside.

His friends and the family's acquaintances always held the temple in high regard, even those who never came. *The superstitious side of them...always odd. Technically up-to-date people tend not to be so open about ancient religious beliefs.* But then Jim had encountered Tuanomena, a being so different from anything else.

"Lem-Jim-Sea, to be with you is Tuanomena's pleasure" was the thought that had rung in their minds when he, his father, and Jim's yet-to-be-born daughter had met Tuanomena.

What the hell did that mean? Just a "nice to see you?" or something else?

A faint purring sound brought Jim's memories back to the station and the cat that used to visit the apartment. *Bad breath! Terrible bad breath! A being strange in ways that no verbally endowed alien could ever be.*

His back felt warm, and he slept.

Suddenly awake, he felt a tickling at the back of his neck. Something purred loudly at his back.

A couple of cats on the station; never cats on the planet.

He was awake with a clarity so sharp the room no longer seemed dark.

If I roll off the bed, the sheet will bring it with me.

He half turned in the bed, throwing the sheet over the purring. Slipping down the side of the bed, he hopped on one foot and shot his hand toward the small table; the lamp flooded the room with yellow light.

Something black and furry was already up the wall and disappearing through the square hole in the ceiling.

Jim sank to his knees, blinked, and stared up.

He reached for his tablet and sent Yarl a message, "Bring forensic sample kits. There was something in my room."

CHAPTER 26

THE GANG

Tella sat tall and white in his robe before Jayde's desk. "What news?"

She glanced at her tablet. "Three gang members, one female, two male. They are booked into one room in the Garden Hotel—not cheap, not expensive, preferred by small business owners."

"Where have they gone on the station?"

Jayde continued reading. "Nowhere much. The Café. A couple of restaurants. The arboretum."

"Do they carry scanners or other gear? Are they tracking anyone or anything?"

"No sign of it. They are like typical visitors. With the exception that they aren't attending any meetings, contacting anyone, or interacting in any way with station personnel."

Tella nodded. "Embedding themselves in the hope of becoming invisible. They are waiting."

"I have our best guys on rotation in Alfie's spare room. I just hope she stays put."

"And Jim is in his room in the temple. We hope he too will 'stay put.'"

Jayde locked eyes with the Neraffan. "You'll need to tell me of any actions you intend to take. Understand this: I will not permit weapons fire on my station."

Tella matched her gaze. "I do understand. Did their luggage contain anything suspicious?"

"Of course not! They wouldn't have gotten aboard."

"Then there are a few possibilities to consider. They have undetectable weapons of some sort. They are waiting for a delivery they think will defeat your security efforts. Or they do not need weapons."

"Okay. I don't think they will get anything through. We're onto them. Anything addressed to them, we'll intercept."

"Indeed. I should add another possibility; they have something already on station waiting for them."

"Again, unlikely."

Tella stiffened. "Please enhance your security on the armory. Change all passwords, recode all the locks."

"I doubt we'd need to do that."

"It is the only stock of weapons on station. That they are rarely —if ever—removed from storage isn't relevant. If the gang knows they cannot bring their own, perhaps they intend to use yours."

Jayde sighed. "Very well."

Jayde knocked on the outer door of Jim's ship. Marhan's voice echoed in the airlock, "Identify yourself!"

"It's Jayde!"

"Are you alone?"

"I am."

The door cracked open, and Marhan slowly peeked out. "We weren't expecting you."

"I know. Something's come up. Are you going to let me in or not?"

The door opened wide and Marhan closed it after her.

Tella met her halfway down the corridor. "Administrator?"

"You were right. We found three blasters missing as we were locking down the armory."

CHAPTER 27

DAY AT THE TEMPLE

Yarl tapped gently on the door, and Jim cracked it open.

"That was quick! Thanks. Did you get them?"

Yarl nodded as Jim let him into the room. He glanced nervously around. "I visited a friend who has access to such things. I hope she is still a friend since I couldn't tell her why I need these so urgently. What sort of 'something' did you see?"

"Smallish, black, furry. Climbed straight up the wall at high speed."

Yarl studied the ceiling for a while before handing three boxes to Jim. "Impossible."

"I know. But then, I've been in space. I've seen a few impossible things."

Yarl smiled. "I don't mean that such a creature might exist. Rather that it might be found in the temple."

Jim ripped open one of the sample kits and carefully approached the crumpled sheet. He drew it back and put his face close. "There you are!"

"What is it?"

"Fur. A couple of odd pieces of black fur." Jim picked them off the sheet with tweezers and dropped them into a sample bag. "Who can analyze these and tell me what it is?"

Yarl hesitated. "I don't know. I can find someone. Perhaps the university in Kallowan?"

Jim shook his head. "No. Nothing speculative. I need the results back...by the end of the day."

Yarl stared but said, "I will try."

"Have Tella contact Robin Stuart, if necessary. There must be someone with the right equipment within a couple of hours' traveling. He might be able to help find them."

Yarl was at the door when he stopped and said, "Do you wish for a different room?"

Jim smiled. "No. I want to know what that thing was. It knows I'm here. I'm sure it'll be back."

"That may not be a good thing."

"I know. It's certainly no cat."

"What's a cat?"

"Never mind. Keep me informed."

"Of course, Jim."

Jim sat on the chair and inhaled deeply several times. *When did I get so comfortable ordering people around?*

The smell of breakfast percolated through to Jim's room. He dressed in the heavy robe again and found his way to the refectory.

Tables occupied one half of the room; stands of food and drink occupied the other half.

With careful navigation, Jim loaded a tray with more than he needed and left without engaging anyone in conversation. He felt a little sad doing so; there were several people whose species he didn't know. *Maybe I'll find you in the library later,* he thought.

Back in his room, he checked under the bed before sitting down to eat.

A loud knock interrupted breakfast.

"Come in!" Jim called.

A tall Meoenan opened the door. His robe, like the one Jim had worn, covered almost everything. He pulled back the hood to reveal the large Meoenan eyes, a wrinkled forehead, and more facial hair than would be normal.

"Who are you?"

"I am Baha, father to Yarl, Master Chatse of the temple, Varzul of the order of Tuanomena. You are Jim Able, The Younger Son of Family Able."

"I am. Pleased to meet you."

Baha strode into the room and sat quickly on the bed, his eyes on Jim's face. "Firstly, you keep Yarl from his work with your requests. Have a care for him. He will never tell you if the time you need jeopardizes his work. Secondly, he tells me you saw something that should not be. In the night. In this room."

"Oh..." said Jim, "I'm sorry. I'll keep what you say about Yarl in mind. He's done good work, getting me here and looking after me. You should be proud of him."

"Of course."

"I saw a creature. Black. Furry. Fast. It ran straight up the wall, leaving no marks. About so big." Jim indicated with his hands.

"What was it doing?"

"Lying on the bed at my back. It came up to my neck. I think that's what woke me. I don't know what it was doing, but it didn't want to be seen."

Baha asked, "Vermin? Looking for food?"

Jim shook his head. "More intelligent, I think."

The monk sighed. "That such a thing could be at large in the temple is impossible. No one else has reported such a thing. Could it have come in with you?"

Again, Jim shook his head. He pointed to his flight bag. "This is all my luggage. I would have noticed."

Baha's large eyes scanned the floor, then he stood and examined the hole in the ceiling. "The light shafts are sometimes narrow but not an obstacle for one of the size you say. They link to each other and to the air shafts, to the public corridors, to our hidden passages...everywhere. It could hide for a long time. I presume it must come out to eat." Baha chuckled. "No visitor to this temple has ever starved, nor has one ever been eaten. Perhaps you will be the first!"

Jim smiled. "I hope not."

"I will alert the kitchens and the shopkeepers on the ground level."

"I'm expecting it to come back tonight."

Baha nodded slowly. "Perhaps. But perhaps not. What can I offer you for your protection? We allow visitors no weapons, of course."

Jim chewed his tongue before saying, "That's not what I heard; your son was preparing to stun me if I left." Baha did not react. "Perhaps you could bring me a stick of some sort. A net? Though it moved so fast..."

"I will have something brought."

The monk strode to the door and opened it. "I hope you otherwise will enjoy your time in the temple."

"Thank you!"

Jim watched the back of the door for a while. *You have something of Sopha Luca about you, Baha. Or maybe his father. All business. Just without the psychopathy.*

Jim sent a message to Jayde Duke on Sonloi-AC. "I'm using a lot of Yarl's time. If it's okay with you, I'd like to continue to do so. I can arrange compensation as needed for him, or I'll pay for a substitute when he can't be at his post in your office. Let me know. Jim."

CHAPTER 28

JAYDE'S DECISION

Around the galley table, Tella, the guls, and Jayde sat in silence.

Betih glanced from face to face. "An interesting dilemma, Station Administrator. Do you wait for them to attack and risk deaths and injuries? Do you arrest them prematurely and risk discovering someone else took the blasters?"

"If I arrest them now, there are Meoenan politicians who will hang us out to dry. The movement to stir up resentment of us 'aliens lording it over them' may have gone underground, but it's still there. I dare not arrest citizens of Sonloi without actual evidence."

Marhan said, "That the theft was so clean, it speaks of inside help."

"I agree," Jayde replied, "that's a separate matter."

"So," Tella asked, "What can we do?"

Jayde looked around the table. "Stay here, on board. All of you. Don't come onto the station. If there is to be a fight—I'm sorry—but it has to be here, away from everyone else."

Tella nodded.

She continued, "There are maintenance passageways—well, crawlspaces—nearby. I'm stationing people in them in advance. But I can't keep them there forever. I hope you realize that."

"Understood," said Marhan.
"Good luck," said Jayde.

CHAPTER 29

THE TEMPLE LIBRARY

Jim ventured to the library after eating breakfast.

The stone walls, a sunny tan color, matched the rest of the temple. The library shelves stood dark in contrast.

Meoenan books traditionally hung from a carrying handle or a hook, the spine being at the top of the pages. Meoenan writing ran from top to bottom and then left to right. Jim and his brother had been brought up to know Standard, English, and Melu, the most common language on Sonloi. The young Jim and Matt had nearly ruined their eyes squinting at the small type Meoena preferred to read.

Jim asked a librarian, "My father, some years ago, spent much time here. I'd like to follow what books he enjoyed most. Can you let me know what they were? Do you keep records like that?"

The librarian nodded carefully, hoping to be polite in her use of the peculiarly human gesture. "We do not. He would have had access to all the books in our collection. What interests you most? Perhaps I can make some suggestions?"

Jim smiled and said, "I'll give it more thought. Thanks."

As he turned away from the desk, a tall female Meoenan rose from one of the ancient and comfortable chairs nearby.

"James Able! James Able!"

"Hello?"

She was taller than most Meoena. Like Yarl's father, she had a wrinkled forehead and more facial hair than would be normal. As she stepped forward, she limped. He could also tell her arms were stiffer than they should be.

She wrapped her warm blue hands around Jim's. Her eyes lowered to be level with his. "James Able! It's so long since I last saw you."

Jim smiled. "I'm sorry, but I don't remember..."

"Oh, why should you! I am Jart, Jart Bregg. I worked with your father. He and I spent much time together on the station. Then, once I retired and came to live at the temple, it was such a delight to see him again here."

"Oh, you live here?"

She nodded, quite naturally. "I do. They are kind to let me. My health is not good, and the environment within mitigates many problems I would otherwise face."

Jim smiled, not quite understanding.

"Did I hear correctly that you want to know what books your father read?"

"I'd like to, if I can."

She spoke softly. "I would love to help. We often read together. How long do you have?"

"Several days, if not more," he replied, matching her tone.

She let go of his hands and clasped hers together in glee. "Wonderful! We'll first find two seats together where we won't be disturbed. Then, I shall form a list of volumes for them to bring to us! Oh, what a delightful surprise!"

Jim blinked but said, "Great! Thank you so much." *I'm not sure this will work. But she seems a nice old lady. And I have time.*

She swept him away from the main room and into an area with smaller rooms, smaller shelves, more lamps, and fewer light shafts in the ceilings. The room she decided upon was triangular, with two walls of half-height stacks, two chairs, and a table between them.

The books looked all part of the same collection: identical hooks, ancient covers, and pages smelling of antiquity.

"We'll make this our launch pad, Jim!" she said almost conspiratorially.

"Thanks! I welcome somewhere to keep out of sight while I'm here because—"

She held up one hand. "We dust off the world's troubles when we enter the temple. It clears the mind."

He smiled. "Of course."

"Now, let us take a moment to join our hearts with the many monks, pilgrims, researchers, questioners, and seekers who are here today, who were here in all the days of the temple, and who will be in all the days to come."

As she closed her eyes, Jim could see a tremble in her hands he hadn't noticed before. Like a weight on his shoulders, he felt a cloud of all those who had come before, much as he had in his room during Betih's lecture.

What am I doing here?

"Now, Jim, have you ever been on The Walk?"

"I have. I can't tell you all the details, but yes, I have been there. I have met Tuanomena."

She gasped and sat back. Withdrawing her hands from the table, she joined them in her lap. "You have been blessed!"

Jim smiled wryly but didn't contradict her.

She continued. "It was your father's goal to learn about The Walk. He so wanted to understand Tuanomena!" She stopped and laughed. "I remember him being so calm and businesslike on the station. So professional, if not—as is so often the way with engineers —a little boring."

Jim laughed.

"But then," she continued, "when I met him again here, he was...on fire! He had discovered a joy in research. He was dedicated in a way I wish more of our young people could be."

"Did he ever explain why he was so interested?"

She looked at him without speaking, then whispered, "He said he couldn't tell me everything that had brought him to that point.

But it became clear we had the same interests. My reading over-lapped with his in many ways."

"About Tuanomena himself?"

"About time. About what our ancestors understood about time. About the building of the temple. He read as many of the accounts of The Walk as he could find, the diaries of pilgrims, the reports from the monks. You were on the Walk. You know it is best described as 'complicated.'"

Jim chuckled. "That's Yarl Breen's favorite expression." He nodded. "I understand some of the complications, yes."

She sat straight up, quite silent, and spread her trembling fingers on the table. "Would it be best to return to the Walk?"

"I don't want to go back up there." *That isn't true, is it?* He continued, "Well, at least not until I've read more—like Dad did."

"I understand. Let me think a while. We should start with...Oh, *The Lirthon*! Yes, that would be good. He found it useful, I remember. We shall read it together, and I can comment for you about where, in more recent years, we might disagree with it."

"*The Lirthon*? What is it?"

"It was written at least three hundred years ago, perhaps a little more. The Master Chatse at the time, one Gror Gute by name, wrote down his—oh, his intuition, yes—and a summary of the knowledge, such as it was then, of Tuanomena. Yes, for you, I think it will be a good starting point."

"Fine. I'm happy to take your guidance."

She reached out and held his hand. "Oh, this is such a delightful meeting!"

CHAPTER 30
RITUAL

Betih lay on her bed in Module Three. She performed a ritual she had neglected in recent days, whispering each question slowly to herself.

"What do I hear?"

Almost nothing. My breath. The snores of my nephew across and down the hall.

"What do I smell?"

The chemicals used in manufacturing the walls, the carpet, the furniture. The scent of humans. Perhaps some slept in here before I did. The smells of cooking that drift up from below and linger long after eating.

"What do I feel?"

My limbs and the stiffness of age. My muscles—softer than they ever were. The bed beneath me. More comfortable than the bed in The Luminary. I should be sleeping on the floor.

"What do I taste?"

Death. My time has come.

"What do I see?"

The dark.

. . .

"Such good questions. Thank you, my sisters, for such training. Now I know."

She slipped quietly past the other modules, descended the ramp, and padded silently along the corridor to the airlock.

She opened the inner door and sealed it again. Then, slowly, she opened the outer door—just enough to pass through—and closed it behind her.

The lights had been dimmed for the late shift in semblance of night.

I know you see me, waiting security guards. I will be gone before you get your instructions.

She moved swiftly down the corridors and into an elevator. Within minutes she was in the lobby of the Garden Hotel.

At the visitors' door, she knocked.

"Who is it?" came a voice from within.

"Both trouble and information," Betih replied.

She heard movement, careful movement, from behind the door.

The safety window drew back, and she stepped away to give them a clear view. She smiled, lifted her ears, cocked her head to one side, and drew her pink robe closer around her.

"What do you want?"

"To come in. To talk. Why else would I knock?"

The safety window closed. She listened to the whispering.

The lock clicked, and the door opened. She stepped into the darkened room.

"Wait there!" The male voice was from behind her at the side of the doorway.

The second male approached her. "You'd better not be armed."

"Search me," she said, "but remember I am old and experienced. If you're going to feel me up, you'd better do it right."

The Meoenan female snorted slightly.

At the searcher's signal, the lights came on.

"Sit down and state your business."

Betih sat on the large chair by a desk strewn with papers, maps, and what might have been diagrams of the station.

"I am Ernot Bard Betwen, Luminant of Tanna Gul. Who are you?"

"You don't need to know our names," she replied.

Betih shrugged. "Nor is there any point in concealing your names from me. The authorities already know everything about you, where you come from, and who you work for."

The air chilled further.

She smiled and looked at each of them in turn, their large eyes gleaming in the lamplight. "Really? Did you think that coming onto this station and asking about Jim Able would not get you noticed? They know about him, they care about him, and they would die protecting him. What are your names? It will make this conversation go more smoothly."

"Call me Galla."

Still standing behind her, one said, "I am Freg."

"I am Hirt," said the other.

"Thank you, Galla, Hirt, Freg. I do not know what instructions you were given. Nor, really, do I care. You have walked into a situation no one on your planet could be aware of."

Galla asked, "What do you mean?"

"You seek Jim Able. I'm sure you did not bring him gifts of fresh fruits from Earth's jungles or even as much as a loaded payment fob. You've been told to kill him, leave the station, and disappear."

"You travel with him," Freg said, "have you come to bargain for his life?"

Betih smiled. "His life is mine."

"Talk plainly!" Galla hissed.

The gul sat back and crossed her feet. "I am an assassin. It is *I* who will determine whether Jim Able should live or die, not you."

Hirt laughed. "Some assassin! Look at her!"

Betih lightly snapped her jaws at him. "Impudent puppy! Show some respect, Hirt, to your elders and betters."

"Prove it," Galla said.

Betih shook her head. "Galla, the role of the assassin is not one to be questioned on any planet. Do not, any of you, think to interfere with my work."

"You're traveling with him. Why haven't you killed him yet?"

She nodded. "A good question. No assassin will kill before making sure the action is justified. On Tanna Gul, he destroyed an entire space fleet. The ships were empty, but he also leveled two buildings that were not. That is where and when I first heard of him. On Hon Hen Flereat, he killed a party of Limarcs. On Stacco Ila 32, a party of Kevar. There are other crimes...I won't bore you! Destruction and death follow in his wake, yet no authority is seeking him; no judiciary has posted a warrant for his arrest. I am making my determination. I say again, do not get in my way."

Hirt said to Galla, "She's raving. Kill her."

Galla looked to Freg for his reaction.

Freg shrugged. "Makes no difference either way. She does it, or we do."

"Makes a big difference," Galla replied, "We get paid for a result. We don't subcontract."

Betih chuckled. "Neither do I."

Galla looked her in the eye. "We could kill you. You and the others are collateral damage to us."

The gul growled. "Careful, blue-skins. Assassins do not allow their kind to be murdered. If you kill me, another will come, not for Able, but for you—all three of you—and probably the ones who have sent you here."

Galla snorted. "We have no proof of what you say. You're an old gul in a pink robe! Hirt's right; you're insane."

"Do I sound insane? I have come here, in the middle of the night, unarmed, to talk to you! In full knowledge of who and what you are." She turned her head slightly. "Though, now I hear myself say that, perhaps I am insane, but not in the way you mean it. That I am an assassin is not in doubt. Who else could perform such tasks, if not someone who does not look the part? How many assassins do you know? What do they look like? Hmm? Tell me!"

They looked from one to the other.

Galla shook her head. "This conversation is a waste of time. You can give us no proof. What do you expect us to do?"

"I expect you to leave. I will deal with Jim Able. Go home, tell your master what I have said."

"He'd shoot us on the spot! We're here to carry out a mission. I hear nothing from you that changes that."

"Then you have another problem to add to those already snapping at the heels of your mission."

"Again, speak plainly! I have no time for riddles!" Galla shouted.

Betih smiled. "No need to shout. I may be old, but my ears still work! How close are you to completing the mission? Do you know where Able is? How will you confront him? The Neraffan, where is it? Perhaps it came in here with me?"

All three froze and glanced around the room.

Betih continued. "The authorities are aware of you. How long before they come and remove you? You have no legitimate business on this station and their patience is short. For that matter, so is mine. I understand your position. My work has similar constraints to yours. In all assassinations, I weigh the chances of success at every step. If I cannot complete my task at any point, I defer. I wait for a better time, or rather, I *create* a better time. This is where you stand now. Your mission has no likelihood of success. Your target has eluded you."

Betih wondered, from her expression, if Galla would reach for a blaster and kill her there in the chair.

Instead, Galla said, "And you? Have you any greater chance of success?"

"I am traveling with him." Betih didn't smile but looked each of them in the eye again.

Hirt punched the wall.

Freg muttered, "You put us in a bad position, assassin!"

"A better position than being carried back to your planet in body bags."

Galla sank a little where she sat on the bed. "There is something to what she says."

Hirt hissed, "No! We just need to flush him out! Let's use her. Keep her here. Do a swap—him for her."

Betih smiled and said, "There is a time for improvisation; this is not it."

"Why not?" Galla challenged.

"Able would not come. Others would."

"And you? You wouldn't survive it."

Betih shrugged. "As I said, I am old. As for the mission, another will take up whatever I do not complete."

Galla shook her head as if she were avoiding flies. "No! When does this end? You're saying he is untouchable! Like he's getting protection from all the assassins of the galaxy until one of you decides to finally take him out!"

Betih said nothing.

"Where does that put *us*?" Galla said, louder than she intended.

"In deep shit," Hirt replied.

"I empathize, I do, but can offer little comfort. As I said, you walked into a situation you did not anticipate."

Silence reigned in the room.

"Wait," Galla said quietly, "assassins carry a mark. Something only they know. Show us your mark. Then we'll believe you!"

Betih smiled. "And the reason it is only known to each other? We do not tell outsiders what it is."

"Us you can tell."

"Not without ensuring you tell no one else."

A knock came at the door. The three froze.

Betih stood and announced, "That is for me."

"What?" said Hirt.

"Who?" asked Galla.

Freg threw back the security window, turned, and said, "No one."

"Nonetheless, it is time I left you to decide what you will do."

"Wait!" Hirt called.

Galla grabbed a blaster from under the pillow next to her.

Betih had the door handle in her claw and swung the door into

Freg's face. She was in the corridor and running before the blaster shot burned into the door of the room opposite.

In the elevator, she sighed and said, "Thank you. Your timing was excellent."

From behind, Tella replied, "We have much to discuss."

Back at the assassins' room, Jayde's security guards moved in.

CHAPTER 31

THE TEMPLE, THIRD DAY

Jim awoke, his neck stiff and sore. As he had all night, he sat on the bed, his back to the wall.

As his dreams faded, he recalled vivid images of the black creature, purring in the crook of his arm, as he showed it the buffet tables.

Once he had stretched and showered, he checked the skin on the back of his neck as best he could in the mirror. Then he repeated his anonymous raid on breakfast and returned silently to his room.

He found a note from Yarl.

"The examination of the sample is complete, but the creature is not known. I am sorry, but the more advanced laboratory cannot provide an answer until next week."

Also, on his desk lay an edition of *The Lirthon*, translated into Standard with large print. Jim put down the note with a sigh, picked up the book, and began reading where he and Jart had left off.

It was not long before Jim announced to the book, "Gror Gute, for a Master Chatse you write like your only other work was a shopping list!"

I don't have the mind for this stuff. Give me a wiring diagram or a bucket full of spare parts and I'm fine. Who can get through this word salad?

Dad. Jart. They've managed to get into it. Something in their minds made the transition from the ordinary to the multidimensional.

Jim sighed, stuffed something bread-like in his mouth, and continued to read.

The Walk, the circularity, Tuanomena's temporal truce.
The Walkers, the kitchen of flavor, a soup of pilgrims.
The Temple, where in space, where else an intrusion.
The Monks, a calm, the sailing crew ignorant of the
weather.

"Thanks a lot, Gror. An illuminating analysis."

Jim stared at the bright square in the ceiling, half expecting a black shadow to cross it, but it didn't change. He checked the time, closed the book, and donned his robe again.

"Okay, Jart, let's hear more about how great Dad was."

In their library nook, Jart scanned several books opened side by side. Jim felt a pang of sympathy as he saw her hunched, bony body. Her shawl was low across her back, and he saw black patches across the blue skin of her neck.

"Good morning!"

"James! Good morning. Did you sleep?" Noticing his gaze on her neck, she brought up her shawl to cover the marks and reached for another book.

"Some, thanks, and you?"

She nodded. "Oh yes. I sleep very well these days, though my dreams are becoming wilder and wilder of late! How far did you get with *The Lirthon?*"

Jim coughed and said, "Not far. It's not the historical treatise I was expecting."

"Ah, no, Master Gute has a unique style. Though, within his words, there is great meaning, I think."

"Any facts? I mean, later on in the book."

Her face came alive with mischief. "Facts? As in engineering data? Archeological finds? Recipes for Jara cake? No, James, it is not that sort of book."

"But Dad got something out of it."

"Oh yes! He read it repeatedly."

"Great..."

"Now..." Her eyes lost focus. "There was something I had to ask you...I wonder what it was?"

Jim smiled. "Can't help you there. It'll come back."

"Yes...Why are you here?" Her eyes were not on him.

"What do you mean? Are you okay?"

She shook her head and frowned. "Yes, I'm fine."

"You know why I'm here. I'm following in my father's footsteps."

"Yes, you must tell me why."

Jim saw her hands shaking more than the previous day. "Are you sure you're okay? Can I get you anything?"

"It's very important..." She gasped, laughed, and said, "I'm sorry. What was I saying?"

"You asked me what I thought of *The Lirthon*."

"Oh yes. There is much hidden within it. I hope you can extract what you need."

They read together in silence for a while, though Jim took in none of the words.

What was that? Is her mind going? Is it a result of her condition? How much should I rely on her? Am I going down a rabbit hole here?

He ventured a question. "Jart, what can you tell me about your condition? What's so beneficial about the environment in here?"

She waved him off. "Oh, it's just old age. The monks keep the temple warm and dry. The damp isn't good for my joints, that's all."

Twice more, during the morning, Jart showed signs of distraction and asked Jim why he was at the temple.

As he raided the lunch buffet, he spotted Baha. Gesturing for him to come over, Jim withdrew to a corner.

"Dear Guest, how can I help you?" Baha said serenely.

"I've been doing some reading in the library with Jart Bregg. Do you know her?"

"I do."

"What's her story? I see she has some kind of bone or joint problem. How's her mind?"

Baha stepped back a little. "It is not polite to ask such questions of another guest. I am surprised at you, Younger Son!"

"Sorry, but you know I'm on high alert right now. She acted a little strangely this morning."

"She is a dear lady. We are happy to have her here."

"And she was a good friend of my father's. I'm concerned there may be something wrong. That's all. Her mind has been so strong and clear, but today..."

Baha, nodding formally, replied, "Enjoy your stay," and left.

Okay, that's me put in my place.

Their afternoon together passed better than the morning. Jim read a passage from *The Lirthon* that said,

> Pilgrim, did you cleanse your feet?
> You washed away the dust of time.
> You are pure.
> You are unfettered.
> You walk not as one.
> You walk without restraint.

That reminds me of something. Who said that—"without restraint"?

Tuanomena said that! "To travel without restraint." That's what he called the T-switch.

"Jart?"

"James?"

"This phrase in here, 'walk without restraint,' what can you tell me about it?"

She looked at him, sat back, and sighed. "Oh, that's a big question! You'll need to read Miqlu...and probably Shur. Though they do have some wild ideas." She leaned into him and whispered, "I must confess I find them hard going." She sat back and smiled. "There's a primer to their works here somewhere."

"Did my father read them too?"

"I think so, though I don't remember him saying much. I wondered at the time if he understood anything in them. It's quite deep Meoenan mysticism."

"Great...I'm not much of one for any kind of mysticism." *But Tella is into all that!* "I'll give the primer a go."

"Wonderful! Though you must tell me how it goes. Don't be embarrassed if you have problems with their ideas. These books are notorious for flushing out those students whose time might be better spent elsewhere."

Jim smiled. "I won't be. Don't worry."

"I forget, did you ever devote yourself to a period of reflection?" she asked, "Were there human rituals of self-discovery when you were young?"

"You mean go on a walkabout, like you guys do?" He chuckled. "No, I'm still avoiding it."

She hung her head, smiled, and said, "It's never too late."

CHAPTER 32

TELLA AND THE GANG

Tella sat bolt upright on a stool. Red flashes from a nearby medical monitor sent occasional sparks of color across its face.

Galla lay in the bed, scowling.

Tella said, "I have the administrator's ear. I can influence much of what will happen to you in the next few days. Once you are off the station, I can no longer help."

"Why should I believe you? What help would *you* give *me*?"

"I will gain nothing from your incarceration on Pec Sonloi. I may yet gain something from your cooperation here. I am willing to trade."

"You know I'm dead if I talk."

Tella sighed. "That is their threat. But, as you now are aware, those sent to kill do not always succeed. We can make it less likely that you will die."

"A life on the run? It's no life."

"If you appeared to die in this bed, there is little likelihood of pursuit. There are planets that would take you. Do you have any family?"

Galla shook her head. "Strange Meoena suddenly showing up

would ring alarm bells. We don't travel much. The color of our skin makes us stand out in crowds."

Tella shook its head. "Your young travel much for religious reasons, I understand. Are you too old for such a thing?"

Galla snorted. "Bunch of nonsense! Pseudo-intellectual losers!"

"But an adequate disguise in your case."

She glanced at the Neraffan and quickly looked away.

"All I want in return is to know who is likely to send someone else after Jim. I just need a name."

Later, back on the ship, Tella made a call.

"Rob Stuart? This is Tella."

"Tella? Hi! Is Jim okay?"

"He is well. I have a job for you."

"Oh, okey dokey. Who do you want me to find?"

"I have someone I want you to lose."

CHAPTER 33

JIM'S INVITATION

Yarl knocked on Jim's door.

"Yarl? What's up?"

"I have a message..."

"From? Looks like it's a problem."

Yarl nodded. "It came through a...high functionary."

Jim smiled. "Your father?"

Yarl indicated "no" and said, "In this case, no. But...Well, a guest is living in a staff room. We do not advertise his presence. Indeed, we are under strict instructions not to talk of him."

"Okay. Please start making sense."

Yarl glared at Jim.

Uh-oh! Never seen that look before. A real flash of your father.

The Meoenan continued, "He came down from The Walk some thirty years ago. I understand he traveled much in the early days after his arrival but has recently become reclusive. He has his food brought to him, and he does not mingle with the other staff."

"Does he have a name?"

"Gror Gute."

"The author of *The Lirthon*?"

"Yes. He has asked that you attend him in his room."

"Perhaps he had wind of my less than favorable review."

"I should add...Master Gute died three hundred years ago."

"Yeah...Is that one of those insane grammatical conditional tenses? 'He will have died...' but just hasn't done it yet."

Yarl smiled.

"How did he do it? Does he have a T-switch?"

Yarl looked away. "We don't know. But, as you perhaps already know, these areas—reserved for staff—are part of the complications of the presence of The Walk above us."

Jim swallowed. "I didn't, no."

Yarl continued quietly, "The physical spaces do not entirely match the configuration of the rest of the building. Neither are the days and nights quite—"

"Shit...it gets worse."

"I once took Administrator Duke to The Walk through the staff passageways and staircases. At Tuanomena's will, it is also possible for visitors to be guided—or in Gute's case, find his way—down from there."

"Wait...Possible for someone on The Walk—from the past—to come into our time? Or any other?"

Yarl nodded.

"Perhaps Sea did it that way?"

"That I cannot say. However, Gute is with us, and it is not generally known. Please be discrete with this information."

"Of course. Did he say what he wants with me? Or how he's even heard of me?"

"No. I am merely to convey his request for your presence."

"Duly done! Thanks. What's your assessment of any potential problems with me seeing him?"

Yarl hung his head. "I don't think he would mean you or anyone direct harm. However, danger exists merely in extending further the group of people who know about him—and those who know about you. That this should occur within the river of complications flowing from The Walk—and Tuanomena's many blessings—makes everyone a little nervous."

Jim laughed. "Well put! Hmm, I guess I'll go and see him."

"Take the stairs to the left. Go up three flights. Turn right. His door has the same sign as yours." Yarl turned and had almost left when he said, "My father will be asking questions of you before your first foot falls back in this room."

Jim nodded. "Maybe he'll be in a mood to answer some of mine."

Yarl almost signed "no" but instead said, "Again, please be discrete with anything you may learn."

CHAPTER 34

JAYDE AND BETIH

Aboard Jim's ship, Jayde sat across the table from Betih.

Marhan listened, just out of sight, on the ramp.

"We agreed on a plan. What the hell were you doing?"

Betih smiled. "What you could not."

"What do you mean?"

"I understand these people, Meoenan they might be, but their type is the same on every world."

"I tried my best to ensure any weapons fire took place off my station. Instead, you provoked a fight in a hotel corridor! A public area!"

"I fired no shot."

"Don't pick hairs!"

Betih laughed and snapped her jaws. With a small growl, she replied, "I prevented a full-scale battle. Your guards are proficient. They contained their opponents in a confined space. And no one died."

"I have a family—in the room opposite—*traumatized*! That's down entirely to you going off on your own. The blame may come to me, but I am going to share as much of it with you as I can!"

"Please do. Then share the credit too. Those three oafs were demoralized when I left them. They were on the verge of panic when your people moved in. They were not the cool killers who arrived on the station. That is what I did. I cut the legs from under them. You cleaned up their droppings, nothing more."

Jayde shook her head and groaned in frustration. "Do not leave this ship again. Do not come onto my station. One whisker out of that airlock, and you're in the brig! Understood?"

Betih's long tongue licked the bottom of her nose.

Jayde felt the challenge to her authority brewing.

"Very well." Betih drew her robe close.

"My assessment of the rest of this crew is ongoing. When is Jim expected?"

Betih shrugged.

CHAPTER 35

GROR GUTE

Jim knocked on Gute's door.

A loud, jolly voice rang out inside, "Come in! Come in!"

Jim opened the door, and a thick wall of incense smoke blew out into the corridor.

"Hello?" Jim coughed, inhaling the sweet, spicy smoke.

"Come, come! Don't stand in the doorway, come in!"

The room was no bigger than Jim's but was decorated quite differently. Dark wall hangings loomed over all. There was no bed, table, or chair, only cushions. Under a large vent in the ceiling, the room's sole occupant sat naked on a bare board.

Most Meoena are taller than their human friends. This specimen, however, was short and fat. Jim had never seen a citizen of Sonloi so enormously overfed.

Gror Gute's bald head sat moon-like on his rounded shoulders. His rolls of stomach fat spread like a terraced garden yet failed to hide his genitalia. The deep blue of the Meoenan skin showed blotches of lighter color at his knees and where his legs crossed and touched the board.

All Meoena fastidiously covered their skin and the lines of white bumps that trace along their limbs. Jim remembered being curious about them as a youth, when he learned the bumps play a large role in Meoenan sexual activity.

The sight of this entirely naked Meoenan was a shock.

Jim pushed back against thinking of Gute as a Buddha—any personification of the spiritual would be strange for the Meoena— but his host was such a mixture of both strange and familiar that Jim's heart rate stayed high, and his balance stayed on the balls of his feet. *Be ready for anything.*

Gror's face split with the largest Meoenan smile, and his eyes— bright, large, and semitransparent—scanned Jim's face and clothes repeatedly.

With a jiggling of his entire body, Gror let out a laugh that filled the room. "James Able! The human! How wonderful. Here you are come to see me!"

"At your kind request." Jim suppressed all attempts at humor. *Meoena don't laugh so much. And they wear clothes.*

"Come closer! Come closer! Sit. Be comfortable."

"You speak Standard well for someone not born to it," Jim commented.

Gror rolled his head. "An unexpected aspect of living on Sonloi in these years. I had not anticipated a future where we would use anything other than our own tongues."

Jim nodded. "It makes so many things possible across the galaxy."

"As I have come to learn." Again, the blue body erupted with laughter.

"You asked to see me."

"Twice! And yet you refused both invitations."

"What? I'm sorry, when?"

"The first night you slept here, I sent one of my friends to greet you." He bowed his head and shoulders low to Jim, revealing a shadow hanging behind his neck and down his back.

Jim felt sick as he recognized several cat-like creatures hanging by their mouths from dark patches of loose skin.

Jim spoke without thinking. "What the fuck are they?"

Raising his head again to laugh, Gror said, "My friends. Most useful creatures. Sit! And I will tell you their story. Relax, James Able. You stand as if you are in some danger. Nothing will happen to you here! You are under the protection of Tuanomena. You are under my protection. You may be, for what it's worth, also under the protection of Master Chatse, Baha Breen. Sit! Sit!"

Under pressure from more laughter, Jim arranged himself on a large cushion.

"One day, I sat pursuing my education," Gror began, in a preachy tone, "as the master always must, when I found a note. A most peculiar note, as you will soon understand. It was written on a shiny paper of a kind I had never seen, but the script was easy to recognize; it was my own! Now, the note had been placed in a rare book, in an obscure chapter, perhaps a place into which only my eyes had ventured for many centuries. I had found a note from myself!" The Meoenan laughed long and hard. "And this was but the start of my strange days. In the note, I told myself to go to a certain room, by way of certain stairs and corridors, when the light of Pec shone down only certain shafts. This I did, of course!" Again, he laughed. "Whereon I found myself transported in time by the blessing of Tuanomena!"

Jim listened without comment.

"But that was merely the first part of the note! The second— and to me more mysterious—told me I must travel the stars. I must go to a planet called Mit Apogan. Do you know this place, James Able?"

Jim shook his head. "Never heard of it."

Gror laughed. "No. Why would you? No one like us lives there. Those who do have yet to find the fullness of *their* languages, let alone discover one standard throughout the stars. But I went. I did, in obedience, what I myself wrote that I should. I found the cave where I was instructed to meditate. And there, James Able, I met my friends. They have no pronounceable name for themselves. Their needs are simple. They like food. And, as you see, so do I!"

Gror's body shook and jiggled in illustration.

"I remember well the night when one first ventured to make physical contact with me." He closed his eyes. "I sat with the choice clear before me: allow it or resist it, let the creature approach my neck or cast it aside." Opening his eyes again to lock with Jim's, he continued, "You chose the latter, I the former. Meditation removes fear, James Able. You would benefit by learning this lesson!"

Jim nodded politely.

"And so, I found in the days that followed, this simple creature was hungry. Its mind unfolded to mine. It did not wish to consume me—let's be clear—no, it wanted me to fetch it some food! How could I resist such a harmless request?"

"How did it communicate?"

"I have since come to understand it sent a projection of its brain into mine through the back of my neck. You may be better versed in the ways of ganglions and nerves than I, but some sort of extrusion passed from it into me. Then, once established, it could connect—better and more clearly as the cells grew—until we shared, through this physical contact, one brain. Its wishes were my wishes. When it fell away from my neck, I could remember. The memories were mine—though the thoughts, in their origin, were not."

Jim swore silently to himself.

Gror laughed long and hard. "Soon enough, I found that my trained mind could perform similar operations on the mind of this more primitive creature. I left Mit Apogan with a brigade of fifty under my benevolent control."

"Lovely," Jim said quietly.

"Now, the second time I tried to communicate with you was through Jart Bregg. Though she seemed to have some trouble integrating my wishes into her conversations with you."

"She was acting strangely."

"Indeed. I send my friends to other people to share what I command them to share. The recipients usually think of my wishes as their thoughts, their memories, their desires. Why should they not? She perhaps has some underlying mental problem that interfered with the process."

"Maybe...And the site where they connect? That doesn't look healthy."

Gror moved his hands lightly to the left and chuckled. "I have had no ill effects."

Jim shifted uncomfortably. "It sounds wrong, Gror Gute, as a member of the temple staff, a Meoenan, as a sentient creature. Surely you realize that?"

Again, the laughter came, and Jim began to dislike it.

Gror replied, "Nonsense! What I do is ethically sound. But when did a human have anything to teach a Meoenan about ethics?"

"Before we start down that long road, perhaps you'd better tell me why you wanted to see me?"

Gror bowed again and seemed to shift a little.

Jim saw a black streak disappear up the wall and through the vent.

"Why? Why would I *not* wish to meet you? You are of the famous family. I have heard so much about you. I remember your father and was present at his first meeting with Tuanomena—a blessing few of our young people receive. I want to hear from you the tale of your own meeting with Tuanomena. What transpired? Why have you not returned before now? We have so much in common between us to discuss!"

Jim nodded cautiously. "But let me begin with a few questions for you, if I may?"

Gror laughed. "Of course! Begin!"

Jim's suspicion deepened that the laughter wasn't kindly. He asked, "Where did that thing just go? You sent it off somewhere."

Gror opened his arms wide. "I sent for refreshments."

"But it...Who to?"

"Somewhere, a member of staff is waking up or falling asleep. They will bring us food and drink. Then they will return to their other duties."

"And they won't realize quite why. And you've been doing this for how many years?"

For the first time, Gror frowned. "I spent several years traveling. But certainly, since I returned! My friends' ministry makes my life here very comfortable."

"How did you meet my father?"

"I sought him out. Having heard rumors of an alien visiting our library, I was concerned. I felt his presence was a matter best left for Tuanomena to decide. I could not trust the temple authorities of the time to do the right thing."

"Did he decide?"

Gror shifted his weight, uncomfortable with the question. "In part. Tuanomena blessed your father. Several times. Whereas I—Tuanomena's humble servant—was given no such equivalent blessing whereby I might have asked my question."

Jim smiled inwardly but said, "You mean Tuanomena appeared and spoke to my father several times."

"Yes."

"But you weren't included to hear what was said."

"I have said so."

That's not what you said at first. So, you don't know about the T-switch; you're fishing for clues. That's what this meeting is about. Jim lied, "My meeting with Tuanomena was unexpected, and I'm not sure I could articulate what happened clearly."

This only received a laugh in reply.

A knock sounded at the door.

"Come in! Come in!" Gror shouted in welcome.

A kitchen staffer brought in two small trays and placed one at Jim's feet, the other at Gror's.

Jim tried to catch the staff member's eye, but he bowed to Gror, turned away from Jim, and left without another word.

"I don't understand how you can use people like this! So, I have to ask again, Gror," Jim said, "how can you think your use of him is in any way ethical? He's obeying your instructions without real choice."

"No! He is quite happy to fulfill his duty. I am a person of rank. This is what he does. In serving my person, he serves Tuanomena."

"But Jart Bregg is not happy. Her mind is sharp, but she's also old and frail. Your 'instructions' to her have caused distress and confusion."

Gror swung both hands to his right, the older Meoenan equivalent of nodding in agreement. "Yes, she is old. That is perhaps the best explanation of her troubles."

"I don't understand why you can't see how wrong that is—using her that way!"

Gror chuckled. "So! Let the student teach the master. You tell me."

"It's intrusive! Simple bodily integrity for each individual is enshrined as a right on every advanced planet. You violate that with your...creatures. Let's start right there!"

"Well, an interesting fallacy. By conflating two distinct arguments, you launch yourself into a river of confusion."

"What arguments?"

"Let us begin with the easiest to deal with. 'Enshrined' you say, and 'on every advanced planet' you say. This is not so. Many planets have written such rules and purport to uphold them in law. But do they do so? I think not. Such documents are clothing and, as such, may be cast off at any time."

"That's disturbingly cynical."

"And for the other, the more interesting argument—'each individual.' Ah, yes, the bane of my earlier life when I sat before class after class of wide-eyed fools, trying to teach them both logic and truth at the same time. No, James Able, I will not let you sweep past that assumption unchallenged. Why should we think all individuals to be of equal rank, of equal status, of equal worth? Hmm? Tell me!"

"Why?" Jim choked slightly. "It's the fundamental principle of civilization. All are equal before the law, and the law is applied equally to all who come before it."

Gror chuckled but didn't reply.

Jim continued, "And in situations where people aren't treated as equals, who decides how the inequality works? Who's in control? The rich? The better armed? People who've proven to be unethical in other matters? No, no, no. Before most races explore space, they have—each one of them—sorted this out."

"Your questions are simply answered, James Able. Those who are *better* decide."

"'Better' in what way? And who defines that?"

At this, Gror laughed a long time. "Do you think, human, you are superior to a Meoenan?"

Jim frowned. "I think we are equals. We may be *better at* certain activities, but our worth as people is not affected by that."

Jim could see Gror breathe in deeply; some of the folds of fat rolled a little.

"But you do, do you not, consider the people of this world less important than those of your own? Tell me this, human! Here is a human child hanging by its fingers at the edge of a canyon. There, three arms' lengths away is a Meoenan child in the same distress. You can save only one. Choose! Choose now before they both fall!"

"I would gladly risk my own life in trying to save them both."

"No, look deeper! In your rush to help, your instincts will bring you to the human child first. You say you have no preference, but that is merely like legal documents and clothes—fluttering away at the first gust of a testing wind!"

"You don't know me very well, do you?" Jim smiled. "If I have such a parochial instinct, that's...sad. It's a judgment against me. It says nothing about the equal worth of those kids. It also says nothing of the one who put them in such danger."

"Each of us," Gror continued, without a smile, "will choose our own. We admit our own are to be preferred. We admit our own are worthier. Is Meoenan knowledge of philosophy not better than human cleverness with mere nuts and bolts?"

"That's a total misunderstanding. Being equal doesn't mean being the same, doing the same things, or even having the same skills! It doesn't even mean we don't have our own emotions, preferences, or prejudices. It's the claiming to be better than me just because you were born on this planet rather than mine; that's what is ridiculous!"

"I am! Meoena *are* superior. That is why we use a multitude of humans to do our work for us. That is why your father was here, learning from us. He understood, finally, as he aged, how much better we are than humans."

Jim was momentarily lost for words. "You taught this shit? And your bosses let you?"

"There are many good people on this world, James Able, who understand these matters more clearly than you ever will."

Jim sat for a moment, aware of the incense, the food going cold on his tray, the sweat on Gror's forehead. Jim became aware of his own stomach, the slight knots, the feeling that was growing in him that the floor was less solid than it had been before. Jim sighed. *These ideas are depressingly familiar. What have I gotten myself into here?* "You bring to mind another question, Gror."

Gror's smile returned.

Jim licked his lips. "Do you know Lert Carn?"

Gror swept his hands right. "I do."

"You know what happened to him. Why he's now in jail on the station."

"I do. I do. Wonderful political theater, his arrest. What clearer image could our people be shown? Aliens causing explosions on our streets, kidnapping one of our leaders. Again, the inferiority of humans being shown so clearly. In your illusory victory, you proclaim your own defeat."

"He kidnapped me and my mother. He killed a human, Alice Brown. And he kept her prosthetic eye as a toy."

Gror laughed.

"He's also behind sending a Meoenan gang called the Parfot after me, isn't he? You could choose better friends."

Gror only laughed again.

Jim sighed. *He's not going to give anything away.* "Why did you ask to see me? Was it just to tell me I'm inferior?"

"No, that is irrelevant. I wanted to meet you. To see why Tuanomena would choose to show his face to you. To you, to your father, to the woman. Why should Tuanomena show such a lapse in judgment?"

Thank you! Now I get it; you're jealous!

Gror laughed and laughed. "What did Tuanomena see in you that I do not? Why did he extend to you what has only ever been extended to us? Who are you?"

Jim heard an echo of the fear voiced by Schpurr, Marhan's dodgy business contact, when asking the same question.

"I'm not sure I can say," Jim said calmly.

Gror sat and looked at Jim.

"I've been reading your book," Jim said, breaking the silence.

"*The Lirthon?*"

Jim nodded, and Gror burst again into almost maniacal laughter.

"What's so funny?"

"I walk here, in these chambers, without restraint. I know my future, and it brings me abundant peace."

"Your future? What about it?"

"*The Lirthon!* My great opus. My defining legacy."

Jim chewed his lip, guessing what was coming.

Gror smiled and, without laughing, continued, "I have yet to write it."

Jim chuckled. "Yeah, time travel is strange, isn't it?"

"And so, I know no danger will befall me here, in this time. I know I will return eventually. And I look forward to returning to my previous life. I will obviously be in good enough health to allow the writing of a long and complex work. I am secure. I am happy. I walk without restraint."

Jim stared at the Meoenan. "That's a lot of confidence for one individual to be given."

"You see how freeing it is! I am far freer in this time—knowing the book will be written—than I could be anywhere else, any time else. This is the great blessing from Tuanomena."

"For you, yes, I see that. But you are in a position to do a lot of damage to this time and for years and years to come. Your lack of restraint can harm the people around you—Jart Bregg, for one."

"I come from a time when space travel was impossible other than with generational ships. I arrived here to see efficient travel and instant communication. I see, in Sonloi's sky, an object built by aliens. I see Tuanomena unstudied, neglected, a curiosity. The conclusion is obvious."

"You want to take your people back. Back to the good old days."

"I want all aliens to go back to their own worlds! Live your lives in peace, but do not trouble your betters."

Jim shook his head. "That is a decision neither you nor I can make."

"We will see." Again, Gror did not laugh. "I live here without restraint. I may do what no one else will dare."

Jim stared at the fat alien again. Gror's self-revelation kept Jim alert and restored the confidence he had felt slipping.

"What no one else will dare." No matter who gets hurt. Jart. Alice. Who else? I see what you are. Thanks. It's obvious what I have to do.

A new sensation shivered through Jim's body: a solidity, a connection with the temple's stone walls around him and the miles of soil and rock below him. He felt as cold as the skin of Sonloi-AC.

You are the first person I could really feel comfortable killing. But no, it's way too early for a decision like that. "One more question, Gror. That business Lert Carn set up. When they kidnapped my mother, was that all your idea?"

Gror's body jiggled with mirth. "In its details, perhaps not. In its overall strategy, yes, of course. I want to know what Tuanomena gave your father. I want to know why you don't have it. I want to know where the woman went. And you, James Able, will tell me everything."

Jim shook his head quickly. "That's not going to happen."

"Yes, you will tell me. You may have to tell one of my friends first, but I will find out. You will sleep, and it will come to you. It will see your memories and then repeat them to me. We will each share what you know. Remember, I have nothing whatsoever to fear and everything to win. You cannot say the same."

Jim's jaw tightened. He stood and left the smoke-filled room.

CHAPTER 36

THE CHATSE

Yarl and his father sat on a couch in the Chatse's office, a large and pleasant suite on the temple's second floor. The sound of traffic in the streets happily reminded Jim of ordinary life outside.

"Why haven't you sent Gror Gute back to his own time?" Jim asked.

Baha nodded carefully. "It is a blessing from Tuanomena that he should be here. Who am I to try and undo what Tuanomena has brought about?"

Yarl added, "How would we do it?"

Baha swung his hands in agreement.

"What about the black...things? Those you could address."

Baha chuckled. "Only you have seen them. You tell us they come out at night and are too quick to catch. Again, what can we do?"

"Have people on the lookout. Investigate. Set traps."

"It is not the place of the temple staff to do these things."

"They are a danger to you and everyone in your care. This guy could be manipulating you in ways you can't imagine!"

Again, Baha nodded, but Jim could tell he did not agree.

Jim scowled and looked around the room. "I'm sorry. I'm expecting too much of you."

Baha said quietly, "Perhaps if you can catch one for us, then I might be in a position to act."

Jim chuckled mirthlessly. "Sure. I'll see what I can do." *There's an easier answer, but Betih wouldn't approve.*

"Jart?"

"James?"

"I'm wondering if we can do something for each other."

"What sort of thing? Do you need more reading?"

"No...nothing like that. I...need you to make a dream come true."

"Oh, that sounds mysterious! Tell me more."

Jim squared himself to her across the table. Her eyes stayed steady on his face.

"I had a dream last night. There was a creature, a small black furry creature, so big." Jim indicated with his hands. "It was hungry. And I was showing it the food laid out in the breakfast room. I held it in the crook of my arm—like this."

Jart said nothing.

"If you're willing...tonight, can you meditate on this image, on my dream? Can you do that? Imagine yourself holding it, as I did, taking the creature for breakfast, caring for it. Show it all the food. Tell it how the food is unlimited." Jim swallowed. "Tell it, it can be 'unrestrained.'"

"I can try that, certainly. How would this make your dream manifest?"

Jim sighed and avoided her eyes. "I'm not sure it is just a dream, and I fear we may be in some danger. You see, such a creature exists. I think it will come to you. I think it has before. But I don't know exactly what it will do."

Jart sat up straight. "Well! I have never heard of such a thing. I know my dreams have been vivid of late. What manner of thing is this creature? Do you think my meditation will summon it? I would be curious to see if it did. You think something will come of it?"

Jim nodded. "Sure. I saw one in my room. And...I don't like the idea of us being visited in our sleep. I think by telling this thing we can feed it, getting it to trust us, we can influence it. I think you have a strong mind, more disciplined than mine. But, at the same time, I don't want you putting yourself in any danger."

"How extraordinary!"

They read silently for many minutes before she asked, "The creature is somehow tuned to dreams? Is that how my meditations possibly call to it? This thing will actually be in my room, you think?"

"I can't say for sure. But, yes, I think so. And I'm sorry to ask you. But I have no one else."

She reached across the books and put her warm blue hand over his. "I'm glad to! And I see no harm in trying. Where could such a creature have come from?"

Jim smiled and shrugged.

Jim sat with his back against the wall all night. He stood often. He performed more push-ups than he had in years. He raided the late-night buffet. During the slowly passing hours, he ached to see the light return to the shaft above. His guilt about drawing Jart further into his business burned him colder and colder in the darkness.

I should have told her the whole story.

But if she can influence it, she can bring it to breakfast, where people can see it...

If I sleep before then, Gror wins. I doubt I could wrestle control of one of those things. I hope Jart can.

But am I treating her no better than he does?

But if anyone can win it over...she is so good natured! Is her mind strong enough? I hope so.

What have I done?

He fingered the small net that had appeared in his room, certain he would be too slow if he had to use it.

. . .

As the first fragrance of food wafted into his room, he threw on the robe and ran to the breakfast room.

Few monks had arrived. Instead of grabbing his food and retreating, Jim filled a plate and sat off to one side at a table. He ate slowly, forced his eyelids to keep open, and waited.

The Meoena should learn to like coffee. That's what I really need.

The room was full of monks, visitors, and conversation when she arrived. All fell silent at the sight of her.

Jim's heart broke at the wounded expression on Jart's face. She was naked above the waist. Her arms were scrawny and twisted. Worst of all for Jim, she looked as if she had been doing battle the whole night.

As the silent room watched, a black ball of fur climbed over her shoulder and settled in the crook of her arm.

Jim left her in the care of temple officials then raced through clouds of anger back to his room.

At least she's still alive. What did I do to her? What did that laughing monster do to her?

He threw open the door and saw two streaks of black dive for cover. He drew the hood tight against his head, grabbed his flight bag, and rushed back out.

Yarl walked calmly toward him, but Jim, fishing in his bag with one hand, announced, "Busy, Yarl! Talk to you later."

"But Jim—" Yarl began. He leaned back against the wall as Jim pushed past him.

At Gror Gute's door, Jim did not stop to knock. The wave of smoke billowed out and rolled back with him into the room.

Gror's eyes widened. He stood slowly and gracefully. "My human friend!" He laughed, and his body shook. He stretched stiffness from his arms in a circular motion.

Jim clicked The Striker open to its full extent. The cold surface of the device again recalled the outer surface of the station, high above.

A quizzical look crossed Gror's round, smiling face.

Jim stabbed The Striker onto the Meoenan's bare chest. They locked eyes, and both felt a slight jolt. Black shadows leaped from Gror's back, up the wall hangings and into the ceiling.

Jim stepped back and, deep under the layers of fat, a short-lived glow lightened Gror's blue skin.

In Jim's mind, the glow echoed the craft of the Raeff's fleet exploding as he flew over them, his ship firing on automatic, doing his bidding without effort on his part.

The Striker is just a weapon, like any other.

Gror coughed, and as his limbs failed him, he whispered, "May Tuanomena curse you, human!"

Jim's grim smile did not change as he watched Gror crumple to the floor and roll onto his back.

He turned quickly, slipped The Striker back into his bag, and closed the door. Incense had followed him into the corridor. In the silence, he could hear the blood singing in his ears.

Yarl and three others found Jim leaning against the wall at the end of Gror's corridor.

"Jim? Are you okay?" Yarl asked, leaning into Jim's face.

"Gror! He's dead."

Yarl gestured to his companions, who moved quickly into the room.

"Had he asked to see you again?"

"Jart Bregg...Gror obviously sent one of those things to her last night."

"Agreed. We now know what to look for. Though Jart has yet to explain how it came to be docile in her arms!"

"I saw..." Jim stood straight and swallowed. "I saw several of them fleeing into the shaft in his room. You'll need to investigate what happened. You don't want rumors spreading."

The Meoenan calmly said, "That would expose the fact of his

presence. I doubt my father will permit news of either his life or death here to reach beyond those who already know."

One of the other monks looked out of Gror's room and caught Yarl's eye. They exchanged several signals Jim didn't follow.

Jim said. "I'll help in any way I can, of course, but I think it would be better if I go back to my ship—right now."

Yarl glared at him, as he had once before, but did not immediately speak. He placed his hand on Jim's shoulder and led him away. "We received word earlier that it is safe for you to return to Sonloi-AC. Do you wish to see anyone while I arrange transport to your flier? Jart Bregg? My father?"

"No. Get me out of here." He choked a little and added, "I'm not safe."

Yarl frowned but did not reply.

Back on the ship, Jim came up the ramp from the flier's storage area below the flight room.

"Jim!" called Tella.

"The monkey is back!" said Marhan.

Betih looked at his face.

"I'm going to lie down for a while," Jim said, "Maybe a year or two." He said nothing else as he walked up the ramp to his module.

Betih said quietly and to herself, "Ah."

Tella called after him, "Jim, something is happening. There is...possibly...a galaxy-wide problem developing."

Jim said without emotion, "Good, there's a galaxy full of people to deal with it."

CHAPTER 37

UNDERSTANDING

Jim woke up in his module to find Betih sitting on his chair and the clothes he had piled there in a heap on the floor.

"You can guess what happened?" he asked.

"I have seen it before. Don't ask me if it gets easier; you won't like the answer."

Jim chuckled to himself. "Great!"

"Were you seen on your way to your target?"

"Yes."

"Fool! A beginner's mistake. Learn from it! Did you speak to the target?"

"No. There was nothing else to say."

"Good! Perhaps now you understand something. Were you seen leaving?"

"No. Yes, I stayed nearby until someone came."

"Fool! But I understand how hard that is. Rehearse your exit in your mind long before. Learn it! Be so familiar with it that you do not need to think. Thinking may not be possible...then. Tell me of the target. Why the hurry?"

"A Meoenan. A temple official. He's been using...creatures to control people. He was behind Lert Carn's kidnapping of my mother. Did Marhan tell you about that?"

Betih said, "Ha!" louder than Jim thought polite.

"He was also...from the past."

"Really?" Betih did not sound impressed.

"And," Jim sighed, "I probably just created a major temporal anomaly."

Betih rolled her eyes. "I know nothing of such things."

"He's the author of a famous book. There's a copy of it, there, in my bag. Only he told me he hadn't written it yet. Now he won't."

Betih paused, then said encouragingly, "Embrace that finality, assassin. Now you understand what it truly feels like."

Jim sat up on his bed. "Actually, I'm pretty sure I don't like how it feels."

"Good! I have said your task is to make sure it happens rarely. Make sure you only accept targets who prove themselves deserving of your attention. Now, perhaps, my teaching makes more sense to you? Yes?"

Jim nodded. "I'm sorry. Yes. What you've said makes a lot more sense."

She rolled her long tongue from her front teeth to the back of her mouth. "Tell me. How did you decide he should not receive a conventional arrest and judgment?"

"He told me he knew he would return to write his book, as I said, in the past. His knowing that left him 'unrestrained.' That was his word. He knew nothing would stop him...had stopped him...could stop him...that he was in no danger from human or Meoena, from disease, injury, or death. He'd already proven himself unrestrained by morals."

"And what did you do to verify this? What investigation did you do?"

Jim snorted. "I've been living it. I told you. He gave instructions to Lert Carn, who went on to kidnap my mother and me and kill Alice Brown. He directly...used a friend of my father's while I was there and probably many others in the temple."

Betih nodded. "So, you will hear no complaint from me.

However, if I know you well enough, I fear you will hear much from yourself as the years go by. You allowed the facts to become mixed with your feelings. It clouded your judgment. I don't say your judgment was wrong; it does not seem to be from what you say. However, you must make the next mission less personal. Take longer. Learn more. Examine more. Do you hear me?"

"I hear you. And yes, I fully expect I'll be beating myself up about it forever."

She stood, but Jim stopped her. "Tella was here earlier. It suggests I shouldn't trust you. It heard you talking to the gang."

She turned her face to the door. "Tella is good. He is quick! I thought I had come to you first."

"Don't call it 'he.'"

She waved a paw. "Yes, yes! It, him, her, I care not! What it heard was misleading." She lowered her head and looked at Jim with one eye. "I was convincing those children of something I needed them to think."

"But there's still a chance you could make me your final target, isn't there?"

She silently assessed him as he looked up, his hair a mess and his shoulders hunched. "Marhan talks of the spirit using you. What do I know? What would the evidence for that look like? How different would it look from my observation that you are a living, walking storm piling up victims in your wake?"

"If I'm dangerous, so is he. So are you! How large is *your* pile?"

Betih laughed and licked her lips. "We will talk more. In the meantime, I promise not to kill you yet."

Jim laughed and laid back. "So comforting! Hey!" He contorted his fingers into the most obscene gesture he had learned on Tanna Gul.

Betih straightened and her eyes widened. She opened the door and left saying, "Really!"

PART FOUR

THE GREAT SILENCE

CHAPTER 38

THE GREAT SILENCE

Jim returned to the flight room to find everyone sitting silently.

"What's happened?"

Marhan snorted. "Bad news."

"For who?"

"All of us. All the worlds."

Jim frowned. "That would take some doing."

Tella began, "Just before you returned, we saw reports of difficulties with long-range communications."

"Network problems?"

"Total network failure."

"That's impossible."

"Agreed."

Marhan said, "Local radio transmission still works to Sonloi and nearby stations. Nothing interplanetary can get through."

Jim sat in the command seat. "What happens when you try?"

Tella replied, "Buffer full. Over and over again. The communications devices remain full, and nothing is resolved."

Jim frowned. "Is anyone suggesting a cause?"

"No. But there is much local speculation."

A knock came from the airlock.

"Who's that?" Jim asked.

Betih answered, "The station administrator. She warned us she might come. Perhaps she has news."

Jim walked down the corridor and let Jayde in.

"Jim."

"Jayde."

"I heard you had a difficult time at the temple."

"I survived. What's all this about comms being down?"

She indicated the flight room and was silent until they joined the others.

All eyes were on her as she stood between the ramps to the upper level.

"A Sonloi ship went out to our nearest communication relay. The device is working fine. It's just not going anywhere. The nodes aren't switching along the network. That's why no communications traffic is moving. The whole network is stationary."

Tella commented, "I have never heard of such a thing."

"Worse is still to come," Jayde said. "While they were out there, they made a dash for clear space. Their D-switch didn't work either."

A deep silence fell on them all.

"Shit," Jim said, almost in a whisper.

Marhan looked sideways at Betih. "We may be stuck here with a planet full of blue monkeys."

"Sounds like it," she agreed. To Jayde she said, "Has anyone any idea of how this could happen?"

Jayde shook her head. "That's partly why I'm here. Jim? This ship is probably the most advanced one currently in the system. Are you willing to experiment and see if you are affected too?"

"What makes you say that?"

"Isn't this a custom PR ship? You know no one else around here has anything similar."

Jim nodded quickly. "Of course. Raeda? Undock and take us to the nearest switch point."

The ship replied, "Airlock closed and sealed. Course set for Pec clear space."

"How long till we can use the D-switch?" Jim asked.

The ship replied, "Five hours, Sonloi time, at full power."

"Full power it is. Proceed."

"Beginning route to Pec clear space."

CHAPTER 39

ICE CREAM

D'Ghil wrote out the phrase in fifteen languages. She even worked out a way of representing it in her mother's outmoded pictographic script, which made her smile a little.

"I just can't catch a break!"

In Standard, the phrase was a simple metaphor—"All I grasp is air."

She pinned the page on the corkboard above her refrigerator. "Well, that's something accomplished today!"

A light knock at the door to her room filled her with dread.

"Who is it?"

"It's me, Danny!"

D'Ghil sighed with relief and grabbed the doorknob.

Danny smiled as she tripped lightly into the room. "Hi, neighbor! You sounded odd just then. Is everything okay?"

Danny's manner, her frizzy hair, her light-brown skin, and her colorful clothes were everything D'Ghil was not.

D'Ghil pointed at the paper on the board and slumped into the creaking chair beside her bed.

Danny read, looked at D'Ghil, and smiled again. "That's what I was afraid of. And why I brought this." She moved a white tub from behind her back. "Ta-da!"

"What's that?"

"Ice cream. Remember, I told you about it last week? I found some!"

"I don't know..."

"Trust me. This stuff is made for times like this. Where's your spoons?"

D'Ghil frowned and shrugged.

"Oh, hell, never mind!"

She pulled the top off the tub and sunk a finger into the ice cream. She held the tub out to D'Ghil and stood, finger in mouth, until her friend did the same.

D'Ghil sighed, then laughed. She cautiously put one scaly, gray digit into the cold substance.

She passed the ice cream under her small nose. *Sweet. Very sweet!* The coldness against her purple lips sent a shiver down her limbs. *Tastes good!*

Through a full mouth, Danny asked, "Well? What do you think?"

D'Ghil nodded. "Good! But cold! So cold!"

"I know! Right? Best bit? We don't have to stop until we've eaten it all and our stomachs ache. Ain't no one going to stop us. To hell with 'em all!"

Danny sat laughing on the edge of D'Ghil's bed.

"Is this a human tradition?" D'Ghil asked.

"One of mine anyway."

"That's nice."

Danny watched her strange friend as they scooped and ate their way into the ice cream. Only when they'd had enough did she ask, "So what's happened? Feel like talking?"

D'Ghil shook the small dome of her head. Her rounded body swayed a little under her loose clothes. "You don't want to know."

"I don't want to pry, but sure, I want to know. We have ice cream; therefore, I refuse to believe life is *that* bad."

"That big assignment fell through. Someone else got it."

"Oh, I'm sorry."

"My estimated turnaround time wasn't fast enough."

Danny frowned. "What? Who says the stuff you do needs speed? I thought it was all inspections and delays and filing paperwork."

D'Ghil nodded. "Mainly."

"And?"

"I've got a lot of expenses. Told you that before. A lot of over-heads. The jobs I have lined up aren't enough. I can't save anything. It's like a treadmill. And this place is more than I can afford, you know."

"I know. Not to say we couldn't all do with moving up to some-thing better. But we're on our way! It's a start. And hey! You got great neighbors."

D'Ghil smiled. "Yeah, you're okay, I guess. But then I got this yesterday."

She showed Danny a message.

"Really? What is this? Some disgruntled customer?"

"No clue. Some random dude who doesn't like me."

"I'm so sorry," Danny said, "Can you go to the police?"—D'Ghil grabbed the mostly empty tub from her and slurped another digit full—"No, I guess not."

D'Ghil answered, "People like us don't get that option. I just have to stay out of sight and hope it blows over."

"But do they know what you look like? Do they know you live here?"

D'Ghil shrugged. "Don't know. That's all I got."

"That sucks!"

"Tell me about it."

"Freega, upstairs. He's got a blaster. Do you want me to ask him if you can borrow it?"

D'Ghil laughed. "No, Danny! Thanks, but no. I can take care of myself."

"Okay..." Danny looked around the small room. "Listen, I am going to tell the others. We can make sure no one we don't know comes up. Guests only allowed when they're escorted from now on. We don't want this creep wandering in off the street."

"You don't have to."

Danny nodded vigorously. "Sure we do! I'd hope you'd do the same for me."

D'Ghil stretched several gray fingers around Danny's brown hand. "Thanks."

CHAPTER 40

LISTENING TO THE GREAT SILENCE

Jim sat in the command seat, waiting for the ship to speak.

"Zero movement."

He had commanded the ship to make one jump as far as the sensors could detect in empty space.

"Raeda, try again."

"Zero movement."

He turned to Tella and said, "Suggestions?"

The Neraffan shook its head. "Return to Sonloi-AC."

Marhan added, "It may be home to us for some time."

Jim looked at Marhan and Betih. Both looked shrunken and defeated. *I wish I could say something that would help.*

"Jayde?" Jim asked, "Are you okay with us staying with you for however long this takes to resolve?"

She smiled grimly. "No. I was, if all this hadn't interrupted me, going to tell you all to leave sooner rather than later. You, or your presence at least, brought criminals onto my station. The actions of your crew"—she glanced at Betih—"resulted in weapons fire that endangered guests. So, no, Jim, I am not okay with you staying. You'll have to find somewhere else to dock. And, going forward, strict protocols will apply to your visits."

Jim nodded. "I was afraid of that. You're right. You're right..."

Betih asked him, "Will your friends at the temple provide you with accommodation if it is required for the long term?"

Jim shook his head. "I doubt it. But it's way too soon to be thinking like that. Someone will come up with an explanation for all this. I'm sure the PR are all over it."

"I am not," Marhan said with a shake of his head. "This is too big a matter for just one ship maker. The whole galaxy has shut down."

"We don't know that. This could be localized. We may have to wait for ships to come in from somewhere things are still working." *I hope that sounded convincing enough,* Jim thought.

"Well, whatever the future holds," Jayde said, "Please take me back to the station. You can visit with your mother while you work out where else to dock or land."

They gathered in Alfie's apartment. Marhan squatted next to Betih sitting in a tall wing chair. Tella stood off to one side, its white robe washing its features into a ghostly blankness.

"How lovely to see you all again!" Alfie said. To Betih, she added, "It's a pleasure to meet you, Betih. Any relative of Marhan's is welcome."

Betih eyed her suspiciously. "Thank you. It isn't usual for Marhan to win such affection."

Alfie smiled back, undaunted. "The first time he visited, he showed rare insight into the artistic process. I appreciated that."

Betih snorted lightly.

"So," Jim interrupted, "there's been no progress communicating with anyone outside the system."

"I may not be able to travel to TMV as I hoped," Tella stated.

"Nor I to Tanna Gul," Betih added.

Marhan growled—to Alfie's discomfort—and said, "You were not going there."

Betih fixed him with a stare. "I am old. I must go into the wilderness. You cannot keep me a prisoner."

Marhan barked loudly. "Prisoner? How dare you?"

Jim held up his hands, "Hey! Keep it down you two. I know we're all on edge, but this is no time to be fighting."

Betih drew her pink bathrobe tighter around her thin limbs.

"Forgive me," Marhan muttered without sincerity.

Someone knocked at the door.

Jim frowned. "Are we expecting anyone else, Mother?"

Alfie shook her head and went to open the door.

Yarl and his father came slowly into the apartment, their eyes scanning each face.

"Yarl? Baha?" Jim asked, "What are you doing on AC?"

Yarl replied quickly, "Visiting you. Seeing how you are after the horrible experience of finding Gror Gute's body. Are you okay?"

Baha added, "Processing such unpleasantness can be difficult sometimes."

Jim frowned. *What's this? What are they up to?* "I'm fine. Thanks. Is there any word on what happened?"

Both swung their hands to indicate "No."

Good.

"Can I get you anything?" Alfie offered, indicating the teapot and small cakes.

Yarl smiled and replied, "Thank you, but no."

"Please take a seat."

The two Meoenan monks sat next to each other on the sofa. Both looked uncomfortable.

Jim swallowed and wondered whether he should speak what was on his mind. *The one thing I don't want to talk about is how Gute died.* "Baha, I learned something that may be a little troubling about Gute."

"Please."

"I can't say in front of everyone else unless you are okay with me doing so. I should say that everyone here has heard about the T-switch."

"Ah"—The monk looked from face to face—"Then, perhaps, they may also know that this Gror Gute had traveled in time to be with us."

"From the future?" Tella asked.

"The past," answered Yarl.

Jim said, "He is the author of a major work of Meoenan theology, *The Lirthon*."

Baha smiled. "A difficult and much-studied work."

"Gute told me—the last time I spoke to him—that he hadn't written it. Yet." Jim watched frowns cross the Meoenan brows. "So his death may be...a complication of Tuanomenan proportions."

Both Yarl and his father glanced at each other, but neither spoke.

"Does the book still exist?" asked Tella.

A look of true alarm crossed Baha's face. "I hope it does. We remember it. Do you have a copy, Jim?"

"Sure. Jart Bregg gave me a copy. I'll check it's still in my ship."

Yarl said, "Please check. We will check in the library when we return."

Jim could see Yarl was not comfortable. "Is there something else bothering you, Yarl?"

Yarl glanced at Baha again. The elder monk turned his hands, palm upmost, but said nothing.

Yarl straightened up and began, "The Walk has gone dark."

"What do you mean?" Jim asked.

"I mean, we can see up through the central core of the temple. We can see no light or movement on the highest level. We also cannot access The Walk in our usual ways."

Baha added quietly, "It is as if Tuanomena has left us."

"Why can't you get up to it?" Jim asked.

Yarl sighed. "We find the passages that took us there are not open. The staircases we used do not lead where they once did."

"What nonsense is this?" Marhan snapped.

Yarl glared at the canid and replied, "All things related to The Walk are complex. What I say is true."

Jim raised a hand to warn Marhan to be quiet. "Do you think this is related to Gror's death?"

Baha answered, "How can we know? Such gifts and blessings as the Walk are at the behest of Tuanomena. But this coincidence troubles us."

"I'm sure. Has this ever happened before?"

"No," Yarl said. "We have never heard of such a thing. We are...lost."

"Much as we are with the D-switches not working," Jim added.

"Is it possible this is your daughter's work, Jim?" Tella asked.

Jim chuckled. "Who knows? It could be. When I talked with her last, she seemed to resent the amount of time she'd spent in the temple. Maybe she's found a way to sabotage The Walk."

Baha spoke into the silence. "We are like novices, not sure yet what is true. We move in a river of uncertainty, feeling the pull of ideas—both true and false—unable to discern which is which."

Marhan snorted.

Jim stood up. "Let's go check on my copy of *The Lirthon*. I'd like to see what facts we have."

On board his ship, Jim brought his flight bag down from his module. He pulled out and opened his copy of *The Lirthon*. "It exists."

Baha smiled, relieved. "Good news. Does this mean Gror lied to you? He must have written it already, though he claimed not to have done."

Jim shrugged. "This exists. So, *someone* wrote it. What evidence do you have that Gror Gute was the actual author?"

Yarl frowned. "This is a matter we can take up with the librarians."

Baha said to Jim, "Your help is appreciated. I already know from the administrator that the problems on board the station have been dealt with. It is most unfortunate that any Meoenan could place a member of the Family Able in danger. Deeply regrettable. Now, if the matters of transportation and communications do not resolve themselves soon, can we find you a safe place to stay?"

Jim nodded. "Thanks. I hope it won't come to that. Between Jayde and my friends here, I think the immediate danger has passed.

Tella gathered good intelligence on where the threat came from. I should be fine."

Before the monks had completed their shuttle flight back to Sonloi, several consoles on Jim's ship sounded with alerts and warnings.

"What is that?" Marhan asked.

Tella moved immediately to sit at one of the consoles. "Messages. Routine alerts."

Jim tapped a few commands at another display. "Messages from the Praestans Rapax. General inquiries about 'service disruption.' The communications net is back up!"

Marhan and Betih both barked in celebration.

Jim sat in the command seat and said, "Who's for another D-switch test?"

Just outside the gravity well of Pec Sonloi, the ship attempted a short jump.

It intoned, "Successful jump. Navigation is functioning within normal parameters."

When they returned to Sonloi-AC, Jayde invited them to the station-wide party to celebrate a return to normal life.

The ship announced, "Incoming message from Davey Able."

"Put it up," Jim called.

Davey's face appeared on the main monitor. "Hi, Uncle Jim!"

"Davey. Glad to see you. Glad to be able to communicate."

"Yeah, right! 'The Great Silence' they're calling it. Everyone is freaked."

"I'm sure. Anyone any good ideas what's been happening?"

Davey looked solemn and shook his head. "That's what's really odd. There's like no one in authority saying much at all."

Marhan offered, "Because they have no ideas and are afraid of their ignorance."

Davey shrugged.

Jim said, "No harm done on your end of things?"

"No," Davey replied. "Apart from Dad having endless meetings. He told me to call you and see what you were up to."

"Ha! Tell him it wasn't me. Okay, Davey, thanks for checking in."

"Sure thing."

"Oh, Davey? Just put together the facts of what happened for me. See if Clo can find someone who knows what they are talking about. There must be someone with some ideas."

Davey nodded and ended the call.

Betih stood in front of Jim and announced, "Lessons resume immediately. Enough delay."

Unable to think of a suitable reply, Jim shrugged and followed her down to the galley.

CHAPTER 41

KATRIGG, THE PLAN

Betih drew with a marker pen across the galley tabletop. She checked briefly that she could erase it easily.

"Now, monkey! Here, this circle is your target. Draw your mission."

Jim sighed loudly. "How many times do we go through this? I know what I did wrong last time."

Betih barked, "Draw!"

Jim said nothing but drew a wavy cloud on the edge of Betih's circle. As he drew a similar cloud opposite, he said, "Cloud. On the way in. Preplanned exit, still with The Cloud. Don't talk to anyone."

"No. Before."

Jim moved further down the table and drew a cartoon book. "Research."

"Where?"

Jim frowned. "That's Rob's job."

Betih sat in what Jim understood to be hostile silence.

"No," he continued, "really. He's brilliant at getting the facts about people!"

"Mere data gathering," the canid countered.

"Research."

"You will meet the target. In what circumstances?" Betih grabbed the marker and drew a neat coffee bowl halfway between Jim's cartoon book and the circle with the clouds.

Jim scoffed. "Sure, I'll sit down with Jack Katrigg—who is expecting me and preparing to kill me—for coffee and donuts. I'll just sit down opposite him and let him shoot me under the table."

"You will meet the target. How?"

"Look, that might work if you don't know them. If they haven't been warned you're coming. In theory that's fine! This isn't going to be like that."

"You will do it. You will always do it. You will find a way."

"No! You're crazy."

Betih drew three stick figures, more dog than monkey, under the coffee bowl. "Consider this. This is you. This is the target. Who is this?"

"The waiter?"

She growled back. "This is the one who tried to kill you."

"Who? You're inventing complications."

"Perhaps she is your tutor, overwhelmed with irritation at you. She decided to give you what you deserve and chose Ch'Garratt as the place to do it. I would sympathize with her! I would help her, perhaps!"

"Crazy! There wasn't anyone else. It was Katrigg. He got into his fancy ship, took off, and fired!"

"I ask again, how will you be sure? How will you hear Katrigg's account of that day?"

"I don't want to hear it!"

Betih smiled. "Now you say it aloud."

"What?"

"You do not *want* to do it. You make excuses not to do something difficult. But the *reason* is because you don't *want* to!"

Jim frowned. "No! What do you mean? Why should I listen to him?"

Betih tapped the third stick figure on the table and said, "To find the identity of this person."

"This fictional person."

"If Katrigg is guilty, find out! If Katrigg is not guilty—and this person is—then you have correctly identified your target and saved the life of an innocent person."

Jim stared at her and made no reply.

Betih added quietly, "I don't care what you want to do or don't want to do. You will take all due care to kill only the guilty. You will meet Katrigg. You will establish his guilt or innocence. Then, you will act accordingly. This isn't a game, monkey. This isn't a matter of what *you* want or don't want."

Jim shifted uncomfortably in his seat. "If he's guilty, he'll lie. He'll cast doubt on what I know. Send me off chasing fictional people. I'll put myself at a complete disadvantage."

"I already said it is difficult. But you are not alone."

Jim pointed to the circle. "Yes, I am."

Betih pointed to the coffee bowl. "No, you're not."

Jim looked off into the distance. "Oh...Someone else could meet Katrigg. Someone he doesn't know. They could find stuff out."

"And, when appropriate, arrange a meeting with you, avoiding the trap Mrs. Katrigg has set for you."

Jim scowled at Betih. "Smart for a mutt, aren't you?"

"I am. But so are you—if you apply yourself. If you're willing to admit when you're wrong, there's hope for you. And there's hope for the ones you would otherwise leave littering the galaxy."

Jim stared at the drawings on the table. He sat up and said, "Will you and I ever get to the point where we are polite to each other, do you think?"

"No. Canids and simians are different. It doesn't mean we can't work together."

Jim nodded and sighed. "Okay."

CHAPTER 42

MIL VARON

Jim spoke before the screen Marhan had set up again in the galley. "This is Mil Varon, a nasty gas giant, but it has this cute little moon, Ara. Jack Katrigg's job, according to Mrs. K., is to collect a small package from a scientific lab, sign reams of paperwork, have the package sealed and certified multiple ways, and take it to another lab in the Laja system."

Rob's voice came from Jim's tablet. "Laja's trouble. Weapons get run through there."

"Good to know. Our job won't be easy. We have to find Katrigg on Mil Varon Ara, probably at his destination, and then follow him to Laja, then home."

Tella added, "Without being noticed."

"Of course. Once we know where he lives, we can think about how to make nonthreatening contact."

Marhan asked, "Are you sure he will return home? Won't he just go on to the next job?"

"Two weeks in between, the way we count it. I'm sure he has a home base for the downtimes."

"You'll need some good gear," Rob said. "Tracking someone

who's switching is notoriously difficult. Especially if you have no idea of even the general direction."

"And yet," Jim smiled, "the Praestans Rapax do it to me all the time."

"Best chance," Rob continued, "is to attach something to his ship. But you'd need unobserved access to it for long enough. That's tough."

"So, that's the job for today. The gear, how to attach it, and how to use it. Assume we'll only get the one chance."

CHAPTER 43

PACKAGE

Jack Katrigg checked his watch. "How much longer must I wait?"

The receptionist smiled. "If you'd like to take a seat, I'll call you when they have your package ready for you."

"I'd rather wait where I can see the packing process. I'm required to verify the contents of anything I transport."

"I'm sure, sir. However, no outside parties are allowed past this point."

"Our client will not accept a package that hasn't been vetted. For that, you need me. You need me inside. You need me inside, now."

"Thank you for your concern, sir. I have explained—"

"Check again. Tap Blik is required to meet me. If I'm not to be allowed in, she must come out here and talk to me!"

The receptionist smiled again. "Of course, sir. Let me call her again."

The reception area echoed with voices and movement. The polished floor reflected the glare of sunshine pouring through windows several stories high. The chrome sides of the reception desk, the doors, and the huge plant pots sent zigzagged shafts of light in every direction. Jack Katrigg hated it.

The receptionist spoke quietly enough that he could not hear the words. The smile remained unchanged. Nothing in her eyes gave any clues.

"Doctor Blik will join you shortly. Please take a seat."

Katrigg said, "Thank you," and she said, "You're welcome," without either meaning it.

Doctor Blik rushed through a double chrome door and made straight for Katrigg. She wore a thin, clean coat that rode up over her mottled red skin. Her sleeves caught against the nodules and deep creases common to her kind. In her left hands, she carried a large plastic tub. In her right hands, two wads of paper.

With an interrogatory wave of her antennae, she called, "Jack Katrigg?"

"I am."

"I.D."

Sighing, Katrigg showed a pass and then, on his tablet, a complex image of dots and swirls. "Enough?"

Blik put her head close to the tablet and blinked her multi-faceted eye several times. "Acceptable."

"If you have completed the packing process, it must be redone in my presence."

"No. You may examine it in its current state. The inner receptacle is pressurized. You may not open it at any time."

"That wasn't made clear in my instructions."

"Not my problem."

"It *is* your problem. I'm required to verify the contents of the package I'm delivering. It's simple enough. I should have been in there to see what you put inside."

"I would remind you that, given the recent disruption in delivery schedules, you are lucky we have this consignment to give you. Even so, there is nothing you would have been able to verify. The contents were loaded by machine under sterile and pressurized conditions."

"Unbelievable! Then we must sit down and go through the

declarations. I will sign only those that accurately describe this situation."

"Of course."

An hour later, Katrigg left the facility. The plastic tub followed him on a small hoverpad.

At the port, Katrigg stopped in the restaurant across the docking bay from where his ship sat in quiet anonymity.

The port showed none of the aesthetics of the science lab. The light from Mil was just as bright, but instead of polished surfaces, the floors and structures were roughened and carved. Swirls, reminiscent of leaves, touched carvings of husks and flowers. Hints of other colors had sunk into crevices, leaving the outer parts dull blues and grays. Years of dirt and grease lay in the corners by every column, by every truss and beam.

Katrigg thought, *So much ornamentation! For what? The knuckleheads who work here don't appreciate it. The visitors have no time to enjoy it.*

He saw no activity near his craft. He thought the time spent in the restaurant was probably wasted, but the routine was good, learned over many such missions. The bay to the left held a small flier similar to Sol Earth's, perhaps large enough for one or two humans. That such a craft should be docked on Ara was of no real concern, but Katrigg noted it. Avoiding humans was sometimes a necessity.

The bay to the right was unoccupied. As he ate lunch, he noticed a technician arrive, enter the empty bay, and return a few minutes later.

As the courier stared through the window, he realized a ship was there. Its hull was so black it looked like a shadow. He could see little of the ship's true shape behind the notice boards and the pillars and struts of the docking bay.

Once lunch was finished and paid for, Katrigg strolled toward the black ship for a better look.

Magnificent! Worth a fortune.

A shadow loomed over his shoulder. Stepping back to put a hand on the hoverpad, he looked up.

"Careful where your curiosity leads you, monkey!"

It was a massive gul, dressed in a military-style black overall, a large blaster at his belt.

"No offense, Sir!" Katrigg muttered.

The gul growled and bared its teeth.

Katrigg backed off. He turned to the next bay and retreated into his craft, the gul's eyes following him all the way.

CHAPTER 44

GHOST

Tella sniffed as it looked around the room. Something had died there and not been removed for some time. A glance at the window was enough to establish there was no chance of ventilation.

Rob smiled as he looked up at the Neraffan. "Used to better accommodation, my friend?"

"I once spent a week naked, living amongst rocks and thorns."

"I'll take that as a 'yes' then. Plenty of incentive to get the job done quickly."

"Agreed. How far away from Katrigg's building are we?"

Rob looked out of the window. He pointed and said, "That's it there. Two blocks."

"Through crowded streets. I will not find it easy."

"Yeah," Rob sighed, "it's a busy city. This neighborhood won't sleep much. Looks like low-paid shift workers, retail and catering staff. See that stream of people coming from the transport node?"

"You are more likely to pass unnoticed than I."

Rob smiled. "Did you just disrespect me?"

Tella stretched out on one of the two beds. "When do we leave?"

"For this phase, I'm staying here and doing more research. You should take a walk once it gets dark."

Tella asked, "Is there any way to approach the building from above? Are there nearby rooftops?"

Rob cocked his head and frowned. "You can see for yourself. It's right there. Maybe you could get up onto that one to the left."

Tella did not move from the bed.

"Or"—Rob continued testily—"you could fly. Do Neraffans have wings?"

Ignoring him, Tella asked, "Is there a basement?"

Rob shrugged. "Subject of upcoming research. I will endeavor to produce detailed plans for both the building in question and its neighbors. Will that suffice?"

"Thank you. I will sleep until you are ready."

Rob muttered, "Great!

In the early morning hours, a tall figure stood outside Jack Katrigg's building, looking up. It wore a dark robe with a large hood, its face barely visible.

Tella took in the scents of the city and the night in a series of calm, deep breaths.

So much to learn. A shame to be hurried.

It hung its head and crossed the road.

Food. Cheap food. Alcohol. Smoke. Sweat. Fear. Deodorizer from the transport system.

A vehicle flew overhead, a large shadow followed by a gust of hot air that became trapped within the tall buildings on either side of the street.

People from several systems. What a wonderfully complex place!

"Learn anything?" Rob asked on its return to their accommodation.

"Much. There are many theories abroad about the Great Silence."

"I'm sure."

"But as for our business, I fear my skills will be of little use. There is no way to approach the building from the street without being seen. There are patterns in the sidewalk, architectural features"—it waved a pale hand—"piles of garbage that would betray my presence. I cannot simply walk inside. What have you found?"

"That's unfortunate. Well, the most important thing I found so far is that Jack Katrigg doesn't live there."

"We saw him go inside and not emerge."

"I know. But I have a list of all the tenants. He's not on it."

"Interesting."

"Now, of course, we should expect him to use other names whenever he needs to. But it opens up the possibility that he's living with someone else, and it's only their name on the list."

"A pseudonym. A partner. Or even a team."

"So, yeah, you really need to get in there somehow and find out."

"Whose names do we have?"

Rob brought up a document. "Ash Freegaman, a Lorit. Del Whit, human. Brian and Sara Hanlan, humans. Dannika Cory, human. D'Ghil Ora Bha, it says she's muwter. But I don't think that's right. Merim Chu and family, about nine of them, Limarcs. Someone called Best Bin, a Homalic whom I'd guess has another identity. One empty apartment."

"What's wrong with the muwter?"

"I think they have trouble with our kind of atmosphere. They'd be carrying a breathing machine. This doesn't look like the sort of neighborhood conducive to that."

"Why not?"

"They tend to be expensive. Around here, gear like that would get ripped off, literally and figuratively."

"So, I need to check that one. I need to see the male humans up close to see if one of them is Katrigg. Jim is unlikely to have mistaken a Homalic. Is it possible the empty apartment is not empty?"

Rob nodded. "And here's what I have so far about the layout inside and the connections between the properties."

Tella watched over Rob's shoulder as he scrolled through images of building plans and a real estate listing.

"Interesting."

Rob rolled his eyes. "If this is what you're into."

"It is. There! A shared access."

"Cables. Probably a network node."

"Accessible for maintenance."

"But could you get up inside from there? It's probably just conduits going into the walls."

"Show me the real estate description again."

"There you go!"

"Hmm. There. Shared garbage disposal. A chute opening on each landing."

Rob raised an eyebrow. "That's risky. I can imagine several opportunities for you to get stuck or injured."

Tella smiled. "I will call you if I need rescuing."

Rob didn't smile back.

CHAPTER 45

TWENTY-EIGHT HOURS

Jim spent many hours pacing the flight room as his ship orbited the planet of Naq Frodin. He hated not being with the others.

We've got Katrigg in our sights. Mrs. T's info was good. I hope they don't blow it down there.

"Raeda, send Davey's report on the Great Silence to my module."

The ship replied, "Documents are ready in your module."

Jim read and reread everything Davey and Clo had gathered.

It doesn't make sense. There's nothing—literally nothing—that could affect D-switches galaxy-wide.

But the whole galaxy had been affected. Davey had compiled accounts from near-Earth sources and from those beyond any human connection. Planets Jim had never heard of reported the same phenomena: no comms, no D-switching. And then, it all started back up as mysteriously as it had stopped.

It doesn't make sense.

Jim began to fall asleep reading the same news again and again until he found a fact. One fact among so many.

The Office of External Affairs—his old employer—had produced a minimally worded statement.

From: Office of External Affairs
To:Public distribution
The Office of External Affairs confirms a recent widespread outage of communications equipment and navigation devices.
The outage lasted approximately twenty-nine hours.
Normal activity has returned.

Please report any similar events immediately.

"Raeda!" Jim called, "Tell me exactly how long the Great Silence lasted, in Earth hours."

The ship replied immediately. "Twenty-eight hours, twenty-eight minutes, and twenty-eight seconds."

"Oh shit!"

"Please restate query."

"Cancel query."

I need to talk to Rolo Kerit. But how will I find him? Rob's busy.

"Raeda, initiate a link to the office of Robins in Unity City. Create a message for the eyes of Robin Stuart only on his return to the office. Use the highest encryption protocol. Embed the message in the image of the can of mackerel."

"Please state message."

"Find me Rolo Kerit. Meoenan. Formerly of Sonloi-AC. Last known on walkabout...Oh god, when was it? When I was sixteen. No one is to know about this inquiry. Do not inform Davey or Clo."

"Message ready."

"Transmit."

"Message sent."

Right, when we're done with this mission, when Rob finds him, it's time for a reunion.

CHAPTER 46

PID

Danny sat on D'Ghil's bed, one arm around the sobbing Merim's shoulders. "It's okay. It's okay." she whispered.

The Limarc dabbed a handkerchief under one eye and tossed her hair back to reach under the other. The white of her bony face caught a flash of color from D'Ghil's lamp.

"A ghost? What do you mean 'a ghost'?" D'Ghil prompted.

"I saw it—by the window on the landing. I came out to throw out the remains of dinner. Tall, still. But I could see through it!"

"Did it say anything?"

Merim shook her head and sniffled.

Danny asked, "Where did it go?"

Merim said, "I don't know! I ran back to our room. The family doesn't believe me. But I remembered what you said...about strangers trying to get in. So, I knew I must tell you. There was someone—some *thing*—in our house!"

Danny hugged her tighter. "Don't worry. Don't worry. We'll get everyone else to look. To keep an eye out."

Danny glanced at D'Ghil as if to say, "What do you think?"

D'Ghil shrugged. "I think we should be careful. Some creatures can become invisible to ordinary eyes. But, together, we can see more than we can alone. I mean, we're from different worlds and are used to different light. I might be able to see more ultraviolet than you can. Maybe you see more infrared. I know Bin smells things I can't."

"It was so scary! My children! How can I protect them if such a creature can walk into our house? I think it has come because of the Silence! Dark forces are at work."

Danny sat up and turned the Limarc mother to face her. "Look, Merim, you are not alone! We're all together on this. We'll help to protect your youngsters too! We're on alert for D'Ghil and—though we don't know this is related—we're on alert for you and your family too. Okay?"

Merim whispered, "May Limal's Servants of Light bless you both and your families."

Rob half sat up in bed. "Back so soon?"

Tella announced, "The empty apartment remains empty."

"Okay. That's good for us."

"I spent an hour with Del Whit. The human is alone and is not Jack Katrigg."

Rob nodded.

"I smelled the air around the doors of the other humans. I cannot conclusively say Katrigg is not sharing with them. I would like to return..."

"I hear a 'but' there."

"I was seen."

Rob rolled his eyes. "How?"

"A female Limarc. She caught me at an unfortunate angle to the light coming through a window."

"Did she raise the alarm?"

"Undoubtedly."

"Shit!"

"I would appreciate suggestions as to our next move."

Rob lay back and sighed. "Best check with the boss, I suppose."

"Or *you* could try and befriend one of the residents and gain access that way."

Rob scoffed, "Nah, that's awkward. Working up one of them and then dropping them once I find Katrigg. He's the one I have to befriend. It'd get too squirrely."

"There may be no best solution." Tella lay down, and they were silent a long while.

Rob said, "I learned more about the building and the landlord."

"Anything useful?"

"Probably not. This city is on the verge of revolution. The whole economic setup stinks. The owner of the building is really screwing the residents."

"The tenants are poor. So much is obvious."

"And kept that way. Doing the numbers on what they earn and what it costs to live—even in a shitty neighborhood like this—there's no way they can get out of it. They'll work till they drop and not be able to afford a funeral."

"A common story for many worlds. Are there signs of social unrest?"

"Oh yeah. The government has been obsessively refining the tax laws and business regulations to close off any avenue of advancement for the underclass. Fantastic resources are being pumped into law enforcement. The free press is a memory for these folks."

"It won't be long," Tella said sleepily.

Tella, in its black cloak, sat in a corner of the local café. Rob sat with his back to the other patrons, partly to conceal his colleague.

"What's the point of this mission, Tella?"

"The point?"

"Yeah. What's Jim going to do once he tracks this Katrigg guy?"

"Ask Jim."

"Been trying to do that; he gets evasive. That puts my antennae up."

Tella frowned but stopped itself contradicting Rob's anatomical claim.

"It is personal for Jim. Katrigg must be stopped."

Rob nodded, unconvinced. "Yeah, yeah. But Jim isn't the kind of guy to take someone out. He's going to hand them over to the OEA or someone, isn't he?"

Tella shrugged noncommittally.

Rob drank from his cup, but his eyes stayed focused on Tella's blank face. "So, I had an idea," he said, putting his cup down with a thud.

"About how to proceed?"

"Sure. After you came back last night...I don't sleep much on this kind of gig. There's not much we can do to help these people—"

"We haven't been asked to."

"—but I thought of a small way we might."

"I will do nothing that might interfere with our mission."

"I could approach the owner."

"Of the building?"

Nodding, Rob explained, "Talk to him about buying the property."

Tella assessed the idea. "You would then have a reason to inspect the inside."

"Indeed, yes."

"You might even get to talk with the residents."

"I might."

"It would take too long. Katrigg's next job is fast approaching."

"Money talks. Sometimes very loudly."

Tella sipped its drink, and Rob almost saw the liquid go down. "I could then return to the ship."

Rob shrugged. "Sure, you kind of blew it already from your point of view."

"I'm thinking of it in terms of efficiency and reducing the chances of being discovered. I do not consider one person's indeterminate sight of me 'blowing it.'"

Rob smiled inwardly. *Ooh, a reaction!* Then he said, "I'd still appreciate having someone watching my back."

"Let's put it to Jim."

"Of course! I'll get him to see it my way."

The office of Ral Pid was on the seventh floor of a building old enough to have no elevator.

Rob, carrying a coat on his arm, was sweating and shaking his head as he knocked on the door.

"Hello?" he called.

"Come in!" a voice called back.

"Hi, I'm Steve Marvelous. We talked earlier?"

"Yes, Marvelous. I'm expecting you."

"You're Ral Pid?"

"I'm Ghen, Pid's right hand, flipper, or tentacle, or whatever!"

Ghen stood up from behind her desk, and Rob got his first good look at her.

She stood seven feet tall, day-glow green hair falling four of those feet. Her skin flashed a scintillating gold, green, and blue. Her dress showed the tightness and lines of an expensive design.

Rob thought, *Scales are so sexy!*

She reached out a hand and shook his.

Two legs, two arms, stereoscopic eyes. But not a primate. She's something new! Are those gills? So hot.

"How can we help you, Marvelous?"

"As I said when I called, I'm interested in acquiring some property. Specifically, buildings on Farq Avenue."

She sat behind her desk again and picked up a large tablet. Shaking her head, she said, "Doubt it! Not an address that's familiar."

"May I?" Rob indicated the only visitor's chair.

"Please." She didn't look up from her tablet.

Rob put his coat over the back of the chair and sat down. He waited and glanced around the small office. *Every expense has been spared—bare walls, cheap furniture. This is a squalid little hole. She's way too good for somewhere like this!*

"Oh! There's one! Not for sale. Sorry."

Rob nodded. "I'm hoping that won't be an obstacle. I represent some investors who are interested in the whole area. They can't pay much over the current valuations, but I know there is a little wiggle room if you understand me?"

She looked up.

Sexy eyes too.

"Not for sale."

"Can you ask Pid?"

"No."

Rob sat silently.

"Was there anything else?" Ghen asked.

"Oh, I think so." He smiled. "When the project goes ahead, I'll be looking to staff up. I can guarantee you a better working environment than this."

Ghen laughed but otherwise didn't reply.

"I could also buy you dinner if you'd like."

"You don't know my tastes."

"I'm up for finding out."

Again, she laughed.

Lovely laugh.

"Is this how you usually do business, Marvelous?"

Rob shook his head. "On special occasions. Meeting you is one of them."

"There are other properties that are for sale. Perhaps I could suggest one of those?"

"No. Just Farq Avenue, thanks. There's a good interplanetary restaurant at the Grinit Hotel, I hear. Have you tried it?"

"On my salary? No."

"Again, I will be staffing up."

"That's nice. But the property is still not for sale."

"Ghen, the place is a toilet. Its lifespan is already in negative figures. Why wouldn't it be for sale? You'll be pouring money into it. More each year. Just to keep—what?—a roof over the heads of a few sewer rats? Come on, I'm a businessman; the numbers tell everything."

"The numbers won't change if the ownership changes, will they?

Why are you interested in buying a toilet? Do humans have a fondness for brick latrines?"

Rob smiled back at her fierce eyes. *Ah, that's more like the real you!* "Sometimes. We can often see the potential in such places. Especially when owned in association with the other neighboring properties. You don't own *them*. You are, however, being dragged down by them."

"Interesting."

Rob drew out his tablet. "I've done my research." He waved the tablet vaguely. "And, before you get too many ideas, you don't know how much of Farq Avenue I already own. Nor will you easily find out. This might be the last building I'm after—the one with most leverage. Or it might be the first—my bargain entry point."

She paused before saying, "I checked you out before I agreed to meet you, Marvelous. Apart from your recent Alien Entry ID, I can't find you mentioned anywhere. You have no real estate license, no history, nothing. Care to explain that?"

Rob didn't reply but checked something on his device. Then he looked up and said, "Certainly not. Let it be evidence of how good I am at what I do."

"And what is that, I wonder?"

"At the moment, I'm acquiring Farq Avenue, piece by piece."

Again, she laughed. "You are persistent; I will grant you that."

"The offer of dinner still stands."

"I'll pass."

"You'll pass." He held up an image of her on his tablet. "Like you'll pass yourself off as your own assistant? Like you'll pass off this hole in the wall as your office, when you actually run your business out of the Harl Center? What are you afraid of, Pid?"

The smile left her glittering face. "That's...quite impressive."

Rob winked.

"So," she replied with reluctance, "who are you? Who do you represent?"

"I'm not going to all the trouble of being invisible just to blurt out my whole story to you. Please don't insult me by suggesting I do."

"I have no intention of selling the place on Farq. Give me one reason why I should."

Rob frowned. "Really? Just one? Okay. Let's go!"

"Go where?"

"To see it."

"Why?"

"Because you haven't. At least not recently"—he frowned —"Ever? I'll give you more than one reason. I'll show you why you want to get rid of it and soon!"

Sitting back, she laughed again. "Why not! Forgive the deception, Marvelous, but one cannot be too careful. This is not a city where one indulges in trust."

"I'm sure."

"My bodyguard will accompany us."

They locked eyes.

"As will mine." He stood and threw his coat to Tella, whose body flushed into view.

"Succaphilosha!" Pid cried, "What's that?"

Immediately, a large security guard burst into the room. In the stony silence, Pid looked from Rob to Tella to the guard then relaxed, smiled, and said to the guard, "Get the armored car. We're all going to Farq Avenue."

CHAPTER 47

FARQ AVENUE

Pid's guard and Tella accompanied them into the building. She knocked loudly on the first apartment's door.

"Open up! I'm Ral Pid, Holder of Rights for this property!"

Del Whit cracked the door, still on its chain, and said, "Who?"

"Ral Pid, your Holder of Rights. Open up."

"Never heard of you. Got some ID?"

"Who are you to ask? I have a right, under your tenancy, to access all rooms at all times for any reason."

"Still need some ID."

Rob leaned forward with his tablet. "Here she is, on the city page."

"And who are you?"

"I'm Steve Marvelous. And I'm thinking of buying this building and acquiring the rights. I'd really appreciate a quick look inside if it isn't too much trouble."

Del looked doubtful but closed the door, took off the chain, and opened up. "You two." He indicated Rob and Pid. "The thugs stay outside."

"Leave the door open," Pid countered. Tella and the guard stood back, shoulder to shoulder.

Del nodded and stepped aside for them to move into his room.

Before Pid could say anything, Rob began, "How's the heating in winter?"

"Nonfunctional."

"Air in the summer?"

"Windows don't physically open even if it were safe to."

"Other utilities? Water, power?"

"Water's clean enough. Power's okay, but access to the network comes and goes. It's slow all the time."

Rob smiled. "Understood. This area didn't get the latest upgrades, did it."

Del snorted.

Rob shot his hand out toward Del and said cheerily, "Thanks for your help! Great job. Much appreciated!"

Del, frowning, shook his hand.

Rob was already back in the hallway before Pid knew the visit was over.

Sara Hanlan, another human, was home, although her husband was not. Rob asked her if vermin climbed up the trash chutes.

"Of course they do! And other things I wouldn't wonder. The sewers back up along this street all the time."

D'Ghil wouldn't let the visitors in.

Pid insisted. "I'm Holder of Rights to this building, and your contract says I can have access to my property at any time for any reason. What don't you understand about that?"

"Bring a warrant from a judge! I don't know you. You've never come here before. You could be anyone off the street. I'm not safe letting you in!"

Rob tried. Checking the list of tenants, he said, "Miss Bha, we only want to ask a few questions. Check your ceiling isn't caving in. Make sure you're actually okay living here. It'll only take a minute."

D'Ghil shook her head. "Go away." She shut the door.

Pid was about to tell the guard to break it down when Rob said, "There's a whole family of Limarcs upstairs, isn't there?"

"What?" Pid replied, "There shouldn't be. Max occupancy is three. Rent is for three. How many of them are there?"

Merim, too, did not want to let the visitors in. Pid's threats scared her sufficiently and she opened the door and retreated behind the table with three of her children.

"How many of you are there in here?" Pid asked.

"Just my husband and our family."

"How many?"

"Seven."

"Anything you'd like to tell us about living here?" Rob asked.

"It's haunted! We're all scared to death!"

"What do you mean 'haunted'?"

"A ghost! I saw it with my own eyes, there, in the passageway."

"Big? Small? White? Dark?" Rob pressed.

"Ghost! I could see through it. So still. So frightening!"

Pid straightened to her full seven feet and looked down at Rob. "Someone you know, perhaps?"

Rob smiled innocently and refrained from glancing at Tella, clearly visible wearing its dark cloak. "Doubt it. Thank you, Mrs. Chu, you've been most helpful."

On the steps outside, Pid turned to Rob. "Right, Marvelous," she said fiercely, "I've had enough! What's your game here? You've seen every room. But you've told me nothing. What's going on? Why was your bodyguard in there before?"

"Why are the Limarcs crowded into that one room when there's an empty one above them?"

"I don't know. Well, they only pay for one."

"The former resident of the vacant room"—he checked his tablet again—"one Soipher Yit Renk died a year ago."

"How sad."

"I thought so. All that rent not being paid. So, I checked. His mother is paying you."

Pid shrugged and said, "Good!"

Rob grimaced. "Not really. She's old and in a nursing home. Probably doesn't know what day it is."

Pid didn't reply.

"And according to one of my informants, regulations passed a couple of years ago designated rent as a 'Tier One financial responsibility.' Meaning, as in this case, if someone dies without the correct paperwork being registered with the Holder of Rights the nearest relative has the rent garnered from their accounts."

"Eminently sensible."

"Yeah, thought you'd say that. Strikes me as a legal means for landlords to get paid for nothing. Renk's dead, his mother can't fill in the paperwork. She may never have known who or where you are or how to contact you. All in all, she's stuffed, isn't she?"

"Your point?"

Rob smiled. "Just call me a bleeding heart. That's why I want this place. To stop you sucking the blood out of people."

"What an ugly metaphor, Marvelous. Most unwelcome."

"I'd like to visit you, in your real office, tomorrow morning. Let's see if we can make a deal. You're better off selling than having these poor strays' plight become a matter of public discourse."

"I think I preferred it when you were trying to flatter me."

"Let's do some business instead." Rob held her eyes with his.

"What a strange creature you are."

"A strange creature with enough money at his disposal to keep you interested."

"Perhaps."

The Harl Center office was everything Pid's other office was not. It had glass walls, a view of the nice parts of the city, fresh-scented air, and fawning staff.

"Welcome to my lair, Marvelous!" Pid called when she saw him emerge from the elevator.

"Thank you. I hope you've had time to review my offer."

"Well, yes. A feeble attempt to undervalue the property. But that's why we negotiate, isn't it?" She showed him her most serpentine smile.

"Indeed. I don't usually conduct my business in public, Pid. Please send your immediate staff on a break."

She waved him to a chair in her inner office. "Do you have your invisible friend with you?"

"Not today."

"How do I know that?"

"To do business, one must make some effort to trust."

"No, I don't think so."

She stood behind her desk and picked up a device half-gun, half-antenna. Scanning the office, she nodded and put it down again. "Now, I know."

"Staff?"

"This will have to do." She pressed a button, and shades came down to cover all the glass of the inner walls.

Rob stood and said, "Good enough." He pulled out the Lascon stunner, ducked, and caught her full-on with its blue flash. He pushed his chair against the door.

For five or more minutes, he scoured the desk, walls, and furniture until he found the safe. He took out a small rod from his briefcase. One end, he pressed over her limp finger to extract her print. The other end, he used to scan her rolling eye.

In the safe, he found more papers than he expected and, almost hidden at the bottom, a leather shoulder bag. He checked to be sure it contained the precious metals and jewelry he was expecting.

"Your emergency getaway bag," he told her prone figure, "Knew I'd find it. Your type is so predictable."

He left the office with a quick smiling word to Pid's secretary. "She's not to be disturbed for half an hour."

PART FIVE

THE COURIER

CHAPTER 48

DENJ WRAM

"Well," said Rob, "that's another world I can't go back to."

Jim handed him a mug of coffee. "Uh-oh, what did you do this time?"

Rob smiled and shrugged. "I guess I led her along. She'll be out to get me. Definitely the jealous type."

Jim laughed. "I won't ask any more. I'm sure I don't want to know the gory details. But you met Katrigg?"

"Probably."

"Rob?"

"No, a distinct possibility. I met most of the residents of the building, and we have images of the others. Whichever one gets on a flight to Denj Wram is our man...or whatever."

"Rob, this isn't the certainty I was asking for!"

"Jim, none of these guys can afford commercial transportation. None of them are going anywhere. They're dirt poor. Whoever gets on that flight is someone hiding in the shadows. Don't worry! We have him."

Jim frowned and glanced at Tella across the galley table.

Tella nodded. "I agree. Robin's methods are unorthodox, but I think his conclusion is sound."

Jim said, "Okay. Let's call the others. We'll go through what the kids found out about Denj Wram."

On the screen in the galley shone an image of a blue planet. Jim said, "It's strongly influenced by a species called Y'Fin—if that's how it's pronounced. I don't know why Earth doesn't have relations with them. They run a kind of empire, and the Denj system is frontier territory."

"You will stand out," Marhan offered.

"Unfortunately, yes."

Betih added, "But then, so will Katrigg if he is a human."

"Good point."

Tella said, "Do you think Katrigg is transporting more weaponry?"

"According to his boss, he's collecting a package and delivering it to the same place in the Laja system he went to last time. So, yeah, probably weapons."

Rob shook his head. "That's bad news. This kind of operation is looking more and more high stakes. That means a greater likelihood of someone else monitoring Katrigg's travels. Other actors with their own concerns who could get in our way."

Jim stared at the image of the planet and then said, "Do you think we should wait? Go to the next job on his list?"

Marhan growled. "Every job Katrigg does carries the same risk to us. He works for criminals. You said Schpurr told you they call on Katrigg most when something bad happens."

"Betih?" Jim asked.

The elderly Gul didn't reply immediately. She drew her robe around her and growled softly. "If you fear being dragged into the misdeeds of others, you must be clever. Do not endanger their goods. They do not care about Katrigg; they care about the package. Your opportunities are before receipt or after delivery. You hear the warnings about not going to Laja. Your choice is made. You must act as soon as Katrigg arrives on Wram."

"Agreed." Jim smiled, relieved. "How does the timing work?"

Tella picked up a tablet from the table. "Two days to the Denj system. We should be there before Katrigg leaves. As soon as we have word of which flight, and which individual is on it, we can prepare our welcome."

CHAPTER 49

IDENTITY

Jim sat listening while Rob was in conversation with Davey Able. "That's not right. Are you sure? Yeah...no problem...Let me know. Hey, your uncle wants to talk."

"Hi, Davey. How's it going?" Jim saw his nephew shrug his shoulders. "Where are you at the moment? That doesn't look like EBMS."

"I'm on Earth! Didn't you know? Clo and I have an apartment in UC."

"When did your dad allow that?"

"Umm..."

"Davey?"

"Mom arranged some time away."

Jim nodded. "Okay. Say no more. How's working with Rob going?"

"Yeah, good."

"So, what's happening on Naq Frodin?"

"Well, we've got one of the Farq Avenue residents booking a cabin on a commercial flight."

"And?"

"Under her own name, not Jack Katrigg's."

"Who?"

"D'Ghil Bh-ha?" Davey read, stumbling on the pronunciation.

Jim glanced nervously at Rob. "Were we expecting that?"

"No. I thought we'd see Katrigg getting the ticket. Are you sure? She doesn't look like Katrigg."

"But how is she financing it? Can you see who paid for it, Davey?"

The youngster shook his head. "That would be a lot more work."

"Okay," Jim said, "hold off on that."

Jim stood and walked around the flight room. "Rob?"

"Jim."

"How did she travel to Mil Varon Ara? As Katrigg or herself?"

"Katrigg."

"Really?" Jim asked, "Then why the change?"

Davey said something neither caught.

"Don't know. Probably not significant."

"Rob?" asked Davey louder.

"Yeah? What's up?"

"She did the same on Ara. She didn't travel as Katrigg."

"What? Then..."

Jim rushed to the screen. "She traveled as herself?"

"Yeah. But the ship was registered to Katrigg. That's how we traced it."

"Then, how do you know it was her?"

"Umm...Clo looked at the Ara Port Control logs. They had some to and fro before she was allowed to land. We saw the feeds showing her face."

"Well done! But why didn't we know this earlier?"

"I could have saved a lot of—" Rob interjected.

"No, no!" Davey said quickly.

Jim leaned into the screen and held up his hand to Rob.

Davey continued, "We didn't know it was her! We only saw— just now—that it's the same person. It looked, you know, like it was just someone else acting as pilot on Katrigg's ship. Didn't know who she was."

"Okay," Jim said reassuringly, "Not a problem. We're learning something about how he—she—works. First question: why is she on a commercial flight and not in her own ship this time? Second question: did Katrigg own the ship at Ara, or was it rented?"

Davey shook his head. "Don't know. I'll see if the Ara logs have the ship's ID."

"Good man!" said Jim, "Call us back when you know."

"Sure, Uncle Jim!"

As they ended the call, Rob frowned. "Even if the ship at Ara was rented, why change? How is she getting off Wram? Is she taking something dangerous on a commercial flight? That's just asking for trouble."

"Not like Katrigg at all. I wonder..." Jim frowned.

"What are you thinking?"

"Maybe someone else is providing the transport to Laja. Part of throwing people—people like us—off the scent."

"Right." Rob nodded. "She'd have to travel commercial since she wouldn't want to leave her ship at Wram—or take a rental, for that matter."

"They're going to smuggle her off, so there's no trail to follow. Katrigg will be there, but no records will show it. Then, if something goes wrong, some other Katrigg will come forward with proof he was somewhere else at the same time, and denying his presence here will have credibility. And no one cares about D'Ghil Bha."

"What a load of effort!" Rob shook his head. "We're sticking our noses in something, aren't we? Someone's gonna be pissed!"

Jim said, more or less to himself, "How do they coordinate that? Who is visible, and who is dark? I think I want to hire a magician."

"You what?"

"Magicians do this sort of thing all the time—what do they call it? Misdirection! Your attention is in one place; the action is in another."

"That's a politician, not a magician."

Jim laughed. "You might be right!"

"But, you know, the real trick is getting someone as ugly as her into a believable human form."

. . .

The arrivals hall at Denj Wram Memorial Spacefield showed no mercy to tired passengers. It was long, loud, cramped, and impersonal.

Rob stood peering through the narrowest of cracks in the best security door his bribes could arrange. Floods of passengers dragged themselves and their luggage across his limited field of view.

Davey's voice whispered in his earpiece. "Within twenty feet of you."

"Give me something obvious to look for. Anyone abnormally tall? Any striking females?"

Davey laughed and replied, "Three Homalics, bright blue clothes, gold luggage. They're like five or six people in front of her."

"That's what I'm talking about! I see them."

"Got her?"

"Not yet."

"Should be right there!"

"Oh, is that her? She's shorter than I thought. But I only got a glimpse before..."

"Are you set?" Davey asked.

"Okay! I'm signing off. Going in."

Within a second, Rob was just another tired passenger in the crowd.

Slowly, he worked his way forward until he was walking directly behind D'Ghil Bha. On cue, Davey set the next phase in motion; the power failed, and the entire arrivals hall went dark.

Rob said loudly, "Not again! This happened the last time I came through here. This is ridiculous."

Someone nearby swore at another passenger and said, "Watch where you're going! Mind my bags!"

The noise of conversations, mixed with swearing, grew in the hall. The temperature rose quickly as no air moved.

Rob chatted with the two humans in front of D'Ghil. "Won't be long, he said, "They'll have us going in no time."

Someone cheered ahead of them. The crowd surged forward.

"See, they opened all the exits. No problem," Rob reassured whoever was listening to him.

He and D'Ghil were almost at the exit, in sight of the officials rushing to control the crowd, when a loud bang sounded from back in the hall.

D'Ghil crouched down over her suitcases. Rob put his hand on her arm. "Don't worry, I'm sure it's—"

Two more explosions poured smoke across the exit doors.

D'Ghil screamed. Rob swore loudly.

"Here!" He held out his hand to her. "Follow me! This way!"

He backed into the security door hidden next to the exits. He picked up one of her bags, and she hurried through the door after him.

The room was empty except for two chairs and the one-way window looking out onto the smoke and bewildered passengers.

"Are you okay?" he whispered.

D'Ghil nodded.

"Wait! Don't I know you?" Rob said quietly.

She shook her head but looked at him more closely.

"Miss Bha, isn't it? I'm Steve Marvelous. We met at your apartment. I was there..."

She dropped her suitcase and her eyes focused on his face. "I remember you!"

"I'm here on Wram looking at other properties. What a strange coincidence!"

He saw her thin arms twitch and swell. Her face filled out behind her nose, and she grew taller. Between the gray scales shone orange underskin.

Her first blow caught him square in the forehead.

"Ow!"

She was behind him, an arm round his throat. He felt the arm enlarging and increasing the pressure. He punched backward into her face. The blow landed, and her grip softened.

Twisting round to face her, his elbow between them, he shouted, "Stop! I'm not here to hurt you!"

"You followed me!"

"No!"

She pummeled his chest with a series of hard and rapid blows that left him staggering backward, coughing.

D'Ghil grabbed a suitcase and swung it at Rob. It caught him under his shoulder as he stumbled away, sending him face-first onto the floor.

She sat on his back and pulled his head up by his hair. "Who sent you? Who do you work for?"

"Agh! Myself! I told you. I b-buy property."

"Die, liar!"

To Rob's relief, other voices filled the room and there was movement by the door.

He rolled over as she leaped off him. Watching in wonder, he saw her muscular form—including dangerous-looking spines protruding through gaps in her clothes—deflate into the more familiar, slightly drooping and rotund outline of D'Ghil Bha. Her gray scales masked the orange skin like a sudden cloud.

"Are you okay?" called one of the new voices.

"I'm fine!" D'Ghil shouted back. "This creep attacked me!"

"Hey, wait a minute! I did no such thing."

A uniformed guard stooped over Rob, grabbed his arm, and hauled him up. "Well, it doesn't look like you were doing too well if you did."

"Officer, I'm entirely innocent."

"We take this sort of thing very seriously, sir. If the lady would like to tell us her side?"

They looked around at the small crowd. D'Ghil and her suitcases were gone.

CHAPTER 50

LAJA

Rob lay in bed, in his module. Jim sat with him.

"She's like a fucking pufferfish, Jim! She's a shapeshifter!"

Jim nodded in agreement. "Yeah, looks that way; your bodycam got some clear images. But that only explains how she can create the human shape. I'm still amazed at the Katrigg makeup job. She must be really good."

"Yeah, great. Everyone else okay?"

"Exemplary job from you all. I'm amazed. I half expected Marhan's smoke canisters to do more damage! A clean job except for the outcome." He stood up and turned to the module's door. "We were so close!"

"Sorry, I blew it."

"Not your fault. It was a good plan. We just move on to the next one."

"We're not going to Laja, are we?"

"Of course. As soon as Marhan has picked up his ship from where he parked it."

"Don't recommend it, Jim."

"Duly noted. You'll sit it out anyway. Doctor's orders."

"Call that thing a doctor?"

"It sorted you out well enough. Don't be ungrateful."

Rob scoffed and replied with an insincere, "Sure."

Marhan sat at the galley table, his face in his paws. "Jim, you cannot proceed. She is aware of us. She will be doubly careful."

Jim sat opposite, his face set in a grim smile. "We know she's there. We know where she's making her delivery. We only have to catch her."

Marhan snorted. "You are outclassed."

"No! Providing a friendly face to rescue her from a crisis didn't work. It was a good attempt. We'll try something else."

"In the middle of a system that draws the worst of the galaxy. It would be better to wait."

Betih stood on the ramp, listening.

Jim said, "I think I underestimated her."

Marhan said nothing.

Betih walked to the table and sat down. Quietly, she began, "A glimmer of wisdom comes to the monkey brain. She is your equal. She is smart and well-qualified for her job. She also has the same rights, the same expectations as you. Why would you ever think differently?"

"She tried to kill me," Jim replied simply.

Marhan interjected, "From what Rob says, she is more than your equal, physically."

Betih corrected him. "That doesn't matter. An assassin does not fight."

"I'm thinking I should meet her face to face and just ask my questions," Jim said.

"She will kill you," Marhan replied flatly.

"Is that what I've taught you?" Betih asked Jim.

"You've taught me to research. I did. But the answers weren't there. D'Ghil lives quietly in a rough neighborhood. There's no way to know if that's a cover or her real life. She can defend herself, but is that because she's been trained as a professional killer or because she's had to learn to look after herself?"

The old canid narrowed her eyes. "Go on."

Jim frowned. "That's...about it."

"You don't even know what species she is!" Marhan exclaimed. He stood and walked to the coffeemaker.

Betih sat, watching Jim.

He glanced at Marhan's back, then looked into Betih's eyes. "Maybe I'm not cut out for this work."

"Does that happen to you?"

"What?"

"That feeling. The feeling you want to give up. Has that happened to you before?"

"No..."

"Think! Perhaps when you met Tella? Where were you? What was the mission? Did you say to him, or to yourself, while you pursued your objective, 'I'm in the wrong job'?"

Jim shook his head. He wanted to say no. He remembered well sitting with Tella in the EIA-rented flier, feeling disgusted with the mission, with the Regdenir, and with his own performance. They had just escaped an attack from Sopha Luca. But that wasn't what Jim remembered feeling bad about. It was Tella expecting him to predict what Sopha Luca would do next.

Fire a rocket at me, and let me do my best. I don't want you putting your expectations on me.

Betih said softly, "Tell me, monkey. Tell me."

"No. It's not like that."

"What isn't?"

Jim sighed. "We were pursuing someone. He'd attacked us and escaped. Tella was on my case to predict his next move."

"And?"

"I thought the whole mission was a failure. I wanted to be done with it."

Betih waited.

"Tella said I had the right skills. That humans couldn't—don't—understand about using the right resources at the right time, or something like that. Then it told me I had empathy for aliens."

"You do." She nodded.

Jim stared at the table. He shrugged. "Maybe, in that case...yeah. But I don't for Jack Katrigg. I thought it was all more straightforward. I thought he was just a criminal—with criminal instincts—someone I could protect others from. But now I've seen her on the logs and the images we got...She's just a kid! I don't understand why...I don't understand why he—she—did what she did. I don't actually care so much about her trying to kill me! I just want to understand why!"

Betih scoffed, "And now, when things are difficult, you think you can't be an assassin!" She leaned forward and continued. "Listen to yourself! You give voice—better than I have been able to—to the reason you will not kill without being sure."

"What do you mean?"

"Find out the 'why'! Yes! This is what I've been saying. *How* you do it doesn't matter. You will treat her with respect. You will find out why she did what she did. Then—only then—decide what you will do about it."

Jim did not reply.

Marhan sat heavily in the chair next to his aunt. "The Neraffan was right; you confuse yourself with all the resources you gather for your work. Perhaps your idea is the simplest and the best. Talk to her. I was being overly cautious on your behalf. But be ready to accept the consequences."

"Like, as you just said, she'll kill me. Just as Mrs. Katrigg planned it."

Betih nodded, and so did Marhan.

Jim continued, "But then, D'Ghil thinks the same thing will happen to her if she meets me. I guess that's something we have in common."

Silence fell over the galley table.

Jim sighed and said, "Go get your ship, Marhan. Meet us at Troom."

It was festival time on Laja Gonlar. Practically speaking, it meant increased hotel rates and extra taxes, but not much else. There were no special events, ceremonies, or shows. Each city permanently hosted its own display grounds. Public transport bulged with patrons, funneling thousands—if not millions—into confined spaces built for the great expressions of Gonlaran culture: cooking and eating.

Katrigg's customer worked in the city called Troom. The kids had found a guest registration under Katrigg's name at the High Note Guest and Reception Centre. The lodging was close to Troom's main tourist attraction: the display grounds that were both permanent fairgrounds and a massive open-air restaurant.

The giant gates reminded Jim of something, but he couldn't remember what.

Have I been here before?

The gates loomed high over the approaching crowd. Two black stone towers thrust a hundred feet or more into the night sky. Every ten feet or so, their stones cradled a basin of flame that roared and occasionally belched smoke into the air.

Hinged between the uprights, enormous dark wooden gates stood forever open to welcome the crowds.

Thousands walked from the public transport stations along narrow paths and underpasses designed to defeat any vehicular traffic. At every turn or switchback, vendors competed for space, offering everything visitors could wish for: glow sticks, hand sanitizers, sealable bags, cutlery, instant chemical analysis kits, water bottles, stimulants, and more.

Jim ignored the merchants. He relished the faint smoke, the lively chatter of his fellow tourists, and the comfort of anonymity.

Once inside the display grounds, the celebrations began in earnest.

The reception area consisted of a huge semicircle radiating from the gates, a flat area where the tourists rearranged themselves along five paths leading to the interior.

Visitor information booths stood ready for the newcomers, but most of the crowd already knew which way to follow to the meat-eaters area or to the plant-only vendors. Those who preferred food alive used the path furthest to the right. Those whose tastes were for the old, fungal, or rotting took the path to the left.

Desserts lay beyond the central, widest, and most frequented path.

Unlike the grandiose scale of the gates, everything inside the boundary was smaller and more intimate. The food vendors worked constantly, some under small canopies, some in long, low tents. Some sold food in the hand; others served at constantly cleaned tables under the starlight. Each displayed small tokens of their own culture, hints of distant planets, religious relics, and swathes of bright fabrics.

Lights burned everywhere: subtle colors to enhance the flavors, bright spots to aid the staff, and small stars at ground level to keep tourists on the paths. But, above all, were the flaming torches on tall poles. Everywhere, they sputtered and flared. Their smoke created a moving ceiling that drifted from dark clouds to glowing banks that broke unexpectedly here and there to reveal once more the starlit heavens.

Jim, still only just inside the gates, could already feel soot settling on his lips, a salty pre-taste of the wonders on sale before him.

Just beyond the information stations, the entertainment also began.

A burst of green flame erupted from a performer dancing for a ring of admiring visitors. He swung around, suddenly dark, and then delivered another jet of flame from his mouth. Jim smiled at the cries of appreciation. He had seen the act before, but not, he thought, performed by a creature with four arms and budding wings.

Just beyond the circle, another gaggle of onlookers watched and listened to a small band playing deep, throbbing music that shook the trampled ground beneath his feet.

A small breeze wafted aromatic meat-flavored smoke over them all. Jim breathed deeply. *Oh, this is so good!*

. . .

Marhan's voice sounded in Jim's ear. "Where are you?"

"Inside. Should I take the dessert path or the meat one?"

Marhan scoffed. "You are not there to gorge yourself! Let me know when you are at the mound."

"Will do. Want me to bring you anything back?"

Marhan didn't answer.

"You know," Jim continued, "I have this strange feeling of having been here before."

"Concentrate!" the canid grumbled.

The mound—or more formally, The Judging Center—occupied the middle of the grounds and was, as befitted its name, raised above the acres of the vendors' tents. One large open-sided pavilion operated as a stage for all major activities: performances, competitions, culinary displays, fights, and quizzes. The five paths into the grounds were mirrored by five wide paths up its tall bank.

Around the mound, seats and benches clung to its slopes, looking outward. The upper ones commanded the best views of the scene below—when the drifting smoke broke enough.

One bench looked north, the highest of a series of semi-circular structures nestled into the grass, renowned as Gonlar's Whispering Slabs. Two people could sit at either end, ten feet apart, and— thanks to the skillful stonework—hear each other's quietest whispers.

Jim finished the climb to find two children sitting at either end of the stone bench, giggling to each other. He stood patiently nearby and felt the vibration of music from a crowded vendor directly below. When the children showed no sign of leaving, he approached one end and loomed menacingly over the bench's carved shoulders. Soon enough, he sat alone on the bench and surveyed the scene.

I'm exposed to anyone with a sighted weapon, but I should be able to see someone approaching—except from directly above. Of course, I'll only be able to stay until someone bigger than me wants this seat and gets fed up with me hogging it.

Marhan asked, "Are you anywhere near being in position yet?"

"I'm here. I'm waiting."

Jim reviewed the message he had sent to D'Ghil at her hotel.

Mrs. Katrigg has manipulated us both.
I suspect she has told you I mean you harm. I do not. I wish only to talk.
She gave me the list of your last and next few jobs with the intention that I
should find you. I suspect she did not tell you that.
Please consider meeting me.
I have researched a public place that would be safe for us both. The exact
description is attached.

▭

He gave her a time. She had sent no response.

Are you going to be here?

CHAPTER 51

JACK KATRIGG

Jim's attention was lost in the crowds below, the smells of cooking that rose to the height of the mound, and the occasional orange glow reflecting on the stone of the bench as torches flared. He was also aware of his increasingly cold seat.

He heard a slight scrape and a soft sigh in his right ear. It wasn't Marhan. He looked left along the bench and there sat Jack Katrigg, the same brown coat, the same well-fed face. There sat the cause of so much misery.

Jim was lost for words.

"I have a blaster pointed at you. You'll be dead before you can try anything," the voice whispered again in the wrong ear.

Jim quietly said, "This bench is wild, isn't it? I hear your voice from the wrong side. Can you hear me, okay?"

"I can. State your business."

"My business? To talk to you."

"Why? I don't know you."

"You only know what Mrs. Katrigg told you?" Jim frowned.

"Who are you?"

"I'm Jim Able. We have met."

"I doubt it. I don't recognize you."

Jim's heart sank. "Do you remember being on Sin Har? At the spaceport called Ch'Garratt?"

Katrigg, who had not moved, swung around to stare at Jim. "I remember it well. What is it to you?"

"I was there."

Katrigg did not reply.

Jim continued. "We met there. I interviewed you. Earth's Office of External Affairs audit, August 2098, by my calendar. You were flying a gold saucer-shaped craft."

"You are an auditor?"

"I was helping out. It was a big audit."

"I was working."

"I know. You signed off on a load of shipment confirmations and tax declarations."

Katrigg laughed, though to Jim, it sounded more like D'Ghil laughed. "You make people fill out paperwork for a living? I should shoot you for that alone."

Despite himself, Jim laughed back. "Sounds kinda dumb when you say it like that, doesn't it?"

"I was working. I did whatever my customer told me to. I don't remember you."

Great, Jim thought, *thanks a lot!* Marhan said something in his ear, but ignoring it, he carefully reached behind his ear and switched off his communicator.

Jim gritted his teeth, breathed a lungful of sweet, spicy smoke, and said, "I need to understand what happened next."

"Why? What's it to you?"

"I was there. I was injured. I held some of your victims...as they died."

D'Ghil didn't immediately reply. When she spoke, Jim could barely hear her whisper. "It's nothing to do with you. I was working."

"What does that mean?"

"I was...I cannot talk about my employers. You can't ask me about that."

"Of course I can! I must!"

"Anything between me and my employers is just that—between us. Not for discussion with strangers."

"It didn't stay between you when you committed mass murder!"

Jim heard her gasp. He said, "I'm sorry. Understand, I get emotional about this. It haunts me..."

"I understand. But it shouldn't. It's nothing to do with you."

Jim felt the weight of the planet spinning under him. *Nothing to do with me?* "I saw you onto your ship. You took off, hovered, and opened fire! What do you mean 'nothing to do' with me? You thought I'd found out about something. You—"

"I can't say. If you shout at me again, I will leave."

Jim closed his eyes. *This is slipping away from me! What the hell is going on?*

D'Ghil was silent.

He glanced at her and saw she was staring down at the tents, crowds, and lights. The scent of trampled grass rose from his feet. "I just want to understand why you did it. I'm not law enforcement. What can you tell me? Surely there's something!"

"Nothing. It's between me and my employer. It's confidential. If I am known to talk, I'll never work again—if I should live."

"Okay. I get that. Some employers are worse than others. Some are engaged in things...well, things we normally wouldn't get involved in. Mrs. Katrigg is a terrifying woman; she has so much power and no sense of responsibility."

D'Ghil scoffed. "Who cares about her? She's in the middle. She's not the customer."

"Wait. What? She didn't tell you to do it?"

"Nothing to do with her."

"Who then? Who was the customer?"

"Can't say."

"Come on! Tell me. I'll leave you out of it. Give me a name."

"No."

Jim put his head in his hands. "I just want to understand how you—how anyone—could open fire on a terminal full of civilians and just fly away. I have to know!"

"I didn't!"

"What?"

"I didn't! Alright? I didn't fire at you. Or them! And I didn't fly away!"

D'Ghil was up and walking away.

"Wait!" Jim called. "Don't go!" He jumped up and ran after her down the slope.

Dew had begun to form on the grass, and Jim found himself slipping. Suddenly he was blocked by a group of people crossing the slope. He skidded to a halt.

They were a group of men speaking English. As they walked by, Jim heard small bells rising from their every step. "Morris dancers?"

"Eh-up!" cried one, "A human!"

This brought a cheer from the others.

"Hi, guys! Can't stop. Bit of a hurry!"

But Jim was surrounded, backslapped, forced to shake hands, and asked a barrage of questions.

He caught a glimpse of D'Ghil at the foot of the mound, turning and disappearing into the crowd.

By the time he had extracted himself from the dancers, she was gone.

Jim turned his communicator back on.

"Jim!" Marhan was shouting.

"I lost her. I had her talking, then I lost her."

Marhan swore.

"I have to find her again, Marhan! I can't let her go."

Sighing, Marhan replied, "We will come in. We will help search."

"Please. I'm sorry. This won't be quick. She's dressed as Katrigg. She looks fully human."

Jim met Tella, Marhan, and Betih in the entrance area. Tella walked with Jim along the main avenue for plant-based food. "You must try and remain calm, Jim. This is a difficult task, but success is possible."

"I had her! I had her talking, and she walked off!"

"She was upset by something you said?"

"I guess I did accuse her of mass murder. She seemed not to like that."

They stopped to glance into a busy tent of laughing people. Orange-tinted smoke wafted out of the entrance. Jim waved the smoke away from his face.

"That might be a good sign," Tella replied as they moved on to the next vendor.

"What might?"

"Her reaction. Perhaps she is not actually a mass murderer."

Jim clenched his fists. "That's what I'm trying to do here—ask her that very question! If she didn't do it, who the hell did?"

"And the calmer you are, the easier the conversation will be."

Jim glared at his tall companion. "Shut up and keep looking!"

Marhan's voice sounded in Jim's ear. "This crowd is too thick. How is it there?"

Jim replied, "Variable. But no sign. Is Betih in position?"

"She is. And complaining."

Jim laughed. "Buy her the charred backside of some animal. She can chew on it while she waits."

Marhan grunted. "I already have."

Jim and Tella stopped at a circular intersection. At the center, a team of jugglers stood back-to-back, keeping various colorful glowing objects in constant motion. Without any apparent signal, they began to weave themselves into a dance, each one taking over and passing on the flying pieces. They increased their speed to cheers and whoops from the onlookers.

Jim's eyes searched the crowd in vain for any sign of D'Ghil.

Tella's hand grabbed Jim's arm as a large creature burst from the path to the left and cut into the crowd in front of them.

A cry of "thief!" sounded from behind. Five human-like people ran after the creature, and the crowd parted for them.

The juggling stopped, and the troupe disappeared to the left, away from the problem.

From the path ahead came more shouting. An alarm sounded, and suddenly, the intersection was flooded with intense white light. As Tella pulled Jim back the way they had come, three things happened simultaneously.

The running creature stumbled and fell. Its pursuers mobbed it and began raining violent blows on its back. Half a dozen police in uniforms and visored helmets came from the path ahead at such speed bystanders staggered and tripped, unable to get out of their way.

Jim watched in horror at the melee that followed. The police showed no partiality, beating bloody anyone who came too close and dragging away anyone they deemed involved.

The lights went out, leaving the flickering of the flaming torches as a dim reminder of something past. The crowd drifted back from left and right, the murmur of comment and conversation gradually rising to its customary level.

Jim muttered, "That was...surprisingly efficient."

Tella replied, "I had wondered about security arrangements here. But based on this system's reputation, I presumed they had none."

"Looks like they monitor everything. And have people stationed to react. Over an area this size, that's a huge operation!"

"And not ordinarily visible. I'm impressed."

"They must have cameras. I wonder if we could hack into their feeds?"

"She would be long gone before you could achieve that."

Jim sighed, "Yeah, you...You go that way. I'll go this."

Tella bowed slightly.

Jim called after it, "Stay out of trouble!"

As the night and their search continued, Jim saw several more incidents like the one by the jugglers, but not as close.

He saw the bright lights silhouetting a large tent crowned with three tall chimneys, their smoke transforming in the light into a towering serpentine monster.

At the end of a row of sweet sellers, he heard the running feet of a crowd moving away from another pool of white light. The alarms wailed, faded, and then music and the sound of voices returned as if nothing had happened.

Twice, he saw medical vehicles slowly crawling through the masses of people and down the narrow paths.

Nowhere did he, or Marhan, or Tella, catch any sight of D'Ghil Bha.

Jim returned, yet again, to the mound. It seemed smaller and less well-kept. The growing daylight showed damage to the grass that couldn't be seen at night.

The smells wafting from the vendor's preparations mixed more with the scent of the trash waiting to be collected.

Where did the Morris dancers go? I could ask them to help look for her...

He sat on a bench—one where no other voices would sound in his ear. He listened to the wash of noises from below.

A band of string musicians played nearby. Jim felt their tunes too lively, too evocative of a fun night out.

I need daytime music. Music for working.

Someone started singing above him in the Judging Center pavilion. Contrasting with the high notes of the performer came a long low sound. It was part digeridoo, part orchestra. The long notes weaved slowly around each other. He had never heard an instrument like it.

He started to walk up toward the pavilion, but the sound didn't become clearer. He turned and realized the musician was below him, somewhere in the alleys between the tents.

This isn't finding her. Giving up? He sighed and began walking down again. *Yeah. At least I can find out what the hell that instrument is.*

He first saw the cluster of brass horns bobbing above the heads of a crowd. As he moved closer, he could see the horns were all part of the same instrument.

Stopping near a busy intersection, the musician stood against a tent wall to play a new piece.

Jim and several others stood in a small circle to listen.

The performer held a long keyed cylinder in front. Two tubes rose from the end to enter his nostrils and a third to the mouthpiece. Large straps over his broad shoulders held the six horns, like flower blooms, in a fan arrangement.

The music mesmerized Jim and his fellow onlookers. Notes came without interruption, weaving both the tune and its accompaniment. The musician's fingers flashed around the keys that clacked slightly as they worked. The ground vibrated with the low tones, and the listeners' spirits soared with the power of the melody.

And yet, captivating though the music was, Jim's attention fastened solely on the creature playing. The purple lips—of skillful embouchure—stood out in clear contrast to the gray scales that occasionally flashed a bright orange beneath.

He watched as the creature, breathing both out and in through the instrument, seemed to be pumping himself up under his skin, rhythmically and continually.

Pufferfish. You're the same species as D'Ghil, aren't you?

At the end of his playing, the musician held out a portable device to accept contributions from the crowd.

Jim set a large amount on his payment fob and made his donation. It caught the musician's eye.

"A word, if I may, when you're free," Jim said.

The musician nodded, wary but also grateful.

After three more tunes the musician removed the pipes from his nostrils and pushed the mouthpiece to one side. He thanked the crowd and then asked Jim, "How can I help?"

"I'm looking for D'Ghil Bha. I'm guessing you know her. There can't be many of you guys here."

Jim caught a flash of his eyes.

"Don't know what you're talking about."

Jim stepped close and to one side, putting his hand on the alien's shoulder. "It's okay. She and I were talking, but we got interrupted.

She said something to me that I need to clarify. No funny business, I promise. Just want to finish our conversation."

"There's a lot of people in a place like this," he replied, "Not all of them can be trusted."

"I agree. I feel the same way. But I'll go along with someone like you—if I have to. I know what you can do when you defend yourselves. A slender primate like me has little chance against a creature like you."

"What makes you think she wants to talk to you further?"

Jim stepped in front of the musician to meet him eye to eye. "Because she's been accused of a serious crime. If she's innocent, I can help her clear her name."

"You're police?"

"No. But I'm highly motivated to succeed where the police failed. I need her to tell me what she knows. That's all. I'll do the rest. I'll see justice done, wherever it takes me. She doesn't need to be involved more than that."

The musician grunted, looked Jim up and down, and said, "You're right. You won't survive if you try anything."

Jim nodded once.

CHAPTER 52

D'GHIL

The musician led Jim along a narrow alley between long formerly white tents that had grayed with soot and mud. No flaps opened along the alley, and the ground was tortured with spikes and ties.

At the end of the alley, he unbuttoned a flap in the wall of a green tent and waved Jim inside.

The tent was large—twenty feet or more to Jim's left, another ten to his right. In front, a wide opening gave onto another tent of similar size, end on. In the further tent were tables in long lines, half full of customers. To his relief, he found himself standing in the kitchen.

"Wait here," the musician instructed.

Jim sat at a table hidden from the main dining area. He watched the staff, ten or more people of various species, working at boiling pots and hissing grills. The waitstaff smiled and chatted over newly prepared plates before turning to deliver them.

The easy morning shift, he thought. *I wonder what it's like at midnight.*

The musician unstrapped himself from his instrument, stacked it by the flap they had come through, and then disappeared into the alley without a word to Jim.

A Kevar, his head wrapped in a bandana, called to Jim from one of the stoves, "You hungry?"

Jim nodded. "And tired. Been up all night."

He laughed, "Happens around here. You with Jax?"

"Who?" Jim frowned.

The cook pointed to the huge instrument against the tent wall. "The Furnan player. Didn't you come in with him?"

"Oh, yeah. Sure."

"I'll get you something."

Jim smiled, but his thoughts were of the last Kevars he saw. He winced at his vision of their bodies, lying where they fell, dead at the hands of his daughter and her goons.

The cook's face was the same white color. His tall, bony frame, typical for a Kevar, looked to Jim to be too thin for his clothes.

Who were they? Who hired them? I should find out. One day. Were they this guy's relatives?

A party of customers in the dining area sang a birthday song, clapping and cheering.

The cook brought over a plate, pausing to glance at the singers. "Assholes! Just after a free cake." He smiled at Jim.

Jim smiled back. "How can you tell?"

"I've been at this a while. Enjoy."

"Thanks!"

Jim looked down at the plate. It was filled with three different foodstuffs, nothing Jim had seen before. The first was a red mash run with a purple streak; the second, a green vegetable with stalks, leaves, and small bulbous flowers; the third, a pile of black eel-like shapes. Jim couldn't tell immediately if they were animal or vegetable.

He tried each in turn. The mash was spicy, with a hot, peppery taste he instantly liked. The purple sauce within it grabbed the back of his throat and had him coughing.

The cook brought over a large glass of water without comment.

The green stalks were sweet, more dessert than anything. The eels reminded Jim of things he had eaten on Turcanis Major V-I: salty, meaty, and filling.

After a few minutes, he called to the cook, "What are these? They're great!"

The Kevar shrugged. "Don't know where they're from. We call them Black Worms. Not to be confused with the Brown Worms; the cooking is different."

Jim asked, "You need paying for this?"

The cook shook his head. "No. Jax is cool."

The Furnan player returned to pick up Jim and his instrument.

Back in the alley, Jim asked, "Why did you leave me there? Where are we going now?"

"Somewhere safe."

"Sounds good."

"For D'Ghil, not for you."

"Right..."

Again, they moved through the tents but not on the main paths. Twice, they crossed through lines of people waiting outside popular vendors. At length, they came to the back of an enormous pavilion.

"What's this place?" Jim asked.

"The Beer Tent. Did you not come here already?"

"Ah...no. I didn't see this. I recognize the smell though."

"In here."

Jax opened a buttoned flap and led Jim into a square area surrounded by canvas and empty but for a table and two chairs. A strong smell of damp grass filled the small space.

D'Ghil sat on one side of the table, in her true form, no longer dressed in Katrigg's clothes. Another of her kind stood against a closed entrance behind her. Jax buttoned the flap after Jim.

"Good morning!" Jim said lightly, "Thanks for seeing me again. Thank you for shedding your disguise."

He heard a noise behind him and turned quickly to see Jax changing shape. His arms grew longer, his chest rounded out, and his legs stretched and widened. All over his skin showed more and more orange. Short spikes emerged from his bare skin.

Across the room, D'Ghil's other friend bulked up equally threateningly to block Jim's only other way out.

"Please sit down," D'Ghil said quietly.

"Thanks. It must take a long time to put all that makeup on."

"You have no idea. What must I do to get rid of you?" she asked.

Jim sighed. "Tell me what happened. You said you didn't fire on the terminal, and you didn't fly away. But I saw you do both."

She shook her head. "You saw me get on board. You saw the ship. What makes you think *I* was flying it?"

In front of her, D'Ghil had been doodling on napkins. She pushed one of them across the table to Jim. On it, he saw a rough diagram of a saucer-shaped craft, lines across its interior.

"What's this?"

"Me." She pointed to the edge of the drawing. "Loading ramp. It leads to the cargo bay. Below the cargo bay, there's nothing but the engines and the switch. Here."

Jim nodded.

"The floor slopes, but the gravity-plating is micro-adjusted to make you think it's flat. Under the other side, there are hidden compartments. That's how it works."

Jim nodded. "Nice."

"The access to the middle section is up the ramp here or the elevator here. How long do you think it takes to walk from the ramp over here, across the cargo bay, up this ramp, just to get up there?" Her voice was getting stronger as she poked her finger repeatedly on the napkin. "Then, access to the flight room is back around here. Stupid design! Probably built with the expectation of fights and mutinies. By the time I got up there—to the flight room—we were nearly in orbit."

Jim sat back and looked at her. "So, who was flying?"

D'Ghil said loudly and slowly, "I can't tell you! I've already said that. They'll kill me if they even suspect I've talked about it!"

"It was registered as your ship, with you as the pilot."

"Of course it was! That's why you were interviewing *me*. That's how it's done! That's how things happen without idiots like you interfering with the real business. The written record, the official documents, they're all a sham...well, when it suits them."

"Why? What were they hiding?"

She poked the napkin again, shaking her head at Jim. "It's not just hidden compartments. Do you know what a magician is?"

"Sure."

"They wave a wand with one hand, and your eye follows it. With the other, they do what? Something you don't see. What was happening in Ch'Garratt while you did your audit, huh? While you made a great show of checking paperwork and ships' records and had hundreds of inspectors counting the cargo, what were *they* doing? They were making a show of complying. They waved their wands and you looked where they wanted you to. You watched me. What were they doing?"

"You tell me."

D'Ghil shook her head again. "I don't know. And I don't care!"

"You must have some idea."

"I have ideas. I don't share them. I don't want to die."

Jim picked up the napkin. "Look, I see your point. They hired you as a front. But you were there; you heard them talk. You know who they are and where they come from. I need a lead. I need to find them. We can stop them doing it again!"

"No. No names."

They sat in silence.

"What species are they? Human?"

She shrugged. "I didn't ask." She almost smiled and added, "You can't always tell, can you? That's how I make my living."

Jim squinted at her. "Fair enough. Probably wouldn't help me much, even if they were."

D'Ghil sighed and said, "Look, don't be so thick! Listen to what I told you. It's a magic trick. What did they do? They had everyone looking at the wand. A big, shiny, golden wand. Big. Shiny. Deliberately eye-catching! Come on, you stupid human!"

Jim blushed. "The golden saucer was the front, not you."

"I was the front of the front. Tip of the wand. They wanted everyone to look at the saucer. And you did."

Jim's eyes focused on the worn grass at the side of the table. "So what was happening at the same time? What else was going on that we didn't notice?"

D'Ghil shrugged. "Don't know, don't care."

Jim thought a long time before asking, "So, where did you go?"

Her skin stretched and flexed in ripples. "Not where you think."

"Tell me."

"I will. But that's it. I won't give you names. I won't see you again. If I hear that you're in the same system as me, I'll kill you."

"If it leads me to...your customer...I won't need to see you again."

"It might. Depends on how smart you are."

Jim shook his head slowly. "I only want the chance."

She drew on another napkin. "Up to orbital height. Then they dropped the decoys."

"Mines."

"Whatever. Then, instead of leaving orbit"—She drew an arc —"round the other side of Har. No one's watching. Almost every eye is on the spaceport. Flying in the dark, lights off, without any transponders. There's a big canyon; I don't know what it's called. They have a facility carved into the wall. That's where we went."

"How did you get off Har? Your picture was everywhere."

"Jack Katrigg's picture was everywhere. No one recognizes me"—she squinted at Jim—"except you."

"So...what? You just got a regular flight home?"

D'Ghil shrank and shivered. "They argued. I don't know exactly why. I mean, really argued. I think one of them had gone further than the other thought they should. Maybe the decoys, maybe the terminal. Don't know." She neatly put the top back on her pen. "I was stranded on that goddam planet for half a year. No money, no ID. I ran for my life from that canyon place. I'd love to tell you exactly who they are. I'd love to pay them back for the hassle. But I won't. I've seen them in action. I don't want to die." She paused. "We're done."

Jim wasn't sure what to say.

"Oh," she added, "Don't go blundering around the canyon

straight away. If someone saw us together here...Make it look like you found it on your own."

"Okay. You think there'll be any evidence still there?"

"Your problem. My guess is they will have wrapped it all up and sealed it up. Probably too much gear to waste but too hot to use for a long while. You might be lucky."

Jim sighed. "Thanks, I guess."

"You're welcome. Good-bye."

Jim didn't get up. He said, "Look at it from my point of view. I saw what they wanted me to see. I saw you. And, yes, I've wanted to kill you. Out of revenge, sure. But also to stop you doing the same thing somewhere else, to other people. The regular authorities completely failed to bring justice to those people."

"Is that some sort of apology?"

"No. While I wanted to kill you, a friend of mine persuaded me that I should make sure you truly were the one responsible—before I did anything too drastic."

"And now you know. Thank your friend for me."

"But I don't know yet, not for sure. All I have is this"—He held up the napkin—"and a forthcoming hike in the Har wilderness. If you're lying to me, I will find you again."

"You can try."

Jim shook his head, smiling. "This isn't how I thought meeting you would go. That we're both still alive is good, right? Mrs. Katrigg didn't get her wish, did she?"

D'Ghil chuckled coldly. "One question. You're human, right?"

"Yeah..."

"Do you eat ice cream with your fingers?"

Jim chuckled. "Wow! Didn't see that one coming. No. Long time since I had any. But in my youth—when we had it—we ate it in edible cones. Oh, and a chocolate stick sticking out the top."

D'Ghil showed no emotion. "You humans are weird. Now please leave."

Jim smiled and nodded, and Jax let him out of the tent.

CHAPTER 53

GONLARAN POLICE

Jim turned his communicator back on and said to the others, "We're done!"

Tella replied first. "Shall we meet at the entrance?"

"Yeah. I'm not hungry right now but I'm buying if you guys want something to eat.

Marhan asked crisply, "Did you kill her?"

"No," Jim replied, "Not yet. Another lead to follow."

Jim heard Marhan's grunt and imagined the roll of the eyes and snap of the long jaw that went with it.

Betih sat on a bench near the wide entrance and its towering doors. As Jim returned to the welcome area, she muttered through his earpiece, "About time! Don't you realize how cold old bodies get when they sit for so long?"

"Thanks for helping."

She snorted. "Where's Marhan?"

"On his way."

Tella added, "You were successful, Jim. You found her."

"I did. I got something, but it may be a wild goose chase."

"A what?"

Before Jim could answer, Marhan caught up to him. To their

alarm, a squad of uniformed Gonlaran police, in a practiced set of moves, surrounded the Gul, confining him in a circle of spears just out of his reach. Two more policemen took Jim's arms and said, "Do not resist!"

As Tella saw the squad emerge from the crowd, it slipped off its robe and swung it over Betih. The Neraffan disappeared into the shadows of the wall and the ceremonial doors. Betih dropped her head, rolled backward over the bench, and walked away, Tella's robe wrapped neatly around her.

A steep slope opened immediately behind the curtain of the nearest information booth, leading to the tunnels below the fairground. Jim's feet were barely on the ground as the police officers gripped his arms and held him up as he was walked down into the tunnel.

Behind Jim, Marhan moved silently—head bowed to avoid the ceiling—twitching at every touch of a spearpoint.

Jim found himself in a chair opposite a Gonlaran interrogator. Marhan, he guessed, was in a nearby room, in the same position.

The interrogator sat reading from a tablet without looking up at Jim.

Jim smiled and relaxed. *At least they didn't shoot us. That's a good sign. I wonder if this is D'Ghil's work?*

The people of Laja Gonlar bore the common likeness of the galaxy's primate-like species: two legs, two arms, bifocal vision. They differed in having no nose in their faces, nor any visible ears. Their stiff hair swept back over their heads and down to their shoulders, giving the impression of a hardened shell.

At length, the officer looked up at Jim. "Name?"

"James Able."

"Planet of origin?"

"Sol Earth."

"Not Pec Sonloi?"

"That's where I grew up."

"Huh! Why are you here?"

"Here in this room or here on Laja Gonlar?"

The officer sighed. "Start with why you came to Laja Gonlar."

"I like food."

"And drink?"

Jim nodded, suspicious of the question.

"Who is the gul?"

Jim smiled and replied, "If you already know enough about me to ask about Sonloi, I'm sure you know very well who he is."

"We do. Confirm his identity for me."

"Ernot Dirl Marhan."

"From?"

Jim scoffed. "Look, let's make a deal, shall we? I won't waste your time if you don't waste mine. You know he's a gul."

"We do. Why are you traveling with him?"

"He's a friend of mine."

"That's unusual."

"What, for me to have a friend? Or for guls to have friends?"

"Sol Earth and Tanna Gul don't have formal relations, do they?"

Jim shrugged. "Don't know."

The officer studied Jim's face. Then he said, "When were you last on Gonlar?"

Jim frowned. "Never. First time."

Marhan's interview followed the same format.

"Name?"

"Marhan. Ernot Dirl Marhan, citizen of the great planet of Tanna Gul. Why have you brought me here?"

"Planet of origin?"

"I told you! Tanna Gul!"

"Why are you here?"

"Your goons forced me in here."

The officer sighed. "Why have you visited Laja Gonlar?"

"To celebrate with my friends."

"To get drunk?"

Marhan glowered. "Perhaps."

"Confirm the identity of the person you travel with."

"Jim Able."

"From which planet?"

"Sol Earth, obviously. Aren't humans distinctive? You need me to tell you?"

"In what way do you find them distinctive?"

"Their physical weakness. Their intelligence. Their smell."

"Yet you travel with it. Why?"

"We are friends."

"How so? Tell me more about that."

"Do you have no friends? The galaxy must be a sad place for you."

"Answer my questions."

Marhan growled and clicked his claws on the surface of the desk. "Then ask me something with some point to it, you puppy!"

The officer studied the canid's face. Then he said, "When were you last on Gonlar?"

Marhan smiled and his tongue licked the left side of his snout. "Ah, now we get to it! You tell me."

Turning his tablet toward Jim, the Gonlaran officer asked, "Who is in this image?"

Jim swallowed and his eyes widened. The image clearly showed Marhan standing under a pillar supporting a blazing flame. Next to the gul was a smaller figure, less distinct.

He thought, *Is that me?* but said, "I'm not sure."

"Look again. Take your time."

"What is this? When was this taken?"

"Was this the last time you were on Gonlar?"

Oh shit! "I'm not sure..."

"You just told me you have never been here before. Is there anything you'd like to say further?"

"I travel a lot. I mean, really, a lot. I sometimes visit a planet and see nothing more than the inside of the spaceport and a hotel room.

I can't be expected to remember everywhere I've been one hundred percent."

The Gonlaran tapped his finger on the image. "Does this not help your memory?"

"No, not helping."

"It looks like you stopped to eat, does it not? Not just inside a spaceport, but at one of the galaxy's finest places to celebrate with your friends."

"I'm not sure that's me in the picture."

"Does your gul friend travel with other humans?"

Jim shrugged. His stomach sank. *That's why it all seemed so familiar.* The officer waited.

Jim sighed and said, "Where was that taken? I'm sure I've never been to Troom before."

"This was taken in Frint. Two hundred miles north of here. Do you wish to tell me the truth now?"

Jim wondered what Marhan was saying in the other room.

Marhan picked up the tablet, looked at the image, and threw it back to the officer. "So, you were waiting for us."

"There is a warrant for your arrest in Frint, where this was taken."

"On what charge?"

"Theft and assault."

Marhan scoffed. "Assault? Who do you accuse me of killing?"

"The complaint comes from Ropan Dru, proprietor of The Stars Bar and Grill, #457, Festival Park, Frint."

Marhan sank in his chair slightly. "He is alive?"

The officer frowned and nodded.

Marhan smiled. "Then I did not assault him. If I had, he would not be."

The officer waited.

"What does he say I stole?"

"Two drinking vessels, one deep bowl suitable for a canid, one upright tankard suitable for a simian."

Marhan laughed for a long time.

Jim said, "I don't remember this occasion."

"Do you have problems with your memory? Are you under a doctor's care?"

"I...I may have been drunk."

"Drunk enough to assault the proprietor of The Stars Bar? And to steal from him?"

"Very unlikely. I'm not that kind of a drunk. Wait! Steal what?"

"The complaint states, 'Two drinking vessels, one deep bowl suitable for a canid, one upright tankard suitable for a simian.'"

Jim laughed. "You mean he wouldn't let us finish our drinks, so we took them with us."

The officer nodded, unsmiling.

"You've seriously gone to all this trouble for a couple of mugs? You're crazy!"

"You admit the offense?"

Jim shrugged. "I don't remember this occasion. I cannot confirm or deny it."

"I shall arrest you and have you moved to the jurisdiction of Frint."

"Wait...you don't have jurisdiction now? So how can you arrest me?"

"I have that power under the Gonlaran Global Code."

"But why? Why bother?"

"The law is the law. Is that not so on Sol Earth?"

Jim stared at him. "I was warned not to come here. My contacts called this system dangerous. Arms smuggling was the main concern." He leaned forward across the table. "Why bother with this? Do you really have nothing better to do?"

"Do you think it helps your cause to insult me?"

Jim sat back again, still staring.

The officer stood up. "I will let you consider your position."

. . .

The other officer told Marhan, "We do not treat this matter lightly. You broke the law on your previous visit. Do you admit it freely?"

Marhan growled. "I admit nothing!" He gestured toward the tablet and the image. "That's your evidence? That's your proof?"

"A human and a gul, working together. A human and a gul, drinking together. A human and a gul, thinking they can behave however they wish, believing they can disrespect our laws. You drew our attention."

Marhan's eyes narrowed. "Ah, I see. That's where this comes from. We drew your attention. Then you found some minor complaint from the past. Then you thought, 'Let's see how lucrative we can make this!'"

The officer sat back and smiled.

Jim was alone in the interview room for half an hour before his interrogator returned.

"Well, James Able of Sol Earth, have you considered your position?"

"Sure. You're wasting both my time and your own."

"I have the authorization for your removal to Frint, right here."

"How much will it cost to make this go away?"

"Oh," the officer began, as if the thought had never occurred to him, "Well, let me think. There would have to be some compensation to Ropan Dru, the proprietor. Perhaps he would be kind enough to withdraw his complaint if you expressed sufficient remorse."

"Okay..." Jim replied cautiously.

"Then, perhaps you could contribute to the Officers' Benevolent Fund in Frint."

Jim groaned inwardly.

"And, of course, you have put us, here, to considerable inconvenience and administrative effort."

"How much?"

"Make me an offer, James Able."

Jim cocked his head and squinted. "The price of a nice meal for the proprietor. Twice as much to the Benevolent Fund. Three times for you and your friends."

"Again, I ask, 'Do you think it helps your cause to insult me?'"

Jim sighed. "Okay, but you include Marhan in this. I'm not letting you squeeze me and him separately. You'd have tried us together. You're not getting two payouts."

The officer smiled and remained still. Then, nodding, he stood, held the door open, and called for Marhan to be brought in.

As they emerged from the back of an information booth to the smoke drifting across the entrance area, Marhan asked, "Are you unharmed, Jim?"

"I have a pain in my payment fob."

Marhan chuckled. "It'll pass. Do you remember Frint, now?"

"No, not at all. But the fairgrounds are probably the same. It did feel somehow familiar."

"That barkeeper was a fool."

Jim laughed.

"And the tankard is at the back of one of the galley's cupboards. I have the bowl in my module."

"I thought you didn't remember much either!"

"Bits have come back. But not in any order. As all good celebrations should be!"

"I don't even remember this planet being on the navigation log when we arrived back at EBMS."

"There were a lot of places on that list."

"Let's get out of here."

CHAPTER 54

DAVEY

A planetary shuttle returned Jim and the others to the Gonlaran orbital parking station. During the trip, he whispered, "Let's go somewhere quiet and decide where we go next."

Marhan said, "The farther, the better."

"Not yet. Let's book your ship and mine two berths next to each other on another Gonlaran station."

Both Marhan and Betih looked doubtful.

"We can make it appear we are leaving the system," Tella commented.

Jim continued, "And unless they are right on top of us, they won't notice where we've actually gone."

They docked in another busy, utilitarian station. Jim relaxed a little amid the constant traffic.

Somewhere quiet is relative.

The others slept, but Jim sat in the flight room, the lights at their lowest setting.

I could have killed her. Like I did Gute. And whoever hired her would still be out there.

He brought up an image of D'Ghil on the display.

Betih was right.

I got lucky this time.

Rob, still sporting bruises from his fight with D'Ghil, was preparing a meal in the galley as they sat at the table.

Jim said, "Okay. I've been gearing up to deal with Jack Katrigg for so long...Now, I learn that it's all way more complicated. I need some time to think."

Tella announced, "Jim, I wish to help you in your task, but it seems the information from the shapeshifter will take some time to investigate. I must go to TMV-One."

"I will remain with you," Marhan said.

Betih added, "I wish to return to Tanna Gul."

"No!" Marhan barked. "You have work to finish here."

"I am old, Marhan. The wilderness calls. You should have more respect for the aged. And for our traditions."

"You have years of life still in you, Betih! You will stay and finish Jim's training."

The elderly canid scoffed, said nothing more, and retreated a little into her bathrobe.

In the quiet that followed, Rob asked, "What training is that, Jim?"

Betih was instantly alert.

Jim winced. "Well...nothing to worry about. Guls have some nifty techniques...things I need to know."

"Like what?" Rob asked as he laid the plates.

Marhan growled.

"Boss stuff," Jim said simply.

Rob stopped—a plate not yet on the table. "You what? You pulling rank on me?"

Jim nodded. "Yeah, I guess so. 'Need to know' and all that."

"Huh!" Rob continued serving. "That's a first."

Jim shrugged, and the guls relaxed.

No one was hungry.

Jim said to Tella, "Did you say you needed to go to TMV-One? You know you can't, right? It's still under precontact quarantine."

"I recreated the Pongret M'dar."

"Yeah, I remember, in a Unity City warehouse."

"I had Pritas read it."

"Whose Pritas?"

"My sibling."

"Your what? You have a brother?"

"No. Nor a sister. We are genderless."

Jim waved his hand. "Sure, I know that! But you have a family? You've never said."

"All Neraffans are born in pairs."

"A twin?" Betih asked.

Tella nodded.

"That explains much," she replied, "This Pritas is the one you trust."

"Of course."

Jim looked from Tella to Betih. "What?"

She kept her eyes on Tella and said, "Tella does not give his trust easily to people. There are nuances to his manner that you probably miss, Earth monkey."

Tella began to correct her pronoun, but she talked over it.

"No one can go through life without at least one person to whom they can confide or rely on in a crisis."

Jim thought, *Really?*

Tella said, "I trusted Pritas with the matter, so I could...resolve things with you, Jim. But now I have lost contact. I must follow. You have support from Marhan, Betwen, and Rob. The time has come for me to leave, at least for a while."

Rob grumbled, "*My* support? He used to."

"Tella, from my point of view, you have a home here—always. And we'll help if you need us. But you can't go to TMV-One. It's under quarantine. You'll be stopped. It's illegal."

"Pritas has already gone. And contact is lost. I have no choice."

Jim put his palms flat on the table. "You are in real trouble with the EIA about my job and your assignments. This is going to make it an order of magnitude worse. You know that!"

Tella cocked its head to one side. "Have such considerations ever stopped either of us before?"

Jim gagged, and Betih laughed.

"You'll need a stealth craft," Marhan said simply.

"Do you know where I can find one?" Tella replied with a poker face.

Marhan snorted and looked away. "Bring it back in one piece, or I will tear you limb from pale limb."

"Thank you."

Jim hugged the tall Neraffan as it said good-bye. "Don't make me come and rescue you!"

Tella replied in a whisper. "Rescuing each other is what we do."

Rob was waiting for Jim in the flight room.

"Jim! I need to get back. Got a business to run, and my boss— well, you know, no pleasing some people."

Jim smiled. "Thanks, Rob. I couldn't do what I do without you."

"Someday, are you going to tell me what it is you really do? When you said you'd sometimes want me to find people for you— illusive people—you called it a 'justice machine.' What do these guls have to do with it?"

"Yep, that's about it. And there's no visible connection to me. That's part of the company's DNA, right?"

"Right. But *I* know about you. So why can't you tell me the rest?"

"To protect you. To protect the kids."

Rob shook his head. "Jim, I've been around the block a few times. This sounds seriously bad. For you, I mean."

"It's complicated, that's for sure."

Rob smiled. "You know I'm going to work it out. I always do."

"Don't. Just accept it. Go make some money helping people."

Rob didn't smile. "Sure. Boss."

"Good man. Let's get you a commercial flight home. There's a new—highly confidential—assignment waiting for you when you get back: a Meoenan I want you to track down."

Jim was asleep when the ship intoned, "Call from Davey Able with urgent priority."

Jim shook himself awake. "I'll take it in the chair. Tell him to wait a moment."

"Acknowledged."

Yawning, he sat in the pilot's chair. "Accept the call."

"Connected."

"Davey! What's up?"

"Hi, Uncle Jim, how are you?"

"Fine, Davey. I was sleeping. Not expecting anything urgent from you. What's up?"

"Well...I had to wait until Rob was on his way back."

"Okay...why? What is it?"

"Well...Clo found something. A couple of things actually."

Jim waited.

Davey continued, lowering his voice, "I dunno...I thought you should see it."

Jim frowned. "See what?"

"A police report with a recording."

"Where from?"

"Naq Frodin."

"Huh! We just went there."

"Yeah. Can I send you this file?"

"Ship, accept the file from this source. Display on this console."

"Acknowledged. Transfer complete."

Davey waited while Jim watched in silence.

The scene showed a smart office interior, similar to any office on an Earth-like inhabited planet. Across the bottom of the picture ran the text "Office of Ral Pid, entrepreneur and property developer,

Harl Center, Compar, Effic, Naq Frodin," followed by the local date and time.

Jim's eyes widened as he saw the female behind the desk, tall, elegant, and sporting extraordinary green hair. Her skin flickered with different colors as she moved.

He frowned, watching Rob walk in and sit down. The female scanned the office with a handheld device and, then, lowered the window shades. The image flickered as the camera adjusted to the lower light.

He saw Rob get up and hold something above his head. The image flashed blue for a split second. When the flash was gone, the beautiful figure with green hair slammed into the floor.

Jim paused the playback and returned to just before the flash. He zoomed in on the device in Rob's hand.

Davey began, "So—"

Jim said, "That is a Lascon stunner. They're illegal in...everywhere."

"Yeah," Davey said, "we researched that bit."

"Who knows about this, Davey?"

"Me and Clo. And the police on Naq Frodin. They have an arrest warrant for someone called Steve Marvelous."

CHAPTER 55

TURCANIS MAJOR FIVE

Tella sat at the controls of Marhan's flier, watching as the navigation computer fed the coordinates of each jump into the D-switch. The Neraffan continued to examine every possibility it could devise for such a fundamental activity to have been so mysteriously interrupted during the Great Silence.

Greater minds than mine will have to work this out.

It turned its attention to Jim's reports from his visits to Turcanis Major Five.

I dare not land on Mainworld immediately. I must find Jim's contact, Madhar Nect. I wonder if she will remember me?

TMV-I, a modest-sized moon, lay below Tella's craft. A large storm stood over the coastal peninsular where Madhar Nect lived.

The Neraffan checked again Jim's record of where he first landed. *It will have to do.*

Tella programmed a descent through the storm, hoping no ground-based observers would detect his passage through the turbulent atmosphere.

· · ·

The vegetation growing in Madhar's field whipped back and forth in the gusts from the storm. Rain hissed through the nearby trees and drummed on the beach.

The wind halted as if catching its breath. Something heavy settled on—and sank a short way into—the soggy ground. Only someone close to the object would have been able to tell it was a spaceship. The rain sputtered into steam on hitting the metal still hot from the descent.

Tella walked the short distance to Madhar's small house. The windows showed no light. The front door was locked.

After trying every window and the back door, Tella stood under the canopy for the front door and watched the rain.

The ground is rich with life. The smell is full of new things. This is a fascinating moon. The sea, too, smells full of life! But there are no Turcanians nearby. She has not been here in many days.

Tella brought tools from the ship and removed the door.

It found the switch for the lights in the small hallway, and suddenly, walls covered in photographs swam with color. Rain blew in from the open doorframe.

Grabbing the door, the Neraffan reversed its work and restored it, more-or-less, to the same state it had found it. The carpet showed a large wet area spreading from the doorway. Tella ignored it and walked through to the kitchen.

A well-stocked refrigerator! Thank you, Professor.

Tella watched Turcanian television programs long into the night. The house surprised its visitor, being both comfortably furnished and warm, while the storm wrapped the building in an anarchic blanket of sound and water.

The morning came with gentle rain and light winds. Tella stood on the shoreline watching waves from the bay rush onto the beach—the water made dark with churning sand.

Again, the smells flowed around Tella's transparent body.

Wonderful! Such an interesting place. Such a pleasant change from being on board a ship.

Once more inside the house, Tella used one of the professor's communication devices to send a message to the Latsin Institute.

madharVnectVlatsinVux
Greetings Madhar Nect.
You have a visitor at Martorn.
We have met before. I am Tella of Neraff.
When will you be here at your house? Or is there somewhere else we could safely meet?
I am aware of the rules of contact that presently place your system in quarantine and that these restrictions have recently been broken.
It is this situation I wish to discuss. Discretion is essential.
madharVnectVmartornVnir

It waited an hour for a reply.

madharVnectVmartornVnir
Greetings Tella.
My house was locked. How did you get in?
Why have you put all our work in danger by traveling here?
The negotiations for our entry into galactic society are at a delicate and difficult stage.
You are aware, you say, of the ship that was seen landing on Mainworld.
Why would you risk another sighting?
Is Jim with you?
madharVnectVlatsinVux

You answered none of my questions.

madharVnectVlatsinVux
Greetings Madhar Nect.
When will you be here at your house?
Is there somewhere else we could safely meet?
madharVnectVmartornVnir

An entire day passed, during which Tella enjoyed walking in the woods and swimming in the bay.

As dusk fell, it heard an engine. Moving quickly into the house, it opened the back door, left it ajar, and took up a position in the main room in the shadows of a corner.

Madhar opened the front door with her key. In her own language, she swore at the damp carpet. In Standard, she called, "Tella? What did you do to my floor?"

Tella waited to know if the scientist was alone.

Madhar walked to the back door and looked outside. Returning to the main room, she swore quietly.

Tella relaxed and stepped into the light.

Madhar's reaction was immediate; she fired her weapon.

Tella felt the barbs attach to its skin and saw, rather than felt, the electrical shocks burst through its limbs. It smelled the carpet briefly before losing what remained of its consciousness.

Tella woke with a headache. "Ouch!"

"You're awake?"

"But hungover. Were Jim and I drinking?"

"He's not here."

"Professor Nect?"

"I am. And you are an unwelcome guest who's made a mess of my house, eaten my food, and endangered the future of my world."

Tella did not reply.

Madhar asked pleasantly, "Can I get you anything?"

"Water. Please."

Muttering, the professor went to the kitchen and returned with a glass. "Here."

Tella sat up, saw its limbs swirling with colors from a blanket thrown over its body, and sank back down with eyes closed.

"I'll leave it here for when you want to try that again."

"Thank you. I'll give it a minute or two."

"Why are you here? And where is Jim?"

Moving as little as possible, Tella answered, "Jim is engaged on other matters. My sibling, Pritas, has come to your Mainworld on a most urgent mission."

"Your sibling? You've come looking for a relative?"

"I have. But more than that. Pritas is searching for more of our kind. We believe there may be a population of Neraffan-jong on Mainworld."

"You're joking!"

"We are a persecuted people. As much as the government of Neraff might show us neutrality within established norms when dealing with us, there are others who will not. If word has spread, any jong on Mainworld are in danger."

"This Pritas came and landed on Mainworld. You have come here. I suppose you hope to follow on to Mainworld." The Turcanian made a buzzing sound. "And then others will come...Do you realize how bad this situation is?"

"I have come first to you for advice."

Madhar said nothing, walked into the kitchen, and was gone for many minutes.

She returned and sat in a chair near to where Tella lay stretched out on the floor. She sipped from a mug, her eyes searching Tella's face from under her pronounced brows. "Tella, how much do you remember about the Regdenir?"

"I remember the discussions Jim and I held with them in the retreat house. I have read Jim's reports of his earlier encounters."

"They are difficult to deal with. They cling to old traditions with a...tenacity that we find...incomprehensible."

"I remember."

"In his dealings with Sopha Luca, Jim saw it close up. They are reluctant, on the whole, to engage with the rest of the galaxy. Some of them have come around—probably the people you met. Some have not."

Tella nodded where it lay. "It is often the way."

"We brought enough of them onto our side, in part, with assurances of the sanctity of Mainworld. They need to know who goes there and what they do. They need to know it ahead of time. That's what they care about. Did Jim tell you they call Mainworld 'Beauty'?"

"He did. He says in one report he came to understand it is sacred to them. Though Sopha Luca seemed to care less for the people living there."

"Sacred. Yes, that's the word."

"Has Pritas then committed sacrilege?"

"Oh, yes. Big time. And here you are wanting to do it some more. And telling me there will be a stream of people coming and stomping all over their holiest place—for them, the holiest place in the universe."

"We must tell them that lives may be at stake. Are they not reasonable people?"

Madhar drank some more. "I thought you said you'd met them."

"I did. I met a delegation of philosophers. I met Margrev Aplar of the Second Order and a couple from the First Order."

"I know Aplar. He's a reasonable person. But, no, he's not typical. When it comes to their attitude to Beauty, there are few who are."

"Even in such a matter of life and death?"

"It's far more important than that. Particularly if they aren't Regdenir lives."

"Ah..."

"Your being here makes it worse, Tella. You must leave. And do it before anyone else knows you're here."

"I must find Pritas."

"No, you must leave."

"I sent Pritas on this mission. I translated the carvings on the Pongret M'dar."

"What's that?"

"A stone platform near Sopha Luca's retreat house. It is ancient. A Neraffan-jong carved its story into the rock."

"A story about being on Mainworld?"

"Yes. I wish events had moved less quickly. I would have liked to make a presentation to your government. But I was delayed helping Jim."

"My government wouldn't have let you come and present anything. Nor would the Regdenir."

Tella sat up slowly. "I find that difficult to understand. Why wouldn't they?"

Madhar watched the colors playing through Tella's skin as it moved. She sat back with a sigh. "I told you things are at a delicate stage. We're almost at the end of the negotiations with Earth's representatives. But the whole thing rests on the more extreme Regdenir being held in check by the First Order. Your Pritas has blown that."

"I'm sorry. How can I talk to them? How can I make them understand?"

"You? Definitely not you."

"What do you mean?"

"You're a gallassidnir!"

"I am?"

Madhar made a buzzing noise that Tella did not understand. "Folk legends—tall tales, if you like. We frighten our children with stories of creatures of glass, see-through and strange. Understand— you guys aren't the stories' heroes. Far from it. We're taught not to trust anyone like you from an early age."

"Interesting."

"Interesting? It's catastrophically unhelpful in terms of what you hope to do. You must go. Think of some other way to help your relative."

"Relatives. Though we don't yet know the size of the population remaining on Mainworld."

"You mean the number could be zero."

"It could."

"Again, you'll risk *our* galactic future—for nothing? For no one?"

Tella sighed and nodded. "I must."

"No, Tella. Not if I have anything to say about it. We're too close. I won't let you get in the way. Especially not on something so speculative!"

"Then, Professor Nect, we have a problem."

CHAPTER 56

INFORMATIONALS

Jim continued to stare at the images from Davey. "How did you find it?"

"Clo caught it. She has a thing she does automatically for every place you go. She sort of checks the gossip to see who's saying what. The warrant has Rob's face, clear as anything."

Jim put his hand over his mouth and swallowed hard to stop himself swearing. Nodding, he said, "Okay, Davey. Delete all references to this. Don't you—or Clo—mention it to anyone else. You've done the right thing showing me."

"Sure, Uncle Jim."

"No, really. You've done the right thing and"—he pointed at the images on the screen of Rob ransacking Pid's office—"what I'm seeing there is definitely something other than the right thing."

Davey nodded. "Umm..."

"What else?"

"That was kinda the ordinary news. There's bad news too. Sorry, Uncle Jim."

Jim rolled his eyes. "Okay. What?"

"The EIA has published an informational about you, asking for any sightings. They want to interview you. It's not an arrest warrant, but almost. Tella has an actual arrest warrant out there. There are several General Briefings from the OEA about you both too."

"Shit! I was expecting something about Tella—"

"And," Davey continued, "another informational from the office of the Regent on Tanna Gul. They want to talk to Ernot Dirl Marhan about an incident at 'The Luminary,' whatever that is."

"What kind of incident?"

"An explosion. Property damage and"—Davey looked off to one side—"a missing resident."

Jim started to laugh but stopped himself. "Did you kids rob any banks recently or get any parking tickets or speeding violations, Davey? Now's the time to tell me. It won't seem so bad."

Davey laughed and said, "No, we're keeping squeaky. Dad watches us constantly, even though he's on the other side of the solar system. Sorry, this is all kinda gloomy stuff."

"Don't apologize. But you've given me a problem."

"What are you going to do?"

"About Rob? Dunno. About Tella? He's gone off to do something worse. About me? I guess I need to disappear for a while. This call isn't traceable, is it?"

Davey shook his head. "'Course not."

"Good man."

"Anything Clo and I can do?"

Jim looked sideways at the screen. "Set up some way of making these calls that Rob won't find out about."

Davey hesitated. "Whoa! That's not an easy one. He's really good. I've learned a whole boatload of stuff from him already."

"You're good too. You'll work it out."

Davey nodded. "Okay."

"Who else has Rob hired for the office?"

"There's someone called Bernie. I'm not sure what she does. She's nice though."

"Bernie? Huh. Send me her details, and whatever Clo can find. Thanks, Davey!"

"No problem."

"Ship! End call."

"Acknowledged."

Jim sat in silence.

Eventually, Marhan stirred from where he had been sitting at the bottom of the ramp.

"I'm sorry, Jim. I should have told you the circumstances of bringing Betih out of The Luminary."

Jim replied without turning round. "Yeah, probably."

"Why is that kind of stunner banned?"

"The way they work. They can stop autonomic functions, like your heart beating or your breathing. They're indiscriminate. You might get lucky and have no aftereffects. But they can just as easily kill you."

"I'm surprised they haven't reached Gul. Many of my contemporaries would be impressed and think those are recommendations."

"You heard all the other news too?"

"I did."

"I'll have to disappear."

"Like the Neraffan."

Jim laughed. "Nice one! Where can we go that's so out of the way no one will reach us for a while?"

"There are places...places where life looks different from ours. The ends of the communication networks are usually empty. Of course, there are more lawless places nearer to the galactic center where many hide. But I think you mean somewhere few others go."

"Yeah. This ship is a good one. But its individuality is its biggest flaw. It's recognizable wherever it's docked."

"Gifts from the Praestans Rapax are—what do your blue friends keep saying?—'complicated.'"

Jim sighed. "We should have let Tella go in this ship and kept yours."

"You keep saying how rich you are. Rent a new one."

"I could do, but the funds won't last forever, and I've got a lot to do yet. I'm happy I didn't kill Katrigg, I mean D'Ghil; we'll call that a win. But I must find the people pulling the strings at Ch'Garratt. I don't know how deep that pit goes. I don't want Tella's legal troubles getting in my way. And I still have my sights on Daum Robertus Graffen. I guess those are my problems, in increasing order of magnitude.

"You mean Rob is a smaller matter? Will you be asking me to kill him for you?"

"You'd do that?"

"My aunt is better qualified."

Jim smiled. "Maybe. That's one I need to think about. I just don't understand why he'd do...that."

"You trusted him.

"And now I don't."

"We all make mistakes, Earth monkey. Learn from them."

"I've been spending a lot of money on building the business in Bunden Street. Rob is key to that. It'd be a huge pain—and expense—to start again with someone else. I need him."

"But I have heard you say the business is separate from you. Not traceable to you. Is that distance not enough?"

"I'm paying for it all." Shaking his head, he added, "If I'm paying him to assault people and rob them, what does that make me?"

Marhan laughed. "My aunt has written several books on such ethical matters. It seems you must learn this from her as well as...your other skills."

"Yeah," Jim replied distantly.

Marhan continued, "If it helps, I am grateful for your trust in me. I hope to remain worthy of it."

Jim turned to the huge canid. "Thanks. You're rude, overbearing, aggressive, and"—he sighed—"I can hear you snore even with your door shut. But, yeah, I trust you. I'm truly glad you're here. I guess Rob will have to wait. I need someone else in place before I resolve that issue."

Marhan gave a small bark and began to lope back up the ramp.

"Wait. Is Betih asleep?"

The canid turned and nodded.

"Tell me again. What is this thing she talks about—going out into the wilderness on Gul? Sounds like she's depressed."

Marhan stiffened and, shaking his head, said, "It is how we die —if no one kills us first. You feel the call. If the time has come, you go into a wild area alone and find your peace."

"And she's felt the call?"

"Long ago. But—irritating as she is—she is too valuable to waste."

"Hmm. I understand. And I can understand her wanting death on her own terms."

Marhan turned and glared at him. "As do I. It is not an easy matter. But I have no intention of giving in to her."

CHAPTER 57

SAFE STATION

Jim sat alone at the control panel near the command seat.

I wonder if D'Ghil is telling the truth. We could probably go to Sin Har. A short trip? Maybe find something about the true owners of the saucer...And the folks at the EIA are after me...No, not going to see them in a hurry. Can't go to Sonloi-AC; Jayde Duke is still in a sulk. Where can we go?

He input a series of locations into the navigation computer but instead of telling the ship to start the route, he stored the information for later.

The galaxy's communications network reached far out into the periphery in all directions. At the end of one long and little-used path, the constantly switching nodes reached a terminus beyond any inhabited planetary system. Nearby, astronomically speaking, a station hung suspended in the dark.

Jim had only been there once.

"Raeda, send a message to the Administrator of Safe Station, Hank Glenfold. Message reads 'I'm coming back.'"

CHAPTER 58

BETIH

After breakfast the next morning, Jim sat with Betih in the galley.

He thought, *You are so impressive. Can't ever admit it to you though. So odd, diminished and old, wrapped in your pink robe—but still more werewolf than anything else. The bad temper isn't so alarming anymore. A lifetime in academia. A professor of ethics. No wonder I'm only beginning to understand your moral outlook. How can I ever match you?*

Looking straight at her across the table, he thought, *Few would take you for an assassin, but here we are.*

She looked back across the table at Jim, who sat smiling. *That vacant, unintelligent smile—so common to simians. How could Marhan be right? He thinks there is evidence of the spirit at work. How can the spirit work in aliens such as this one? Few would take you for an assassin,* she thought, *but here we are.*

Jim asked a question. "Do you think I did the right thing, taking D'Ghil Bha's word that she wasn't responsible for the carnage at Ch'Garratt?"

Betih shook her head slowly. "I cannot say. It was you who talked with her. Are you a fool? Are you easily persuaded against the truth?"

Jim coughed. "I...hope not. No. I don't think so."

"Then, in all seriousness, do not ask me what I think. An assassin must have confidence in their own ability. There is only so much I can teach you. Are you not ready to make your own decisions?"

"I...I was relieved when I didn't have to kill her. And I was disturbed that I so easily killed Gror Gute. I still don't share the certainty you and Marhan have about me being a good candidate for this work."

Betih snorted. "This is what I have taught you. It seems you *have* learned something. No assassin will kill unless it is absolutely necessary. You will be sure. You will investigate and insert yourself next to your target long before the night comes when their life must end. Then there is no more doubt, no more words, no more debate. Of course you feel relieved when that moment does not come. Of course you feel—what did you say?—disturbed when it does. You should feel more than that. In Gute's case, you did little investigation. You did not place yourself close enough to evaluate the target properly. You will feel disturbed forever; death is undoable."

Jim shook his head. "You see? That's why I don't think I'm cut out for this."

Betih stood suddenly, her chair crashing behind her. Her paws hit the table with a snick from her claws. "Are you deaf as well as stupid, monkey? What you say *is* what qualifies you! The doubt, the concern, the unease you feel, all these *are* your qualifications!"

Jim chewed his tongue before saying quietly, "Marhan explained about your wanting to go off into the wilderness of Tanna Gul and die."

Still standing, leaning on the table, she spat back, "What of it?"

"I don't want you to die. I need you here. I'm not ready."

"You have Marhan. You have your transparent friend, Tella. You have the tools. You don't need me."

"Tella is working. Marhan? Yes. I'm glad to have him around. But he isn't you. Give him these tools, and he'd slaughter his way across the galaxy."

She laughed. "True. Never lend them to him."

Jim looked up at her.

The ancient assassin looked down at Jim. "You are not alone. You should not be alone. There is help all around you. We deal in death, but don't forget that ordinary life goes on all the while. You will get help from others. You *must* get help from others."

Shaking his head, Jim replied, "One, you say it's a secret. Marhan wasn't supposed to know you were an assassin, nor me. Two, it's a dangerous job. Involving other people puts them at risk."

She picked up her chair and sat down with a sigh. "Yes. Involving anyone in our business puts them at risk, a risk you may not be able to explain to them. I know. You must weigh the risks to them against the risk of letting someone live who must be stopped. It's never a simple matter. One can never say with certainty, 'in risking this one life, these ten lives, I might save twenty others.' Lives may be of equal worth in some ways, yet not in others. But remember, it is not your job to make such judgments."

"How do you—did you—decide such things?"

"For that, you must ask Marhan more about the spirit. Does the spirit not guide us? Do we not feel the guidance in our hearts?"

Jim squinted at her, not sure if she was being serious. "I don't know. Do you believe I'm in some way divinely inspired?"

She squinted back and mimicked his words. "I don't know."

Jim thought, *That isn't helpful,* but said nothing.

Marhan loped down the ramp into the galley and joined them at the galley table.

"I have received a summons. I must go to Tanna Gul. As Davey reported, General Dol, the regent himself, has asked to see me"—he waved his long paw vaguely—"about how Betih came to leave The Luminary."

Jim smiled. "And the property damage. And the injuries."

Marhan shrugged. Normally a dominating figure, he held his long limbs close and his head down, ears flattened against his head. "It could be difficult if he chooses to make it so."

"Why go back? Do you need to keep the Regent sweet?"

"Sweet? He is cunning and unscrupulous, both a politician and a general. Sweet is not a word to use."

"But he's the one paying you off, right? Allowing you to be here."

Marhan nodded. "True. He worries that I may still have influence."

Betih said, almost under her breath, "He wants to know if the Luminants still support you."

Jim frowned. "And now they don't. Because of the..."

Marhan growled back, "Some may still."

Jim paused, looked at Betih, and asked, "Are you going with him?"

She smiled and licked her tongue along the length of her mouth. "It would make it easier for Marhan if I did. I could say I came willingly, and the problems are to be hung on the tails of General Dol's enemies."

"Great! So that's what you're going to do?"

"No," Marhan replied flatly.

"No." Betih nodded.

Jim looked from one to the other. "What's going on?"

Into the silence, Betih said, "I taste dust and death in my mouth. If I go to Tanna Gul, I will not return."

Jim stared at the pattern in the tabletop. He got up and worked with the coffeemaker. When he sat down, they were both watching him.

"Okay. Marhan, you must go back. Keep all the friends you can. Betih, you must give Marhan your support. Make sure he's in good standing with the Regent." Before Marhan could object, Jim leaned forward across the table to him. "And make sure you don't let her out of your sight. Tie her up and gag her if you have to, but bring her back. She's not done here."

Marhan nodded but said nothing.

"Remember, monkey," Betih said quietly, "I could kill you where you sit."

Jim nodded in reply. "Remember what we were just talking about? That avoiding unnecessary death is just as important, if not more so, than the killing part. Neither your death nor mine are necessary. You might prefer death to living on an Earth monkey's ship, but that's just preference, not a necessity."

"You flatter yourself if you think my preference for death is relevant to being with you. I am old. I have heard the call. Marhan understands. I do not expect you to."

"No," Jim said, "I do. I do understand. But I'm also selfish and don't want to let you go. Your nephew wants his aunt to go on living. Why wouldn't he?"

Betih looked Jim full in the face and then gave Marhan a sideways glance. "I've said all I have to say about it. If I go to Tanna Gul, I will not return."

To Marhan, Jim said, "We'll go to Tanna Gul. I'll drop you off. While you're there, I'll go to Safe Station and sort out getting us a berth for a bit. I expect to see you both on the other end." He smiled at the elderly canid.

CHAPTER 59

TANNA GUL

Some spaceports are built in the hearts of great cities. But not all. In the case of the Tanna system, it was decided, for the safety of visiting aliens, the best option would be a neutral and uncontested moon. The sister planet to Gul and Jorr, Falt, bleak and uninhabited, possessed one moon with almost nothing to recommend it except the closeness it offered and the disdain in which both parties held it. A quiet rock was a useful sanctuary in a system that had known wars—on each planet and between them.

And so, on Tanna Falt Traplec, the spaceport sat without atmosphere, a hub for interplanetary traffic connecting with local traffic but providing no reason for any visitor to linger.

Jim landed his ship in a cloud of fine dust and waited for the docking tube to guide itself to his airlock.

"Okay, Marhan, keep in contact. You know how I worry." Jim smiled at the large canid.

"I will let you know if and when she misbehaves."

Jim laughed. "That's exactly what I mean." To Betih, he said, "It'll all work out. Just come back to the ship for a while after."

"Good-bye, Earth monkey. Use my tools well. Pass them on to a worthy successor when you, too, reach the end."

Jim narrowed his eyes and wondered whether to argue. "Whatever, Betih. See you later."

"Come with us," Marhan said suddenly.

Jim winced. "I can't. You know I didn't have a...happy time...when I was there last."

"Destroying the Raeff's fleet and being present at his death brought you no joy?"

For a moment, Jim was uncertain if the canid was being sarcastic. "It was a mission. I lost an expensive ship. I was pursued. I had responsibility for a young PR monk caught by gul troopers, who laughed as they shot him. I may have succeeded in my mission...but go back there? No thanks."

He waved them both up the ramp and through the airlock. Once the door had closed, he sat slowly in the command seat. "Raeda, show me the current political analysis of Tanna Gul and a description of any subgroups among the Luminants."

"Acknowledged."

The shuttle from Traplec landed in the sprawling city of Brurass. A uniformed driver met Marhan and Betih and escorted them to a waiting vehicle. The noise of the journey made Marhan smile.

"I had forgotten how badly we drive," he said to Betih.

She shouted, "It seems to be worse than before. I hope the crash sheets are up to it."

As if by command, the vehicle next to them drifted from its lane and sideswiped them.

"Apologies!" called the driver. He smiled, adding, "I won't go after him."

"Please don't. We're in a hurry," Betih called over the sounds of the metal sheets screaming as the vehicles again bounced off each other.

. . .

Through rocky canyons and across a wide area of sandy, burnt ground, they traveled to a temporary government camp outside the city. Flags of Tanna Gul, the country of Muthlec, Tanna Jorr, and the family crest of the previous Raeff fluttered inconsistently in the hot breeze.

Marhan sniffed the air as he stepped out of the vehicle. At once, three armed guards stood around him.

"Come with us!" commanded one.

"Am I under arrest?" Marhan rose to his full height.

"No, but the Regent wishes no delay."

"Bring the Luminant," Marhan replied.

The Regent's office was in a dark, one-story hut that Marhan thought was rather stuffy. *He needs to spend more time with his people.*

"Ernot Dirl Marhan! It is good to see you again."

"General Dol."

"Though part of our prior deal was that we would not meet."

"True." Marhan stopped and said nothing else.

"Please sit." The Regent sat behind a desk overflowing with papers and binders. He waved a long paw over them, saying, "The business of state. How would you have fared with all this shit?"

"I would have done what I could and delegated the rest," Marhan said quietly and without emotion.

The Regent laughed. "An engineer's response."

Marhan fixed his eyes and smiled.

An aide burst through the door. "Sir! Apologies. The car has left, and the Luminant Professor is still in it."

Marhan was on his feet. "Fools! What did I tell you?"

The Regent shouted, "Where did she go? Who is the driver?"

The aide shook his head, his ears flat against his skull. "The driver was thrown from the vehicle as it left. We do not know where she is going."

Marhan let out a yell and grabbed the aide by the shoulders, throwing him against the wall. "Fools!"

· · ·

The Regent had Marhan ride with him in the parade of vehicles fanning out from the compound. Their eyes searched the rocky wastes seeing only bleak and uninterrupted desolation.

Marhan growled in frustration. "She is gone. She is too clever to be found."

"Why? What does she want?"

"To die. She has heard the call."

"Why didn't you tell me?"

Marhan shrugged. "I did not give her permission to leave."

The Regent laughed. "I wouldn't have dared to try that with *my* elders. You thought you could sway a senior Luminant? An academic of such long service? You are braver than I give you credit for."

"Your staff are slow and stupid!"

"Of course they are!" he snapped, but then more quietly added, "It would be dangerous to surround myself with anyone else. How do you think I survive this job?"

Marhan said nothing in reply.

At length, Dol said, "Do any of the Luminants still support you?"

Marhan sniffed. "They might. Those who Betwen could sway were loyal. Any who understood Paun Mic Loff was insane would support me—or you—or anyone who could bring us back to common sense."

"And so, you see my problem."

"What problem?"

"Some still believe the previous Raeff to have been divinely sent. They are united. Those who think as we do...we are divided. Some regret you did not fare better in your attempted coup. Some think I am a fine interim choice. Some think the Raeff's child should lead. And the Luminants...seek to profit from such division."

"They haven't found a new Raeff?"

"No. No sign. No one is showing the requisite...insight."

Marhan laughed at the general's choice of word. "The deeds of our last Raeff shook my faith. My aunt's also. Yet we still believe the spirit will lead us."

Dol sighed. "I admire that belief." He stared out at the burnt landscape. "But I do not share it."

They rode on in silence. Marhan eventually asked. "Do you have a point in talking with me? Was it necessary that I come here in person? That I risked her so...my aunt."

The general's long snout rose up and down. "I do. I regret not seeing her first." To their driver, he called, "Return to base."

The driver did not return them to the Regent's office. Instead, they arrived at a small tent on the far edge of the compound.

"What is this?" Marhan asked.

"The point. This is where you were to report after the formalities were over." He grabbed Marhan's shoulder tightly as they stood by the vehicle. "Know this; you are free to go. I will ensure the Luminants will file no charges against you. The affair at The Luminary is forgotten."

Marhan nodded. "Thank you."

"But do not return," he hissed, "Our agreement is still in force. You will not interfere in Gul politics."

"I...am called elsewhere. You have nothing to fear from me."

The general nodded but gave Marhan a sideways glance and a low growl that reinforced the threat.

Marhan ducked under the outer flap, and the general followed him into the tent.

A young figure in a variation of the general's uniform sat picking food out of his mouth. His snout was shorter than a gul, and his fur neater and shorter than gul hair. The youth's eyes were on Marhan with an intensity the gul found unsettling.

"Hi, Marhan. Pleased to meet you."

Marhan swallowed. "You are Larc?"

Larc smiled. "Shouldn't that come with some sort of formal address?"

Marhan drew himself up and added, "Sir."

Larc laughed and said, "Sit down! If you haven't heard, I don't do things that way. Relax. Please sit."

With a suspicious glance, Marhan took a low bench and sat opposite the former Raeff's son.

"I've made it a point to find out about you, Marhan," Larc began.

Marhan waited.

"My Regent is good at telling me what he thinks I ought to know. For the rest, I read a lot." Larc waited long enough for Marhan to smile at the general's discomfort.

Larc continued, "I hear you travel with someone called Jim Able from Sol Earth."

"I do."

"I've met him. And the Neraffan Tella."

"I know him also."

"Hmm. Shouldn't that be 'it'?"

Marhan shrugged. "Whatever."

Larc raised a sharp, extended claw. "Tella, I have much respect for. It saved my life. Jim Able, I only met briefly. Tell me about him."

Marhan frowned and chuckled. "I don't know where I'd start with that question."

Larc nodded. "Leave us, Regent."

"Sir?"

Larc waved him away. "And the guards. I'm safe enough with members of the Ernot family, aren't I?"

The general sputtered. "I'd rather not put something like that to the test."

"Out!"

The general and several guards left the tent.

Immediately, Marhan asked, "Why? Why do you need to know about the Earth monkey?"

Larc got up and went to a side table. He arranged a mug and a bowl and poured a thick, fragrant drink from a thermos flask. Giving Marhan the bowl, he said, "L'hala pur gah."

Marhan squinted back. "I forget."

Larc smiled and said, "I say 'L'hala pur gah,' and you say 'L'hala ar di.'"

Marhan grunted and repeated, "L'hala ar di."

Larc waited until Marhan had licked some of the liquid from the bowl. Putting the mug to his lips, he sucked some up and rolled it in his mouth. "First, I'm sorry about your aunt. Jorr traditions are different, but I salute her and her life. Second, Jim Able? Because you travel with him. Because he single-handedly destroyed my father's fleet. There are rumors that you later explored on your own in the wilds around Traknho Base at his behest. He is obviously an 'Earth monkey' to be reckoned with."

Marhan licked along the side of his mouth. The figure before him was not physically threatening. His youth and his genetic makeup gave him an appealing aspect. *But,* Marhan thought, *Being the hybrid offspring of a Gul father and Jorr mother...makes you unpredictable. Dangerous. Keeping the rituals of Jorr—with this "L'hala"—here on Gul, you are holding fast to your special place in this system.*

Larc watched Marhan slowly working out how to reply. *A weight-control engineer with political aspirations thanks to his Luminant connections. How much of your life is your own? How much is the influence—the manipulation—of others?*

Marhan spoke softly. "Jim Able was sent to interview me by the Praestans Rapax. I thought I would see him only once. He returned to free me from the place they held me. I owe him."

Larc smiled. "Tell me about that."

Marhan shook his head. "I have neither desire nor need to talk of the Praestans Rapax. But Jim...did something unlooked for. Something good. I have witnessed similar actions in different contexts. He is not what I expected from his kind. I have heard previously he was present at your father's end. Does his presence not hold significance? He acted and acts...with spirit. Some would say, 'as a Raeff would.' As a Raeff should."

Suddenly, Larc understood. *A Raeff? An alien Raeff?* He had expected to meet a politically savvy engineer. But the clouds of gul religion overshadowed the tent. *Okay. Not a weight-control clerk. Nor a pawn of the ambitious females of The Luminary. A true believer. That makes you unpredictable. Dangerous.*

"Am I a Raeff?" Larc asked.

Marhan squinted at the youth, understanding that the question drew him to the edges of a precipice. "Does the spirit blow through you?"

Larc replied, sounding to Marhan more like the teenager he appeared to be, "How would I know?"

Marhan, reacting to Larc's tone, answered quickly and with some force. "Do you ask questions no one else asks? Do you see a path no one has yet walked? What follows you? Death? Life? Joy? Do you act at all? Or do you sit picking your lunch from your teeth and making mocking judgments about those brought before you?"

Oh, shit. I underestimated the fire in you, didn't I? Larc smiled and didn't reply at once. He looked the large gul up and down. "I'd like to have you around. What would it take?"

"You have all the advisors our world can offer. You do not need me."

"I said I'd *like* to have you around; I didn't say I *needed* you."

It was Marhan's turn to smile. "You are clever. I had heard as much, and now I see it. But I also know always having what you want is the biggest danger you face as you grow."

"Don't patronize me."

"Literally, someone had better. You need a father. You need a paternal influence who can guide you. I will not—I cannot—perform that role."

"I could order it. I'm sure General Dol would find a way to persuade you."

Marhan barked a laugh. "No. I have made my bargain with the general. I will not interfere in gul politics. I will not stay. I will not try—or appear to try—to influence you. I have other tasks to perform."

Larc weighed what to say next. "What if I *am* the next Raeff? It has happened before in gul history, where the son of a Raeff was equally"—he chose his words deliberately—"gifted by the spirit."

Marhan said simply, "Then my home world is in safe—if oddly shaped—paws. That would be a good outcome."

Larc laughed. "You know how irritating you true believers are, don't you?"

"I have been told."

"I saw the horrors my father inflicted on this planet and on Jorr. Was that the work of the spirit? You know...I don't know if I believe in the spirit at all. Does that shock you, Marhan?"

"You are young. You are untested. You are...unique. Everything about you is shocking. And yet..."

"And yet...?"

"The spirit has ways of making itself known. If not to you, then to those around you."

"Why wouldn't you want to be one of those...one of those around me?"

"I do not."

The hybrid gul-jorr sat up straight on his stool. To Marhan, it seemed as if Larc had come to some conclusion about him.

Larc said, "My mother is a scientist and a good one. I was raised in an academic institution on a planet that holds science in high regard. And yet, here I am, heir apparent—at least for now—to a ruined world that still is...what shall I call it?"—he shrugged and raised his paws slightly—"still in the shadow of superstition. Don't take offense; I don't mean any. But I hope you can see my problem."

Marhan grunted. "I hear similar words from the Regent. But General Dol's problem is a political one. Yours is a religious one—since you call the evidence of the spirit 'superstition.' I now know why the Luminants are unsure if they like you."

"I think your aunt might have. I'm sorry I didn't get to meet her."

Marhan looked at the ground. "The galaxy is worse off today. The general's staff are fools!"

Larc nodded. "Shall we leave it there, Marhan? We'll meet again. Say to Tella that I would welcome a visit."

Marhan looked Larc up and down, grunted, and stood.

"I also want you to bring Jim Able here. I feel...drawn...to see him again after what you've told me."

Marhan frowned, shrugged, and said, "I will ask. But I don't think he will come."

CHAPTER 60

FAMA

Jim's ship followed a long line of communications relays into sparsely populated space.

He wondered how Marhan was handling Betih. *I can see them coming to blows. Guls are so unsubtle.*

His ship intoned, "Approaching Safe Station."

"Show me."

A small bright dot appeared on his view screen. Nothing was yet visible through the observation window.

"Contact Safe Station Arrival Control."

"Acknowledged."

"This is Safe Station Arrival Control. State your business."

"This is Jim Able of Sol Earth requesting docking. Please send my greetings to Hank Glenfold."

"Stand by, Sol Earth craft. Messages may be sent once your status is confirmed."

Jim remembered his first visit. He never worked out whether what was behind the voice of Arrival Control was organic or mechanical. Its timbre and intonation sat exactly between the two. The formality could be rigidity either acquired through discipline or inherent in automation.

Jim waited for half an hour.

"Sol Earth craft, Jim Able. This is Safe Station Arrival Control."

"This is Jim Able. Is there a problem?"

"Please proceed to docking arm thirteen. Image follows."

Jim told his ship, "Accept the image and display it on the view screen."

"Acknowledged."

An image of Safe Station appeared. The huge egg-shaped station hung in the blackness, only faintly lit by distant stars. A red dot flashed regularly at one end.

"Ship, dock with the arrival arm as indicated."

"Acknowledged."

Previously, the arrival arm had seized Jim's ship and deposited it amongst the other craft on the station's outer hull through a series of maneuvers of its articulated joints. This time, an arm swung him onto a dark and otherwise unpopulated area of the hull, which immediately sank into the station's body. A door, sliding overhead, blocked out the faint view of the galaxy.

"This is new," Jim said to himself.

"Please restate query," the ship asked.

"Cancel query."

The ship shook slightly as something connected to the outer airlock.

The ship stated, "Safe Station is requesting docking."

"I've got it," Jim said, walking up the corridor and opening the outer door.

He was presented with a glass sphere that contained a couch and two single seats bolted to a skeletal scaffolding. He sat in one of the seats and fastened the seatbelt.

He tapped a command into his tablet, and the ship sealed the outer door.

Immediately, the gyro ball shot back and downwards. Jim had bewildering flashes of tunnel entrances and lit intersections interspersed with unpredictable lengths of disturbing darkness.

Suddenly, a large hall, bright with lights, opened around him. The gyro elevator stopped, and the clear door opened. He stood again in the Welcome Area, where staff from Safe Station examined every visitor.

A uniformed greeter—a human—called out, "Welcome to Safe Station. Return to your ships now if you carry any explosives or weapons. This is your only warning. You will be allowed no further into the station until you have been searched and screened. Line up behind the barrier in an orderly fashion. Harassing or threatening staff is punishable. Welcome to Safe Station."

Jim, with several other new arrivals, stepped forward to stand before high desks occupied by station officers from several worlds. The officer interviewing Jim looked down and asked, "Your business?"

"Jim Able, Sol Earth. Here as a private citizen. I sent word ahead to your administrator."

"Stand still. I will return." From his position, looking upward at the officer and her desk, Jim couldn't see where she'd gone.

Other visitors came and went and were processed and cleared while he waited.

"Jim Able, Sol Earth." The officer had returned.

"Still me."

"You are clear to enter. Take this."

Jim reached up to take a small device that fitted neatly into his palm. Rounded at each end, it looked like a small model of the station itself. "What does this do?"

"It will direct you to your accommodation. You may receive further communications through it; I don't know what's been programmed into it."

"Okay. Thanks."

"Next!"

Jim made his way to the main body of Safe Station. Vast walls of windows and balconies overlooked an enormous oval plaza. At one end gleamed a waterfall several stories tall, surrounded by landscaped gardens.

Jim remembered the bar that looked out behind the waterfall. He breathed deeply, and the smell of the water and the humus around the plants brought back more memories. *Crazy thing to do in a station! All that water, all the greenery. No one does this in a space station. It makes Sonloi-AC's arboretum look like a scale model.*

As he admired the glass and the natural-seeming light, the device in his hand lit up briefly and vibrated.

"Hello! What do you want?"

The otherwise black exterior of the device now showed an orange light on the left-hand side. Jim turned in that direction and the light moved to the front and turned green. *Nice!*

He followed the prompting to an open-topped train car that took him, at high speed, down through the gardens and stopped at the base of the waterfall.

The device led him up a long curved ramp through fragrant flowers and through a gentle spray from the thundering cascade of water forty or fifty feet away.

Jim found himself in the same bar he remembered. The long panoramic windows opened to a view of the waterfall and, at its edges, the rest of the station's long open interior.

Without thinking, Jim slid himself onto a barstool and ordered a beer.

He noted the other patrons: several humans, a few species he didn't recognize, and a table of Mallans.

At the far end of the room was a giggling party of Homalics—circular eyelids in a large loop of upper and lower eyebrows, triangular noses, double rows of sharp teeth, and fur on bodies and faces. They were young, female—as far as he could tell—and getting drunk.

Sometime during his third beer, a voice called from the doorway, "Jim Able! Jim! It's good to see you again."

"Hi, Hank! I was beginning to think you didn't want to see me."

Hank said enthusiastically, "Far from it, Jim. Just a bit busy with...stuff at the moment."

Hank was dressed like a gardener. His beard had turned grayer than Jim remembered. His eyes were no less bright and searching.

Jim slid off his stool and took Hank's hand. "It's been a while."

"Sure. But we knew you'd be back."

Jim nodded. "Thanks for the discrete docking."

"No one will see your ship. It's a fancy one. You know I want to know all about it and how you come to be flying it. But I'll wait."

Jim nodded again. "It's not a quick story; that's for sure. How's Fama?"

Hank lost his smile. "She's fine. Busy right now. She'll catch up with you later, okay?"

"No problem. So, it was you told this thing to bring me here?" He tapped the locator device on the bar.

"Good, aren't they? One of our guests came up with the design after getting lost trying to find their room a few years back."

Jim smiled. *Guest? That's what you're calling them? The young people with special talents?*

Hank put his hand on Jim's shoulder and steered him to a table. "So, tell me. Why have you come back now? What's been happening."

"You always did get right to the point, didn't you?"

"It helps when you're running something like this place. You in trouble?"

Jim shook his head. "Not really. Well...not yet."

Hank waved off a waiter but otherwise watched Jim's face.

Jim continued, "Ran out my welcome with my brother; he'd been letting me dock at his place. Don't want to push it too much at my mother's."

Hank waited.

"I'd like to find somewhere to dock my ship where it won't be noticed."

Hank said quietly, "Fama told me. That Praestans Rapax ship is a one-off. Easily recognized, easily followed. She said it wouldn't suit you for long."

"First time I've had a place to call my own, in a way. And, yeah, it came with certain...disadvantages."

"Look, Jim, I don't know the details. Don't need to tell me. But tell Fama. She's been watching you. You know she has."

Jim smiled. "I guess so. My nephew's girlfriend is gifted in that way—finding people. I remember Fama has a head start over everyone else."

"Just tell the locator 'to my room,' and it'll take you there. Settle in. Work out how much you want to tell us."

Hank stood and held out his hand. "Welcome back."

Jim stood as well. He shook Hank's hand and watched him stride out of the bar.

More beer.

He stood looking down at his half-empty glass. *No. I have a room* Hank said. *Better go see what it's like.*

He watched as his hand picked up the glass. He drained it and said to the locator, "Find my room."

Well, this is about as far from the bar as a visitor can go. Jim's room was at the other end of the station.

One entire floor, close to the high domed ceiling, ringed the station's central hollow. It was above the administration offices, above The Square—the official meeting place for the station's business—and above all the other floors with guest rooms.

These rooms must be for high-level dignitaries...or people they want to keep out of the way. Yeah, that'll be me.

The "room" was several large spaces. Jim went straight out onto the balcony. He had an unrestricted view of the entire operation.

Nice!

Just inside the balcony doors, he found a long table. Arrayed along it were the most sophisticated comms units he had seen: one for using the public nets, one for ultra-secure directed traffic, one that looked like it made toast. *I'll come back to you. It's a good start, Hank. Thanks.*

Jim lay down on the bed.

He woke to a knock on the door. Still blinking, he opened to find a small female alien with pale skin and silver hair swept back over her head in two rows.

"So what am I, fish entrails?"

Her eyes caught him by surprise, even though he remembered

them well—emerald-green eyeballs with pools of jet black that moved in a not-entirely natural way, as if she had learned to master seeing her way through a bewildering fog.

"Hi, Fama, come on in."

"Unless you're too busy."

Jim hung his head but smiled. "I heard *you* were busy. I was being patient."

"What does Hank know?" She stepped quickly into the room. "You're looking well."

"As are you." *But you're older. More lines on your face.*

"Thanks for the welcome and the stunning accommodation. Do I need to pay you for this?"

"Of course not!"

"I can. I came into some money recently."

"I know. First contact reward. Is it all official yet?"

"Nearly. Contact is established enough that the powers-that-be paid up."

Fama nodded quickly. "Yeah, they don't pay it out if they think they'll have to take it back."

"That's what I'm hoping."

"So congratulations on that. And for the briefings from both the OEA and EIA—a double achievement. You've a wanted gul living on your ship. And, then, there's the Neraffan." She shook her head. "Interesting company you keep, Jim Able."

Jim shrugged. "That's life."

Fama walked into the kitchen area and began to make a drink. "Only just, from what I hear about you being attacked on Flereat— really though, what in the name of all the gods were you doing there?—and again at Ila. You've had a couple of lucky escapes. I, of course, want all the details. I want to know how you did it. I want to fill in the truth behind what I read on the nets."

Jim nodded. "How long have you got?"

He was surprised by her answer. "As long as you need, Jim. You're home here."

Fama made a drink, mixing a powder from an unmarked glass jar, producing a pot full of bright blue steaming liquid.

Jim sipped it. "Whoa! What is this?"

"Tark. It's good for you. Even for humans."

"Nice."

"I stocked your cupboards. Shopping is best on level ten, if you ask me. But I go through phases of liking the more exotic stuff on the lower levels."

"I...I don't know if I'm moving in yet. I'm really grateful that you've set all this up."

"When you're ready, of course. I suspect you're here now because you're hiding from someone."

"No. But I'm not going back to Earth for a while. I want to let all that blow over before I go. I'm the proud owner of an easily identifiable ship...and I'd prefer to live unnoticed for now."

She stared at him before answering. "The ship is no problem. But many people come into the station. If they know what you look like, they can easily report seeing you. It won't be like you've disappeared."

"But you vet everyone who comes here. And you monitor them. I'd be safer here than anywhere else I can think of."

Fama looked back at her Tark. "That's what we do. And yes, within limits, you're safe inside the station. That's not the issue though. Let's talk about what you want to do out there."

"You and Hank are good at coming straight to the point, aren't you?"

"Don't see any reason not to."

"Okay. Straight to the point. Well...I can't tell you everything. You'll have to give me a bit of space there. I'll be doing work that sometimes...takes a while. Projects, I guess. I'll need to come and go unnoticed."

Fama drank but said nothing.

Jim continued, "I'll need good comms systems. I see Hank's already set me up there."

"You'll need to talk to your friend in Unity City."

"Rob? That's him. I've set up a business to find people. Had some early successes too."

She frowned. "Where? Who did he find?"

"A guy who was enslaved in some clandestine factory at the Hawkins Array. Freed some others too."

"Hawkins Array? That was you?"

"Well, no. It was Rob. But that's the business. He did good first time out. He tracked the guy down. Someone had fitted controllers on him and the others, so they worked like robots. Nasty business."

Fama nodded. "Business. No one risks doing that sort of thing unless they can make a lot of money at it."

Jim nodded in reply, wondering where she was going.

"So they did. And now they don't."

Jim frowned. "No. I guess they don't. Quite right too. Isn't that what law enforcement is all about? Rob called them in to clean it all up."

Fama's eyes scanned his face. Again, he felt the movement seemed slightly artificial. *Or are you just seeing differently from me?*

"I hear things. You know that."

"Sure."

"I hear the police at Hawkins Array were out of their depth before all this. Now it's worse."

"They always were understaffed."

"Yeah. Now they're under attack."

"What? What do you mean?"

"Things aren't going the way you maybe hoped. At least one big organization lost a distribution hub, staffed by the cheapest labor, embedded in a hugely popular—you might say 'strategic'—location. They'd like revenge and they're trying to take it out on your friends on Hawkins Array."

Jim looked away, toward the window looking out at the station, but he didn't see it. "Not really friends. I worked a job there once."

"What did you think would happen?"

"I thought the bad guys would get locked up. At least the slaves were freed."

Fama nodded and said, "Of course. Good outcomes. But not the story. Not the whole story."

Jim chewed on his tongue before saying. "No, I guess not. But I'm not sure you can know before you start investigating something.

You don't know where you'll go, how bad it'll be, or who might be behind it."

"Right. That's my point. The Hawkins people knew their limits. Dealt with the things within their power. The other things, even if they knew full well what was happening, they left alone."

"Yeah. I can see that. But no one should be forgotten, left to that sort of fate. That guy's sister was looking for him. Someone should have helped her. Helped him."

Fama got up. "Yeah, I was right. I said you were one of us."

"What? I mean, who?"

"We help people who don't have anyone else able or willing. We do what we can. But Safe Station doesn't stay that way by sticking fingers up the noses of criminal gangs. We don't willingly cost the nameless and the faceless guys behind those gangs large amounts of money. That's, after all, what they care about."

"Right."

"I'll be back. Let's talk some more."

Jim frowned. "Okay. Sure."

What was that? Is she telling me not to get involved...in anything?...Ever? I don't get it.

CHAPTER 61

HANK

Hank silently sat with Jim, listening to the waterfall outside the bar.

"So Fama was talking to me," Jim said.

"Yeah, sorry. She does that."

"No, I mean...she's concerned, I think, about me causing trouble for you guys."

Hank nodded. "Not my department. She does the worrying. I dig up the dead plants and put in new ones."

Jim smiled. "Amongst a few hundred other things."

Hank shrugged.

"If I stay here, I don't want to bring you any problems. I just need a bolt hole. Somewhere to keep out of sight."

"Ain't nowhere completely safe, forever trouble-free. You plant something from good stock, water it, fertilize it, talk to it. The bugger still dies on you."

"I can't see you talking to plants."

"Why not? They make better companions than some people. But don't take what she says the wrong way. She's seen a lot. She sees the patterns in things. She's seen people go down slippery slopes of their own making"—he lifted his hands a little and rocked his two index fingers from side to side—"and seen people climb back up. Maybe she knows the difference between the two?"

Jim shook his head. "You two don't talk like anyone else I know. You're so direct...until you decide to be hard to follow. I've spent my life around engineers and bureaucrats. You want to lay that out for me?"

Hank laughed. "Nope. You spent at least part of your life around your mother, didn't you? Did she lay things out like a technical manual? Bet she didn't. She's an artist, right? Bet she's a good one too."

"You've never met her. She's a force of nature."

"So are you. So's your brother."

"You know Matt?"

"Not met him, but I've heard about him."

"Yeah, we are quite a family, I guess. But I don't think of myself in those terms."

"Maybe that's what my wife is telling you. Your actions have consequences. Maybe more so than a lot of people's."

"Hmm. I guess...in some ways, they might. But I'm just an ordinary guy."

Hank laughed and laughed again.

Jim said, "When I was here before—the first time—you were having a bit of trouble with some plants."

Hank nodded.

"What happened? Did they sprout again?"

"Sure. We gathered up all the seeds, as best we could. Gave them a place to grow out beyond the inner shell with the kind of environment they like. One or two still surprise us, coming up somewhere inconvenient."

"Ever managed to communicate with them?"

Hank shook his head. "No. And those things that came looking for them haven't been back. But we're ready if they do."

"The galaxy is a strange place sometimes," Jim said.

Then Hank said, "Do you know anything—have you heard anything—about the Great Silence?"

"Except for how long it lasted. No one I know has any clue."

Hank nodded.

"But," Jim continued, "it's a worry. The idea that the galaxy could just stop." He shook his head. "It doesn't bear thinking."

"Ain't that like life..." Hank smiled.

"Got a gardening metaphor for it?"

"Not yet. Workin' on it."

Later in the day, Jim received a message from Marhan.

"My business is concluded. Shall I rent a ship, or will you return for me?"

I won't ask, but that's a "me," not a "we." What happened?

CHAPTER 62

ABOUT BETIH

Jim wanted his question to be gentle, quiet, and respectful. But his voice betrayed him. "What happened?"

Marhan hung his head. "She did what she said she would. The fools couldn't stop her. I...didn't stop her."

They walked slowly from the airlock down the corridor to the flight room. Jim sat on the command chair, and Marhan sat on the bottom of the ramp up to the sleeping modules—just out of Jim's eyesight.

They both looked out onto the dust and darkness of the Traplec spaceport.

"Now what do I do?" Jim wondered.

The silence lasted until Marhan said, "I met Larc, the hybrid child."

"How is he? Is he safe?"

"I think the Regent protects him. The boy is clever. Being half-Jorr, I don't trust him of course."

"The first time I met him, he ripped out his father's throat. Not something you forget in a hurry."

Marhan made a coughing bark and said, "That was the half

that's pure Gul. It's what many of us would have done given the chance."

Jim turned with a grim smile. "I...I was going to say that's not how humans do things. But that wouldn't be quite right, would it?"

Marhan looked up at Jim's face warily. "You have your moments. Oh, and Larc says I should bring you to meet him again."

"Really? Any reason?"

"No. I think he is curious about you. No arrangements were made, no timetable suggested."

"Okay." Jim turned back and was quiet again.

Marhan rose to go to his module, but Jim said, "She's truly gone? No chance of getting her back from...wherever she went?"

"She overpowered the driver. They found the vehicle. Beyond that, she left no trace. It is...our way. I admit it was right and proper"—his voice caught—"and sad."

Jim sighed. "I feel like I just started at a school only to have the whole place burn to the ground."

"You people have funerals and hold parties for the dead, don't you?"

Jim nodded. "Usually."

"We howl and move on."

Jim closed his eyes and said, "Yeah."

PART SIX

THE TRUTH

CHAPTER 63

SIN HAR

"Where are we going?" asked Marhan.

Jim replied, "Sin Har."

"Not Safe Station?"

Safe Station would be the safest choice. But it feels like retreating. We'll both mope about if we don't keep active. Damn you, Betih! How could you do this to us?

"Not yet."

Jim stood at the display to the left of his command seat. "Here. Here are my notes from my meeting with D'Ghil Bha. See what you make of them. I don't want to spend longer on Har than we have to. But she said there may be evidence there...evidence of who the people are, who tried to kill me at Ch'Garratt."

Marhan nodded and sat in front of the display.

Jim sighed and said quietly, more to himself than Marhan, "I could do with a drink."

Marhan snorted. "My aunt's death is nothing to celebrate."

Jim frowned. "There's more than one reason to drink."

"No. Celebrations are joyous, shared...excessive. Drowning sorrows in quiet corners helps no one."

"Maybe not. But—ask anyone—it's what I do."

"You have this ship"—he gestured to the display—"this golden saucer to find. A lead to follow. Let that be your distraction if that's what you need."

"It doesn't sound nearly as much fun. But it's probably for the best."

After a long conversation with its orbital authorities, Jim steeled himself for a return to Sin Har.

"What's it called again?" Jim asked Marhan.

Marhan read the display and replied, "The Steep Abyss."

"Ha! Abyss? I love the marketing hype."

"Are these Har people given to exaggeration?"

"Actually, no. They're sensible people, generally, very polite."

Marhan frowned. "I won't like them."

Laughing, Jim said, "With any luck, we won't meet anyone."

Some spaceports are built in the hearts of great cities. Ch'Garratt is one. The city itself is large enough to be clearly seen from orbit. The orderly ways of the Har can be seen in Ch'Garratt's construction, its decoration, and its efficiency.

Such orderly ways had resulted in the terminal's rapid reconstruction and return to operations.

For Jim and the others injured in the blast, the effects lingered far longer.

Exactly on the opposite side of the planet from Ch'Garratt spread a lightly populated area with no cities and no spaceports. When viewed from orbit, except for the thin line of the abyss, it showed featureless brown by day and featureless black by night.

They flew over trackless scrubland of dwarf bushes, sandy dirt, and the occasional startled creature. Without warning, the ground disappeared and reappeared just as quickly.

"What was that?" Jim shouted. "Raeda, slow us down and turn around."

"Reducing speed. Reversing course."

Marhan was standing up against the window. "There! The Steep Abyss."

Jim ordered, "Raeda, hover over the canyon."

"Acknowledged."

True to its name, the far wall of the canyon fell steeply from the scrubland into the shadow.

"Raeda, turn us around to see the other wall."

The ship turned slowly.

The deep trench opened below them, curving toward the north. The west wall's upper reaches had just begun to glow in the morning sunshine. Ferns and small trees filled narrow shelves, gently waving in the early breeze.

"Take us down halfway."

"Acknowledged."

The east wall blocked the sun, and the ship's internal lights immediately brightened.

"Do we know which part of the canyon the facility was built into?" Marhan asked.

"No. How long is the canyon?"

Marhan shrugged.

Jim called, "Raeda, give me the canyon statistics."

"The canyon designation begins where the walls reach more than three hundred feet. There are forty-two miles where the height varies between three hundred feet and half a mile. For a further twenty miles north the wall height averages two hundred feet and is called the Brother Abyss. The temperature—"

"Stop," Jim called. "We'll have to fly it all. D'Ghil gave me no clue where to look, except it's built into the wall."

Marhan nodded.

"Raeda, plot a scanning run for the whole length of both abysses. Retrieve my personal file called 'Golden Saucer.' We're looking for a cave or opening large enough for that craft to enter and be concealed."

"Acknowledged."

"Begin when ready."

The ship lurched upwards into the bright sunshine and spun south.

Jim sat in the control seat, resting his chin on his hands and drumming his left foot to unheard music. He glanced left and right at the steep rock walls passing on either side.

Marhan stood forward by the windows. "There is nothing here. Some vegetation down on the floor. I see no sign the Har come here."

"No, probably too difficult. I guess they have backpackers and tourist groups."

"Wait! There. Up above."

Jim jumped up and followed where the canid pointed.

On the west wall, two tiny figures stood on a narrow path, looking down at the ship as it passed.

"So, someone's here."

"Friend or foe?"

"Raeda, are those people Har?"

"Affirmative."

"I wonder what they're up to?"

"Please restate query."

"Cancel query. Continue scanning for caves."

"Acknowledged."

The canyon sank deeper and darker. The glow of sunlight from the upper west wall grew brighter but showed them little of the ground below.

. . .

After many minutes of steady flight, the ship slowed and rotated to face the east wall. "Candidate cave detected."

Jim and Marhan strained to make out the differences in shadows along the wall.

"Lights! Let's see it."

The exterior lights transformed the gloom. The wall became a colorful canvas of lines and streaks almost parallel to the canyon floor. The darkest lines stopped and started, sometimes wide, sometimes thin. Jim could see rocks sparkling with gold and silver amid patches of greens and blues.

A bright red layer, scored into the wall, ran just at the height they hovered. Above this was a thin black shadow.

"Is that it?" Marhan asked. "That's an opening?"

"Raeda, Is the area above the red rock layer an entrance?"

"Affirmative."

"Can we fit?"

"Clearance two feet."

"Slowly then. Take us in."

"Acknowledged."

CHAPTER 64
THE BASE

At first, the gray interior of the cave—in contrast to the colors of the canyon outside—made Jim think it was foggy.

"Raeda, increase the lighting outside."

"Acknowledged."

"It doesn't help," Marhan grumbled.

"The floor looks flat. Raeda, set us down."

"Acknowledged."

"Scan for other ships."

"No contacts."

"Any signs of machinery?"

"Negative."

"Just a cave, then?" Jim wondered.

"Or are things well hidden?" Marhan countered.

Jim nodded. "We'll soon find out."

In the cool air of the cavern, their breath made clouds around them as they moved away from the ship.

"It smells old," Marhan said.

"And a little damp."

. . .

The cave spanned a hundred feet back into the rock but much farther to the left and right. The back wall was an unmarked rock-face, and the floor a smooth layer of rock with only small grit and pebbles scattered across it.

"I wish Tella were here," Jim said.

"So it could hide to its heart's content?"

Jim chuckled. "No. When we first went to the artificial asteroid where we met you, it could tell from merely looking at the surface that it wasn't natural. I couldn't distinguish it from the rest. But Tella could."

"You think this place had been manufactured?"

"Sure. It's also too small to hide anything like a ship for very long."

Marhan snorted and walked to the back wall. Jim followed, searching the ground for traces of wheel tracks or footprints.

The cave echoed with the deep toll of a metal plate. Marhan struck the wall again and shouted, "Here! This is not rock."

Jim was at his side. He reached up and rubbed his hand over the surface. "But made to look like it." He pointed to the right. "You go down that way and see when the sound changes. I'll go over here."

Marhan nodded and strode away. Every few steps, he hit the wall with his clenched paw. Jim walked the other way. Each time they hit the wall, the sound was the same.

Jim's fist hit the wall with a soft thud when they were two hundred feet apart. "Here!"

Marhan walked farther on until he, too, hit the rock. "And here!"

"Look for a mechanism of some sort." Jim called, "Probably hidden under a cover."

Many minutes passed in silence as they each searched for some protrusion, indentation, or switch.

Marhan called back, "Nothing!"

"Nor here." Jim stood back to appraise the wall again. He stepped back farther, looking from end to end. Still saying nothing, he walked away toward the ship. The ship's lights shone over him as he sat on the floor roughly opposite the center of the metal door.

Marhan muttered and slowly loped back to join him. "Are you tired by our activities?"

"No. Just thinking."

Marhan sighed and waited, sitting on his haunches.

"You fly in. Just as we did." Jim held his hands parallel to the floor. "You set down out here." He lowered his hands. "No. Why do that? There's no tracks or conveyor out here. You have to fly farther in once the doors open." He raised his hands again. You have to open it remotely."

"Or have someone waiting to open for you."

Jim nodded. "True. But what about when you've all left? When there's no one home?"

"In that case...I would make sure there is another way in."

"Right. You need a way in from above. Or a way out to the surface if there's an emergency. But for a ship? There must be a signal—sent from the ship, received by the door."

"We have access to neither."

"Right. Without access to the door mechanism, there's no way of telling what the signal might look like."

"We could destroy the door."

Jim didn't reply. He continued to stare at the plain metal made to look like rock.

"When you built the Raeff's fleet at the Traknho base, no one saw you do it, did they?"

"No. We erected the canopy to make it look like a lake."

"They would have had to do the same here. I mean to build...this. I'm guessing there's a whole lot that's worth concealing behind there. I'm sure they didn't fly it all in."

Marhan nodded. "Up above. A flat area big enough to land a freighter, a large ramp, somewhere to keep construction vehicles."

"That's what we're looking for. Easier to find than a door control."

.   .   .

Back aboard, Jim asked the ship, "What's the optimal placement of an access ramp for a facility behind the metal door in the cave?"

"Please specify parameters of 'optimal placement.'"

Jim sighed. "A ramp angled for the safe use of large construction vehicles descending to the cave's depth."

"Analysis complete."

"Show me."

The ship displayed a map of the surrounding flatlands with an area colored to show the possibilities.

"Okay. Take us up above this area. Scan for equipment, entrances, disturbed soil"—with a glance at Marhan, he added —"canopies or covers."

The ship backed out of the cave mouth and swept up over the canyon wall.

"There it is," Marhan said, pointing out the front window.

"Where?"

The ship intoned, "Candidate site located."

"I don't see it," Jim said, frowning.

"Much of the ground is a different color from the rest of this scrubland. There are two long lines—there to the north and coming down this way," Marhan said.

"Got it. If that's the ramp entrance, it's buried under the sand. Raeda, set us down just to the east of the site."

"Acknowledged."

"Scan for a door, a hatch. Is there an opening?"

"A shaft, four feet square, is covered by a hatch."

"Yes! That's our way in, Marhan."

The canid nodded and smiled.

The scrubland surrounding the canyon stretched for mile after mile. The short bushes clung to the ground as if fearful of becoming airborne. What life there was moved with caution, precision, and speed.

Marhan and Jim stood above a small square hatch covered in

fine dust. Around it, camouflage nets hung from piles of rocks, covering dirt and broken machinery.

"It, too, may need a signal to unlock it," Marhan said.

A strong breeze blew, swirling dust around them.

Jim shuddered briefly. He hated sudden breezes, particularly ones carrying dirt and grit. The sensations of being on a planet sometimes contrasted uncomfortably with the clean orderliness of life on the ship or a space station.

Jim reached down to brush the sandy material from the hatch. "Looks like a manual lever."

He grabbed the inset handle, pulled it outwards, and failed to make it turn.

"Shit."

Marhan leaned over, wrapped his long paw over the handle, and, bracing himself, pulled. The mechanism shuddered with a grinding screech. The hatch opened, and small piles of sand hissed into the opening.

Jim looked down. "Huh! A ladder. How quaint."

"Remember, this is our only way out," said Marhan grimly.

"I know. I know. Flashlight set?"

The canid held up his flashlight and indicated the blaster at his waist.

Jim shrugged. "Here we go."

The climb down the ladder was short. The last rung left them on a flat footpath, a rock wall on their left, and a short drop onto a sloping roadway on their right.

They followed the path, taking stairs down at regular intervals as they descended.

Marhan repeatedly drew his flashlight beam across the walls and ceiling. "This is good work. Our engineers have built many underground facilities like this."

Jim nodded. "Yeah, I guess money wasn't much of an obstacle to the folks in charge."

Marhan chuckled. "Perhaps like you—independently wealthy."

Jim smiled and said, "I'm thinking an order of magnitude or two more than I can muster."

The last set of stairs deposited them against a metal wall, blocking both the path and the ramp.

"This is the same as out in the cave," Marhan said.

"We haven't traveled far enough for it to be the same door," Jim replied.

Two human-sized doors were visible, one to the left and one to the right.

Jim asked, "Which way?"

Marhan shrugged. They went to the left-hand door. It was unlocked but opened with reluctance.

Jim moved the beam of his flashlight across a large, bare room.

"Nothing."

Marhan sniffed the air. "My guess is no one has been here for a long time."

They crossed the room to another door which led to a staircase going back up.

"What the hell is this place?" Jim said.

The staircase led them into a large office area of desks, dark monitors, and dusty chairs.

They explored carefully. Jim tried to switch on a monitor but without success. "Offices are the same on every planet. I'd hate to have to work in one."

"I did," admitted Marhan, "They are the breeding grounds for revolution. And also for depression."

Marhan kept to the right-hand wall where no furniture obstructed the way. He trained his light on the wall to see an area of long slats. "Ah. Here we have something."

"What?"

He held the flashlight in his jaws and reached up to force a slat to turn. The metal strip buckled but would not turn.

"This is powered somehow."

"What is it?"

"It covers a window."

"Right. We need the power back on. Where would you install a safety cut-off?"

"Within easy reach."

Within a few minutes, they found a cupboard on the same wall as the window slats. Mounted within were several panels of switches and miniature lightbulbs, dark and unlabeled.

"What do you think?" Marhan asked.

"Complicated setup. There's probably a correct order to follow when starting up from cold."

Marhan stood back and let Jim examine the panels and look down their sides and farther inside the cupboard.

"Oh, that'll do." Jim stood back and took the tablet out of his pocket. He pulled the tablet's small extendable plug and, pulling out the cable to its maximum, reached in with it to the bottom of the lowest of the panels.

Images flashed across the tablet's display, too quick for Marhan to see. "What is this?"

"Umm...a hacking program I wrote. Not really finished yet, but this part may be useful. It's trying all the standard protocols used to maintain equipment like this. If it finds one, the system reacts—Oh, there we are..."

The flashing images had stopped, and a small window showed three input fields.

"This is an odd one." Jim typed nonsense into all three input fields. There was no reaction in the window or over at the panel. "Okay. I need to let it work its magic." He propped the tablet against the cupboard door and entered several more commands.

Marhan moved his light from the tablet to the panel and to Jim's face. "How long?"

Jim shrugged and smiled. "Are we in a hurry?"

Marhan replied with a growl, "That depends on who knows we are here."

Jim waited while Marhan explored more of the office—opening drawers and cupboards, occasionally muttering in his own language.

A small orange light lit up near where Jim's device was plugged in. "Got something!"

Marhan was quickly at his side but growled with frustration. "You have an orange light."

"I have a *stand-by* light. That means there's activity along this row." His fingers flicked each switch. Several new lights lit in the rows above.

"Be careful!" Marhan said, "Do you know what will happen?"

"If it's booted into diagnostic mode, almost nothing will happen. Only the most basic services will be running. It will default to the safest settings."

"And?"

"And? I have no idea. I don't even know what kind of system this is. I'm guessing it has to do with the power. The fact that there are no labels tells me it's all so obvious no one ever needs to be told."

"Ha! Except us."

"We're special."

One small light behind them in the room's ceiling began to glow faintly.

Jim looked away from the cupboard and up the wall next to the slats. A small panel protruded from the wall with a single button. He reached up and pressed it.

The window slats rotated ninety degrees, making only a soft rattle in the quiet.

"Power is on," Jim noted.

Marhan put up a paw to bend a wider gap between two slats. "Ah..."

Jim stood next to him and looked through the window.

A huge open area spread out below them, several stories deep. Small lights in the roof reflected faintly off the ships parked across the floor.

Jim let out a long sigh. "There it is."

"The saucer."

"The saucer."

"What do you make of the others?"

"Hmm. Personal flier, older style. That larger thing is an orbital shuttle, generic—the sort of ship no one would notice."

"Those small ones interest me," Marhan added.

"One-man fliers?"

"Or something from a dwarf species."

"Could be. Could be."

"We need to get down there quickly. Whatever you need to do must be done before anyone can react to the power returning."

Jim looked up at Marhan's face. "Which way do you think?"

"We saw only the freight door as we came down the ramp. This way." He indicated a door at the other end of the office.

Jim nodded. "I hope I can disconnect..." He unplugged his tablet from the panel and glanced nervously up at the light. It remained glowing.

Their descent to the hangar floor was marked only by the echo of their footfalls on the staircase.

They walked quickly and quietly to stand silent in front of the saucer-shaped craft.

"It's exactly as I remember it." Jim paused to fish a napkin out of an inner pocket. Marhan looked over his shoulder.

"You drew this?"

"No. D'Ghil gave it to me. Can you see the cargo ramp? That's where she went in...that day."

They walked slowly toward the ship. Large and sleek, it stood on delicate legs, its curves perfect and uninterrupted by external units or antennae. The gold surface that had impressed Jim when he had first seen it, seemed dull and dirty in the low light.

Around the other side, they found the cargo ramp extending to the floor. Wrapping material lay in bunches, stringing from torn boxes whose empty shells littered the ramp and floor.

"Someone has been partying," Jim said.

Marhan glanced around. "Same with the other ships. We're not the first visitors."

"Let's go up. Carefully."

Marhan drew his blaster and followed Jim up the ramp.

Cold air greeted them inside the saucer.

Marhan sniffed the air. "Something is rotting in here."

"Careful where you walk."

Their flashlights showed a wide cargo bay, the ceiling only a foot above Marhan's head.

Consulting D'Ghil's drawing again, Jim pointed across the cargo bay. "Over the other side, another ramp goes up to the next level."

"Her information is good so far," Marhan commented.

Nodding, Jim said, "I had a feeling she was being truthful. I think the people who own this ship served her badly when they brought it here."

A faint noise came from outside the ship, across the hanger deck. Marhan swung around to look back to the loading ramp. He switched off his flashlight.

Jim hit the switch on his and stood in the pitch black, listening. He heard Marhan breathing but nothing else.

They stood long enough for Jim to become even more aware of the vulnerability of their position inside a ship with only one exit in a facility where the way out was nowhere close.

"What do you think?' he whispered.

Marhan moved in the dark. His voice came quietly, near Jim's ear. "I think we should be quick. I do not know what caused the noise. It could be wildlife; it could be trouble."

Turning the light back on, Jim checked on the drawing. "Up there."

They ascended to the ship's next level up a narrower and curving ramp.

Marhan pointed at the wall as they passed. "Blaster damage."

Jim looked at the black streaks crisscrossing the metalwork. "Both directions. Not just an accidental discharge."

"Didn't she say they argued?"

"She did. I hadn't understood she meant...this."

"Where now?"

"This is the middle level. Flight room access round the other side."

"The further in we go, the more trapped we may become."

Jim smiled grimly. "No choice. I need to see the flight room. I need to find some clue about the owners. When we've done that, I want to get into the other ships too."

"If we have time."

They walked through more debris, empty crates, and the sites of more blaster fire.

A narrow spiral staircase led from the middle level to the flight room under the dome atop the saucer.

Marhan muttered as they moved carefully up the stairs.

"What did you say?" Jim asked quietly.

"I begin to see the artifice in this design."

"What do you mean?"

"The flight room is highly defensible. I presume there is an elevator as well. But no sane attacker will try this way if you secure *that*."

"True."

Small creatures scuttled into the shadows as they entered the circular flight room.

"Company," Jim commented with a smile.

"There must be something for them to eat."

"The smell is worse here."

Several furry bodies launched themselves down the stairs, squealing.

Marhan followed their path with his blaster.

Jim turned his flashlight around the room. "Do you recognize this technology?"

Marhan grunted. "No. It seems inconveniently small for a gul."

Jim examined the two command seats. "Someone's been eating the stuffing out of the cushions."

They looked at the banks of instruments—some ripped partly out from their mountings.

Marhan asked, "Can you start these stations as you did the power outside?"

Jim's light caught a small plaque on the wall. "Might not need to."

Walking around the instrument banks to the otherwise bare part of the wall, he read out:

THIS ship
    CRAS.du.nun.me.1245.9980.5467
    MADE in bar.el.ion
    ALL that is good and profitable
    THIS to all in traveling thus

Marhan laughed. "Did D'Ghil tell you what species her employers were?"

"She wasn't precise. They appeared to be human. But this...style of writing I know."

"And?"

"Daa Hobb is the planet. I think the people call themselves Tuc. I had to read stuff from them sometimes at the OEA. Not sure if they *can't* write Standard properly or *won't*."

"I've heard of them. They are not like us."

"Right." Jim recorded an image of the plaque. "But I guess they keep records and, with the right inducement, might tell us who commissioned the ship."

"Perhaps those small craft outside are theirs. Can we go now?"

"There's more to find. I'd like to stay longer. But..."

Marhan drew himself up to his full height and said, "It is time to leave."

Jim nodded. "Sure.

All was quiet until they emerged once more onto the wide cargo ramp.

A strong voice from the darkness said, "Raise your hands in the air. Do not attempt to resist."

Five figures in flowing robes approached the ramp, one from ahead, two from either side, all pointing blasters.

Marhan growled softly.

Jim called out. "Identify yourselves. We mean you no harm."

"It is you who are strangers here. It is you who must identify yourselves" came the reply.

Jim waited, a smile forming on his lips.

"Are these Har?" asked Marhan quietly.

"Count the fingers. Eight is usual."

"Is this your ship?" Jim asked.

"It is not yours."

"No. But I need to find this ship's owners. Is that something you can help a stranger with?"

"This is a wild and dangerous place, at the very border of civilization. Answer our questions, or your families will not find your remains."

"How rude. I have never heard Har so unwelcoming to visitors."

The lead figure laughed. "We are not Har."

"You seem to be. You are tall, eight-fingered, and speak Standard better than I do. If you aren't Har, who are you?"

"For purposes of classification, we are Sin Sojan. We do not recognize the Har as the representatives of our species. We do not accept their ways. And you cannot expect to use their crippling politeness against us. You will now answer our questions."

Jim nodded.

Marhan whispered, "You know these people?"

Under his breath, Jim replied, "Not a clue. Better do what they say. For now."

They moved down the ramp. Jim raised his hands in the air. Marhan watched and did the same. As they walked, Jim said, "I am Jim Able of Sol Earth. My friend is Ernot Dirl Marhan, of Tanna Gul. Your name?"

"Jim Able. Sol Earth. I know that name. I know of no one from Tanna Gul."

"Lovely place," Jim lied, "you should visit."

"I will walk ahead of you until we reach our vehicle. The others will move behind you. They will kill you if you try to escape. Remain silent."

Marhan growled but said nothing.

Jim turned off his flashlight, dropped it in a pocket, and took out his tablet. As they walked across the dark flight deck to a far door, he entered commands to order his ship into a full security lockdown.

Their captors guided them up a staircase lit by small openings drilled in the canyon wall. They emerged back onto the surface to the bright sunlight, heat, and swirling dust.

A camouflaged bus waited, engine purring, alone near the canyon's edge. Both Jim and Marhan glanced round to check on Jim's ship. It squatted—out-of-place and easily spotted—several hundred feet away. Another bus hovered next to it.

"Where are you taking us?"

He received no answer except for hands pushing him into the bus.

They made Jim sit in the first seat on the left and Marhan opposite on the right. *What a cheap vehicle,* Jim thought.

The seats were threadbare, and the windows were smeared with dirt. Several upright handholds were dented and marked. The noise of the engine was louder inside than out.

Jim glanced over to see Marhan frowning. "Nice ride," he commented, "Rich fittings." He stroked the material of the seat.

Marhan smiled and nodded.

"Silence," the lead Sojan repeated.

The bus may have been old and dirty, but it was fast. The bare land flashed by them as they followed the canyon's edge south.

Half-an-hour's journey brought them to a single-storied building surrounded by large tents. The same low bushes clung to the ground. The same sand blew into Jim's eyes as they descended from the bus.

The building was cool and quiet. They entered a vestibule, and the lead Sojan ordered, "Place your weapons on the table. No tricks."

Jim chewed his tongue but nodded. Marhan reluctantly placed his large blaster on the table. Jim placed his next to it.

Instead of being taken into another room, they were hustled out across the sand and brought to the sudden edge of the canyon.

"When you came to the Steep Abyss, which side did you come from?" asked the Sojan leader.

"The south," Jim replied, hoping to irritate his questioner.

Raising his arm and pointing, the Sojan asked, "Did you visit the western lands across the Abyss?"

"No. Why would we?"

"We live on the edge of civilization. Some still live in the west. They are even more of a danger to visitors than we are. Answer me truthfully and count yourself lucky we found you first."

"And who are you?" Jim asked with a smile.

"I am Starf, Hunga of Matta."

"I am Jim Able of Sol Earth, and I'm pleased to meet you, Starf. What's your business with the golden saucer?"

"This is our planet. This is our home. These lands are our lands. You are the stranger. It is you who must explain your presence here."

"I registered our presence with the Har authorities when we entered orbit. They were nice enough to allow us to enter your atmosphere and land where we chose."

This was met with general derision.

"We do not give Har license to invite aliens to break into our facilities, examine our vessels, to delve into things that are private."

Jim frowned. "So, you're what? An independent nation? Not under Har law?"

"We believe the Har to have wandered from the truth."

Marhan asked, "Who enforces the law here? You or the Har?"

"We do. You can expect no help from them. If we find fault with you, we will send you to the bottom of the Abyss."

Both Jim and Marhan looked around. They could see the shadows lower in the canyon but not much more. Small sand spouts whirled around their feet and disappeared over the edge. The Sojan moved closer around them in a threatening semicircle.

"I'm sorry," Jim said, nodding. "I was unaware that Har

authority wasn't recognized here. If I'd known, I would have come to you first."

"To do what?"

"I said already. I need to find the owner of that golden ship."

"What business do you have with them?"

"You must be aware of what they did."

"What do you mean?"

"The attack on Ch'Garratt Terminal Two. The deaths. The injuries. The destruction."

"What is that to you?"

"You said you'd heard of me. I can't think of any other reason you would. I was one of the survivors."

The Sojan shook his head. "That does not yet explain why you and...a gul broke into the Mattadrah base."

"Hmm. 'Mattadrah Base.' Okay, so it has a name."

The Sojan didn't reply.

Jim continued, "I don't think you own that ship. You know its history and my name, and if you were responsible for the Ch'Garratt business, you'd have probably killed us already."

Marhan added, "But you own the base, don't you? It was you who built it."

Jim's heart was racing at the thought of the long drop. His mind was racing through the details D'Ghil had told him. *They hired D'Ghil. They attacked Ch'Garratt. They flew up to orbit and then round to hide here. They were using the base already. This was an established hideout. Why is it in disuse now? That's a whole lot of investment going to waste.*

Starf was answering Marhan. "We build strong and well. We know the ground. We know the rocks. We know the ways of the Steep Abyss. We know how to be one with the land."

Jim nodded once and smiled at Marhan's salient insight.

"Here's what I think." He glanced at Marhan. "I think they paid you a lot of money to build Mattadrah Base for them. And, yeah, you did a nice job. A lot of work...not just the construction but the keeping it secret, making sure no one comes here...But then something went wrong. Something to do with the attack on Ch'Garratt. That's what I'm trying to find more about. We don't know them. We don't have any ties to them. And since they almost killed me, I'm no friend of theirs, am I?" Jim paused, thinking quickly. "They haven't come back. That much is obvious. They left a mess. And"—he held up a hand to ensure he had their attention—"they've stiffed you for the parking fees, haven't they? They haven't been back, and they haven't paid you what they owe."

Starf looked uncomfortable. "You are looking for revenge?"

"I'm looking for *them*. What I do when I find them is my business."

Marhan spoke up. "The base is a mess. More money to clean it, to make it useable again. You need someone who will use it. Someone who will pay you."

Jim frowned but didn't interrupt.

The canid straightened up to his full height and continued. "My friend has a ship—you saw it. Like the saucer, it is easily recognized. This would be a good place to keep it. I am wealthy—even for a gul. I will buy this base from you and give it to my friend."

Starf glanced at the Sojan to his right. "Even if you were serious, a contract is still in force."

Jim jumped in to say, "Tell us who with. I'll go and negotiate with them directly."

The Sojan laughed and said, "And kill them? How will that help us?"

Marhan said, "I want the base. I promise they will not die without ending their contract with you first."

To Jim's surprise, the Sojan all found this amusing. Indicating the canyon's edge with his thumb, he asked, "Can we discuss this somewhere more comfortable?"

Their captors relaxed, lowered their weapons, and stepped aside for the pair to return to the building.

A courtyard, covered with a thin semitransparent roof, sat in the center of the building. Jim noticed the patches of dust and sand piled by the winds on the roof's corners and seams.

The air inside was cool and clean.

The Sojan arranged chairs in a circle inside the courtyard and made Jim and Marhan sit opposite Starf.

As they removed their robes, Jim could see some physical differences between these residents of Sin Har and those he'd dealt with before.

Starf's skin was dark, possibly tanned or wind burnt. Where the Har's eyes were widely spaced, his were closer together. His nose seemed narrower and better able to avoid breathing in dust.

Marhan sat and watched the Sojan's fingers, finding the subtle motions of eight digits unsettling.

Jim tried to get control of the conversation before Starf. "Tell me, please...help me understand the difference between yourselves and the Har. It's a real surprise to me."

Starf sighed and replied, "They are the dominant people, much to our regret. Their politics and their industry overwhelm our world, while we keep to the traditions of our ancestors as much as we can."

Marhan snapped his jaws. "You have blasters and hoverbuses. You build technologically advanced bases in the rock."

"We live in their world. We share the galaxy with you, even if we travel rarely. We teach our children Standard, and mathematics, and engineering. We buy and sell. Of course we do! How else could we survive?"

Jim nodded. "But that doesn't mean you like it."

Starf bowed in agreement.

"So, how can we help each other here?" Jim asked. "We need information. You need better tenants."

The Sojan smiled and narrowed his eyes at Jim. "First, we must understand who you are and how you came here. How did you find a secret and well-hidden base? How did you start the emergency power systems we had powered down?"

Jim smiled and asked, "How long since you heard from your customers?"

Starf held his hands up, all the fingers wide, and said, "All information has a price."

Jim replied, "I agree."

Marhan growled again. "And the base currently earns you nothing. You maintain a home for vermin."

To Marhan, Starf replied, "It currently costs us nothing." To

Jim, he said, "For negotiations to begin, you must show us proof of your identity, your authority to negotiate, and your ability to back your desires with the appropriate funds."

The Sojan at Starf's right spoke up. "Our ways of doing business have deep roots in our past. Hospitality has not been forgotten. We protect what is ours, but if someone comes humbly as a friend, he will find welcome with us."

Jim smiled. "Great! We'd like nothing more."

Marhan shifted uncomfortably in his chair.

The Sojan waited in silence.

Jim thought, *Shit, they're waiting for me, aren't they?* "You saw my ship. You recognize the manufacturer? It's a Praestans Rapax custom build. Marhan's ship is also one of their designs. Don't imagine I will show you the numbers in my financial accounts merely to satisfy your curiosity. Perhaps you will appreciate that we prefer quality over pretentious design and unnecessary flash in our choice of ships."

Starf smiled.

Jim asked, "Who are they, your tenants? Are they humans?"

"The makers of that ship were not human, no."

"I already know that. It's from Daa Hobb."

The Sojan looked at each other in surprise.

Jim pressed his advantage. "But you didn't have to deal with *them*, did you? The owners are physically like me, aren't they? Respectable businesspeople? Reliable payers—at first?"

"These are good questions." Starf waved to a Sojan standing in the doorway to the courtyard. "Bring food. We will set a table here." He indicated the center of the semicircle.

Marhan put his long face next to Jim's shoulder and whispered, "This will take days."

Jim replied, "I don't care. It'll be worth it."

They sat in silence while noises came from a kitchen nearby.

A young Sojan, leaned over the shoulder of one of the others, her eyes partly hidden under her hood. "May I ask a question?"

"Of course," Jim replied.

"Is the Great Silence likely to return? What do you hear in your travels?"

Jim shrugged. "I haven't heard anything. No one knows. No one knows how, or why it happened."

She nodded and was about to say something else but suddenly, all the Sojan sat straight in their chairs. Looks of alarm spread across their faces. Jim asked, "Something wrong?"

Marhan stood quickly and turned to the main door.

Within a breath, a rush of people filled the doorway, several other doors to the courtyard flew open, and more people flooded in. The courtyard was suddenly full. The newcomers' robes were styled like the Sojan's but of a lighter color, streaked with a dark camouflage pattern.

Physically, the newcomers seemed the same as the Sojan, but their weapons were knives, swords, and clubs.

They took each Sojan by the arms. No blows fell. No one spoke.

"What's going on?" Jim asked quietly.

A rustling behind him made him turn back to the main door.

Dressed in the same robes but with a bright purple line across her face, the newcomer said, "Are you hurt?"

Jim answered, "No. Who are you?"

She stepped to one side and ushered Jim and Marhan out, through the vestibule, and back out to the heat and sunshine.

"Who are you? Where are we going?"

He got no answer.

By the bus, large lizard-like animals stood in a rank, each held by a rider whose face was hidden by a hood.

Marhan and Jim had no choice but to hurry towards the beasts as the crowd of strangers swept them along.

Marhan began to say, "I cannot get on one of..." but he found himself pushed and pulled up into a second saddle behind the rider.

The whole party was moving in moments. Jim couldn't see which animal Marhan was traveling on. He regretted not picking up his blaster from the table as they left.

The animal smelled of dung. Its skin was bare and wrinkled. The head and body stayed low to the ground, but its wide feet reached out, quickly and determinedly, with increasing force and speed. The saddles, Jim guessed, were some sort of leather with a grip immediately in front of him, for which he was soon grateful as the beast lunged, lurched, and twisted.

Apart from the snorting of their rides, the whole party moved south quickly and with hardly a sound.

Bushes and stunted trees rose ahead, along a depression at right-angles to the canyon edge. The whole party swung to the left, heading down a path into the trees and back toward the canyon.

Rock walls pressed close as the track steepened, the sound of the beasts' feet and dislodged stones echoing as they rushed onward.

Jim was amazed at how sure-footed his ride seemed around the sudden twists of their path. The light from above lessened; the lower they went, the more uncomfortable he became. *How far down are we going? We're getting further and further from the ship.*

Without warning, he found himself ducking under a low arch. The animal followed its troupe in swinging hard left immediately through the arch.

The canyon spread out to Jim's right. They were all in deep shadow while sunlight glared off the wall opposite. He incautiously looked down to see the canyon floor a long, long way below.

They moved in single file along the canyon wall. At length, they made a sharp turnout around a group of spikey bushes, and the terror of the drop moved to their left side.

It may have been an hour or more before they reached the canyon floor; Jim couldn't tell.

Marhan's ride drew up next to him, and he called, "How was your descent, monkey?"

"Much as yours, I guess. Not something I enjoyed."

"The beast's smell turns my stomach."

"Agreed. I don't like being so far from the ship."

The canid stretched his neck to look up, and swore.

The female with the purple face paint called to them. "Don't worry. You are safe now. You have reached the Free Nations. You are under our protection."

"Thanks. I think. Who are you?"

"We will talk soon."

The line of beasts and riders crossed the canyon floor from the dense shade to the bright sunlight. Jim and Marhan instantly became hot, finding the air still and heavy.

They were taken over three clattering streams and into the cover of a wide open-mouthed cave.

"We will rest here and speak," she called as she jumped from her mount.

Jim and Marhan were helped down more slowly.

Jim's eyes searched the cave and then the view of the canyon floor. The presence of water here at the base of the Steep Abyss allowed many plants to grow and thrive. He could see the work of natural erosion in sweeping curves of the rock. To Marhan, he said, "You'd never know this place was here."

Marhan nodded. "Better concealed than the base, and that was well done."

Several others, also sporting the purple face paint, gathered in a circle.

"Come and sit with us. You are safe here."

"Umm...I'm not sure we were unsafe up top," Jim commented.

Several of them laughed.

The leader took Jim's arm. "Sit. You've asked questions, and we have not replied. Now we shall."

"Thank you."

They all sat on the ground. The leader filled a wooden bowl with water, took a sip, and passed it on to the robed figure at her left.

When it came to Jim, he found he was glad of it and had to stop himself draining the bowl.

Marhan licked at the water suspiciously and passed the bowl on quickly.

Jim spoke up. "You said this was the Free Nations. I see you are not Har. You look like Sojan. What shall we call you?"

"*Turra* is the name we prefer. We are not Har. The Sojan are closer to us in our history but far from us in the present."

"What danger were we in?" Marhan asked.

"Good question. First, tell us your names, and we will tell you ours."

"I am Jim Able, from Sol Earth. You can call me Jim."

"I am Ernot Dirl Marhan, from Tanna Gul. You may refer to me by Marhan."

All the other heads in the circle nodded once. All repeated the names in unison.

"I am Leller, Hunga of Far Place."

"Pleased to meet you, Leller," Jim said.

As they each introduced themselves, Leller sat with closed eyes. Then she smiled and opened them again to look at Jim. "We saw you travel through the Steep Abyss. We saw you turn and enter the Sojan cave."

Jim nodded. "Yes, we were looking for a ship—a golden, saucer-shaped craft. And we found it inside."

"We saw the Sojan come. They took you to their brick camp. We do not allow them to mistreat those who first travel through our lands. All must pass freely between the sea and the Har lands."

Jim frowned. "We didn't travel through your lands. We flew through the canyon."

Leller smiled. "You deal much with the Har, I think. And yet they taught you nothing of the Free Nations."

What can of worms is this? He said, "I hadn't heard of the Sojan, the Free Nations, or the Turra before today. You're right."

"The Har have strayed from our traditional ways. They have taken over our world and traveled beyond the skies to worlds like yours. We have no part in what the Har do."

Marhan asked, "Do they make you live out here, in the wastelands?"

This caused the Turra some amusement.

"We have good relations with the Har. Many years ago, our fore-bears made The Agreement with them. These lands are free. We choose to live here. And, for us, they are not 'wastelands.' Your world must be very different from ours if you think so."

Marhan shifted on his haunches. "Not as much as you might think."

"So, what is the difference between you and the Sojan?" Jim asked.

"They were part of the Free Nations once. But they have strayed into the ways of the Har. They use Har technology. They use Har currency. They act like Har. They have become different from us."

"Okay, I see. Thank you."

"Under The Agreement, we live in all the land from the sea to the Steep Abyss. However, the Sojan have tried to alter the terms. Their land is to the east of the Abyss, and they try to divide the rocks and the grass in ways that make no sense to us. They say, 'The wall of the abyss is yours, but all behind it is ours.'"

Jim frowned and smiled at the same time. "So, the base is theirs, but the entrance is yours?"

Leller shook her head slowly. "They say the grass that grows on the eastern wall is ours, but the roots that grow into the rock are theirs. They built the base from behind the wall to the edge, and they claim it as their own."

Jim nodded, expecting more.

Leller continued. "We have the rights and the responsibilities for the Abyss. No one can fly into the base without flying through the canyon, which is ours. You flew into our protection, and then they took you."

Marhan barked a short laugh.

Jim said, "Okay. So, I understand you don't like the Sojan. I understand there are disputes between you. Why did you bring us here?"

"For your safety."

"We were negotiating with them. You interrupted that."

Leller laughed. "They cannot be trusted. The tricks they try to play on us, they would play on you."

Jim smiled. "We weren't with the Sojan long. But I know the Har are scrupulously polite in all they do. They...make it difficult for some visitors. When a direct answer is needed for a question, they can rarely give it, or, at least, will take a long time doing so."

This the Turra also found amusing.

Leller answered, "We often talk of why it is. They wrap themselves up in lies and half-truths. We prefer honesty."

Jim was finding the floor uncomfortable but straightened up to say, "Really?" Glancing at Marhan, he said, "Then please, let's be as honest and straightforward with each other as we can."

Leller nodded. "Very good."

Jim took out his tablet and began, "Can I show you some images—"

"We would rather you didn't use your machine. Use your words to describe what you wish to tell us."

Ugh! "Okay...I'll do my best."

With another glance at Marhan, Jim hunched his shoulders and stared at the floor while he thought of what to say. "Some time ago, a ship came to the Har spaceport called Ch'Garratt. It was the golden saucer. The ship attacked the spaceport. Many were killed. I was one of the injured. I have recently come to know that the ship came here just after. I think it's been hidden here since."

Wanni, the Turra next to Leller said, "I know of this. I saw the golden ship."

"Great! So you know about it. I met someone—who I thought was both pilot and owner but wasn't either. I'm trying to find the true owners of the ship. I want to find who was flying it...who fired on the terminal building."

"Why? What makes you come here to try and find them?" Wanni asked.

Jim locked eyes with him. "That's my business. But, so far, they have escaped all justice. I want to balance things out."

Leller said, "We appreciate the concept of balance."

Marhan interrupted to ask, "Did you see them fight? We saw blaster marks through the ship. What happened?"

Wanni glanced at Leller. "Yes. I saw them fight. There was a battle, and several died."

"And?" Marhan pressed.

"They fled. Many fled the base. Some went east. Some came to us."

Jim stuttered. "Th-they came here? To you? Who came?"

The Turra were all silent.

Jim waited, but no one spoke. "I thought we were being honest with each other?" he said, a little sharper than he intended.

Leller smiled. "Will you continue that battle? Have you come to finish what was begun that night? Do you come here from one side or the other of a conflict that has nothing to do with us to bring more death to our lands?"

"No," Jim said.

Marhan nodded and growled. "We are not part of that fight."

Leller stood up. "How can we know that? These troubles are not ours. Do not bring them here."

Jim quickly said, "No, we won't! That's not our intention. I'm looking for information, that's all. The ship's owners are long gone...gone somewhere else, and possibly are putting other people in danger. They need to be stopped. But to do that, I need to know who they are."

With a gesture from Leller, the other Turra stood up. She announced, "We will think about what you ask. Thank you for your words. Please wait outside."

Biting his tongue, Jim followed Marhan out into the sunlight. They sat on a fallen tree trunk that spanned one of the streams.

Jim said quietly, "I don't think this is going well."

"How can you tell? They ask much but say little. I have learned nothing about them except they are afraid of us."

"Afraid? How can you tell? Why would they be?"

"'How' is easy. Like all creatures, their smell changes as they react to something they fear. We scare them, but I think the fight at the base scares them more. "The 'why' question is an interesting one. While they seem accustomed to conflict, something about that battle was different."

Jim quietly said, "Okay. So, we'll ask more about that...gently."

. . .

Leller called them back into the cave to sit again in the circle. She began, "You ask for information, Jim Able. Yes, we have some. We don't know if what we can tell you will be useful to you. And we hesitate for good reason."

Jim glanced at Marhan, who was studying the Turra carefully. "Please, go on."

"We live here as our ancestors did. The Sojan...are a warning to us of what will happen if we stray from our ways and accept the ways of the Har. We see in them what we might become."

Wanni spoke. "We use what we can make with our hands. We eat what we hunt. We reap what we grow. The Har and the Sojan no longer do this. Your people no longer do this."

Jim nodded. "You're right. Our cultures are built on the division of labor, on specializations. But surely you trade with them? Are you really self-sufficient?"

Leller smiled. She replied, "Each generation wrestles with this. That is a conversation that will last for centuries. We stand on the edge of the Abyss and watch you, all of you. The problems you have with each other, the wars you wage, the destruction you cause, and we see the consequences of your culture."

Jim sighed. "I can't say I disagree with you. But it's the culture I live in. I can't live like you—outside it all. I have a role to play—an opportunity, if you like—to make one small thing better. If I can find the owners of that ship, bring them to justice, and stop them hurting other people...I think it's worth trying. Will you help me?"

"At what cost to us?"

"What do you mean?"

"We cannot make a shirt that protects us from a blaster shot. We cannot make a house that protects us from a missile. What if we help you and those people come back to confront us? What will we do?"

Marhan sighed and nodded.

Jim replied, "If I'm successful, they won't be able to threaten you."

"We don't know you. We don't know what you will count as

success. Is it not better that we have nothing to do with you and those you pursue?"

Marhan asked, "Was the battle not contained in the ship or the base? Did they continue the fight here?"

The Turra were silent, looking from one to another, deciding who should speak next.

Wanni held his hands wide and began. "It was night, the darkest hours. Our watchers saw the ship come, fly through our canyon, and enter the base. We heard the raised voices echoing from the cave mouth. Then the blaster fire." Wanni's eyes searched the ground. He reached down, scraped at the dirt with a finger, then held it up and said, "Do you know these insects?"

On the end of his finger, a small multi-legged insect rose, indignantly waving its antennae. He leaned forward so Jim and Marhan could get a better look. "They live in vast colonies under the ground. If you disturb them, they can swarm."

"Like ants on Earth," said Jim nodding.

Marhan also nodded. "We had such things."

"The aliens and their Har friends, as they ran from the base, seemed to me like these, scurrying each in his own direction. Their blaster fire was the same, even hitting the western wall."

Leller continued the story. "Some made their way down the Eastern wall through the rest of the night. Others took vehicles and headed into the Sojan lands. Some stayed, stripping the base and loading their machines into other ships. They flew out at midday."

Wanni added, "They threw thirteen bodies from the cave mouth onto the canyon floor and would have let them rot there."

This triggered a shudder in the other Turra around the circle.

Leller went on. "The ones who flew away, we could do nothing for. The ones who fled further into the Sojan lands we could do nothing for. The dead, we buried. Those who came down the canyon, we welcomed and brought up to our camp. Eight individuals: one Har, two Sojan, two humans, two Peerin, and one other."

Jim thought fast. "The humans—were they the owners of the saucer?"

Leller shook her head. "I think not. They talked of receiving orders, orders they did not like."

"The other one—you didn't identify the species. Was it a shapeshifter? Gray skin but orange underneath?"

Leller and Wanni looked at Jim in surprise and alarm.

"How do you know this?" Leller asked quietly.

"I met her." *Don't say anything more. Don't want to mention she gave away this location.*

"The seven we escorted south. There is a road the Har sometimes use. We left them at the buildings there."

"She stayed with you, the shapeshifter?"

"She was troubled. We helped her as best we could."

"Okay. That makes sense. I think you did a good thing."

Marhan asked, "What did they say to you about what happened?"

This question made Leller uncomfortable. She asked in return, "Would you have us tell others what we say here? Should we treat you differently than we treat them?"

Jim frowned. "Point taken. But I think they will have talked about who the owners were. Probably, they will have talked—at least amongst themselves—about what triggered the fight. Maybe even about who went where."

"We know," Marhan said, "there were two people in charge. The configuration of the seats in the flight room shows it. Usually, there is only one pilot's command seat. In the saucer, there are two. Were they a couple? Were they business partners? What planet were they from? These things you can tell us without betraying any trust."

Leller nodded but was silent. Then she said cautiously, "One, the male, was injured. The trouble began when he found out something the female had done. Each had supporters, it seems. The female took her people across the Sojan lands. It was the male and his people who threw down the dead and flew away."

"Definitely humans?" Jim pressed.

She frowned and thought. "Yes. That is what they said."

Jim sighed. "Thank you. This is a great help."

Marhan asked, "Did they leave anything with you? Documents? Devices? Did they pay you for your kindness to them?"

Wanni laughed. "We do not take payment for hospitality. If not given freely, how is it hospitality?"

Jim pressed, "But did they leave anything? Is there anything they discarded here?"

Leller frowned. "Do you wish to unbury the dead? Their corpses are in the ground. You know we have no use for devices, nor documents, nor money. Whatever they had is buried with them."

Jim looked at Marhan and sighed. "Thank you. We have learned several things we didn't know before. The ship, made by the Hobb Tuc, was owned by a human couple. Their relationship was such that each had their own armed supporters or staff. If he was injured, perhaps *she* was the one who acted at Ch'Garratt in a way *he* didn't like."

"Hobb Tuc?" one of the other Turra asked, "the Manocka?"

"The what?" Jim replied.

Leller said, "Do we mean the same people? They are not like us —longer limbed, covered in fur."

"Blue and gray. Large ears," Jim offered.

"Yes, we know of them. Our ancestors met them long ago. We have tales of their trickery, their guile."

Jim nodded, cautious about saying more. "I've seen pictures but never met any. They are known to be difficult to deal with."

"We say the same of humans."

Well, that explains a lot. Is that why I seem to be missing something? Jim almost smiled. "I hope you won't say it of me."

"We will see from your actions, Jim Able, and those of your companion."

Jim grinned and nodded. *Hospitality with a threat running through it. Nice.*

Marhan growled.

Jim looked round the circle. "Thank you for your time, your words, and your hospitality. Are you sure we may do nothing for you in return?"

Leller considered his question. "Nothing is required in return. If you develop any sway with the Sojan, have them close the base in the western wall. Stop them flying through the canyon. Have them leave us in peace."

Jim nodded. "If I ever have an opportunity, I will try. But I don't think the Sojan we met will listen to us now."

Marhan said, "I do not trust them. We must return to our ship soon; it stands up there unprotected."

Another Turra, who had not yet spoken, said, "A moment." She rose, went to the cave mouth, and gestured with what Jim guessed to be a mirror. She stood and stared up at the edge of the western wall. Returning to the shade of the cave, she said, "The Sojan surround your ship."

Jim glanced at Marhan and said, "Is there a flat area on the canyon floor big enough for my ship to land?"

Leller nodded. "Half a mile north from here, the sand is flat after the rains."

"Then please take us there. With your permission, I will bring the ship down. Then we will leave."

It was a pleasant path between the canyon wall and the nearest stream. Jim enjoyed the fresh, clean air, unlike the dust and grit of the land above.

Quickly assessing the size of the sandy area, Jim took out his tablet and ordered the ship to turn on the external cameras.

About sixty or more Sojan sat in groups of three or four in a circle around the ship.

"Okay. Raeda, have they made any attempts to get in?"

The ship replied, "Fifteen attempts have been made. Superficial damage to the rear outer airlock."

"Lift off. Descend into the canyon to the flat area near my location."

"Acknowledged."

Jim watched the Sojan leap up in alarm as the ship's engines fired, pushing clouds of dust up into the air.

They watched as the ship, black against the bright sky, traveled down the exact center of the canyon between the towering walls to land with a quiet "whoosh" on the sand.

Eight Sojan warriors clinging to parts of the ship dropped instantly to the ground, bringing blasters to bear on Jim, Marhan, and the Turra.

CHAPTER 65

TURRA

Silence fell on the canyon floor.

The Sojan stood tall and silent, their blasters rock steady in their hands.

Almost without sound, darts flew from the eastern wall. The Sojan fell together.

Leller stood in front of Jim. "Remember—if you ever come here again—we do not allow such weapons as those blasters in our land."

Jim swallowed at the implied threat. "I understand. I'm sorry you have more bodies to bury."

"That is not your concern. The Sojan know better. Look to yourselves. Do not involve us in your affairs and you will find us, as you have, hospitable friends. Do not become our enemies."

Marhan offered, "Do you wish us to remove their blasters?"

Leller nodded. "Please."

Jim held back from the work of stripping the dead. Without comment, Marhan took the blasters, various communicators, and other devices onto the ship.

As he closed the outer airlock, Jim looked back at Leller. To Marhan, he said, "I don't think I've ever met a group of people I understand less. We speak the same language but see things so differently."

Marhan replied quietly, "They are skilled in many ways. They are efficient. But they are insular. Those are dangerous qualities to combine."

"Let's get out of here."

CHAPTER 66

JIM'S SHIP

"Where to?" Marhan asked with a smile.

Jim brought up the image of the maker's plaque from the golden saucer. "Wherever 'bar.el.ion' is."

"How will we find it?"

"I didn't have Rob Stuart create Robins for nothing. He has everything he needs to track this down. It will be somewhere in a public record."

"I thought you no longer trusted him."

"True. But until I work out what to do about his thieving, I'm not letting the infrastructure go to waste."

"You always wait. You procrastinate. Guls act swiftly. If it were me, I would have ripped out his throat and been done."

Jim groaned. "I know. I want to find the right answer. It may not involve spilling blood; it might. But I hope there's another way."

Marhan yawned. "Wake me when we get there."

"Sorry I've kept you up."

With a growl, the canid disappeared into his module.

___

From: Jim Able, Sol Earth, private citizen.
To: ROBINS, Unity City, Sol Earth

Hi Rob,
I need you to find me where a ship was made and who by. All I know is
from the maker's plaque:
THIS ship
CRAS.du.nun.me.1245.9980.5467
MADE in bar.el.ion
ALL that is good and profitable
THIS to all in traveling thus
All signs point to the Hobb Tuc, but I don't know how far their businesses
spread or if anyone else butchers Standard that way.
Thanks,
Jim

Rob replied within an hour.

From: ROBINS, Unity City, Sol Earth
To: Jim Able, Sol Earth, private citizen

Okay. Easy enough.
Bar.el.ion is a Tuc manufacturing center. I can't tell if it's all one business
or some sort of hub for different companies.
Get a translator. Those guys are weird.
Rob.

From: Jim Able, Sol Earth, private citizen
To: The Manager, Bar.el.ion, Daa Hobb Grynd.Af

Hello, I am Jim Able, a private citizen of Sol Earth. I am seeking information about a human who owned or commissioned the following craft from you.

CRAS.du.nun.me.1245.9980.5467
MADE in bar.el.ion

I am neither a law enforcement officer nor involved with any legal action or litigation.

If you do not have any information, please consider telling me who else I can contact.
With appreciation of the friendship and cooperation between our worlds, I give you my thanks.
Jim Able

To Jim's astonishment, the reply came within minutes.

From: aa.tro.fl, Head of Security, Bar.el.ion, Daa Hobb Grynd.Af
To: Jim Able, Private Citizen, Sol Earth

YOUR message has gained our attention.
THIS ship is known to us.
TRAVEL now to Jal Nas 6.
HERE will you meet.
ER.te.bse of Bar.el.ion
HE the authorized representative.
HOW will we know your ship?

ALL that is good and wondrous in our skies.
THIS to be yours in your goings.

What? Why there? This isn't going to work.

Reluctantly, he sent an image of his ship.

"Marhan! Wake up! What do you know about Jal Nas?"

A low grumble came from Marhan's module. Eventually, he came down the ramp to the flight room. "What did you ask?"

"Jal Nas. Jal Nas 6, to be precise. Do you know it?"

The canid shook his head. "No. Who lives there?"

Jim said, "Raeda, what's the profile of Jal Nas?"

The ship replied, "Jal Nas is a planet known for its volcanic instability. It is home to the Nurcer. Nurcer traders are associated with the Stap Bal Ird Trading Alliance."

"Show me a Nurcer."

The display nearest Jim changed to an image of a small, wheeled chamber with darkened windows.

"Any image of the occupant?"

"No other images are on file."

"Do they accept visitors to their station Jal Nas 6?"

"No information on file. Shall I contact the station administrator?"

"No. Set a course to Jal Nas 6. Begin when ready."

"Acknowledged. Beginning route to Jal Nas 6."

"Raeda, how long will the journey take?"

"Approximately thirty-six hours, twenty-five minutes."

"And why are we going?" Marhan asked.

"Because the Hobb Tuc asked—told—us to."

Marhan read through the Tuc message. "It will be somewhere few go. We will stand out. If we appear with backup, it will be obvious."

"Right. This ship is unusual anyway. Maybe that will work both ways."

Marhan nodded thoughtfully. "Perhaps that is their reason. It may be merely an efficient way of making our meeting secure."

"What did Leller say about them? 'Trickery' and 'guile,' wasn't it?"

Marhan barked. "We can compete with them in that!" He sniffed the air as he looked around the flight room. His grin fell, and he hung his head.

"What?" Jim asked kindly.

"I must clear the module she used. I will pack up her belongings."

"No hurry."

"May I store them in your cargo hold?"

Jim nodded. "Of course."

"This ship is empty without her."

CHAPTER 67

THE TUC

Jal Nas 6 only nominally orbited its planet. As Jim's ship drew close, the star and three other planets were small, bright specs in the blackness. The planet Nas showed huge scars from volcanic activity. Jim noticed the glint of many orbiting stations. Station 6 spun slowly in its remote orbit, emitting nothing but a navigation beacon.

"Unusual," Jim said.

Marhan nodded but didn't reply.

"Raeda, contact the station administrator. Ask if berths are available."

"Acknowledged." Almost immediately, the ship reported, "No berths are available. Bookings can be made at selected times. No bookings are being accepted."

"Maintain this distance. I suppose we have to wait for our Tuc friends—"

The ship interrupted. "The vessel Dran.ve.hep.mo is requesting to dock."

"Show me."

The main viewer changed to show a wide, flat craft approaching the rear of Jim's ship. To the left and right, its wings held both engines and armaments away from a compact main body. Underneath, Jim saw what might have been huge grapples. *Are those landing legs or for grabbing other ships?*

"This may be riskier than I thought."

"Show them nothing but your face," warned Marhan. "I will be quiet."

Jim drew the small screen from the left arm of the pilot's seat and made sure nothing of the inside of the ship was visible before ordering, "Raeda, let me talk to them."

"Acknowledged."

Marhan moved to stand in front of Jim and behind the screen. Within a few moments, a furry face appeared before Jim. He could see nothing of the inside of the Tuc ship behind.

"You. Jim Able."

"I am Jim Able. Who are you?"

"Er.te.bse. My name: Er. Representative of Aa.tro.fl, Head of Security. His place Bar.el.ion. Our place Daa Hobb Grynd.Af. Your place Sol Earth."

"That's correct. I'm from Earth. I'm here to talk about the golden saucer."

A quick look of alarm crossed the Tuc's face. "We come aboard. Open channel may be listened."

Jim glanced at Marhan. "Okay...Who is we? How many of you?"

Jim wasn't sure but thought the expression under the fur was of confusion.

"We come aboard. Eight. We the crew."

Jim swallowed. "No weapons."

Again, the confusion. "No weapons. No harm we mean you."

Jim nodded. "You may dock. Raeda, dock with the approaching ship."

"Acknowledged. Standard docking protocols established. Docking initiated."

Jim ended the call, opened the side of his pilot's seat, took out a blaster, and attached it to his belt.

Marhan said, "I will remain out of sight but will be listening."

• • •

Jim stood halfway up the corridor to the airlock. He called, "Raeda, open the inner airlock."

"Acknowledged."

The inner airlock opened to show several creatures in a huddle. Cautiously, they moved into the corridor and down toward the flight room. Jim waited, arms crossed, almost on tiptoes, geared up for the unexpected. He heard them whispering but couldn't catch what they said.

One Tuc stepped ahead of the rest. "Praestans Rapax. A custom ship. Jim Able a rich human in flying thus."

"Are you Er?"

"Er." He made a theatrical bow.

The Tucs' fur varied from dark blue to gray as the light and shadows changed. Jim noted it was more hair than fur, coarse and long. Their limbs were thin, and the fur stuck out—making their joints look angular, almost sharp. Their bodies, like their ship's main section, were small in comparison. Each was dressed the same in black shorts and a loose black sleeveless jerkin.

Jim thought, *Being so thin would be unhealthy for a human. I wonder how strong those limbs are.*

Er stood in front of Jim and rose to his full height, but he still had to look up into Jim's face. The Tuc's face stuck out a little, not like the snout of a Gul but more pronounced than a human. His huge tufted bat-like ears dominated his head.

"Welcome aboard," Jim said, smiling.

"Welcome!" Er echoed. The word was taken up by the others and repeated several times.

"Can I offer you drinks or food?"

Er's head turned quickly to his fellows. "Drinks, Hobb!"

"Hobb Yoy!" they replied in chorus.

Smiling more broadly, Jim led them into the flight room and down the ramp to the galley.

Er jumped onto the chair at the end of the table, feet on the seat, squatting on his heels. Two others jumped onto the tabletop, standing tall and scanning their eyes across the ceiling and cupboards. Another leaped onto the counter next to the coffee machine. The other four stood next to each other, shoulders slightly hunched, watching Er.

Jim called, "Please! Sit or stand around the table. What do you drink?"

Er's face lit up with a grin. "Drinks. All kind. Alcohol. Marjus. Ollan root. You are from Sol Earth. Do you have Earth caffeine?"

Jim nodded. "I do." He turned to the coffeemaker and the Tuc on the counter who had ignored what he'd said about sitting at the table. "Sit over there. I'll make coffee."

"Coffee!" the Tuc replied, "Hobb!"

The others all replied, "Hobb Yoy!"

The Tuc didn't move. Jim pointed to the table and didn't move. The Tuc hung its head, its ears twitched, and it jumped down.

During the making of the coffee, Marhan came slowly down the ramp.

The first Tuc to see him shrieked. Before Jim could say anything, they had leaped across the room, putting the table between them and the canid. "Rak Yoy! Rak Yoy!"

"It's okay! It's okay!" Jim called. "He's a friend. You're in no danger."

Er pointed at Marhan. "Gul. Why is it free? A danger to your ship!"

Jim stood at the table. "No. He's not a danger. He's my friend. Sit down. I'm sorry we alarmed you."

Er's hands reached out and held the arms of the two Tucs on either side. Jim could see they were all breathing heavily.

"Gul. Human. Together."

"Sure. Why not?"

Er's eyes flashed from Jim to Marhan and back again.

Marhan said quietly, "I am Ernot Dirl Marhan. I mean you no harm. You are Jim's guests. Nothing will happen to you here."

Er still held his companions' arms; his mouth was open, but he said nothing.

Jim asked, "Would you prefer Marhan went above again?"

Er nodded vigorously. The others quietly whispered, "Hobb Yoy."

"Sorry, Marhan. We'll catch up with you later."

The canid growled softly, smiled, and went back up the ramp.

Jim turned to the cupboards, took out nine mugs, and arranged them on the table. The Tuc hadn't moved.

"Please, relax. I'm sorry for the surprise. I didn't know Marhan would be a problem."

Slowly, Er climbed back onto the chair. "Alas, a human with a gul."

One of the others said something Jim didn't catch. Four of them immediately stood to attention behind Er. The other three sat down on the other chairs.

Jim brought the coffeepot and a stool to the table and sat with them.

"Can I ask why you reacted that way? Have guls harmed you in the past?"

Er shook his large ears. "Guls. Much trade they make in Lakweed. Many dangers they make for customers. Stories. Warnings. Never seen one before."

"I understand. I've met some scary guls. This one, though—Marhan—is okay. You don't need to worry."

"Unexpected."

"Sure. So are you. I've never met Tuc before."

The Tuc opposite Jim at the table smiled and said, "Also scary. Stories. Warnings."

"I've heard a few things." Jim smiled back. "I know you make ships. What do you think of this one?"

There was a buzz of clipped words and grunts between them all. Er replied, "Jim Able. Rich. Human with good taste. Good ship of much recommendation."

"Thank you." He passed around the coffee mugs. "Tell me of the golden saucer. It's also a fine ship."

Their attention was solely on the coffee. They sniffed the coffee. They sipped their mugs. Glancing round each other, they downed the mugsful in unison shouting "Hobb Yoy!" One Tuc was a small beat late and received a sharp elbow in the ribs and a snigger from his colleagues on either side.

Jim sat wide-eyed.

Er shook himself. "Coffee! Good drink. Good host. Good Jim Able."

"You're welcome, Er. You're all welcome."

There followed a series of exchanges in their own language. Jim watched their faces but couldn't read their expressions.

Er nodded and said to Jim, "Golden saucer. Unique ship. Number you tell us. This you know from being within. What did Jim Able do? Where is our ship?"

"I found it."

This caused a stir amongst them all.

"Bar.el.ion seek it," Er said, "Jim Able will, for the sake of good relations, tell us where."

Jim hesitated. "May I tell you the story of the first time I saw it?"

Er nodded quickly. "Story. Tell it well."

With another cry of "Hobb Yoy!" they all got up from where they were and sat close together on the floor with Er in the middle, and where, despite all the knees and elbows, they could all see Jim.

"I was helping Earth's Office of External Affairs with an audit on Sin Har." This, to Jim's brief confusion, amused the Tuc. "One of the people I interviewed flew into the spaceport of Ch'Garratt in a golden saucer. It caught everyone's eye. Beautiful craft. We all thought it was expensive. As auditors, we immediately thought the owner was either a successful businessperson or a criminal."

The Tuc laughed and chatted amongst themselves.

When they'd finished, Jim continued. "Inspectors went aboard, checked everything, and declared all was in order. I escorted the person I thought was the pilot back onboard."

Jim drank more coffee before going on. "The ship took off. At the same time, a police flier lifted off too. The saucer fired on it and brought it down. Then the saucer fired on the terminal."

His audience was still and silent.

"A hundred people died. More were injured, myself included." Jim scanned their upraised faces, all eight pairs of ears flattened at their tips. "I want to bring to justice whoever was flying that craft that day. I'm hoping you can help me."

Er didn't reply but stood up. His companions jumped up, and they turned to huddle together. Their staccato words and grunts, Jim thought, were agitated. Their words sounded angrier than their simple alarm at seeing a gul.

Er turned to Jim and said, "A saying. Unfaithful in small, unfaithful in big. Criminal, not businessperson. This we know. This all know."

"Okay. What can you tell me? You asked me 'Where is *our* ship?'. Is it yours? I had heard two humans now owned it."

"Ownership by contract. Payment made. Trade. Reciprocation."

"Go on."

"Breach of contract. Payment unmade. Alas, no trade."

"They stole it?"

Er's ears moved slowly. "False payment. The ship. *Ours,* not *theirs.*"

"Oh, I see. They stiffed you!"

This caused some laughter in the Tuc. *Okay, that's a Standard phrase that has stronger connotations for them.*

Er was nodding. "Embarrassment and hurt. The 'golden saucer' as you say. Great work in its designing. Great work in its building. Expensive, as you say. Beautiful, as we all say."

The Tuc replied, "Hobb Yoy!"

Jim waited.

Er waited.

The Tuc all waited.

"That's my story," Jim said, "the next part is where you tell me who the humans are and, preferably, how I find them."

Er didn't look at him. Nor did the others.

"Come on! If they went back on a contract, why haven't *you* gone after them?"

Er slowly moved back to the table and squatted again on the chair. Hanging his head slightly, he said, "No profit we make. Even his name well-known. No action possible."

"Why not?"

One of the other Tuc said, "Rak Yoy," but the others didn't echo it.

"Wait. What? He's someone like Marhan? Someone so scary?"

Er said, "Alas, no profit can be made for myself, for my crew, for bar.el.ion, for the Tuc. Only trouble. Endless legal problems. Maybe death."

Jim drummed his fingers while he thought. "Okay. I get that you've written it off. You're not pursuing this person because he's too much trouble, too dangerous. You can't do it. But maybe I can."

Er shook his head. "Your reasons are sure? Yes. Power? No. Even with riches enough to buy this ship? No. You cannot do it."

"You don't know me. I don't have to have power—or riches, for that matter. I only need the determination. And some information."

The Tuc made a noise Jim hadn't heard from them before—a low growling wail. No one individual led it. Rather, it came from within each and all of them.

"What's the matter?" Jim asked quietly.

"We do not think this way. Others often do. This we know. Here we see danger. Here we protect our own. We would protect you, Jim Able. One person. Alone." He shook his head again and several of the others did likewise.

Jim smiled at their concern. "I have a job to do. Someone once asked me why I would travel the stars alone. I'll give you guys the same answer I gave her: sometimes no one will go with you."

Er looked round at his crew. "We cannot help. We are not your crew. You are not our crew. Our crew is part of bar.el.ion. You are not Tuc. For us...together is better."

Jim stood up and towered over him. "Like I said, I need the information. I'll tell you where the ship is if you tell me who the humans are."

Er looked away.

Jim pressed, "Do you want it back or not?"

Er and the others, with no enthusiasm, replied, "Hobb Yoy."

Er took out a device from an inner pocket of his jerkin.

Jim thought, *You could have had a weapon in there, and I wouldn't have seen it.*

The Tuc tapped at the device and then gestured to Jim. "An image."

Jim picked up his tablet from the counter to see if they could connect.

As the image of two humans appeared on his screen, Jim dropped the tablet on the table and staggered back. He covered his mouth and groaned. "Oh...that's not possible!"

Er stood up on the chair and the others shuffled back a pace or two. "He is recognized, this person?"

Jim shook his head. "Not him, no. But I know the woman next to him very well."

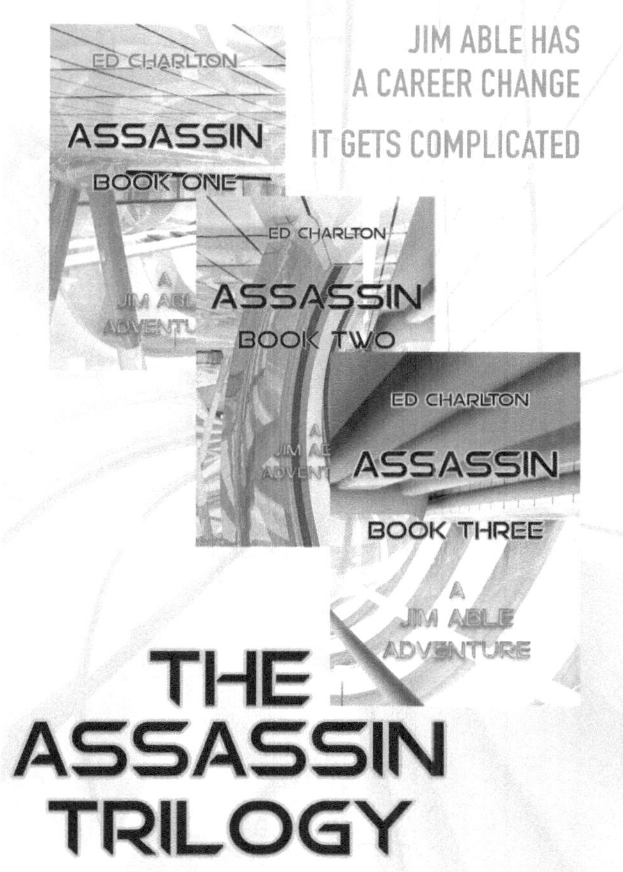

More tales of quirky aliens, flawed humans, and heroes who work in outer space. Jim Able takes action against the hidden schemes of criminals, governments, and interplanetary corporations.

Book One

Jim's Target: Jack Katrigg, the courier who destroyed Ch'Garratt Spaceport Terminal Two with Jim in it.

Can Jim find an ethical solution to the problem of justice denied?

Book Two

Jim's Target: The power couple who have caused so many of Jim's problems.

Is learning the truth more important than life or death?

Book Three

Jim's Target: Is it the Praestans Rapax monk, Daum Robertus Graffen, or his entire organization?

Welcome to the network.

Available at edcharlton.com

Visitors from Earth witness the shocking downfall of Aleronde. They share an unexpected role in this catastrophe with a mysterious figure from the past who unpicks the fabric of the Aleronden empire with that most dangerous thing: an idea.

Read *Aleronde the Great* and its two prequels, *The Problem with Uncle Teddy's Memoir* and *Saint John's Ambulatory*.

The Problem with Uncle Teddy's Memoir tells—through letters, emails, and Uncle Teddy's own manuscript—a troubling tale of empire, slavery, and betrayal. Reading the memoir forces two friends to reexamine their childhood experiences of abduction.

Saint John's Ambulatory reads like a murder mystery, but there are aliens in every shadow. Only one man has evidence of extraterrestrials on Earth, but now, he's dead.

In *Aleronde the Great*, the significance of Uncle Teddy's memoir and the Ambulatory are revealed, and one small act of kindness unleashes trouble of galactic proportions.

The Aleronde Trilogy at edcharlton.com

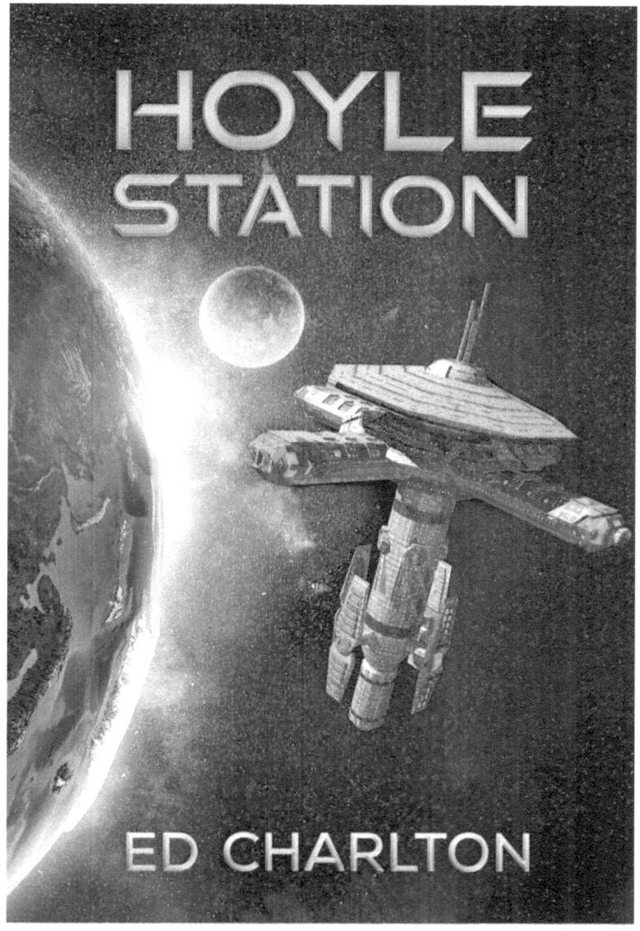

How to murder someone on a space station

and get away with it

Hoyle Station is a murder mystery with a cast of thousands, some of them human.

And there are many questions. How has a member of Earth's Historical Guild so completely vanished? Are the Recorders who run the business of the station as helpful as they seem? Who are the aliens watching from the dark of space?

Hoyle Station

Subscribe to Ed's free monthly newsletter!